About the Author

Kiltie Jackson grew up in Scotland, moved to London and then finally settled down somewhere in the middle.

She now lives in Staffordshire with six cats and one grumpy husband.

Her debut novel 'A Rock 'n' Roll Lovestyle' was released in September 2017.

When Kiltie sat down to write her debut novel, a series was the last thing on her mind but here we are That's what happens when you're not paying attention!

If you would like to read more about Kiltie, you can find her on the following:

Website: www.kiltiejackson.com

Facebook: www.facebook.com/kiltiejackson

Twitter: www.twitter.com/KiltieJackson

Instagram: www.instagram.com/kiltiejackson

Also by Kiltie Jackson

A Rock 'n' Roll Lovestyle

An Artisan Lovestyle

An Incidental Lovestyle

A Timeless Lovestyle

Kiltie Jackson

All the characters in this book are
fictitious, and
any resemblance to actual persons, living
or dead,
is purely coincidental.

Jeff Rowland appears with the permission
of Jeff Rowland – Artist.

ISBN-13: 978 - 1999866631

For

Margaret and John

xx

ACKNOWLEDGMENTS

Before I begin name-dropping all the fabulous people in my life and who support me on this journey, I would like give a massive thank you to my wonderful husband, Mr Mogs, for coming up with the initial idea for this story. We were on a day out when he suddenly began talking about a person coming forward in time but who could find no record of their previous life. I thought it was a great concept although I confess, when he began yakking on about paradoxes, my eyes did glaze over! The seed, however, had been planted and, while I have no paradoxes to offer, I hope I have done some justice to the concept he had in mind. Thank you, my love, for the idea, the support and for finally coming to terms with being a writer's widower. The understanding you give makes it easier to stay focused.

I also offer my thanks to my very bestest friend, Kym Woods, who reads everything I write and never falls asleep when I'm bouncing my ideas off her. You are a truly awesome lady.

To my mum, my sister & my mother-in-law who are my 'forever cheerleaders' – for always spreading my name to whoever will listen and encouraging me every step of the way, I thank you.

This path I travel brings with it many friends in the writing community who are always there to hold hands, lift us when we stumble, celebrate the successes – no matter how small – and who send virtual cake and coffee when the self-doubt kicks in; Samantha Curtis, Emma

Cooper, Stuart Dunne, Anita Faulkner, Becca Mascull, Jane Issac, Sumaira Wilson – thank you for the laughs, the love and the memes.

A massive bucket of thanks goes to two special men in my life – John Hudspith, my long-suffering editor and Henry Hyde, my fabulous cover designer. Between them, they ensure the end package is worthy for public consumption.

These days, most self-respecting authors are members of several online book groups and I am no different. The Fiction Café Book Group is my online home, followed very closely by Chick Lit & Prosecco. If you want to find me just 'chilling out on line' then these are the places to be.

And finally, to you my darling readers, I give the biggest thanks of all. I can't begin to tell you how much of a thrill it is to receive your messages of support, read your reviews, and have you badger me for the next book as you turn the last page of my latest offering. You make it all worthwhile and these are just a mere handful of those who regularly shout my name from the roof-tops: Sue Baker, Michaela Balfour, Melanie Thomas, Mark Fearn, Kathleen Becker, Karen Harrison, Emma-Louise Bunting, Kate Baker, Sharon Conquer, Mandy Coomber, Meghan Gibbons, Melissa Evans, Miriam O'Brian and Emma-Louise Smith. Thank you so much for all the recommendations – every one is always deeply appreciated from the bottom of my heart.

Chapter One

Lower Ditchley - 1860

Molly Smythe gently flapped the front of her sky blue cotton dress in an attempt to draw some cooler air up around her legs. She'd been standing at the kitchen table for two hours, helping her mother bake bread and cakes for the coaching inn next door. The heat from the oven, combined with the hot, sticky, July weather, had made the temperature within the cottage unbearable. She picked up a nearby tea-towel, soaked it in the basin of cold water and dabbed it against her throat and forehead before soaking it a second time to hold against her cheeks. She didn't need to look in the mirror to know they were hot and flushed – she could feel them through the wet rag.

'We're nearly done, love. Once this batch goes in, you can head off out for some fresh air.'

Molly looked over at her mother who was pummelling the dough with a vigour that left her feeling quite drained just watching.

‘Are you sure, Mother? What about the clearing up? I can’t leave you to do that on your own.’

‘Don’t you worry about that – it’s a glorious day out there, go for a walk and enjoy it.’

‘Tell you what, why don’t I go over towards the river and see if some of the blackberries are ready to be picked. With this heat, they should be ripening any time now.’

‘I would say that is a very good idea.’

Molly smiled at her mother as they began dividing the last of the dough into the baking tins. She glanced at the pile of linen, waiting for her attention, on her sewing table by the window. She really should be getting on with that so it could be returned to the manor house but… Her mother was right – it was far too nice a day to be stuck inside. She’d make a start on it after tea.

Half an hour later, Molly was in the pantry, stretched up on her tiptoes, attempting to locate her fruit basket on the top shelf, when she heard raised voices from the yard. She leaned to the side, trying to see out of the small window, but it faced the wrong direction. She raised herself up on her toes again and felt along the high shelf with her hand. Her fingertips brushed against the woven basket and, after a few seconds of trying to get a hold, one of her fingernails caught on a loop and she was able to drag it forward to the edge of the shelf. She pulled it down and sneezed loudly when she inhaled the cloud of dust that came with it. Once the basket had been given a good wipe down, she placed it on her arm and made her way round to the yard at the side of the house, heading towards the voices which were growing louder by the minute.

‘I have told you, sir, that until you settle your outstanding bill, I am unable to do any further work for you.’

Molly saw her father was speaking with Damien Featheringstone, the son of the local landowner, Lord Featheringstone. While his father was a kindly man, Damien was not. He was rude, arrogant and showed no respect to anyone, least of all the villagers who resided in Lower Ditchley. He gambled and drank to excess and the rumours were that he'd run up a huge amount of debt. Molly knew how much he owed her father so suspected there was a great deal of truth in the gossip.

She edged her way carefully along the side of the wall in an attempt to pass by without drawing attention to herself. Damien was an absolute boor and she didn't want him to see she was going out alone. Even though he was now married, with a child on the way, he still believed himself to be quite the ladies' man and there was a risk he would foist his unwanted attentions upon her again. It seemed to be that the more she said no, the more of a challenge he considered her to be. She'd been rejecting his advances for almost twenty years but the message wasn't sinking in. Although she was more than capable of defending herself against him, it was too hot a day for that much effort. It was far better for her to simply avoid his attention altogether.

'So, what are you proposing I do? My horse is lame and needs to be reshod?'

Molly heard her father patiently explain to Damien that he could take his custom to the blacksmith in Upper Ditchley, three miles along the road. Damien's blustering reply on the poor quality of that man's work was the last thing she heard before turning the corner onto the high street and out of earshot.

Damien did have a point though, she mused, as she crossed over the road to walk across the village green – her father was definitely the best smithy in the area and a little smile of pride slipped across her face at the thought. The superior standard of his work brought in custom from all the surrounding villages and there were even visitors to the coaching inn who made a point of stopping there on their travels so he could attend to their horses.

Molly forced the thoughts of Damien Featheringstone from her mind as she made her way along the footpath at the side of the church, heading towards the grounds of Ditchley Manor. She passed through the small wooden gate and took the path to the left, through the trees. Lord Featheringstone didn't mind the villagers coming onto the manor land but he preferred them not to come within the vicinity of the big house. The path she was on would lead her to the windmill on the far side of the estate. It was a walk of almost fifteen minutes but, as most of it was through woodland, the shade of the trees would provide some shelter from the blazing sun, making her jaunt quite pleasurable. She thought about old Seth, who worked the windmill. He was getting on in years and the villagers had had more than one discussion over what would happen when he could no longer work it. His wife, along with their only child, had died of the fever many years ago, long before she was born. He hadn't remarried and there didn't appear to be anyone to take over the business from him. The villagers were concerned over where they would purchase their flour if the mill was to close. Mind you, if there was any truth in the talk of the new train system growing further, and the ability of these machines to transport goods faster than horses or boat, then the villagers may not be too badly affected when the time came.

Up ahead, the path forked and she opted to go right. The left-hand path took her up towards the windmill but that was in an open clearing and today she was looking for the bramble bushes further down the river. Five minutes later, she arrived by the side of the water. It wasn't flowing terribly fast and she almost fancied that it too was feeling the heat of the day and so was having a lazy meander along its route. Even though the river was lower than usual because of the hot weather, Molly still couldn't see the riverbed. The water was at its deepest for the two miles either side of the mill and she'd grown up being warned not to go in because of the strong currents under the surface. The story was that a child had jumped in many, many years ago, got caught up in the current and drowned. Every child in the village had grown up hearing this story and while some occasionally disobeyed their parents, Molly had never had any interest in going into the water. She'd been quite content with the occasional paddle in the pond on the village green and gave a small shudder as she looked into the bottomless, murky brown depths. She was more than happy to keep her feet firmly on solid ground and she turned her attention to the bramble bushes behind her. She could see a good number of the berries had ripened but she knew she would get better pickings further down the path where the trees were less dense and the sunlight broke through. She could pick from these bushes on the way back if need be.

It didn't take Molly long to fill her basket and she began strolling back up the river path. She walked around the bend and spotted a kingfisher just as it dived into the water, sending gleaming ripples towards the banks. She was surprised to see the sunlight dancing on the water at this part of the river – the trees here were particularly thick and dense and the sunbeams would have to work hard to cut through them. The light was coming from somewhere though and the shimmering silver was quite mesmerising. Molly could feel herself being lulled into an almost semi-hypnotic state and it took a concentrated effort to shake her head and rid herself of the sensation. She steadied herself against an old, hollow tree stump next to the path and, with a small laugh of confusion, she turned to continue making her way back. She was tired and it was time to go home.

She'd only been walking a few minutes when she heard voices up ahead. She peeped over the bushes and saw Damien Featheringstone walking in her direction, while talking to Stan Alderly, his friend and henchman. Whenever Damien perceived someone had done ill by him, he would instruct Alderly to exact some kind of revenge upon them. While everyone knew he did this, there was never any proof which would see him face charges. Alderly was a sly, brainless thug who merely did as he was told. He had a nasty streak running through him and he never questioned the acts he was asked to carry out. Not wanting to meet these two in an area where she was alone and vulnerable, Molly quietly slid in between the bushes and hunkered down, breathing as quietly as she could so as not to alert them to her presence.

'—can't get away with talking to me like that, just who does he think he is?'

'He forgets his place, Damien. One day you'll be lord of this land and he should respect that.'

'Hmm, I can't see that happening anytime soon. The old fella is in ruddy good health and looks like he'll be around awhile yet.'

'Do you want me to teach him a lesson? Put him in his place?'

'I think a lesson is required. Something which will teach that blacksmith not to refuse my business. By the time he recovers, he'll be begging me for my custom.'

'Not a problem, Damien, I'll see to it tonight.'

'Good! Now I must get home. Audrine's bloody parents are coming to dinner and I need to get dressed.'

As the voices gradually faded away, Molly knelt behind her bush, shaking with anger at what she'd overheard. She had to get home as quickly as possible and warn her father of Alderly's intentions. She couldn't, however, move from her hiding place too soon and run the risk of being seen so she forced herself to wait a while longer. Once she was sure it was all clear, she stood up and made to step back onto the path. In her haste, however, she hadn't considered that her crouched position had sent her lower limbs to sleep and the resulting numbness caused her to stumble. She staggered against a bramble bush and her dress became snarled upon its thorny branches. The backwards tug pulled Molly off balance, causing her to trip over the thick roots of the tree by her side and, the next thing she knew, she'd lost her footing and was falling towards the river. She felt the cool air of the river on her back a mere second before she landed in the water. The shock of the cold water squeezed a yelp of surprise out of her before she sank below the surface. She kicked her legs but could feel nothing beneath her feet. She broke through the surface again and tried to scream but she timed it all wrong and instead of taking in air with which to emit her cry for help, all she got was a vast mouthful of water. As Molly felt herself sinking further down, she became aware of a tugging sensation around her legs and hips. On no, not the current, she thought. She could feel it pulling her down deeper into the middle of the river. The water was flowing much faster down here and she was dragged along several feet before her head screamed at her to try and get back up to the surface. Using her last reserves of energy, she kicked her legs hard and thrust her arms out to the side. Instinct was taking over; it was all she had left. She managed to break the surface once more, take in one last gasp of air and let out the loudest scream she could manage before she was pulled back down again into the icy depths below.

Chapter Two

Lower Ditchley – Present Day

Charlie Rowland was sitting at his large, mahogany desk situated in front of the open, full-length windows. There wasn't much of a breeze in the air but the little there was, had made its way into the room and was gently lifting the corners of the papers laid out in front of him. His elbows were on the desk and his head was in his hands as he stared at a vast array of photographs. He gazed at them for several minutes before letting out a sigh, straightening up in his seat and, pushing the pictures away from him, he lifted his head to look out of the window where his eyes settled on the vista of lightly swaying barley fields in front of him. He let the view soothe him and calm his agitation. The sound of the river working the water wheel below him, and the soft roar of the water splashing, finally brought a smile to his face. He loved this old mill and being here always calmed his restless soul.

Last year, when Sukie and Pete Wallace had approached him with a view to rebuilding and renovating the old flour mill on their property, he'd initially been unsure if it was a project he wished to undertake, but when he'd taken a walk out to the old building and had stood in the clearing beside it, he'd felt an extraordinary sense of peace flow through him. Something about the mill and the surrounding area seemed to talk to his inner soul and he'd agreed to take on the job. He'd designed a building which embraced the charm of the original mill yet made it more practical as a property that would be comfortable to live in. His friend, Robbie, had moved up from London to set up a small business with a local man, Matt, and they specialised in restoring and renovating the older properties in the area, for the one thing the Cotswolds had in abundance, was old, old properties. The three of them had worked together on the mill project and, when the last nuts and bolts had been put in place, Charlie realised he'd fallen completely in love.

He'd asked Sukie what her plans were for the property and when she'd replied that the intention was to rent it out as a writer's retreat, he'd offered to take it on as a long-term rental. A price had been agreed and it was now his bolthole when London and the pressures of work became too much for him. In some ways though, he was using it as a writer's retreat for he was working on creating a book of old British architecture. His father had loved photographing the old, historical buildings around the country and had always talked about, one day, putting a book together. Unfortunately, he'd died before he'd had the chance to do it so Charlie had picked up the baton in his memory. Right now, however, he was struggling to decide which photographs to use and he could feel his frustration mounting.

'Oh, sod this, I'm going for a run,' he muttered aloud, as he pushed himself up out of the chair and moved around the desk to pull the French windows closed. He'd once made the mistake of going out and leaving them open and had returned to find two pigeons pooping all over the kitchen worktop. He wasn't going to make that mistake again.

He pulled on his trainers, set the fitness app on his phone to "run", put it in his pocket and, after some star jumps and stretches, set off at a brisk pace down the path which ran alongside the river, only slowing down as he approached the old hollow tree stump. The tree must have been very old, for its roots spread across the path, and Charlie was always cautious when he ran past, taking care not to trip and fall. He glanced at the river and saw the silvery shimmer of the sunlight dancing across the ripples of the surface. He did a slight double-take for this part of the wood was quite thick and dense and any sunlight which managed to break through was usually quite muted. Today was a particularly bright day though, he reckoned, and clearly the strong sun had managed to penetrate through the foliage. He gave the matter no further thought as he picked up his speed again and ran for a further two miles before turning to make his way back.

Charlie was just coming around the bend, on the approach towards the old stump, when a scream suddenly ripped through the air.

'HELP!'

He put on a burst of speed and was just in time to see a flash of pale blue disappear under the sparkling surface of the river. Without hesitation, he kicked off his running shoes, took the phone from his pocket and threw it down beside them, before diving into the river. He felt the icy cold attack his muscles and the pull of the under-current against his arms as he swam around, trying to find whoever had fallen in. He opened his eyes to look but couldn't see anything for all around him was darkness. The sunlight which had dazzled the top of the water hadn't been able to send its warmth or light down into the deep, dark depths. His lungs were beginning to burn from holding his breath when, a brief second later, his arm brushed against something soft and he quickly grabbed hold – it felt like a skirt or a dress. Charlie pulled it towards him and the movement of the water changed as a body bumped up against him. He wrapped his arm tightly around it and kicked with all his might to take them both back up to the surface. As soon as they broke through, he gasped as the last dregs of air left his body and he dragged in more. He instinctively assumed the life-saving position and made his way back to the riverbank where, using the gnarly roots of the trees, he pulled himself and his rescue victim out of the water.

When they were both on dry land, Charlie lay for a brief moment to regain his strength then stood and turned to pull the person he'd rescued further away from the water. He grabbed his phone and, with a trembling finger, he made a few swipes.

'Hi, Sukie, I urgently need your help. Could you come down to the old hollow tree by the river as quickly as possible – bring the buggy and lots of blankets, I've just pulled a woman out of the water.'

As he knelt to attend to the wet, bedraggled figure lying in front of him, Charlie glanced back at the river and noticed the flowing water was no longer shimmering and was, once more, the dull, dark hue he was used to.

Chapter Three

Charlie was cradling the woman in his arms, his teeth chattering loudly, when Sukie arrived beside him, holding towels and blankets in her arms.

'Charlie, what on earth…?'

'Quickly, wrap her up. I got her breathing again but there's a blue tinge around her lips. That water is bloody freezing.'

'Here, open this for me while I rub her down with this towel. And what the hell is she wearing?'

Charlie ripped the packaging off the space blanket Sukie had thrown to him and looked at the long pale blue dress which adorned the woman lying in front of him.

'It's a bit over the top for a hot day like today. Maybe she's a bridesmaid at a wedding or something?' Charlie gave a small shrug as he shook out the thin, thermal foil.

'I don't know, Charlie, but right now, it's not important. Are you okay to carry her over to the buggy? We need to get her back to the house right away. I told Laura to call the doctor before I left and to prepare one of the bedrooms.

Was there a handbag or anything lying around that might give us a clue as to who she is?'

'I've had a quick look, Sukie, but couldn't find anything. It's possible it may have fallen in the river with her.'

'No problem, we can get the info from her when she's back with us. Right, are you ready to lift her?'

Sukie tucked the thermal blanket around the woman a bit more securely and then led Charlie back to where she'd parked the buggy. He carefully edged his way onto the seat and placed the woman on his lap with her head against his shoulder. Sukie fussed about as she quickly wrapped another space blanket around them both before getting into the driving seat to take them all back to the manor house.

Laura, Sukie's housekeeper, met them at the front door.

'I've prepared the Blue Room for you, Mrs Wallace, I hope that's okay?'

'That's perfect, Laura, thank you. Did you manage to get a hold of the doctor?'

'Yes, he's on his way. He was over the other side of Upper Ditchley when I spoke to him but he said he'd get here as quickly as he could.'

'Thank you, Laura, that's great.'

Charlie was already carrying the woman up the stairs and Sukie followed him. He went into the bedroom Laura had mentioned and was about to put the woman on the bed when Sukie called to him to wait.

'Let me put a couple of towels on the bed first to prevent it getting wet.'

Sukie quickly got some towels from the en-suite and, once Charlie had placed the woman down, she chased him out of the room.

‘Go and have a hot shower to warm yourself up. Use your old room down the corridor. There’s a guest bathrobe in there so you’ll have something to put on when you get out. I need to get this lady out of these wet clothes ASAP and you don’t need to be here for that. Go on, shoo!’

As soon as the door closed behind Charlie, Sukie set about removing the sodden items from her unexpected guest. With each item that came off, her eyebrows rose further and further up her forehead. It was bad enough with the sturdy, brown boots but who on earth wore thick, cotton stockings in the middle of a July heatwave? Once the dress came off, Sukie had her work cut out with removing the old-fashioned stays, petticoats and drawers. She couldn’t help but wonder if the woman had jumped into the river on purpose in an attempt to cool down – she must have been close to collapsing from heatstroke with this lot on.

Laura had had the sense to warm some towels on a couple of hot water bottles and Sukie used these to briskly rub the cold figure up and down in an attempt at keep the poor girl’s circulation going. She then put the white cotton nightdress which Laura had found onto the prone body. The woman was tiny – even smaller than her best friend, Elsa – and Sukie had no problem manoeuvring her into it. She had just eased the woman under the covers when she began to stir. A small moan slipped through her lips.

‘There, there, you’re okay. Take it easy, the doctor is on his way.’

At these words, the woman’s eyes flew open. ‘No doctor,’ she gasped, ‘no doctor.’

‘You have to see a doctor, you nearly drowned.’

‘We can’t afford the doctor…’

‘It’s okay, you don’t have to pay. The doctor is free.’

‘Free? How is that so?’

‘It’s the NHS – it gives free medical treatment. Are you here on holiday?’ Sukie’s curiosity was growing by the second. The woman spoke perfect English and there was no hint of any accent but her lack of knowledge of the NHS plus her unusual clothing had Sukie wondering if she was a tourist – perhaps someone from warmer climes as that would explain the stockings and, at a push, the additional layers.

‘I see.’ The woman was silent for a few minutes as she looked around the room, taking in her surroundings. Sukie sat by the side of the bed, watching and wondering who she was, while at the same time noticing she hadn’t answered the question about being on holiday. Now that some colour was coming back into her cheeks, and the deathly pallor was receding, Sukie saw she was really quite pretty. She had the darkest brown eyes Sukie had ever seen and they matched her hair which was just as dark. It had been necessary to unpin it, in order to towel-dry it, and Sukie had been impressed by how long and thick it was. She’d actually been a little bit envious for she’d always wanted waist-length hair but hers would never grow beyond her shoulder blades. As if the hair wasn’t enough, the woman had perfect, English-rose skin, and a petite nose. Her mouth was a little on the large side but this suited her slightly rounded face. She wasn’t what was considered by some to be beautiful but her prettiness would make you look twice if you passed her in the street.

‘Where am I?’

The quiet voice pulled Sukie back to attention. ‘You’re in my home, Ditchley Manor, which is in a small Oxfordshire village called Lower Ditchley.’

‘Your home? Where is Lord Featheringstone?’

‘Err, yes, my home. Lord Featheringstone died many years ago. Did you know him? Are you a relative?’

The brown eyes gazed at Sukie for several long seconds before the woman replied, ‘I am tired now, I think I will try to sleep.’ She closed her eyes and turned her head away, leaving Sukie feeling even more confused as she picked up the wet clothing she’d removed and took it with her when she left the room.

Chapter Four

Lower Ditchley – 1860

'And you have looked everywhere? Did you go down to the river?' Alice Smythe looked at her son and husband through worried eyes. It was now late evening and Molly hadn't returned home from her walk.

'Yes, I went to the river but couldn't see anything. It was getting dark though and the lamp didn't give off much light.' Albie shrugged his shoulders; his sister was a grown woman and, at thirty-five years of age, she was entitled to some kind of life that didn't have to always be accounted for. She had a fiery nature and had grown up moaning about a woman's lot in life. She thought it highly unfair that men were entitled to so many more opportunities and Albie agreed with her. When they were younger, she could climb the trees quicker than most of the boys in the village, she could shoe a horse far better than him and her seat on a horse was one of the best in the county. Knowing Molly as he did, he wondered if she'd taken herself off on a small adventure. It wouldn't be the first time and he said as much.

'I know,' said his father, 'but she does usually tell us first and her horse is still in the stable. You know she doesn't go too far afield without Chestnut.' His father put his hand upon his shoulder as he spoke and gave it a gentle pat.

'I suppose…'

'John?' His mother looked to her husband.

'I asked in both of the inns but no one has seen her today. The vicar said he has been out and about around the village all day long but doesn't recall seeing her either. How long has she been gone now?'

Alice glanced at the wooden clock on the mantle. 'She went out just before three so that's over seven hours now.' She looked back at her husband. 'John, I'm really worried…'

'Hush now, she's a capable woman, she'll be fine.'

Albie watched as his father put his arms around his mother to comfort her. He could see from his father's expression, however, that his words were said merely to soothe his wife – he himself had no belief in them.

'Look, why don't you both head off to bed, I'll wait down here for her coming home.'

'Oh, I couldn't sleep for the worry,' replied Alice.

Well I damn well could, thought Albie, although he didn't voice this. He worked in the smithy with his father and they'd been busy all day. The heat of the summer's day had only added to their discomfort and now, all he wanted to do, was lie on his bed in front of the window and hope there was enough of a breeze in the night sky to cool him as he slept.

'Mother, come on, do as Father says. You'll feel better in the morning after a good night's sleep. Things always look better in the morning, isn't that right, Father?'

His father threw him a grateful smile. 'Yes, lad, that's right.' He placed a small kiss on his wife's cheek. 'Goodnight, my love.'

Albie followed his mother up the stairs and, when he glanced back, he saw his father pull one of the chairs out from the kitchen table and put his feet upon the fender in front of the unlit fireplace as he prepared for his vigil.

The small oil lamp had gone out and it was dark when John Smythe awoke with a start. What was that? He'd heard a noise… Suddenly, he began coughing and he realised the air was thick with smoke. The noise he'd heard was the whinnying of the horses in the stable next door.

The last remnants of sleep swiftly left him as he felt the scorching heat and it dawned upon him that the cottage was on fire. In an instant it hit him that Albie and Alice were upstairs and he had to get to them. He turned around and stumbled over the chair he'd been sitting on. He could hear the roar of the flames as they consumed the wooden timbers on the outside of the cottage. He knew that, once they reached the roof, it would all be over for the thatch would go up like a tinderbox. It was so dry due to the current hot spell and they hadn't had rain for several weeks. He reached out his hand and felt for the kitchen table, using it to guide him towards the stairs, all the while bent over with coughing as he did so. He paused for a moment to grab the tail of his shirt and, ripping it off, tied the cotton material around his face. He reached the bottom of the stairs at the same time the fire reached the roof. There was an almighty "whoomph" as the flames found new fodder to feast upon. The torrid heat engulfed him as he desperately tried to climb up to rescue his family.

After what felt like an eternity, and with lungs screaming in pain, John reached the upper floor. Above his head, an angry red curtain ran the length of the ceiling and he had to crouch low as he made his way to the nearest bedroom. Sparks were raining down upon him and he could feel them scorching his skin like a million pin pricks. He opened the bedroom door and let out a howl of grief for he was too late – Albie's bed was fully alight from top to toe and he could see the outline of a figure through the flames. He turned and crawled towards his own bedroom where Alice would be. The door was open and, as he entered, he bumped against something on the floor. He ran his hand along it and, realising it was his wife, John slipped his arm through hers and began dragging her behind him, back in the direction of the stairs.

They had just reached the top step when there was a loud creaking noise and the roof of the cottage caved in. A large fiery beam flew in his direction and hit him with tremendous force on the side of the head.

He was already dead when the floor beneath him collapsed and he, along with the remains of his family, fell down into the flames below.

Chapter Five

Lower Ditchley – Present Day

Molly lay on her side, looking out of the bedroom window. The manor house was quiet and the moonlight floating through the glass panes told her it was now night. A doctor had visited several hours earlier and, after a quick check-up, he'd declared her none the worse for her "adventure" – his words, not hers. He'd left some medication – auntiebotics he'd said, or something like that – just in case she'd picked up anything nasty in the water. He'd said they were a precaution. Although, how on earth could he stop a disease that was already in her body? What kind of silly notion was that?

Since speaking with Sukie, after the doctor had left, Molly had worked out that something wasn't right. She knew which bedroom, within the manor, she was in for she often helped out when Lord Featheringstone was entertaining and having house guests. She'd been in this bedroom only a few months before and it had looked nothing like it did now. It was with this realisation of "wrongness" that she'd gone quiet and had barely spoken since, deeming it to be in her better interest to say little until she had worked out what had happened after she'd fallen in the river. The last thing she needed was to speak out of turn and be bundled off to an asylum for having lost her wits.

She closed her eyes and was on the verge of dozing back off to sleep when her brain suddenly brought her back to full alertness. She sat upright as a wave of sheer panic flowed through her. 'Nooooooo,' she moaned. She'd just remembered the conversation she'd overheard in the wood. She had to get home and warn her father of Alderly's intentions.

Molly threw the bedcovers back and looked around quickly for her clothes. Unable to see them, she glanced down at the over-long cotton nightdress she was wearing. It would have to do. Pulling one of the top covers off the bed, she threw it around her shoulders and made her way to the door. She opened it slightly and peered out into the hallway. A small lamp, sitting on a table halfway along, was lit but there was no one in sight and everything was quiet. She tiptoed out of the room and felt soft carpeting beneath her bare feet. She hadn't been able to find her boots either but time was of the utmost importance so bare feet would have to do. Molly moved towards the stairs, wincing when a floorboard creaked beneath her, and hurried down them as fast as she could. She found her way to the library for it would be easier to slip out of the French windows in there than to open the large front door. Within a few moments, she was running across the lawn towards the path which would take her to the churchyard and the village. Her long hair streamed out behind her and the cover around her shoulders flapped against her back. She scrunched up the front of her nightdress in her hand, thus allowing her legs more freedom to move and to avoid wasting time by tripping over.

'Oh, blast! Open... open!' she exclaimed, as she reached the gate and fumbled with the catch, her haste making her fingers numb and unwieldy. Finally, she was through and, not bothering to close it behind her, Molly flew past the church, her head down and her breath coming in short gasps. She pulled up suddenly and raised her head towards the sky. She could smell smoke! Something was on fire!

Her fear for her family added flight to her feet and she began running again, faster than before. She burst out of the lane that ran between the shops which looked over the village green. She didn't stop to consider her whereabouts, only one thought was on her mind – *I must get home, I must get home, I must get home...*

With the last of her strength, she crossed the green until she was facing the front of the coaching inn...

Except... There was no inn!

Molly, having used her final ounce of energy, could barely hold herself up. She stood barefoot on the grass, swaying as she stared at the building across from her. The faint stench of smoke was still in her nose but, as she looked about her, she could see no flames, nor the signs of anyone panicking. In fact, as she looked around a second time, she began to notice that while she was still in her home village, it was no longer *her* home village.

She took in the large bookshop where the inn used to be, the bakery in the place where the entrance for the stables behind the inn had once been and the road just a few feet in front of her which was blacker than coal and as smooth as glass. It was not the dry, dusty, rutted and lumpy roadway she had crossed a few hours earlier.

She let out a moan and slowly slipped sideways as her mind began to blacken out, no longer able to deal with what it didn't want to know. The last vestiges of reality were just about to leave when a strong pair of arms slipped beneath her and picked her up.

'There, there, it's okay, I've got you.'

Charlie had been unable to sleep. The excitement of the day, if you could call it that, should have had him out for the count but, instead, he was wide awake, going over and over the events which had led to him now lying under the roof of the manor rather than in his own bed back at the mill.

Sukie had insisted he stay the night for she wanted to be close by should anything happen. He'd tried to explain that the doctor had been more than satisfied with him after his check-up and he did plan to take the antibiotics he'd been given but Sukie was having none of it. Charlie had known her long enough to know that arguing was not worth the bother so he'd given in gracefully and allowed her to fuss over him.

His thoughts returned to the woman he'd rescued. All they'd been able to glean from her was that her name was Molly Smythe and she lived in the village. When the doctor had left, Sukie had turned to him and said she'd believed she knew everyone in the village but she'd never seen this woman before. 'Maybe she's a relative who's visiting,' had been his reply. This had appeased Sukie slightly and, with a small shrug and a 'Maybe…' she'd gone off to see about making them all something to eat.

Charlie, however, didn't think this although, truth be told, he didn't know *what* to think. When he'd held the woman in his arms earlier, the strangest sensation had flowed through his bones. He couldn't say what it was or how it had come about, but it had created an unsettled feeling within him which had not yet eased.

He was pondering on this when he heard the smallest of creaks. It was so slight that, had it not been the quiet, early hours of the morning, it would have gone unnoticed. He immediately slipped out of bed, hurried over to the bedroom door and placed his ear against the cool wooden panel. He sensed, rather than heard, someone passing by on the other side and he opened the door just in time to see a hint of something white moving towards the stairs. He ran back into the bedroom to pull on the clothing which Laura had returned, washed and dried, earlier that evening before making his way down the stairs. He reached the last step and hesitated, not sure where to go next. He held his breath, his ears straining to pick up any noise and was rewarded when the lightest of squeaks floated towards him. He knew exactly where to go – the library. He'd spent many hours in there, during his stay at the manor a year earlier, and he knew that squeak well.

When he entered the library, however, the room was empty. He switched on a couple of lamps but no one was hiding in the shadows. It was the sway of the curtains which directed him to the windows and, upon pulling them back, he noticed the French windows were slightly ajar. He looked out and saw Molly, a small white ghost in the moonlight, running across the lawn. He slipped out of the door, pushing it to behind him, and went after her. He didn't think she was ready to be out of bed yet and knew the doctor had ordered her to have a few days of rest.

It didn't take long for Charlie to see they were heading towards the village. With his long stride, he could easily have caught Molly up but he purposely lagged behind, curious to see where she was going. Maybe her mystery was about to be revealed.

He soon reached the mouth of the lane and the village green was spread before him. Charlie stopped to loiter in the shadows. He could see Molly clearly in the streetlights, her white nightdress a beacon for her movements. He watched her stop in front of The Cabookeria bookshop and then stand, swaying, on the grass as her head turned this way and that. He moved out of the shadows and, crossing the road, began to walk towards her. When he saw her shoulders drop and her body beginning to fall over, he sprinted the last few yards between them and caught her in his arms just before she hit the ground.

'There, there,' he said, 'it's okay, I've got you.'

Chapter Six

The darkness slowly began to recede from Molly's head and her eyelids eased themselves open. The side of her face was pressed against something soft and warm and when she looked up, she could make out the underside of a pale chin with a dark sky behind it. She closed her eyes again – this felt nice, it felt safe, it felt... Like she was being carried!

Her eyes flew open and she wriggled around in an attempt to release herself from the arms which held her.

'Unhand me at once, sir. Please put me down.'

Eyes which shone in the moonlight looked down at her and a soft, gentle voice replied, 'No, I can't put you down. Your feet are bare and bleeding and you'll hurt yourself further if you try to walk.'

'I'll hurt you, sir, if you do not take your hands off me this instant.'

'Very well, if you insist.'

'I do insist!'

Molly felt her legs being lowered until her feet were placed on the ground. The arm around her back moved away and she was, once again, standing on her own two feet. Except… they really hurt!

When she'd been a child, she'd spent many summers running wild around the village in a shoeless state, much to her mother's chagrin. "What will people think?" had been her constant cry of horror. It would seem she'd gone soft in the ensuing years for the pain was bringing tears to her eyes. She could see the silhouette of the manor house in the distance and remembered her run from there, only a short time ago, towards the village. She recalled the smoky smell which had spurred her on but now, when she gave a quick sniff, the acrid scent was gone and all she could smell was the freshness of the night. Molly looked at the man standing beside her. He had a slender build and was considerably taller than herself, although he didn't tower over her. His hair glinted in the moonlight and his face was not displeasing to the eye. She couldn't discern his eye colour but it was not dark, she could tell that much. A small smile was sitting on his lips. He didn't look cruel. In fact, she would almost go as far as to say he looked kind.

'Hi, Molly, my name is Charlie and I pulled you out of the river earlier today.' His voice was still gentle and Molly felt her guard drop slightly, although it was not decent for her to be standing out of doors in just her nightclothes with a man she did not know. Whatever would people say?

A hand was thrust in front of her and, despite her reservations, it would be impolite to decline or ignore it. She carefully placed hers within it while saying, 'Then I owe you my thanks, sir, for rescuing me and for your bravery and courage.'

'Please, call me Charlie, and it was no trouble. I'm glad you are alright although those feet are going to need some attention now.'

'Sir, we have only just met and I cannot call you by your name, although you invite me to do so, as it would be most improper.'

'Would it be "improper" if I insisted upon it?'

'Well, yes, it is, but if you insist, then I feel I should oblige… Charlie.'

'That's better. Now, do you think you can walk?'

Molly carefully turned back in the direction of the village and took a couple of steps but faltered when the pain shot up her legs. She stopped, took a deep breath and waited until the pain had eased before trying again. She managed two more steps before letting out a small moan.

She looked at Charlie who hadn't moved from her side. 'Sir… I mean… Charlie, it would appear I am in need of your assistance after all.'

Charlie smiled and his white teeth twinkled down at her. 'Put your arm around my neck, hold the throw tight with your other, and I'll carry you.'

'Throw?'

'The cover around your shoulders. We call it a throw because you throw it over things.'

'I see.' Molly pulled the throw more tightly around her body as she tried to preserve whatever modesty she had left, and allowed Charlie to pick her up once again.

When he turned back towards the manor, she made to protest but he spoke across her in a firm tone.

'Molly, I think, for the time being, it would be better for you to stay at the manor. It is not up for discussion.'

Molly's first reaction was to argue against him but she held it down for she realised Charlie was right. After what she had seen tonight, she needed to find out what had happened to her and it was better for her to do this somewhere where she was safe.

The fight left her then and she relaxed into Charlie's arms, allowing him to carry her back to the manor.

Chapter Seven

'Here, drink this, it'll warm you up.' Charlie placed a cup of hot tea on the table in front of Molly.

They were in the manor kitchen and, having just boiled the kettle for a second time, he was pouring it into a plastic basin he'd found in the scullery. He sprinkled in two spoons of salt along with a splash of cold water to bring the temperature down. He picked it up, placed it in front of Molly's chair and gently placed her feet inside. She flinched, pulling her feet out again but then placed them back in with a slight moan.

'Is the water too hot? Or is the salt stinging your cuts?'

'I think maybe both. The water feels hot because my feet are cold and the salt is definitely stinging but I know it helps.' She gave him a small, grateful smile. Charlie felt something inside him clench slightly at the sight of it. Not wanting to be caught staring, he stood up and retrieved the first-aid box from the cupboard before sitting opposite Molly at the table.

'Molly,' he tried to speak as softly as he could, 'we need to talk about things. Something here is… off balance…

Am I right?'

She hesitated for a moment before nodding. 'Yes, you are correct, but I don't know why things are different, although they are.'

'In what way? How are they different?'

'Since you carried me in here, I have been watching and looking and I can see many things which I neither know nor understand. You boiled water but did not place the kettle on the stove. You have made tea in the teapot, and poured it out without a strainer, yet there are no leaves floating in my cup. We have light above our heads but I do not understand how it is there. These are only some of the questions I have in my head. Am I going mad? Is this all happening in my head like a dream?'

'No, Molly, I can assure you this is not a dream. I am real, you are real and all of this around you is real.'

'Then what has happened to me?'

Charlie thought for a moment before he answered. He was beginning to have an idea as to what may have happened but… nah… surely not… could it have? He leant forward.

'Molly, I'm going to ask you what might seem a strange question but please, if you don't mind, could you just answer it for me?'

'I shall try, sir.'

Charlie nodded. 'Good. Can you tell me what year it is?'

'Why, it's 1860.'

He gasped. It must be as he thought. Somehow, Molly had travelled through time and from a year when, if he knew his history correctly, the very notion hadn't even been thought of.

'Molly, there's no easy way to tell you this, but you're now in the twenty-first century.'

Molly let out a small laugh. 'Oh, sir, you are talking silly talk. How could I possibly be in the twenty-first century?'

'I'm not certain,' Charlie said, 'but somehow, it appears that you've travelled through time.'

She laughed again but it slowly petered out as he sat, saying nothing. 'You are not pretending, are you? You are not mocking me, are you, Charlie?'

'No, Molly, I am being completely serious. You appear to have travelled forward in time.'

'How has that happened? I don't understand. Is this travelling through time thing common? Do people now do this in the twenty-first century?'

'No, they do not. Although they would like to.'

'Then, please tell me, how am I in your time and out of mine?'

'I really, really do not know.' Charlie thought for a moment before asking, 'When you went out walking today, did you see, or notice, anything unusual? Something you've never seen before.'

He watched as she scrunched her eyebrows together, thinking about all she had seen that afternoon. Eventually, she replied, 'No, I cannot say that I did.'

'Let's think this through together – everything was normal for you until you fell in the river, yes?'

She nodded at him.

'But since I've pulled you out, everything is different?'

'Yes, that is correct.'

'Did you notice anything unusual about the river today? Was there anything you may not have seen before?'

'No, it was just the same as always. I was surprised to see the sunlight shining on it where the trees are at their thickest, just by the old hollow stump, but it was a very bright day—'

‘I saw that too! And I thought the same – it was unusual to see sunlight on that spot. Maybe it wasn’t sunlight. Maybe it was a time portal or an anomaly!’

‘A what?’

‘A time portal, or an anomaly, is kind of like a door to another period of time. There was a television programme about such things a few years back – I never for a moment thought there could be any truth in it.’

‘And still you speak of things which I know nothing of.’ Her reply was made in the driest of tones and her face was tight.

‘In the programme I saw, the thing they called an anomaly, was silvery and shimmering – just like the river today.’

‘We’ll return to this “programme” thing in a minute but, first you must tell me, are these “anomalies” common in your time?’

Charlie looked at Molly, his earlier surprise now replaced with total seriousness. ‘No, they are not, not at all. In fact, I have never heard of a real one ever having been discovered and, if the news gets out about this one, I think it will cause a whole heap of trouble, let me tell you!’ He pulled his chair round closer to Molly and, placing a towel across his lap, he lifted her right foot out of the water. She went to pull it away but he grasped her ankle firmly, but gently, and put it back on the towel.

‘Molly, I need to clean this and put some antiseptic on it to prevent any infection.’

‘But, sir…, I mean, Charlie, it is indecent. You barely know me yet you are fondling my feet.’ Molly pushed the nightdress along her leg towards the ankle Charlie still had in his grip.

‘Sorry, Molly, I didn’t think. We need to attend to your wounds though – some of these cuts are quite deep and it will be awkward for you to reach down to do it yourself.

Please, let me help.'

Her reply rode on the back of a sigh. 'Oh, alright! I suppose it must be done.'

'Thank you.' He picked up some cotton wool and began to gently cleanse the dirt from the sole of her foot. 'Why don't you tell me about yourself while I do this? It might help if we know a little about each other. I see you're married.' He inclined his head towards the slim gold band adorning the wedding finger of her left hand.

'Not anymore. I am widowed.'

'I see, I'm sorry to hear that.'

'It happened fifteen years ago so I am no longer sad about it.'

'That's a long time and you still wear your ring – you must have loved him very much.'

There was silence for a moment before Molly replied. 'I suppose I did at the time. I was very sure it was the right thing to do, but now…' Her voice tailed off.

'May I ask what age you were, if it's not too rude?'

'Tommy and I were wed when I was eighteen. I buried him when I was twenty. We'd known each other all of our lives and he took an apprenticeship with my father. One day, there was an accident at the forge and an anvil dropped on his foot. It had to be removed but then he developed poison of the blood and it killed him.'

'That's awful,' Charlie said, 'I'm so sorry.'

'Thank you. But as I said, it was a long time ago.'

'Have you considered remarrying?'

'Is that an offer, Mr Charlie?'

Charlie looked up with surprise at the flirty change in her voice. 'I'm sorry…?'

'Well, you are sitting there rubbing my feet, that really is quite intimate for someone I have only just met.'

'Errm… Umm…'

The sound of hearty laughter filled the kitchen and he

smiled as Molly threw back her head and roared. It was a few minutes before she could speak again.

'Charlie, I am jesting. I have no desire to marry again. I like being a widow.'

'You do?'

'Yes, it gives me a degree of freedom and respectability I would not otherwise have as a single woman or a wife.'

'So, Smythe is your married name?'

'No, it was Robotham, but I was married for such a short time, and with moving back in with my parents after Tommy's death, everyone reverted back to calling me Molly Smythe as that is what they were used to. I prefer it, if I am being honest. "Robotham" had too many syllables. I am perfectly happy being "Smythe". And I am also perfectly happy with my life. Or rather… I was!' She looked around the kitchen before looking back pointedly at him.

'Good point,' he said, 'well made. Right, that's your feet sorted. I think we should return to our beds and try to get some sleep in what is left of the night. Tomorrow, we'll need to have a long talk and see where we go from here. It would be best to do it with clear heads. Come on, I'll carry you up.'

Charlie quickly tidied everything away, swung Molly up into his arms and, after talking her through how to operate the light switch, took her upstairs and placed her back on her bed. When he returned to his own room, he sat with his head in his hands for several minutes wondering what on earth had happened and, more importantly, what the hell was he going to do about it?

Molly lay in bed once more, looking out at the stars in the sky. Her head was swimming with what she had learnt

– how could it be possible to move through time? She didn't understand. Although, if she was being truthful with herself, there was now a lot which she didn't understand and she really didn't know how she was going to manage or what she was going to do. Was it possible for this to be fixed?

Her heart began to race and she sat upright as her breath came out in short gasps. Since Charlie had brought her back to the manor, she had fought hard against the desire to just close her eyes and scream and scream and scream. The panic built up inside her, her stomach was clenching in fear and she could feel the control she'd maintained thus far beginning to slip away. She was surely in a nightmare… Except… Nightmares were usually things of horror and terror and, while she was in a strange place with strange people and surrounded by even stranger things, it was a kind place and she had been looked after and cared for. For the very briefest of moments, in the kitchen with Charlie, she'd even managed to forget her situation and had laughed. She clung tightly onto this thought and replayed the scene over and over in her head, willing herself to draw in deep breaths, slowly but surely, until her breathing began to return to normal and her heartbeat slowed to its usual steady pace.

That's more like it, Molly Smythe, she told herself, *There's nothing to be gained from getting hysterical.*

She concentrated on counting her breaths, slowly in and slowly out and, when she finally lay down and pulled the lovely soft sheets around her, she soon slipped into a deep and dreamless sleep.

Chapter Eight

Lower Ditchley – 1860

Damien Featheringstone stood at the back of the crowd gathered on the village green. Dawn hadn't long broken and the full extent of the fire's wrath was beginning to come into view. The Smythes' cottage was completely burnt out. Two of the roof timbers were still in place, pointing up towards the sky like blackened, knotted fingers, tendrils of smoke swirling around in the gentle breeze. The stench from the smoke could be smelt as far as the manor, for it was that which had woken Damien when it curled in through his open window in the early hours of the morning.

Already, the rumours were beginning to rumble through the watching villagers as they wondered upon the whereabouts of the family. Had they perished in the fire? Had they escaped but were lying injured somewhere? Should a search party be organised to look for them?

Just then, the owner of the coaching inn came out of the front door, staggered over to the crowd and into the arms of his wife, as tears streamed down his face. 'We're ruined, Betsy, we're ruined,' he wailed against her shoulder.

'What is the damage, my love?' she asked him. 'How bad is it?'

'The stable building is still standing, thanks to my father's foresight to rebuild in brick, but the inside has been almost burnt out and the roof is in a bad way. The inn, however, has been badly damaged at the back. It's a miracle the whole building didn't go up.'

'That's because you were sensible, my dear,' Betsy replied through her own tears. 'You had the wisdom to ensure buckets of water were kept close by and, by wetting the building, you stopped the fire taking a greater hold. If only Patrick had been able to escape…' She let out a loud sob.

Betsy and her husband were busy trying to console each other as Damien walked away. He'd spotted Stan Alderly and he needed to have a word with him. In fact, he needed to have *several* words.

He sidled up behind Stan and whispered sternly in his ear, 'Meet me in the woods in fifteen minutes.'

He'd already moved on by the time Stan turned around.

'You stupid, stupid fool! What the HELL were you thinking?' Damien was pacing up and down in the clearing, trying to figure out what to do next. The villagers weren't stupid and it wouldn't be long before someone remembered the altercation he'd had with John Smythe, yesterday afternoon. His parting words had been that Smythe would regret what he'd done and the scene was now firmly imprinted in his mind.

'You told me to teach Smythe a lesson,' Stan whined. 'Something that would make business difficult for him, you said. I thought this was the best way to do that.'

Damien whirled around and towered over Stan. 'Are you honestly trying to tell me that you thought setting the man's home alight, in the middle of one of the driest summers we've had for years, was really the best way to go about it? Common sense alone should have steered you away from that path!'

Stan didn't reply and his silence only angered Damien more. He returned to his pacing, trying to form some kind of plan that made sure no one looked towards him or Stan as being the root cause of the disaster. He'd always been good at getting himself out of trouble – his nanny had said it was his one special gift – so, surely, he could devise a means of halting this one at the gate. He wandered over towards the river and stared down into the water, waiting for an idea to come that might have some merit. It wasn't long before something began to take hold. He allowed it to grow some more before he turned to voice it aloud to Alderly. As he did so, his foot brushed against something and, when he looked down, he saw a rattan basket lying on the river path, spilt berries lying around it. In a moment of panic, he quickly looked about to see if someone was hiding in the undergrowth but then he noticed the berries looked slightly wilted and breathed a sigh of relief at their less than fresh state. He didn't stop to wonder how or why they were there but got a small degree of satisfaction from venting some of his anger upon the basket when he kicked it into the river.

He walked back to Alderly. 'Right, I have a plan. It's not great but it just might work. We allow the villagers to talk about this today but, from tomorrow, we forbid them to do so. We'll say that it does no good to anyone for them to keep talking about the incident and it would be best for everyone if they tried to forget about it and carried on with their lives. The sooner everything returns to normal, the better it will be for all.'

‘But people are bound to talk, Damien, it’s what they do. Even I know that.’

‘Then we make sure they’re too frightened to talk. Get you and your cronies to put it about that anyone caught speaking of this will be evicted from their homes and excluded from the village.’

‘Your father would never do such a thing – you know he wouldn’t.’

‘You and I both know that but the villagers don’t. We’ll make it appear as though the order has come from the old man – he doesn’t want discontent within the village and wants normal life to resume as soon as possible. Anyone who doesn’t abide by it must leave.’

‘But what happens if the Smythes turn up?’

‘Stan, I think it is a more than fair assumption to say the Smythes almost certainly perished in the blaze. If they do turn up, then everyone is happy and all is well. If they try to point a finger, we can redirect the blame by saying they hadn’t properly banked down the fires in the forge that evening.’

‘What if their bodies are discovered when they clear the rubble from the cottage?’

‘I read, once, that if a fire reaches a high enough temperature, then whole bodies can be incinerated with almost nothing left behind. Let us hope this was the case last night. In time, they will be forgotten about but only if no one talks. You can make up for this mess by ensuring no one does. Have you got that?’

‘Yes, Damien.’

‘Good. Now go and get it done. I’ll wait here a while longer to ensure no one sees us together.’

An hour later, Damien stepped inside the village church.

‘Hello, Mr Damien, what brings you here today?’

Damien turned, startled to see the vicar of the parish standing in the vestibule behind him.

‘Oh, vicar, you gave me a start. I wasn’t expecting anyone to be here.’

‘I’m just leaving now. I’m going over to the Smythes’ place to offer up a prayer and give some comfort to the villagers. It’s a terrible state of affairs.’

‘Indeed, it is. I am here to say a prayer for them too. John Smythe and I may have spoken heated words to each other on occasion but I would never have wished this upon him.’

And, in that once sentence, Damien knew he’d dealt with the concern over yesterday’s argument. The vicar would come down on his side if anyone raised any questions. ‘Now, vicar, please don’t let me keep you. I’ll stay here awhile and do what I need to do.’

‘Of course, Mr Damien, of course. Goodbye.’

The vicar set off on his way and, a few minutes later, Damien opened the door a crack and peeped out to ensure he really was alone. Seeing the vicinity was clear, he closed the door again, ran down the aisle of the church and made his way behind the altar to the vestry. He tried the door and, finding it unlocked, slipped inside. He looked around the shelves of books adorning the walls on two sides of the room and hoped that what he wanted would be sitting on one of them.

It didn’t take long to locate what he was after – the records book which held the details of all births, marriages and deaths within the parish. He opened it to find the entries had petered out just over five years ago. The new vicar was far more organised than his predecessor and had clearly adjusted to the new system of centralised registration which was held in London. The previous vicar had been old and set in his ways and his scrawl was very much evident right up to the last entry. Damien let a small sigh of relief fall from his lips. If the last entry was five years ago, then no one would likely notice its absence. He shoved the records book underneath his coat and, after moving the remaining books on the shelf along to hide the gap, quickly left the room and the church.

Once back in his bedroom in the manor, he put the book on the top of his wardrobe. When the cool nights drew in, a month or two from now, he would dispose of it in the fire. After all, if you are trying to eradicate the memories of a family from local history, then where better to start than by destroying the book which held the evidence of their existence in the first place.

Chapter Nine

Lower Ditchley – Present Day

The knock on the bedroom door woke Molly the next morning. The sunlight, signalling the arrival of another warm summer's day, was blazing through the window and onto her face. It took several attempts to open her eyes against the glare.

'Molly, are you awake? I've brought you some breakfast.'

'Come in,' she mumbled and attempted a smile when Sukie appeared with a tray in her hands.

'Hey, how are you feeling today?' Sukie's voice was soothing, which Molly appreciated. Her bare-footed foray last night had sapped what little energy she'd had left after her escape from the river and she'd been in the deepest of sleeps when Sukie had awoken her.

'Umm, somewhat tired right now,' she replied.

'Oh, Molly, I'm sorry, did I wake you up? It's almost ten o'clock and I was worried you'd be lying here thinking we'd forgotten about you.'

‘It’s alright, I wouldn’t normally sleep so late.’

‘You had quite an eventful day, yesterday; it was bound to knock you for six. Don’t worry about it.’

‘Err, Sukie, I need to use the chamber pot…’ Molly felt her face grow hot as she spoke. She desperately had to go although Sukie didn’t seem to notice her embarrassment.

‘Of course, I’m so sorry, I should have told you where to find it yesterday. The bathroom is over in that corner.’

Molly drew in a sharp breath in order to contain her surprise – that “corner” was the airing cupboard where all the blankets for this floor in the manor were kept. This was going to be interesting.

She carefully moved back the sheets and was gingerly placing her feet on the floor when there was another knock on the door and Charlie’s head popped around it.

‘Oh good, you’re awake. A-a-ahh, where do you think you’re going on those feet? You need to rest them…’

‘She also needs the loo, Charlie,’ said Sukie, ‘and what has happened to your feet, Molly?’

Molly looked at Charlie with uncertainty, not knowing what to say.

‘Let’s give Molly a few minutes to refresh herself, Sukie, and then we’ll talk.’

He picked Molly up and carried her over to the door in the corner which he pushed open with his foot. ‘Can you put the light on please, Molly? Just pull that cord there… That’s it, perfect.’

He made a show of being clumsy and closed the door behind him, closing them both in the small room which was definitely no longer an airing cupboard.

‘Right, Molly,’ he whispered, ‘is there anything in here which you’ve never seen before and don’t know how to operate?’

Molly looked around round – The main thing was the white, shiny, raised bowl by Charlie’s legs. She pointed at it shyly.

'That's the toilet.'

'That is a toilet?' she exclaimed. 'How does that work?' In her wonderment, Molly's embarrassment had faded away. That was, until Charlie whispered to her how it worked.

'Oh, I see.' She could feel her cheeks burning up again.

Charlie quickly pointed out one or two other little curiosities before slipping out the door and leaving her alone.

A few minutes later, after watching the flush of the toilet with childish glee and being utterly amazed by the water coming out of the taps on the sink, she hobbled back into the bedroom where Charlie and Sukie were waiting for her return.

Charlie picked her up and put her back on the bed, saying as he did so, 'I've told Sukie we have something important and highly confidential to share with her. Before I tell her, are you alright with her knowing your secret?'

Molly looked up at him, her dark brown eyes full of hesitation. 'I… I suppose we have to…' she whispered eventually.

'How about I tell her, while you eat some breakfast? You must be starving by now.'

Molly nodded and looked down at the tray Sukie had laid across her lap.

'I didn't know if you preferred tea or coffee so I brought you some hot chocolate instead. Everyone likes hot chocolate and it's really nice with croissants for breakfast. Go on, eat up.'

Molly assumed the "cwass-ont" was the golden-brown pastry thing on the plate in front of her. Fortunately, the hot chocolate was less of a surprise. Charlie was sitting slightly behind Sukie and he made a dipping motion behind her back. Molly got what he was "saying" and, tearing off a small piece of the pastry, she dipped it in the warm drink before eating it. When she placed it in her mouth, she didn't know what to expect but oh my… This was delicious! She let out a small moan of pleasure and closed her eyes in order to enjoy the sweetness of the beverage combined with the flaky, buttery sensation of the pastry to the fullest. It was one of the nicest things she could ever recall eating. She did like sweet goods but they were a rare treat. Sometimes, when she'd been helping out with dinner parties at the manor, cook would share out any leftovers and these occasionally included cakes and desserts but none of them had ever tasted as delightful as this. She opened her eyes as she swallowed and quickly set about devouring both the pastry and the drink.

While she ate, Charlie took the reins and began filling Sukie in on what had occurred, and been discovered, through the night. When he'd finished, Sukie turned to Molly and simply looked at her. It took her a couple of attempts to speak but finally she said, 'Is this true?'

Molly nodded. 'Yes, it is. I don't know how it happened but Charlie's explanation does sound the most plausible given the circumstances. I don't know what amonlys are but I think it's what I saw.'

'It's called an anomaly, and, this time yesterday, I'd have said they were a work of fiction but now… I don't honestly know what to think.'

'I think we're all in agreement with you there, Sukie, but, no matter how weird it feels for us, think how poor Molly must be feeling. Do you know just how much we've advanced in the last one hundred and sixty-odd years? If we were to go back in time, we would know – or have a good idea at least – of what we were looking at and what to expect but, to come forward? That is just mind-blowing.'

Sukie was still watching Molly. 'You seem rather calm

about all this, Molly, if you don't mind me saying. If I was in your situation, I rather think I'd be a quivering wreck.'

'It is God's own truth, Sukie, that last night, when Charlie brought me back, I was very close to giving in to the fear inside me, but then I thought of how kind you have both been to me and I realised that becoming hysterical would be of no benefit. It would serve us all far better if I tried to maintain a level head and we all worked together to sort this out. Besides, hysterical women get locked up in asylums – I really do not have a desire to experience that.'

Sukie leant forward and placed a hand on top of Molly's. 'Well, I'm pleased to say that's one thing we've finally done away with these days although I do agree level heads all around would be the best way forward.'

Just then, and without warning, Molly let out the largest of yawns. 'Oh, my goodness, I am so sorry. Please, excuse me.' She could feel the mortification rushing back to her cheeks.

Charlie laughed. 'Hey, don't worry about it. You've been awake half the night, it's no wonder you're tired.'

'Look, why don't you spend the day in bed, Molly. You've had quite an ordeal – you need time to adjust.' Sukie stood and picked the tray up from Molly's lap. 'Get some more sleep and I'll bring another tray up to you at lunch time. You need to rest those feet – I wouldn't recommend walking on them today.'

'I don't want to be any trouble…' She wasn't aware she was clenching and unclenching the bedsheet until Charlie placed his hands over hers.

'It's okay, Molly, don't you worry about anything for now. We'll cross that bridge once you feel better.' His kind tone eased her turmoil and the panic which had started bubbling inside her again, subsided.

She lay down and let Charlie pull the covers back over her. She was asleep before he and Sukie had left the room.

Down in the kitchen, Charlie sat at the table while Sukie put Molly's breakfast things in the dishwasher.

'What are you thinking?' he asked her.

'Charlie, I really don't know what to think. It all seems so… I dunno… Weird? Strange? Fanciful? I can't think of a word to best describe it.'

'Do you think she's telling the truth?'

'Do you?' Sukie turned from the sink to look directly at him.

There was a small pause before he answered. 'I think I do.'

'Why?'

'It's the way she reacted when she saw the shop. The way she almost collapsed on the grass… It was clear she'd had a shock.'

'Maybe it was done for effect. Maybe she did it to fool you.'

'She didn't know I was following her, Sukie. I was quite a way behind and she never once looked back to see if I was there. I don't think her reaction was faked.'

'Hmmm.' Sukie pulled her phone from her pocket and began typing a text.

'Sukie, what are you doing? We can't tell anyone about this. If what she says is true, the media will hound her and the authorities will be questioning her until the end of time, trying to get information—'

'Charlie, hush!' Sukie interrupted him. 'I'm aware of that and I certainly don't want to be bringing unwanted attention to the situation, which is why,' she held up her phone, 'I am telling Laura she can have the two-week holiday she asked for along with some extra days to prepare for it. The less people around here who know about Molly, the better.'

‘Thank you, Sukie. Sorry for thinking otherwise.’

‘Hey, no worries. I understand.’

Charlie stood up. ‘Right, I’m going to head back to the mill, get changed and then take a walk along the river to see if I can see anything out of the ordinary. I’ll pop back in a couple of hours.’

‘Charlie, go home and sleep. Molly’s not the only one whose night was interrupted. Come back tonight for dinner.’

‘Good idea,’ said Charlie with a smile. He was struggling to suppress his yawning and the thought of crashing in his bed for a few more hours was very appealing. ‘I’ll see you this evening.’ He dropped a peck on Sukie’s cheek before heading out into the early heat of the day.

Chapter Ten

Molly ended up being confined to her bed for another three days. The cuts on her feet were too tender to walk upon and she'd declined Charlie's offer to carry her down the stairs. She felt safe in this room and wasn't quite ready to face life beyond it. She knew she would have to soon but she'd prefer it to be when she was more in control and not dependent on someone else to move her around.

On the fourth morning, she was sitting by the window when there was a knock on the door. Sukie popped her head around and smiled when she saw Molly by the window.

'Hey, you're up. How are you feeling today?'

Molly returned the smile. 'Much better, thank you, in every way. My head feels clearer and my feet are definitely on the mend. They're still a bit sore but it's bearable now.'

'I can give you a painkiller which will help, if you like.'

'Thank you.' Molly didn't know what a painkiller was but she liked the sound of it.

'Now, I suppose we need to sort you out with some clothes.'

‘My dress—’

‘Is very nice but not practical. For a start off, it’s hot and it cannot be comfortable. It will also make you stand out and people will notice you. We need to make you blend in as much as possible. We can’t risk you coming to anyone’s attention for that would create a big bundle of grief we really don’t need.’

Molly had noticed that both Sukie and Charlie’s attire was very far removed from her own. For a start off, Sukie wore breeches – something that was unheard of in her time. She nodded as she saw the sense in Sukie’s words. She had already been so kind, the last thing Molly wanted was to bring trouble to her door. ‘I agree but my dress is all I have.’

‘Come with me. I’ll have a rummage in my wardrobe and see what we can find to fit you. You’re quite a bit smaller than me so it might be a challenge.’

The next couple of hours were spent sorting out what Molly would and would not wear – the five-pack of thongs was quickly rejected in favour of some more sturdy items. Molly stared at the skimpy underwear in amazement.

‘Women actually wear these things?’ she asked. ‘Are they comfortable?’

‘They aren’t too bad, especially under jeans and trousers.’ Sukie grinned at Molly’s bewilderment. ‘I’ll be honest with you, Molly, you’re going to find women’s clothing far more liberating than what you’re used to.’

‘What on earth is *this*?’ Molly held up a bra which Sukie had laid out on the bed.

‘It’s a bra.’

‘A what?’

‘A bra. It’s for these.’ Sukie pointed towards her own breasts. ‘Look…’ She lifted her T-shirt to show Molly how it worked.

‘Oh, my goodness! Is it comfortable?’

'Well… It's still a relief to take it off at the end of the day but when I look at the contraptions you wore in your time, you won't hear me complaining.'

'I see.' Molly held it against her chest with a smile. 'Well, I'll give it a try.'

Sukie picked up the pile of clothes she'd gathered together and placed them on the bed. 'I think we'll be able to adapt most of these to fit you. Fortunately, I seem to have a thing for cropped trousers which will probably be full length on you. Tops are easier so there's a number of T-shirts, blouses and sweatshirts in there. Now, we just need to sort out some footwear. What size are you?'

'Size?'

'Yeah, shoe size?'

'I don't know, I have never been told. I just wear whatever boots my mother brings home. If they are too big, I use paper to make them fit.'

'Blimey! I must say, Molly, being with you is beginning to teach me just how lucky we are these days. Here, stand up a second, put your foot next to mine.'

Molly did as Sukie instructed and looked down at their feet. Hers was quite a bit smaller than Sukie's and her toenails were rather plain next to Sukie's vibrant purple ones.

'Sukie, what has happened? You have bruised your toes…' she exclaimed in horror.

'That's nail polish. I usually have it on my fingernails too but it was chipped so I took it off. You must have had nail polish in your day?'

'No, I don't think we do. I've never heard of it.'

Sukie turned to face her and took hold of her hands. 'Molly, are you coping alright? It seems to be that almost everything is alien to you – your poor head must be feeling totally swamped. We call it "sensory overload" when the body experiences too much new stuff all at once.'

Molly felt a lump in her throat in the face of Sukie's concern. On one hand, she was finding all these new experiences exciting but, on the other, there were so many of them. There was no respite and she felt like she was being bombarded. She said as much to Sukie who replied, 'You must tell me when you're struggling to cope. We'll sort out a place for you with minimal twenty-first century "things" in it and you can escape to it when you need some time-out. I mean… when you need a break.'

'There's no need to do that, I can go to my bedroom.'

'You're not spending all your time in your bedroom. We'll take a look at the rooms downstairs and find one which you feel most at ease in. Now, go and try these clothes on and choose an outfit to wear. While you're doing that, I'll try to locate the trainers I bought online which turned out to be the wrong size. If my memory serves me well, they might just fit you.'

Sukie put the bundle of clothes in Molly's arms and pointed her towards the bathroom before turning back to dive head first into the wardrobe.

Molly hesitated for a moment, wanting to say something more but not knowing what – after all, how many times could she keep saying thank you? A few seconds passed before she gave a small shrug and turned away towards the bathroom. There were times, she was learning, when it was simply better to say nothing.

Chapter Eleven

Molly stared in wonder at the bowl in front of her on the kitchen table. The crackling sound emanating from it kept making her giggle. She had yet to try this "breakfast cereal" Sukie had put in front of her and she was bracing herself for that first mouthful.

When Sukie had asked her what she wanted for breakfast, and had offered to make her some toast, Molly had declined, saying she wanted to try something new. She'd been taken aback by her brave step forward and put it down to the feeling of the clothes she was wearing. Sukie had been right when she'd said they were liberating – they felt really good. She felt totally free and light. She hadn't realised until now just how much extra weight she had to carry when wearing her chemise, corset and under-petticoats. And then there was the weight of the dress on top of that. While not so bad during the summer, when the dresses were made of lighter cotton, in winter the heavy fabric was sometimes almost knee-buckling.

Molly glanced under the table. She was wearing a pair of trousers that Sukie had called "Capri Pants".

Apparently, they were supposed to stop somewhere between the knee and the ankle but, with Sukie's extra height, they came all the way down to her ankles. Molly couldn't imagine wearing anything so risqué it would show off her naked legs but she did concur the trousers were very comfortable and walking in them was so much easier. She felt a small flicker of resentment towards the society she lived in where women had to suffer so much discomfort in order to comply with the expected social niceties. Who had decreed it should be so?

The new "underwear" was also nice, even the bra-thing which Sukie had said felt even better when removed at the end of the day. On top of this she wore a T-shirt. It was loose-fitting, had sleeves which came down to her elbows and was doing a good job of keeping her cool. Even though Sukie had said it was growing hot outside, and had opened the kitchen door to let some fresh air in, Molly had never felt this comfortable in all her life. Sukie had also taken the time to show her around the bathroom and had explained what all the different bottles and sprays were for. She had washed the smell of the river out of her hair using a strange liquid called "shampoo" and then Sukie had helped her to dry it with a noisy, blowing thing called a hair dryer. She had liked *that*! She hated washing her hair as drying it was so tedious. She had to sit in front of the fire for hours, brushing and brushing and brushing it until it was dry. It was a moan of hers every time that she wasn't allowed to cut it short – why could men have short hair but women could not? She'd mentioned this to Sukie who told her that a great many women of this generation had short hair and no one thought badly of them.

Of everything she was wearing, however, it was the shoes on her feet which she couldn't keep her eyes off. Sukie had called them "trainers" and they were the best thing Molly had ever seen. When she had put them on, they had turned out to be an almost perfect fit. What Molly hadn't expected was that they felt like she was walking on air! There was no weight in them, even though they looked like they should be so heavy, but it was the bouncing sensation that had taken a bit of getting used to. She'd tripped a few times when she'd first put them on but after walking up and down the hallway a few times, she had gotten used to them. It was like having springs on her feet.

When dressed, she'd looked in the mirror and had barely recognised herself. Her hair was dressed in two plaits down her back and, combined with the new clothes, she looked quite different. She appeared carefree and relaxed, not strait-laced and uptight. In some ways, it reminded her of her youth when she'd been allowed to break from the conventions and expectations and her life had been so much simpler.

'So, do you like Rice Krispies?'

Sukie's voice broke into her thoughts.

'I haven't got as far as trying them yet, I'm still listening to them.' She pulled the cereal box towards her and looked at it closely. It was so bright and colourful and had immediately grabbed her attention when Sukie had shown her some breakfast options she may not have seen before. When Sukie had said they were her children's favourite breakfast, that had been reason enough to persuade Molly to try.

She put a small amount on her spoon, closed her eyes and put it in her mouth. Her eyes quickly sprang open when she felt the popping sensation against her tongue. Sukie, who'd been watching her, burst out laughing. 'Yup, that's exactly the look Drew gave me the first time he tried them!'

Molly crunched down and swallowed. She gave Sukie a wide grin as she said, 'I think I need to use your word here – WOW! Is that correct?'

‘Yes, Molly, that is quite correct and I think the twins would agree with you.’

Sukie placed a teapot and two mugs on the table and sat down opposite Molly. She poured the hot drinks and waited for Molly to finish eating.

‘I really liked those,’ Molly said as she placed her spoon in the empty bowl.

‘You can have more if you like…’

‘Oh, no, thank you. That would be greedy.’ She pushed the bowl away and pulled the mug of tea closer.

‘How long have you lived here, Sukie? Has the manor been in your family a long time?’

‘No, it hasn’t…’ Sukie went on to explain how she and her husband Pete had come across the building one day when it was in a sad and run-down state. It hadn’t been occupied for many years and was fast becoming a derelict ruin. She and Pete had fallen in love with it that first day and, having purchased it within a few weeks, had set about trying to restore it to its former glory.

‘You must be quite well-off to have done all that. Are your families high up in society?’

‘Not at all,’ Sukie replied. ‘I used to work in an office but my husband, Pete Wallace, is a world-famous rock star.’

‘A rock star? Do you mean he is a geologist?’

Sukie looked at her in confusion for a second or two and then broke into a fit of giggles. ‘No, he is not a geologist, he’s a musician. A very famous musician. A “rocker” is a person who plays a certain style of music although the term is often used in a broader spectrum.’

‘I see.’ Molly felt a little hurt that Sukie was laughing at her and this was conveyed in her slightly drier reply. ‘Well, in my time, a “rocker” is a type of chair. Usually found next to the fireplace and occupied by older people so please forgive my confusion.’

Sukie began giggling again. ‘A rocking chair… Of course, it is!’

‘Why do you laugh at me, Sukie?’

She watched Sukie’s face change from merriment to serious within seconds. ‘I’m sorry, Molly, I am not laughing at you, I promise. There are many words from your time still in use today but their meanings may have changed or expanded. Now, when I think of my husband, “the rocker”, I suspect I will have a vision in my head of him sitting in a rocking chair with a pipe and slippers rather than bouncing around a stage making music!’ Sukie grinned as she stood up and walked over to the fridge where she lifted off a photograph held there with a magnet and handed it to Molly. ‘That’s my husband.’

Molly looked at the picture in front of her. ‘Is this a photograph of him?’

‘Yes, that’s right. You know what it is?’

‘I do. Last year, Lord Featheringstone arranged for a man to visit the manor and take photographs of the family. Everyone was talking about it and some of us went to watch them being done. The picture was hung up in the lounge after that. It didn’t look like this though. No one was smiling and it was not this colourful.’

‘I think I may have the picture you are talking about – I believe it is up in the attic. Colour photographs are more common now although some artists use black and white, or sepia which was the norm in your era, to create special effects and atmosphere.’

‘Your husband is very handsome. What does his music sound like?’

Sukie took the photograph and returned it to the fridge door. ‘Come with me and I’ll play some for you. That’ll be easier than trying to describe it. I must warn you, though, it’ll be very different to what you’re used to.’

Molly followed Sukie out of the room, saying as she went, 'Sukie, *everything* is very different to what I'm used to. I think I would be more surprised now if it wasn't!'

Chapter Twelve

Charlie made his way to the manor. He'd called Sukie earlier to say he'd be over just before lunch. He should have been in his office in London but he hadn't wanted to leave Sukie to deal with Molly on her own. By pulling Molly from the river, he felt responsible for her welfare although he knew some might say differently. He'd been able to deal with his morning clients via conference calls and his secretary had moved his appointments around, thus freeing him up for the rest of the week. There were some advantages to being your own boss!

He was looking forward to seeing Molly again – something about her appealed to him although he couldn't say what that was. He admired the strength of character with which she was handling her situation and couldn't even begin to imagine what she must be going through. Worse than that, though, was he didn't know if they would be able to get her back to her own time. He'd sat up late last night, reading up on anomalies and time travel on the Internet but, as no one had ever managed to actually achieve it – or if they had, they weren't letting on – all he had to go on were loads of theories and suppositions. It seemed that the only chance they'd have would be if the anomaly Molly had come through should reappear and for her to go back the same way she had come. When, or if, that would ever happen however, was another story. His plan for today was, if she felt up to it, to go for a walk back along the river and see if they could see anything which might give them some hope of resolving the situation. He was also looking forward to chatting with Molly and learning more about her. She was good company and an intriguing woman and not just because she was almost two hundred years old!

He let himself in through the open back door and, finding the kitchen empty, wandered along the hallway towards the lounge. He was just opening the door when he heard Sukie's voice saying, 'Oh my goodness, Molly, are you okay?'

Charlie flung the door wide and saw Molly lying on the sofa. She was panting heavily; her face was flushed and there was a sheen of sweat on her forehead. He rushed to her side. 'Molly, Molly, what's wrong?'

He took one of her hands and felt for the pulse which was racing under his fingertips. He looked at Sukie. 'What's happened? What have you given her? Did you make her take something for her sore feet?'

'I gave her some Junior Aspirin—'

'You did WHAT? You stupid woman! Don't you realise that she might not be able to take modern drugs? Her body hasn't adapted over time the way ours have. Now she's having a bad reaction and we need to bring the doctor in again. How on earth are we going to explain that?'

He didn't see Sukie's hand approaching his cheek but he certainly felt it land there. The sting of the slap stopped him in his tracks.

'THAT,' she said, 'was for calling me stupid. And this

one,' she slapped him hard a second time, 'was for THINKING I'm stupid. Now calm down and let me explain!'

Charlie stood rubbing his sore face as Sukie talked.

'Firstly, I made a point of giving Molly only a very small dose of painkiller for the very reason you stated. It was a fraction of a standard dose—'

'Well that was clearly too much because look at how she's reacted to it!' Charlie pointed at Molly, too flustered to notice she was now sitting upright and that her colour was returning to normal.

'Charlie, Molly and I were dancing. That's why she's all hot and bothered. It had nothing to do with anything else. Look at her now, she's fine.'

Charlie looked at Molly again and saw that she was indeed quite fine and was sitting watching him with a bemused look in her eye and a big smile on her face. 'Dancing?'

'Yes, Charlie, dancing.'

He looked at them both in confusion.

'I asked Sukie what kind of music her husband created and she said it would be easier for me to listen to it.' Molly smiled up at him. 'I confess it was a horrible cacophony of noise at first but, after a few minutes, it began to sound better and then it began to sound good. So good, in fact, that I wanted to dance to it. I asked Sukie if this was her favourite music and she said no, she liked a band called Green Day?' Molly looked to Sukie for confirmation and Sukie nodded that she was correct. 'I asked her to play her favourite piece of theirs to me. She then taught me one of your modern dances called "Air Guitar and Headbanging".' It is very fast and that is why you found me lying on the sofa as I tried to get my breath back. I do thank you, however, for your concern over my health. The medication Sukie gave me is very good though as I no longer have any pain in my feet. Do you like my new trainers? I think they're wonderful.' Molly waggled her feet in Charlie's direction as he sat down in the chair opposite the sofa.

'Yes, they're lovely.' Charlie felt his racing heart begin to slow. He was surprised by the force of his reaction to seeing Molly looking unwell and also at the relief now flowing through him at the explanation given. He rubbed his face again – his cheek was still smarting from Sukie's slaps.

'Sorry I called you stupid, Sukie. That was quite rude of me and totally uncalled for. I was panicking and didn't think. I know you're anything but stupid.'

'Not a problem, Charlie, but I'm not going to apologise for slapping you. You needed bringing to your senses.'

'I can see that, but did you have to hit me *so* hard? You pack a good punch, lady!'

'Ahhh, the joy of carting four-year-old twins around; you develop a good set of biceps.'

'Talking of the twins, where are they?' Charlie looked at Molly who was still waggling her feet and admiring her footwear. 'Have they met Molly yet?'

Sukie looked at her watch. 'They're at playgroup for another hour. I thought I might introduce everyone this afternoon.'

Charlie looked at his hands hanging between his knees for a moment before he replied to Sukie. 'Do you think that's a good idea?'

'I'm not sure I get your meaning, Charlie. Why not?'

'My concern is that the more people who know of Molly, the harder it becomes to keep her secret. The twins are little chatterboxes and may say something which people might question. I was thinking this over last night and I was going to suggest that it may be better for Molly to stay with me at the mill. She could have the spare bedroom.' He turned towards Molly who was now paying close attention to the conversation. 'Molly, I think it would be easier for you to adapt to your current circumstances in a smaller environment and with fewer people around you. You mentioned that you were familiar with the mill and, even though it will look quite different to what you knew, I think the essence of it is still there and it may bring you some comfort. We can also discuss what to do next.'

Molly looked from Sukie to Charlie. 'I would be alone with you, at the mill?'

'Yes, you would. But you'd have your own bedroom and bathroom.'

'And would that not be considered improper?'

Sukie moved to sit beside Molly. She took her hand as she replied, 'Not now, in this century. I understand it would have been considered so back in your time, but we're far more relaxed these days. I can also vouch for Charlie's good intentions. He would never behave towards you in a manner that would be inappropriate. He's a good man who only wants to help. If, however, you don't feel comfortable with Charlie's suggestion, you are most welcome to stay here. It's not a problem.'

Charlie gave a small cough. 'Erm, Sukie, I think it might be a problem. Aren't you guys heading off to Austria next week?'

'Oh crap! Yes, we are. I'd forgotten about that.'

'I'll stay with Charlie,' Molly said, 'I don't want to cause any more trouble.'

'You're not causing any trouble!' Sukie was quick to give reassurance.

'Thank you, Sukie, but I think Charlie might be right. Being in a place I know well may be more beneficial. While I may have helped out in the manor, I was never a guest here so it does feel wrong. I think being at the mill is a good idea. As long as you don't mind, Charlie?'

‘I don’t mind at all. I just want to help you, Molly, the best that I can.’

‘Well, in that case, it would be best to pack up your belongings and go now, before the twins return because they will ask questions.’ Sukie gave Molly’s hand a squeeze as she got up and made her way to the door. ‘I hope you’re feeling strong, Charlie, because Molly has a few more belongings now for you to carry.’

The two women giggled when Charlie rolled his eyes and replied, ‘Well of course she has! I’ve yet to meet the woman who knows the art of travelling lightly!’

Chapter Thirteen

Molly walked along the tree-lined path through the woods, her head thrown back as she gazed up at the tall canopy of leaves far above her head. Charlie kept pace beside her, carrying the two holdalls which Sukie had filled with clothes and a few toiletries.

'This is so… strange,' she whispered.

'How so?'

She looked at Charlie and tried to find the words to explain. 'I have walked this path many, many times over the years. Seth, the local miller, lost his wife and family before I was born. When he grew older, my mother took him under her wing and looked out for him. I would come this way at least twice a week to visit him and check everything was okay. Now, as I look around me, everything is still familiar but also different. Young trees are now old trees, and the old trees are now ancient. Trees which were once thin, and almost bare, are now thick and leafy. The roots on the path are where they always were but they're bigger and thicker. It all feels both right and wrong.'

'I can understand that.' Charlie nodded. 'I should also tell you now, so you are prepared, that the mill is no longer a working mill. From the outside, I think it will look the same, maybe a bit better as it was all freshly painted last year, but the inside has all changed. I design buildings and Sukie asked me to rebuild the mill last year because it had nearly all fallen down.'

'I see. How different is it?'

'All of the mechanical workings have been removed. The sails still turn but they no longer grind the stones. The water wheel also turns but, again, has no machinery attached. Removing all the workings means there's more space and it no longer looks like a mill inside. It just looks like a normal house. Well… a house with round walls and a funny shaped roof.'

'It sounds interesting. I am looking forward to seeing it.'

Within a few minutes, Molly was standing looking at the windmill in front of her. Once more, she was experiencing the strange sensation of seeing something so familiar look so different. The sound of the river flowing over the water wheel was one she'd heard so many times and, when she closed her eyes, she could well believe she was back in her own time. Opening them again was a sharp reminder that she was not. The mill no longer looked old and shabby – the fresh paint had certainly given it a new lease of life and the sails, which had once been falling to pieces, were all repaired and now moved idly in the mild summer breeze.

Charlie led her to the front door and stood back for her to enter. The first thing she noticed when she walked in, was how bright and fresh it was. She immediately recognised the two large stones in front of her although they were the only familiar items around her. A pale wooden staircase with glass bannisters followed the curve of the wall and led upwards. The stone floor beneath her feet was pale grey – this was the first time she'd ever seen it without wheat husks all over it. As she looked around her, Charlie sat on the mill stones and pulled off his shoes. She followed his lead and laid her trainers beside his. He pointed to the stairs. 'Would you like to go up first?'

Suddenly feeling a bit shy, Molly shook her head. She also wasn't sure about those stairs – they didn't look all that sturdy to her. She would rather see Charlie go first so she could be sure they were strong enough. If they could take his weight, then she'd be okay.

Charlie was almost at the top by the time she was satisfied the staircase was safe to use. She walked up slowly, enjoying the feel of the smooth, cool, wooden treads underneath her soles. The new trainers Sukie had given her were really good but they made her feet hot and sweaty. She was happy to take them off for a time.

As her head rose above the stairs, and she walked into the main living area, she was unable to suppress the gasp which escaped from her lips. Charlie had not been jesting when he said it would look different. Gone was the vast column of iron which had attached the sails on the rooftop to the mill stones below. The large vats and funnels which the grain had been stored in and passed through were also gone and there were no sacks of grain lining the walls, waiting to be milled. With all the traditional interior removed, the room was no longer dark, crowded and poky, it was now big, bright and airy. Pale grey panelling lined the lower half of the walls while the upper walls were painted white. The solid wood doors on the two loading docks had been replaced with French windows and the sunlight beamed through to light up the room. At one end was what appeared to be a kitchen. The cupboards were the same pale grey as the panelling and, although there was no kitchen table, it looked as though a large slab of wood had been placed on top of the floor cupboards to provide a space where food could be prepared. There were also cupboards on the wall above the white tiles. These too, were pale grey.

She turned to look behind her and saw a tidy seating area with a cream sofa, two matching chairs and a small wooden table stood upon a large cream rug. The floorboards beneath her feet were dark and highly polished. There were three smaller windows dotted around the room and each had a brightly coloured vase sitting on the deep, rough, windowsill. Each window had a small brass curtain rail above it which suggested curtains would be hung there in the colder months.

'So, what do you think?'

She turned towards Charlie who was standing by a writing desk in front of one of the French windows. 'It's beautiful. It is difficult to take in how different it looks. Seth would not believe his eyes if he were to see it now.' She smiled. 'I can barely believe it myself.'

Charlie beamed at her words. 'Let me show you the bedrooms upstairs and then I'll make us some lunch.'

This time, when Charlie led the way upwards, Molly didn't hesitate to follow right behind him. They arrived on a small landing with three doors to their right.

'This door here,' Charlie gestured to the door nearest to them, 'is my bedroom. The door at the other end is the spare room, now your bedroom, and the door in the middle leads up to the roof space.' He talked as he walked and, after opening the second bedroom door, he stepped back to let her go in first.

The room was big enough to accommodate a double bedstead and two small bedside tables. There were two doors which she took to be cupboards for storage. Charlie stepped past her and placed the holdalls on the bed. Molly immediately walked over and moved them onto the floor.

Honestly, she thought, *one hundred and sixty years later and men still didn't think!* Charlie grinned at her actions as he stood beside one of the cupboard doors. 'This is a combined wardrobe and dressing table.' He opened the doors to reveal hanging space behind one door and a small dressing table, complete with a mirror and stool, behind the other. Above the mirror were three small drawers. 'If you press this switch here, the mirror lights up.' He hit the switch with a flourish and Molly's own eyes lit up at the miracle in front of her. She bent down for a closer look and was astonished to see her face reflected back so clearly. There had been good mirrors in Sukie's home but none like this. Surely such a mirror would only encourage vanity? She made a mental note to avoid the use of this feature if possible. She straightened up and walked over to the second door which they had walked past when coming into the room. 'What is in this cupboard?'

Charlie smiled at her again. 'That's not a cupboard, it's a wet room. Go on in.'

'What is a "wet room"?' Molly slowly opened the door.

'Press that switch just there, near the door handle,' Charlie pointed to the wall, 'and then you'll see.'

Molly did as she was instructed and saw the light come on as she opened the door wider. 'Oh, it's a water closet.'

'Well… not quite. It's a bit more than that.'

Molly stood looking around the small space. In the corner was an overhead shower, a sink was located next to it and opposite the sink was a toilet.

'It works like this.' Charlie walked over to the glass door between the shower and the sink and pulled it along until it had doubled in length. 'You stand on the other side of the glass, turn on the taps and water will come out of that overhead piece above you. This is called a shower.'

'I know what a shower is, Charlie. We had one in our cottage.'

‘You had a shower in your cottage?’

‘Well, not right inside it. Father built a lean-to against the side wall with a small water tank above it. He made some pipework and a valve thing in his workshop and also something which looked like that.’ She pointed at the showerhead. ‘In the summer months, it was my brother’s job to keep the tank topped up with water from a nearby stream. It was self-filling at all other times with rainwater.’

‘How did it work?’

‘Easy. You turned on the valve, water came out and you got wet. Turn the valve off, soap up and wash then turn the valve on again to rinse off. It was so much quicker than filling the bathtub although also much colder.’

‘I have to confess to being quite surprised as showers didn’t become common until the twentieth century.’

‘My father is always coming up with different ideas. Some work, some don’t. The villagers say he is a bit strange, but in a nice way. He was adamant that I attended school every day until I was fourteen and, after that, he ensured I continued to read books and he would often make me write out his invoices so that I could practise my handwriting. He insisted my education be as good as Albie’s, my brother.’

‘He sounds like a man ahead of the times,’ said Charlie.

‘He is a good man, that is what he is. Anyway, back to this wet room – where does the water go after this shower?’

Charlie pointed out the drainage area and the slight slope in the floor which ensured the water drained off where it was supposed to.

‘So simple and yet effective,’ replied Molly.

‘Indeed!’ Charlie grinned again. ‘Right, how about you take a few minutes to sort yourself out up here while I go and prepare us some lunch? Would a cheese sandwich be okay?’

‘That would be very nice, thank you. I won’t be too long.’

Chapter Fourteen

Charlie was slicing the cheese when he heard a small cough behind him. He jumped at the sound. He'd been deep in thought and hadn't heard Molly come back down the stairs. Mind you, being so tiny and also barefoot, had gone some way towards giving her the element of surprise. 'Hey, is that you settled now?'

'I suppose I am, for now. Can I help with anything?'

'Not really, I'm almost done, although you could pop the cheese back in the fridge for me.'

'The what?'

Charlie looked at Molly and counted to three beneath his breath. The novelty of being in the company of someone from another century was rapidly wearing thin. As they stood in silence, he saw a look of sad uncertainty begin to move over Molly's face and this reminded him that whatever frustration he was experiencing must be tenfold, nay *twentyfold*, for her.

'Right, Molly, what I'm going to do is show you around the kitchen, tell you the name of the items you are not familiar with and what they do. Stay here a minute…'

He stepped over to his desk and returned with a pen and some Post-It notes. Holding them up he continued, 'I'll write the names on these and stick them on, or beside, each item. Now, before you ask…' He held up his hand as he saw her mouth open, presumably to ask a question, 'I am not going to explain *how* every item works. The truth is, most people today *don't* know how most things work – they simply just take it for granted that it will.' He walked over to the fridge. 'This is a fridge, short for refrigerator, and it keeps things cold. Very few people know exactly how it does it, it just does. I'll write both names on the Post-It note for you.'

It took Charlie over twenty minutes to guide Molly around the kitchen and, when he'd finished, it looked like a pink Post-It explosion had occurred. Molly, however, had a wide smile on her face and she appeared more relaxed.

'Do you feel that has helped?' he asked.

'Oh yes!' Her wide smile confirmed her words. 'To know that most people in your time don't understand exactly how things do what they do is a big weight off my shoulders. I was trying to understand everything new and how it could do whatever it did and it was making my head all faint. Now, I only have to learn what something does, or what it is for – that is much easier. Now, can we eat, please, my stomach is rumbling?'

'Of course,' he laughed. 'You grab that plate with the bread and follow me.' He picked up the plate of cheese with one hand, a bowl of salad with the other, and made his way to the second set of French windows, which he'd opened earlier. He placed the food on the table sitting upon the small cast iron balcony which overlooked the river. The large water wheel turned only a few feet beneath them.

As they sat down, Molly told him how Seth, the miller in her time, would sometimes let the children of the village sit on his little loading docks and dangle their feet above the wheel to catch the cool spray when the summers were hot.

'Seth sounds like a nice man.'

Charlie waited as Molly swallowed her mouthful before replying, inwardly impressed by her impeccable manners. He'd come to notice how correct she was in almost everything she did. He hadn't yet heard her use any swear words or blaspheme and yet she'd had every reason to do so. She always said please and thank you and had waited for him to be seated at the table before beginning to eat. It was refreshing to be in the company of someone *so* ladylike and he found himself making more of an effort to behave like a gentleman. Good manners were a rarity in the twenty-first century – he'd just begun to realise this since Molly had come into his life.

'He is a nice man. Although maybe I should say "he was" as, by now, he has probably been dead for a long time.' A shadow of sadness flitted across her face and Charlie, keen to keep her spirits buoyant, leant over the table. 'I was thinking that we could take a walk along the river, after we've eaten, and try to figure out what happened. Maybe, if we're lucky, the anomaly will still be there, or have returned, and we can get you back. What do you say?'

'I'd say that sounds like a very good idea, sir.' She bestowed one of her bright, happy, smiles upon him and Charlie felt a small glow of elation spread through him as he basked in the warmth of it.

He returned her smile as he replied, 'Then let's eat up so we can set about trying to solve the mystery you have become.'

'So, you think this is where you fell into the water?'

Molly looked around her. The woods had changed considerably in the last one-hundred and sixty years. Much more than she'd expected.

'I think so… I am not sure… It is all so different now. More overgrown. I'm sorry.'

'Hey, don't worry about it. Let's walk on and see if there's anything you recognise further along.' Charlie put his hand on her shoulder and squeezed it gently. It was the very same gesture her father used whenever he felt she needed comforting and Molly felt some of her frustrations flow away. It wasn't her fault the trees and bushes around her had continued to grow and spread from her time until now. That was nature and that's what it did.

Thinking of her father, however, had made her suddenly feel quite homesick. She'd never been apart from her family for this length of time. Even when she'd gotten married, the honeymoon had only been two nights away. Her marital home had been two rooms above the stables, converted by her father so that Tommy could be close by to continue his apprenticeship. She'd seen her parents every day and, when Tommy died, she'd moved back into the family home. It suddenly hit her that she might never see them again and a wave of grief passed over her. She was so immersed in her thoughts that she only realised Charlie had stopped walking when she bumped into his back.

'Oomph!'

'Oops, sorry, Molly. You okay?'

'Yes, I'm fine. Why have we stopped?'

Charlie stepped to the side and pointed to a gnarly old tree stump which came to an abrupt halt just above her head.

'Oh my, it's the old stunted tree!' she exclaimed.

'You recognise this?'

‘Yes! I do. It is considerably more weathered than the last time I saw it but yes, I know it. The tree was hit by lightning when I was a child. It split apart up there,’ she pointed at the jagged top, ‘and fell over the river. For a short time, it served as a bridge but, as winter began to draw in, the villagers agreed it had little use as few folks wanted to go to the field opposite and so it was chopped up for firewood.’ Molly placed her hand upon the old trunk in front of her. ‘No one bothered to chop this bit down and it was left behind. It is…’ she hesitated. ‘It is sort of comforting to see it still here. To know that something else has lasted this long.’

‘Well, this is where I pulled you from the river.’ Charlie pointed to the water flowing past. ‘That is where the river was all shimmery and silver-like.’

Molly looked around her and then back at the river. ‘Yes, that’s correct. The old tree has helped me to get my bearings.’

She turned to face back up the path towards the mill and began to slowly retrace her steps, talking aloud as she did so. ‘I remember being mesmerised by the shimmer on the river and used the old tree trunk to steady myself. I began walking along but hadn’t gotten far when I heard voices. I recognised one as Damien Featheringstone’s and so ducked down behind some bushes to avoid being seen.’

‘You didn’t like him?’

‘The man is a boorish thug. He may be in line to inherit a title but that does not make him a gentleman.’

Molly came to a halt and looked carefully around her. ‘I think, although I can’t say for definite, this is where I fell in the river. There was a clearing here, albeit a small one, where I was able to hide. I tripped over a tree root and it was that which caused me to fall.’ She knelt on the ground and carefully pushed some of the brambles to the side and, by doing so, revealed a large tree root sticking prominently above the earth. She looked at it for a moment, thinking of all that had occurred since she'd last been there, before gently releasing the jagged branches which were beginning to dig into her arm and stood back up. She turned to look at Charlie and, as a wave of tired emotion swept through her, she whispered, 'This is where I fell in. This is where it all happened.'

Chapter Fifteen

Charlie looked at Molly's forlorn face and, unable to help himself, he pulled her into his arms and hugged her tightly. 'I don't have any fancy words, Molly, that might comfort you and I am trying my best to understand how you must be feeling but the one thing I can promise you is that I will do everything I can to help you get back to your own time. That's not a promise to say it *will* happen but it's a promise that I will try.'

He felt her relax against him and knew he'd helped her a little. It wasn't much but he hoped she understood that he wouldn't desert her. He was "in" for as long as she needed him.

Before he could say anything else, she straightened up and stepped out of his embrace. 'Thank you, Charlie. Your kindness and understanding are quite precious to me and I do appreciate it. If I do not always show my gratitude, please know it is always there.'

'Oh, shush now! There's no need for that!' He tugged one of her pigtails and smiled.

‘Hey! Stop that!’ She swiped his hand away but smiled back. The tension was broken and the atmosphere was immediately lighter.

‘Right then, let’s check this all out.’ Charlie walked over to the edge of the riverbank. ‘So, you’re quite sure this is where you fell in?’

‘Yes, I’m sure.’ Her reply was firm.

‘Okay…’ Charlie began to walk along the path. A minute later he stopped. ‘This is where I pulled you out, and that,’ he pointed to the middle of the river in front of him, ‘is where I first saw you, when you cried for help.’

He stood looking into the murky water and then looked up to where Molly had gone in. He did this for a few minutes, as various thoughts ran through his mind.

‘Right, this is what I *think* may have happened. It’s only a theory, mind. When you fell into the river, you went into, let’s say, “ordinary water”. If you’d managed to get out at the same spot, everything would have been okay and you’d still be back in the nineteenth century. However, the undercurrent not only pulled you under the water, it also pulled you downstream a few feet and brought you to this point.’ He pointed towards the middle of the river again. ‘Now, we both agree that this is where the river was shimmering and I suspect the time portal, anomaly, whatever you want to call it, was sitting on top of the water. If you had surfaced over there,’ his finger swung round, pointing a bit further down the river, ‘the chances are, you’d still be in your own time. But, because you came up right here, right in the middle of the shimmer, you came up through the portal and crossed into the twenty-first century.’

Molly stood beside him and followed his hand as he moved it about while listening to his explanation. ‘I think I understand, Charlie. I think you are saying that, when the shimmer was lying on the water, the side *under* the water was in the 1800s but the side *above* the water was in the twenty-first century. Is that correct?'

'That is exactly it.'

'So, to simplify, it was like stepping through a door – one room is the nineteenth century, go through the doorway, and the other room is the twenty-first century.'

'Yup! You've got it. While I am not an expert, I strongly believe that is what happened.'

'And you say this is an unusual thing to happen? It is not common in your time?'

'Not at all! Time travel – that's what we call it – is something a lot of people talk about and make films about—'

'Films?'

'I'll get back to you on that one.' He smiled gently as he carried on talking. 'But, as far as I know, being able to time travel has never been proven. Or, if it has, the powers that be are doing a good job of keeping it a secret.'

'I see. So, how am I going to get back? I need to get back, Charlie, I know that Damien Featheringstone is planning some sort of revenge upon my family and I have to get back to warn them.'

'Well, I think that, when the shimmer returns, your best bet would be to dive into it right here where we are standing, and then, staying underwater, you swim upstream to where you fell in. I think that will take you back.'

'I agree that sounds like a good plan but there are two problems, Charlie.'

'Which are?'

'One – we don't know when, or if, the shimmer will return and, two – I can't swim!'

'You can't swim?' This was the one thing he hadn't given any thought to – he'd just assumed that, with growing up quite close to the river, Molly would be able to swim.

'Surely you must have realised, Charlie. If I'd been able to swim, none of this would have happened.'

'Actually, I thought maybe you'd hit your head and had gotten confused or something. It never crossed my mind that you couldn't swim.'

'It is unseemly for ladies to swim, Charlie. So, what do we do now?' Molly looked at him as though he had all the answers. How could he disappoint her by admitting he didn't have a clue!

'Well, until you learn to swim, and you will need to learn – unseemly or not – you're going nowhere so I suggest we head back to the mill, crack open a bottle of wine, have something to eat and put together a plan of action. Does that work for you?'

'It doesn't look like I have any other choice. And, having seen that "thing" you called a cooker, earlier, let me tell you right now that you are doing the cooking! Okay?'

'Okay!'

Charlie smiled again and the journey back to the mill was made in silence.

Molly heard Charlie whistling as she walked down the stairs from her bedroom. When she walked into the lounge, she saw him in the kitchen, bustling around the cooker thing.

He turned around and smiled when he saw her standing on the last step.

'Hey, you okay? Come and get a glass of wine. I thought I'd make spaghetti bolognese for dinner. It's the one thing I can cook that has a zero risk of disaster. Do you like pasta?'

'Erm, I don't know.' Molly returned his smile. 'What is it?'

Charlie went over to the larder and came back with several jars in his arms which he lined up on the counter.

'Pasta comes from Italy and is made of water, eggs, salt and a special type of flour. You can get fresh pasta which is, as the name suggests, freshly made but the most common variety is dried pasta, which is what we have here.' He pointed to the jars. 'It is also made in different thicknesses and different shapes. While they all have lovely sounding Italian names, most people in the UK call them bows, shells, spirals, twists and spaghetti. The pasta is cooked in hot water until soft and then served with a sauce of your choosing or, quite often, just plain with melted butter, black pepper and Parmesan cheese.'

'Those are pretty.' Molly pointed to the jar containing the pasta bows. 'May I try those? Would that be okay?'

'Of course, you can. There are no rules when it comes to pasta – although some people might try to say otherwise but just ignore them – you eat it the way you like it. A bolognese sauce is essentially minced beef, onions, tomatoes and herbs. And, just like the pasta, many people may add other ingredients to suit their own tastes. Personally, I like to keep it simple. Come, have a smell.'

He took her hand and guided her round to the bubbling pot on the cooker. She looked in and, as Charlie stirred the mixture, a small burst of steam popped in her face and brought with it a cacophony of smells which, despite their strangeness, had made her mouth water. She took another deep intake of breath before stepping back.

'That smells delicious.'

'Good. I hope you think the same when you taste it. Now, how about a glass of wine? Would you like red or white?'

Molly gave a small shrug. 'I'll let you choose, Charlie,

as I've never had wine. They used to serve it at the dinner parties up at the manor but the servants never got to taste it. It was kept under lock and key and the beady eye of Mr Shankton, the butler.'

'Well, as you're a novice, we'll start with a white wine and take it from there.'

He poured her a glass from a bottle he'd taken from the fridge and handed it over. 'Go and have a mooch around while I finish up here.'

'Mooch?'

'A look around. Be nosy.'

'Oh, alright. I will.' She took the glass holding the yellow-ish liquid and wandered across to the shelved alcoves directly opposite the kitchen. There were photographs of Charlie – some on his own and some with people who were clearly his family. The resemblance was easy to see. She looked over to him. 'The last time I saw these shelves they were holding spare parts for the grinding machinery. The shelves were covered in oil and all kinds of dirt and rust.'

'That's how they were when I found them. A bit of sandpaper and elbow grease soon got rid of all that. I tried to keep as much of the original mill as I could.'

Molly moved along to the next alcove. She took a tiny sip from her wine glass and was pleased to find the contents tasted rather pleasant. She took a second, larger, sip.

'Be careful there, Molly, just take small sips for now. If you drink all that on an empty stomach, you'll end up getting tipsy. It's stronger than you realise and you're not used to it.'

Molly could already feel the effect of the wine flowing through her. She was feeling quite relaxed and saw the wisdom in Charlie's words. She put the glass down on the nearby table and went back to look at the books sitting in the other alcoves. She pulled one down from a shelf and was looking through it when Charlie called over, 'Do you like to read?'

'Yes, I do, very much. I don't get much spare time but, when I do, I like to lose myself in a book. So many adventures and places I will never see but which I can picture in my head. I can travel the world without ever leaving my chair.'

'Do you have a favourite author?'

Molly held up the book in her hand. 'Charles Dickens. His stories are so engrossing and he's such a nice, kind man. He has a beautiful reading voice.'

'You've *seen* Charles Dickens? In the flesh?' There was no mistaking the awe and wonder in Charlie's voice.

'Yes,' she replied with a smile as the memory came to her. 'It was late October 1858. He was doing a tour of readings around the country and he stopped overnight at the coaching inn in the village on his way to Leamington Spa. Betsy, the landlady of the inn, came to fetch me as she knows I like his books. I was a bit shy at first, him being a famous author and all, but Betsy dragged me over and introduced me after he had finished eating. He asked me which of his books I'd read and what was my favourite. When I told him it was Oliver Twist, he opened the bag by his side, took out a copy and began reading from it. The whole pub went silent as we listened to the story being told in the way it was meant to be, for only the writer of a story knows exactly how it should sound. He read for about an hour and you could have heard a pin drop. It is one of the nicest memories I have.'

She looked from the book back to Charlie. His mouth was hanging open and his eyes were almost as wide. 'Why are you looking at me like that, Charlie?'

'I just can't… I can't… You *MET* Charles Dickens! That is amazing! I'm so jealous.'

‘But lots of people have met him.’

‘Yes, Molly, but none of them are alive now to tell the tale. This is an event which, for you, is fresh and recent but, for me, it’s something I can only read about in history books and try to imagine what he was like. Your story has just left me reeling, that’s all.’

Molly looked back down at the book in her hand. *Great Expectations* – she hadn’t read that one. ‘May I read this one, please? Do you mind?’

‘Of course not, Molly, you can read any of the books there although one or two are more modern so it might be worth asking first before you start those. They may require some explaining.’

‘Thank you.’

‘You’re welcome. Now, dinner is ready to be served if you would like to take a seat at the table.’

Molly put the book back on the shelf and went to sit at the small dining table.

Charlie put a steaming bowl of pasta and sauce in front of her. She was once again taking deep breaths and allowing the wonderful aroma of the herby sauce to infuse her senses. She opened her eyes as Charlie sat down across from her.

‘Senora,’ he said, ‘your first Italian meal. What do you think?’

Molly took one of the sauce-covered bows and carefully placed it in her mouth. Immediately, the flavour travelled across her tongue and up to her brain. She had never tasted anything like this before. She didn’t have the words to describe to Charlie how good it was.

When she had chewed and swallowed, she answered simply, ‘I like it very, very much.’

Charlie smiled at her. ‘Molly, you may never be able to travel the world but I can at least let you see what the world tastes like.’

‘In that case, Charlie,’ she replied, while heaping more pasta onto her fork, ‘I have to say the world tastes rather wonderful.’

Chapter Sixteen

'Okay, my babies, I'll see you later. Have a lovely time.'

Sukie watched as Drew ran off into the playgroup room to join his friends. Poppy, his twin sister, however, stayed where she was and looked up with her hands on her hips.

'Mummy! I have said before that I am *not* a baby anymore. I'm a big girl now.' Her little face was screwed up in annoyance.

Sukie hunkered down until she was eye-level with her daughter. If it wasn't for her husband's bright, emerald green eyes looking back at her, she could have been forgiven for thinking she was looking at a mirror image of her younger self. The resemblance between her and her daughter was uncanny – not only on the outside but also on the inside. Her mother, Beth, often laughed when Sukie relayed tales of Poppy's mischievous antics, telling Sukie that she had been just as bad when she was a child. 'The apple didn't fall far from the tree there, dear.'

She looked at the pint-sized human in front of her. 'Poppy, I know you're a big girl now but you and Drew will always be my babies. Even when you're forty years old and ancient, I will still call you my babies.' She placed a gentle kiss on Poppy's tiny button nose. 'I love you, my little Poppy-flower,' she whispered softly.

Poppy smiled, leant forward and placed a kiss on her nose. 'I love you, Mummy-duck.' She gave Sukie a quick cuddle before turning and running off to find her brother.

Sukie waved when Poppy looked back before going through the door.

'They grow so fast, don't they? I can't believe it's only a year until we're sending them off to school.'

Sukie looked to find Jeremy, the vicar, standing beside her. The playgroup was held in the church hall and run by his wife, Sarah. Their two boys were best friends with the twins.

'Oh, don't say that, Jeremy. I'm trying not to think that far ahead.' She gave a small grimace.

'You and me both, Sukie!' Jeremy gave a mock shudder. 'Well, have a good day, I must get on and sort out my sermon for Sunday. The Lord himself performed many miracles but he's yet to answer my prayers for the weekly sermon to miraculously write itself.'

Sukie laughed at his joke. Jeremy was at the vestry door when Sukie suddenly had an idea. She quickly walked after him, calling his name as she did so.

'Jeremy, sorry, but do you have a minute. There's something I want to ask.'

'Sure, what is it?'

Thinking quickly on her feet, Sukie replied, 'I've been considering delving more deeply into the background of the manor and maybe trying to put together some kind of family tree which I can put up in the library. I know we're not tied to the manor through blood but I don't want its history to be forgotten. I wasn't sure where to start but then I remembered that the records of Births, Marriages and

Deaths were often kept in the parish church until the mid-1800s. Do you still have those old record books and, if so, would you mind if I had a look through them?'

'Why, Sukie, what a wonderful idea. I quite agree that an old building like the manor should have its past recorded. I believe we still have those old books and you are most welcome to look at them. Come with me, I'll show you where they are.'

Jeremy led her to a small room adjoining the vestry which was shelved from floor to ceiling and filled with books. Most were old bibles but there were also many theological books covering different topics contained within the Holy Book. Sukie breathed a small sigh of relief that Jeremy had bought her cover story. It wasn't a lie as such, she had considered doing some kind of historical tree for the house, it had simply never gone any further than a vague thought.

'Right, let's see… Where did I put them?' Jeremy looked at Sukie before turning to cast his eyes across the shelves. 'I had this room converted to a book storage room when I first moved here because there were so many, and out there,' he gestured with this thumb towards the vestry, 'was so overflowing it was a health hazard. Books piled high all over the place. It took some amount of effort to clear it all up and catalogue them properly but I got there in the end. Ah, here we are, parish records. There's one book for each century starting from the 1200s. Not that you'll be needing any that old. You'll be after 1600s onwards.'

Sukie looked over his shoulder at where he was pointing. The dates were clearly written on the spines of the thick, heavy ledgers.

'Erm, I can't see one for the 1800s Jeremy. I was going to work backwards as I thought that might be easier.'

'No, you're right. Now that you mention it, I recall that

I couldn't find it when I moved everything. I did check all the other shelves and cupboards in the vestry office but to no avail. Our parish records cease on the 31st December 1799. You might be able to fill in the gaps from the information online. If memory serves me right, they began to centralise the records in London around the 1840s to 1850s. The first half-decent census was run in 1851 and you can often gather a lot of information from them. It's about fifty years you need to try and fill in. It shouldn't be too difficult.'

'Good idea, thank you, Jeremy. I'll let you know when I need access to these in the future.'

'You're very welcome, Sukie, any time.'

With a smile, Sukie let herself out and walked slowly up the aisle of the church. She slipped into one of the pews and sat thinking, the peaceful atmosphere helping her to straighten out her jumbled thoughts. It wasn't that she disbelieved Molly's story – there were many factors which lent credence to its honesty – but it all just seemed so far-fetched. Time travel? Honestly? Sukie had had a notion that, by seeing Molly's name in the parish records, it would help her overly-logical brain to accept the situation but that possibility was no longer an option. She let out a sigh and made her way out to the vestibule.

The bright sunlight blinded her after the cool gloom of the church and she quickly closed her eyes while rummaging in her vast handbag for her sunglasses. When she found them and put them on, the first sight she saw was the beautiful angel gravestone which was situated only a few yards from the church door. Whoever lay there, was clearly someone of means, she thought. Gravestones of that ilk didn't come cheap now, never mind back in 1689 when Ezra Greenway had breathed his last. Despite the lichen which now covered the greater portion of the gravestone, Ezra's name and the dates of his birth and death were still clear and easy to read. Sukie suspected Jeremy had probably had a hand in that, clearing the gravestones as a mark of respect to those who lay beneath them. She turned to walk away and was halfway along the path when she came to an abrupt stop. She looked around her and took in all the gravestones in the church yard, many of which showed clear signs of having been there for more than a couple of hundred years. She walked to the end of the path and veered left when she reached the church gate.

For the next three hours, she walked slowly through the gravestones, reading every one and making occasional notes on her phone. Eventually she came back to where she'd started. She stared at the small, discrete headstone of Miriam Farmer for several minutes before pulling her phone from her pocket. She gave a few swipes and then waited.

'Hi, Charlie, it's Sukie. Look, can you come up to the house, we need to talk?'

Chapter Seventeen

Sukie placed the tray of cold drinks on the kitchen table and sat down. She looked at Charlie and Molly sitting across from her.

'Charlie, Molly, there's no easy way to say this so I'm going to come right out with it.' She looked directly at Molly. 'Molly, I can't find any record of you or your family living in this parish.'

Molly let out a small gasp of shock. 'But there must be, there must be something. I've lived here all my life. I know my birth was registered in the parish book because it was used as proof when I got married, which should also be in the book…'

Sukie took in the look of dismay on Molly's face. She leant over the table and took a hold of her hands. 'I'm sorry, Molly, but the book of records for the 1800s is missing. Jeremy, our current vicar, wasn't able to find it when he cleared the church up. I then had the idea to take a walk through the graveyard. I did find one gravestone for a "Molly Smythe" but it was dated 1848. There were no more after that. While I didn't expect to find one for you, given that you're here, I thought there might be more recent family graves.'

'Molly Smythe was my grandmother. I was named after her. There should have been a stone beside it for Albert Smythe, my grandfather.'

Sukie brought out her phone and looked at the photograph she'd taken. The gravestone next to Molly's did indeed say Albert Smythe.

'Look, Molly, I know this is coming across as though I don't trust you or your story but that's not the case. It's just so extraordinary and my brain is struggling to take it in.'

'What about the national census records, Sukie? Have you checked those? Do we know when they began doing the census?'

Sukie repeated the information Jeremy had passed on to her that morning. 'The thing is, Charlie, I don't have the time to be trawling through those right now. We're off to Austria at the weekend and I need to get everything organised for that. As of now, the mystery of Molly's family is yours to solve.'

'But I have to get back to London. I've already taken extra days away from the office, I can't take any more.'

'Then you'll need to take Molly to London with you.'

'I can't do that!'

'Why not?' The tone of Molly's voice stopped both Sukie and Charlie in their tracks.

'Molly, we need to solve two mysteries here. One, what happened to your family and, two, how to get you back to your own time. If we're able to return you to 1860, it's better that you go with as little information about the twenty-first century as possible. This is to make your life easier because it would be very easy to slip up and reveal things you shouldn't. We don't want you ending up in some kind of asylum because people think you're mad.' Sukie smiled at Molly, hoping her words didn't come across as hurtful.

'I back what Sukie's saying, Molly. You already know more than is safe for you. London is quite different to this little country village and, if you go there, you'll see a kind of life that you may struggle to keep to yourself.'

Sukie watched Molly as she processed what she and Charlie had said. She only had to hope that she saw the sense in their words.

Finally, Molly spoke. 'I do understand what you are both saying to me and I do accept your reasoning. It does make perfect sense. However, the way I see it is, we have no choice. Sukie, you will be in another country in a matter of days so your involvement with me is about to come to an end. Charlie, you believe you have a responsibility towards me because you pulled me out of the water. In that, you are wrong. You could not have known what you were doing so you can take no blame. It is something that happened and now *I* need to deal with it. I would appreciate any assistance you can kindly give me, but I have no wish to impose upon your life any further. Somehow, I will try to resolve the matter on my own.'

'Molly, helping you is not the issue here. I'm scared that the lifestyle changes which have occurred over the last one-hundred and sixty years will be too much for you to comprehend.'

'Well, Charlie, that is a risk I am going to have to take. I have no other choice.'

Charlie looked at Sukie who just shrugged. She understood where Molly was coming from and, truth be told, if she were to find herself in a similar situation, she would most likely have the same attitude. When it came to her family, she would do anything to save them, no matter the risk to herself.

'Charlie, Molly's right. There's no other option. She needs to stay with you, wherever you are.' She turned to

Molly. 'It looks like you're off to the big smoke, Molls. You had better prepare yourself, gal, because believe me when I say, you ain't never seen anything like it before.'

Molly and Charlie had said their goodbyes to Sukie and were walking back to the mill. Suddenly Molly stopped and turned to Charlie. 'I need to go to the village.'

'What? Why?'

'I need to see my home, Charlie. Or where my home once stood. I might be able to glean some information from somewhere that will help me to find where my family went.'

'But what if you say or describe something that no one else could possibly know. It's far too risky, I can't allow it.'

'Mr Charles Rowland, I would like to point out to you that you are not my father, my husband or my master. You do not get to dictate to me what I can do. If I say I am going to the village, then *I am going* to the village. Is that understood?'

'But—'

'Charlie…' Molly glared at him.

'Okay, okay! We'll go to the village. Please, just promise me you'll be careful about what you say. Remember it will have changed greatly since you last saw it.'

'If I do speak out of turn, then we can use Sukie's excuse from this morning about researching a family tree. I'll say I've found some old family diaries which have descriptions of the village in them. Will that do?'

Charlie grinned at her. 'Yes, it will. It's quite clever actually.'

‘Thank you. I’m not stupid, you know. Just because my knowledge is from a different time, it does not mean my faculties are impaired. Please remember that.’

‘Come on then. Let’s go. We can have lunch in the tearoom.’ Charlie looked at Molly. ‘You should like it, it’s supposed to be Victorian. You can give some feedback.’

‘Now then, Charlie, how would I know what a Victorian tearoom should look like?’ Molly smirked.

The birds in the trees above them suddenly soared into the sky as the sound of Charlie’s laughter roared through the air.

Chapter Eighteen

They turned on the path and made their way towards the village. Molly looked with interest at the doctor's surgery and the chemist next to it as they walked by but said nothing. When they came out of the lane and onto the high street, she stopped to look around while taking several deep breaths as her mind worked on absorbing how the village, which she knew so well, could look so familiar and yet be so different.

She stood gazing out over the village green for a few moments then placed her hand on Charlie's arm. 'Charlie, I am trying not to ask too many questions because I understand it is becoming tedious for you to always be explaining the answers but I do really need to know, what is that?' She pointed to the shiny black box-like thing beside her.

'That's a motor car. It is the current day mode of transport. This has replaced the horse and carriage as people's means of travelling. It is considerably faster and, I believe from films I have watched, considerably more comfortable too.'

‘How does it work? What makes it move if there are no horses to pull it?’

‘See that long bit there at the front,’ Charlie pointed to the bonnet, ‘that is where the engine sits and it does all sorts of jiggery pokery which makes the car move.’

‘I’ve heard of engines. They were attached to trains back in my time and I do believe they were much bigger than what you suggest is in that small space.’

‘Once upon a time, they were very big – and some still are depending on the job they’re doing – but as time has passed, we have learnt how to create the same power from something smaller.’

‘I see there are several of these “motor cars” here – does everybody have one or just rich people?’

‘Most people now have cars. They’re very popular.’

‘Do you have one, Charlie?’

‘Yes, I do, and we’ll be using it when we go to London in a few days.’

‘Then I will let you know how it compares to a horse and carriage. I will tell you if your assumption is correct that it is more comfortable.’ She smiled up at him. ‘Now, let me take a walk around my village and see how it is today.’

They’d only walked a few yards along the pavement when Molly stopped and let out a small exclamation. ‘Oh my, Hilda’s Haberdashery is still here? I can remember the day the shop opened.’

‘Do you want to go inside for a look?’

Molly hesitated. ‘Yes, I do but I won’t. I think I might speak out of turn which would not be helpful.’

‘Did you frequent this shop often?’

‘Yes, I did. I am a seamstress. I often help out with alterations and, occasionally, creating new gowns for the ladies of the manor. I also carry out repairs although they are usually for the village folks as they cannot afford new clothing when something gets damaged.'

She turned away and continued walking along, stopping occasionally to look in a window or peer through a doorway. It was when she reached the French restaurant that she spoke again. 'What is this?'

'It's an eatery where they specialise in serving food from France.'

'I see. Can I assume from this that we are not currently at war with France? We do seem to fight with them rather a lot.'

'No, we're not at war with France and haven't been for many years. Well, not with guns and cannons anyway. We may still have the occasional spat with them but it's only verbal and we both work hard at maintaining a civilised relationship.'

'That is good to hear. War is such a waste of lives and money.'

'I quite agree with you on that, Molly.'

They'd reached the bottom end of the village green, by this point, and it was only a few more yards to walk and she would be standing in front of the building that had once been her home. Molly glanced at the red glass box thing next to her but decided not to ask Charlie what it was. It could wait. Now that she was this close to home, she just wanted to see it. She picked up her pace and walked briskly along the narrow roadway only stopping when she came to her home. Or rather, where her home had once stood. The house now in front of her was built of brick and had a tiled roof. The old cobbles were still on the ground but they were the only remnants of what had stood there before. A high wall prevented her from seeing where her father's workshop had once stood. She sensed Charlie coming to stand behind her. He placed his hands gently upon her shoulders.

'Are you okay?' he asked quietly.

The lump in her throat prevented her from replying so she gave a small nod of her head. What words could possibly express the pain she was feeling inside?

'I can see this is not your home, Molly. This building is not old enough.'

'How do you know that?' she whispered.

'I'm an architect. It's my job to know these things.'

'Do you know what happened to my home?'

'I don't but we can try to find out. My brother owns the shop on the village green and the lady who now lives in this house, Sam, works in the bakery. They might know more about its past. Come, let's go around.'

Molly stared at the house for a moment longer before turning away and following Charlie back towards the village green.

Charlie stopped when he reached The Cabookeria and waited for Molly to catch up. Her eyes were red and he could see she was trying not to cry. When she was by his side, he took her hand and gave it a little squeeze. 'You're doing good, Molly, you're doing good.'

She gave him a watery smile and he watched her carefully as she took some deep breaths. He couldn't even begin to try and comprehend what she must be feeling inside. He guessed she was most likely feeling that way too – unable to understand the myriad emotions she was experiencing.

'Please tell me how this building has changed. I know it's several centuries old so it must have been a part of your life.'

'It was a very big part of my life. There,' she pointed at the bakery window, 'that was the customer entrance to the stables at the back of the building. My father's forge was directly opposite as you walked through, adjoining the stables on the right. This,' she waved her hand towards the shop, 'was the inn. Betsy, the innkeeper, was a good friend. This was where I met Charles Dickens. I would often help out when it was busy so I know the building well. Or, maybe I should say, I *knew* it well. It looks very different now.'

'Well, my brother and his wife own it now and they might have some information on its past. I know when they bought it, it had previously been an ironmongers and had been for over a hundred years. I know very little of its history before that but, hopefully, Jeff and Jenny will know more. After you…'

Molly stepped through the door and he watched as she took tentative steps forward. Her head was turning this way and that as she took in all the books lined up along the walls. Jenny, his sister-in-law, ran the bookshop and Jeff had an arts, crafts and antiques centre up on the first floor. The tearoom in the conservatory at the back was the domain of Sam who also owned the bakery. Their shop had only been open just over a year but it was very successful and had breathed new life into the village.

Jenny was standing by the till doing some paperwork. It was unusual for her not to have called out a cheery greeting as they'd walked in, she was always full of smiles for her customers.

'Hi, Jenny, how are you doing today?'

She looked up, clearly startled. 'Oh, Charlie! You gave me a shock. I didn't hear you come in.'

'Clearly,' he grinned at her. 'I was wondering if you might be able to help out with some information regarding this building's past life. My friend, Molly, is doing some family research and I guessed you might know more about it.'

'Oh, I see, erm… well… I… Look, do you mind talking

to Jeff about it, he's upstairs. I'm a bit busy down here.'

Charlie glanced around the empty shop. 'Err… sure. Will do. I'll catch you later.'

'Yes, later…' Jenny wandered off to straighten some perfectly straight books on the table by the door.

He called Molly and let her lead the way up the stairs.

'Be with you in a moment…' a muffled voice called out from behind one of the shabby chic armoires in the corner.

'It's alright, Jeff, it's only me. No rush.'

'Charlie!' Jeff's head popped out upon hearing his brother's voice. 'Hang on two ticks…'

'Need a hand?'

'No, I'm good, thanks.'

Molly was walking slowly around the room, picking up some of the knick-knacks lying around.

'Hey there, little bro, great to see you.' Jeff walked over to Charlie and gave him a hug. 'What brings you here? Shouldn't you be back in London by now?'

'Going back in a few days, I'm helping a friend to research some family history. Jeff, this is Molly. Molly, this is my brother, Jeff.'

'Very nice to meet you, sir.' Molly dropped a slight curtsey. Jeff looked at Charlie in amazement.

'She's in an amateur dramatics society – they've got a production in a couple of months so she's practising for her role.'

'I see. Well, it's very nice to meet you, Molly.' Jeff gave her a small bow.

Charlie rolled his eyes – trust his brother to ham it up.

'We're here looking into Molly's family history and were wondering how much you know about the past of this building. I recall you saying it had been an ironmongers for many years but do you know anything prior to that?'

His brother thought for a moment before replying. 'Not really. I know it started out as a coaching inn and I recall the estate agent saying something about a fire…? The building on the other side of the courtyard was the stables but they've been sealed closed for many years. It's on the agenda to open them up and have a closer look but we haven't gotten around to it yet. We've been rather busy with this place. You should ask Jenny, she's into her history and stuff, she's most likely to know more.'

'Ah, I was going to but she was really distracted when I spoke to her. Is everything okay?'

'Oh, silly me, of course.' Jeff hit his forehead with the palm of his hand. 'She's seeing Mandy tonight.'

'Ah! How's that going?'

'It's been slow but they're getting there. Mandy's adoptive mum has been great and she's worked hard to bring them together. This will be the first time they've been alone and Jenny intends to share the contents of the sea-chests with Mandy – the proof that she never forgot her daughter and that she always loved her. She's hoping it will help to close the void between them.'

'I'll keep my fingers crossed. They're both lovely people, they deserve to find happiness together.'

'Cheers! Sorry I couldn't help more with your research.'

Charlie waved his hand. 'Don't worry about it. It's fine.' He glanced at Molly and saw the distress on her face. 'Would you mind, Jeff, if we took a wander down the lane for a closer look at the stables. I think it would help Molly to feel she'd somehow connected with her family.'

'Sure, not a problem although I don't think there's much to see, it's all so overgrown along there.' Jeff looked at Molly. 'May I ask what your family connection is with the village?'

Before Charlie could say anything, Molly replied, 'I understand my family – going back a few generations – were the blacksmiths for the village.'

‘Right! That’s interesting. Well, the stables would certainly have some of your historical DNA in them, if that’s the case. Good luck.’

‘Thank you, Jeff.’

Footsteps sounded on the stairs and two American accents floated up towards them. ‘Right, time I was back to work.’ Jeff smiled at them both.

‘See you soon, big bro.’

‘Thank you for your help.’

‘Anytime, Molly.’

Charlie waited for the visitors to clear the stairs before indicating that Molly should go down first. At the bottom, he guided her towards the tearoom. ‘Let’s have some lunch before we go any further.’

He caught Sam’s eye and mouthed he was after a table for two. A few minutes later, they were sitting along the glass wall of the conservatory with menus in their hands. Charlie leaned over the table with a grin and whispered to Molly, ‘Right, let’s see what tasty new morsels we can thrill you with today.’

Chapter Nineteen

Molly turned to look once more at the shop they'd just exited. She wondered what Betsy would say if she were to see it now. The inside was so different and she'd liked the fresh, clean feel of the building. It was a long way from the dark, smoke-filled hostel she'd worked in only two weeks ago. When they'd sat down at the table by the window, in the tearoom conservatory, Charlie had spent several minutes describing to her how it had come to be discovered when Jeff and Jenny had first bought the shop and that it had since become quite the tourist attraction in the village. Molly had confirmed the beautiful glass structure had not been there in her time. In truth, Betsy would have loved something like it, but it greatly reduced the size of the courtyard so would not have been possible. The angle of their table, however, meant she'd been facing out into the courtyard and it had been quite disconcerting to sit eating lunch while gazing out at the stable block which now looked so different.

The large archways that had once held solid wooden doors were all bricked up. Faint black singe marks could still be seen in the stonework above them. The roof appeared to have holes which had been shored up with old planks of wood. It was a far cry from the smart building Betsy's guests had housed their horses in.

The hardest part, however, was seeing the wall that had been built right where her father's workshop had been. It ran from the end of the stable wall, across the courtyard to where the tunnel entrance had once been. The same tunnel entrance which was now the bakery. She'd spotted a roof peeking over the top of the wall which suggested that area had also become part of the bakery.

'Are you ready? Shall we make our way rou—'

Molly turned to see why Charlie had stopped so abruptly and saw him walking quickly towards two elderly ladies sitting on a bench by the duck pond. She hurried after him and arrived by his side just as he was bidding them good-day.

'Rose, Doris, my two favourite women. How wonderful to see you both!' With an exaggerated bow, he bent over and kissed both of their hands.

'Oh, get away with you, laddie,' one of them said, making a mock swipe in his direction. The other giggled and blushed a sweet hue of pink.

'Molly,' he turned to her, 'Meet Doris and Rose.'

She greeted them far more demurely than Charlie had done. Doris had been the one to chit-chat back at Charlie.

'Molly, let me tell you now that, whatever Doris doesn't know about this village, isn't worth knowing. She's lived here all her life, haven't you, gorgeous.'

'Charlie, give me any more of your lip and I'll be living here far longer than you will!'

Molly guessed, from the way the three of them laughed at her comment, that this form of mockery was a common thing between them. She found herself warming to Doris – any woman who backchatted a man in this manner was a fine woman in her books.

‘Doris, I’m glad we’ve bumped into you, you might be able to help us. Molly here is doing some family research and we’re trying to find out more information regarding the old coaching inn and the blacksmiths forge that used to be behind it. Do you know anything?’

‘Oh now, let me see…’ Doris scrunched her face up in thought. After a moment, she replied, ‘I’ll be honest with you, Charlie, I can’t say that I know all that much. The rumours are that there was a big fire in the stables and someone died. His ghost now haunts them and on dark nights, when the moon cannot be seen, his spirit can be heard screaming through the bricks. It’s the same noise he made on the night he died because the intensity of the flames prevented anyone being able to rescue him.’

‘Do you know who died in the fire?’ Molly held her breath as she waited for Doris to answer.

‘Erm… Peter? Paul? Something like that?’

‘Patrick?’

‘Yes, that’s it! Patrick. How did you know that?’ Doris looked at her through narrowed eyes.

‘Oh, I’ve… erm… been reading some old diaries and I remember that name being mentioned.’

Doris nodded and Molly breathed a small sigh of relief. That had been close.

‘Do you know anything about the blacksmiths who lived next to the stables?’

‘Sorry, lass, I’m afraid I don’t. No one has ever mentioned any blacksmiths. Maybe it’s the one up the road in Upper Ditchley – I know they go back a long way. Family-run business that one, been there for years.’

‘Thank you, Doris.’

Charlie looked at Molly. ‘Well, ready to have a closer look?’

‘A closer look at what?’

‘The stables, Doris.’

‘Oh no, lad, you don’t want to get too close to them – the ghost will get you.’

‘I don’t think there’s really a ghost, Doris,’ Charlie replied, giving her a soft smile.

‘Then why has no one ever opened the stables up and done something with the building? Because they know there’s a ghost inside, that’s why.’

‘Doris, the building has most likely remained closed because the previous owners had no use for it and, due to the covenants on the land, no residential property can be built there.’

‘Hmmph! You with your fancy talk! Covenants my arse! It’s the ghost, I’m telling you!’

‘Well, Doris, if we suddenly go missing, never to be seen again, then you can rest easy knowing you were right.’

Doris huffed as she replied, ‘Well, lad, don’t say I didn’t warn you. You young ones have no sense of danger these days. Always looking for the next big thrill. Let’s see how much you enjoy being dead when the ghost gets you. That’ll teach you a lesson.’

‘I’ll be sure to come and let you know, Doris, if that happens.’

‘Argh! Don’t you dare come and haunt me, young Charlie! I’ll run you through with my walking stick if you do. Come on, Rose, let’s go. I don’t want to be here when they let that Patrick one loose.’

As Rose stood up to follow, she turned to Molly and said in her sweet, soft, voice, ‘Good luck, Molly. I hope you find out more about your family. It gives us stability when we know how our roots are planted.’ She smiled before making her way along the pathway to catch up with Doris.

Charlie looked at her with a smile. ‘Still want to get up

close and personal with the stables?'

'If you mean, Charlie, do I still want to have a look at them, then the answer is yes. I do wish you would stop talking in riddles, it is very confusing sometimes.'

She could hear Charlie snickering behind her as she turned on her heel and began to make her way back towards the lane which led to the stables.

Charlie stepped forward to walk alongside Molly. 'This Patrick fellow, did you know him?'

There was a brief moment of silence before she answered. 'Yes, I did. He was a lovely, kind, gentle man. He was a bit simple but he had a way with the horses. He loved them and they loved him. His parents both died when he was in his twenties but the village took care of him. Betsy allowed him to board above the stables and he would often go down in the night to help settle any horse who was nervous from being in unfamiliar surroundings. It saddens me to know he died in such a tragic way.'

'Well, Doris has corroborated what Jeff said about a fire.'

'It's strange, but the night you followed me to the village, I was sure I could smell smoke. It was so strong and I followed it. When I came around from my faint though, it was gone.'

'Are you suggesting the fire happened the night you came through time?'

'Well, I did overhear Damien Featheringstone ordering his lackey to administer some kind of justice upon my father as retribution for showing him up earlier that day…'

'Surely he wouldn't have set fire to the stables? That would be madness.' Charlie shuddered at the thought. He was fully aware that, with their thatched roofs and timber frames, any fire breaking out back in the 1800s would have been even more terrifying than it would be today.

'We both know that, Charlie, but Stan Alderly is not known for his intelligence so goodness only knows what he could have done.'

'Molly, I don't want to upset you, but is it possible your family died in the fire?'

'Of course, it is possible, Charlie, but why are there no graves? Why is there no record of us ever being here? That makes no sense.'

'Some fires can burn to such high temperatures that anything within them just disintegrates. Maybe there were no bodies to bury.'

'In that case, a memorial stone would have been laid. It was the way of the village to always remember the dead.'

Charlie didn't say anything further – there were no such stones in the churchyard so the mystery remained; what had happened to Molly's family?

Molly came to an abrupt halt in the middle of the lane and walked over to the stone wall of the stables. She laid her hand upon it and felt the coolness seep into it. She waited for a few minutes, her eyes closed tightly, sure that something else would flow through her. She wanted the brick to speak to her, tell her what she needed to know. She wanted it to connect to her. When it didn't, she walked away in disappointment. Charlie had stood off to one side and his silence told her that he understood. When she stepped away, he walked over to her side.

'Anything?' he asked.

'Nothing.' There was a small catch in her voice and she coughed. 'I need to get inside. Maybe then I will learn more.'

‘That, I’m afraid, is impossible. We can’t start hitting the brickwork with a sledgehammer while the shop is full of customers. I think Jeff and Jenny would have something to say about that!’

‘Oh, we don’t need a hammer. Or, if we do, it will only be a small one.’

‘I’m not sure I understand…’

Molly looked up at Charlie. ‘Do you really think a building this size only had one means of getting in and out? Come, follow me.’

She walked further along the lane, past the stable building and along the side of a tall, brick wall where the brambles and weeds were thick and high. The lane had only been cleared part of the way to allow Jeff access to the flat above the shop when he’d lived there. Beyond that, it had remained a wilderness.

‘How much further does this lane go on for?’

‘Oh, not far at all. Just beyond the end of the wall. On the other side is where the carriages would be kept overnight. Now… somewhere along here…’ She pulled the long sleeve of the T-shirt over her hand and began pushing and stamping the overgrowth away from the wall. A few seconds passed and then Charlie was by her side, doing the same. It only took them a couple of minutes to clear enough of the greenery away to reveal a large wooden gate the same height as the wall.

Charlie gave it a push but it stood firm.

‘It would have been locked from the inside to prevent any theft.’ Molly was prodding the wood as she spoke. ‘This bit, however, is soft and pliable,’ she pushed the lower section more firmly, ‘and I think that, with a bit of force – or a good hefty kick – we can break through it.’ She glanced up at Charlie with a look of assumed innocence.

‘We can’t do that, Molly, Jeff would kill me!’

‘Oh, Charlie, where’s your sense of adventure? Are you

trying to tell me that you've always been a good boy who has never broken the rules? I would find that very hard to believe.'

'Molly, why do I get the feeling that you're not the strait-laced, well-behaved, Victorian lady I had you pegged as?'

'I really don't know where you got that idea, Charlie. I was quite the tomboy in my youth. I could climb the trees and ride the horses far better than most of the boys in the village. My father often says I am the bane of his life. I don't think he knows that I take his words to be a compliment…' She stopped speaking. A heartbeat of time passed and then she spoke again. 'I have that wrong. I should have said I "*was*" the bane of his life…'

'Hey…' Charlie stood up and passed her a tissue from his jacket pocket. She dabbed at her eyes for a moment before looking at what Charlie had given her. 'Paper handkerchiefs?' she asked incredulously.

'Oh, didn't I tell you, a few things have changed around here in the last couple of hundred years…'

The look of assumed innocence on Charlie's face was exactly what was required to make a burst of laughter jump from her lips. Unable to stop herself, Molly doubled-over as she succumbed to his humour. When she finally pulled herself together, although the odd snort was still escaping from her mouth, Charlie asked her, 'Feeling better now?'

'Yes, I do. It is often said that laughter is the best medicine, I can see why that might be.'

'Good. Now stand back, I'm going to give this gate a "good, hefty kick" and see what happens.'

'You, sir, are a gentleman.'

'Hmm, we'll see about that once I've given this thing a bit of welly!'

It took three "good, hefty kicks" to splinter the wood and a few more tugs to make a gap big enough for Molly to squeeze through. She unlocked the gate on the other side and Charlie was able to push it open just enough to be able to join her.

He looked around him and immediately saw the greater destruction the fire had wrought on this side of the stables. The brickwork was cracked and he could see, through the soot which had seeped into the stone, that there were areas where the mortar had crumbled away and the bricks were dropping down on top of each other. He really wouldn't like to vouch for the safety of the building. Molly, however, had no such qualms and was already trying to tug open one of the stable doors.

'Molly! Stop!' he shouted as he ran over to her. He batted her hands away from the handle she was pulling on.

'Let me open it!' she yelled at him.

'No! Look at the bricks above you! If you open that door, you will most likely bring half the building down. This door is the only thing holding them up right now.'

He pointed above her head to make her see the sense in his words.

'Oh! I'm sorry, Charlie. I just wanted to get inside. I really need to see inside.' She looked up at him and the pleading in her eyes was too much for him. He'd always been a pushover when faced with women's tears.

'Then come with me, let me look and see if I can find an entrance which looks more stable. Ha, ha, get it… "Looks more stable…" I should be on the stage, I should.'

Molly gave him a dry look. 'Yes, Charlie, the first stage out of the village.'

'Ooohhh, hark at you with the snappy retorts!' He was relieved when Molly gave him a silly grin. She was back on track. But he was constantly on edge, always aware of how she was reacting and responding to everything around her. It was exhausting. He guessed that, in some way, this must be how mothers feel when they're sending their children out into the world – never knowing how they'll react, what dangers might come their way and will they be equipped to protect them if required.

He stepped away from the fire-damaged building, pulling Molly by the hand to ensure she didn't touch anything while his back was turned and made his way into the centre of the yard. The weeds had grown up between the cobbles and he had to mind his footing. He was roughly halfway across when he turned and, putting his hand up to shield his eyes from the sun, took a good, long look at the structure in front of him. His gut was telling him to walk away – it was too unsafe to be messing around with. His head was telling him, however, that he had to try and find a way inside that would allow Molly a quick look. She needed to do this and he understood why. As he looked about him, he was surprised that no one had made mention of this area. Now that he cast his mind back, it had been marked on the plans for the shop but it hadn't been a priority for investigation at the time. He could see the apex of the roof of Sam's cottage on the other side of the wall opposite where they'd entered. It was possible that she too was unaware of what lay here as the wall would have blocked the view from the upper rooms of her cottage. He turned back to the stables. It seemed that the only point of entry, which was least likely to bring the roof down onto their heads was the door nearest to the gate where they'd entered. He could see from the blackened bricks that the fire had been more intense at the other end, close to Sam's cottage. That area was by far the most damaged and the wall was taking most of the weight of the unaligned bricks above it.

‘Stay here!’ He gave Molly a firm look to match his firm tone. She seemed to understand for she gave a small nod and made no move to follow him as he walked away.

Once he was in front of the door, he saw he’d been right to choose this one. There was a large gap along the top so, if opened slowly and carefully, nothing should be dislodged. He took a hold of the handle and began to gently pull it towards him.

Chapter Twenty

Lower Ditchely - 1860

Lord Eustace Featheringstone stood looking at the burnt-out shell of the blacksmith's cottage and workshop. It appeared, to his inexperienced eye, that this was where the heart of the fire had been. It was two weeks since the disaster and it was only now possible to get close to the remains. They had smouldered for several days until the hot weather had finally broken and the rain had fallen in torrents, extinguishing the heat from any last embers buried underneath.

'Is there any news of the family?' he asked his son, standing by his side.

'No, Father. No one has seen them since before the fire.'

'Do you think…' The words choked in his throat and he had to wait a moment before trying again. 'Do you think they were inside? Do you think they perished in the blaze?'

'I really don't know, sir. It is possible, I suppose, although it is also possible that they have left the village for good and the fire broke out after they'd gone. Maybe the furnace wasn't extinguished properly…'

Eustace looked at his son. 'Why would John and Alice be leaving the village? This is the family business and has been for centuries. The only way John Smythe would leave here is feet first, in a wooden box!' He peered into Damien's face. 'Have you been up to your old tricks again? Did you have something to do with them moving away?'

Eustace knew of his son's antics – the gambling, the whoring, the bullying and intimidation. His look of innocence only made him more suspicious.

'No, Father, I did not. I have simply heard rumours that John was in debt. It might be they did a disappearing act to escape from those he owed. In fact, the more one thinks about it, it's possible he set the buildings alight on purpose. Feigning death would be an excellent means of getting out of trouble.'

'Damien! How dare you speak in this manner. John Smythe was an upstanding man and would never resort to such underhand tactics. I refuse to believe the words you are speaking.'

Eustace turned to look at the blackened mess in front of him. His eyes followed the line of destruction to the stables. The gable end nearest to the blacksmith's cottage had suffered the most and you could follow the path of the flames from the marks left on the bricks. The courtyard had saved the inn, and its guests, from also being victims although the heat from the flames had scorched the back walls and blown out the glass in the windows. The only casualty, that they knew of for certain, had been Patrick, the stable boy. He'd managed to release the three horses that had been stabled there that night but a beam had fallen on him before he'd been able to escape himself. The villagers had all heard his screams but they'd been unable to save him. Patrick had died a hero and Eustace had told the vicar he was to have a proper burial and to send the bill to the manor for settlement.

He turned to take one last look at what was left of the cottage. Alice's father, Martin Browning, had once been a close friend but, when Alice had run off with John, after meeting him while accompanying her father on a visit, Martin had stated he no longer wanted to maintain a friendship with him. Eustace had felt this was rather unfair as he'd had nothing to do with the elopement but Martin was a stubborn man and would not listen to reason. He'd had his heart set on Alice marrying a certain wealthy young buck from London and had been embarrassed by her actions. Father and daughter had been estranged ever since.

Eustace had kept an eye on Alice and her family from afar. Her daughter Molly had been a bright, sparky little thing with a keen mind. He'd tried to encourage her the best he could and allowed her the free use of the manor library – an offer she'd taken full advantage of. He would miss seeing her curled up on the chair by the French window where she would slip in and sit whenever she had some free time.

In a back-to-front way, he kind of hoped there was some truth in Damien's assertion that John Smythe had done a moonlight flit because the alternative was really too painful to consider.

'Damien, could you liaise with the workmen to get this rubble cleared away. Ask them to take care and to look out for any remains. I would also ask that all entrances to the stables be bricked up and a wall built across this part of the yard to secure the back entrance to the inn. The last thing we need is the village children venturing into these ruins and the whole lot coming down on top of them.'

With a heavy heart and a heavy gait, Lord Eustace Featheringstone turned and walked away, not caring if anyone witnessed the tears flowing down his face.

Damien Featheringstone watched his father walk off. Stupid old fool, he thought. What difference did it make if the family had died or not? What was it to him? He was just a silly, sentimental old man who'd lived far longer than he should. The sooner he passed away, the better. The villagers here had had it too easy for far too long. He would sort them out. He'd charge them proper rents and proper taxes for their homes and businesses – it was time the manor began to make a profit from its tenants.

He walked over to the workmen standing to the side, waiting to be given their orders. 'Which of you is the foreman?' he barked.

A tall, surly looking man stepped forward. 'That would be me, sir.'

'A private word, if you please.'

Damien walked the man away from his team. When he believed they were well out of earshot, he passed on his father's instructions for the stables and the new wall. When he was finished, he added some instructions of his own. 'I need you to keep a close eye out for any human remains within the building. There's a small chance it may have been occupied at the time of the fire. Should you find anything, you *must* keep it quiet and tell no one, only myself. We don't want to upset the villagers any more than they have been already so my father has requested your utmost discretion in this matter. Please package up anything you do find and pass it only to me. You understand? *Only* to me. No one else.'

The man nodded his understanding. 'Of course, sir, not a problem, sir. And… err… Will there be remuneration for this discretion?'

'Of course.' Damien handed over a small leather purse which bulged with coins. 'You will receive the same again when the job is done and anything of interest is in my possession.'

The man's hand took a hold of the purse and Damien tried not to shudder when the grimy fingernails raked against his skin.

'It will be as you wish, sir.' He pocketed the purse and turned back to his men, shouting out orders as he walked towards them.

Damien stood watching the activity for a few moments. When he left, a small smirk played on his lips. He'd done well today. The nugget of doubt he'd placed in the old man's head about Smythe running away had been inspired. And as for getting the foreman in his pocket… Well, it only proved again that money talks. It wouldn't take long for the workmen to remove the remains and build the wall. Once they were gone, he'd be in the clear.

Chapter Twenty-One

Lower Ditchley – Present Day

Molly sat nursing the mug of hot chocolate in her hand, pulling the throw tighter around her shoulders. She hadn't been able to stop shivering since they'd left the stables. Charlie had tried to talk her out of looking inside but she'd refused to listen. Her stupid pig-headedness had overruled the common sense which had urged her to walk away. Oh, how she wished she hadn't been so stubborn…

Molly waited impatiently for Charlie to come back out of the ruined stables. She was anxious to get inside and see it for herself. She didn't realise she'd been holding her breath until he carefully exited through the small opening of the charred stable door and she ran over to him. 'Well? Can I go in? Do you think it is safe?'

He rubbed his eyes before answering her. ‘Molly, I think it’s safe enough but it’s a real mess in there. I honestly think it would be better for you not to see it. I don’t think you’ll benefit from it.’

While her head agreed with him, in her heart she knew her own eyes had to observe the remains of the building where she had practically grown up. It was the only place which hadn’t been touched or altered by another human hand since the last time she’d seen her parents. Her memories had been removed from the coaching inn, they’d been flattened and replaced in the shape of Sam’s cottage and they’d been boxed up and shipped out when the manor had been emptied upon the death of the last Lord Featheringstone. This building was the last one standing that had any chance of speaking to her; of filling some of the void in a heart which kept being broken every time she gathered new information on the events of the night she’d fallen through time.

‘I have to go in, Charlie, I have no choice.’

‘Fine,’ he sighed. ‘I don’t know why I bothered trying to dissuade you. Come on.’

As Charlie held the door back for her to slip through, he said, ‘Stay close to me and be very careful where you place your feet.’

She nodded and stepped through the tight gap. Blinded by the change from brilliant sunlight to the darkness of the stable interior, she closed her eyes, moved slightly to the side and waited for Charlie to join her. When she felt him by her side, she took his hand and opened her eyes. As they adjusted to the gloom, she realised it wasn’t as dark as she’d expected it to be. There were a number of holes and gaps in the roof and the sunlight was streaming through them, providing them with spots of light. The slim black box that Charlie always kept in his pocket had a light in it and he turned this on so they could see where it was safe to place their feet.

They'd entered the stable at the side of the horse stall furthest from where her father worked. This was the door the stable hands used to get water from the pump out in the yard and to take out the old straw and manure.

She looked towards the stall – although the wood was heavily charred, it was still standing. She placed a finger on the wooden wall and felt it crumble beneath her touch. She quickly pulled her hand away, lest she cause any further damage.

Charlie led her around the stall and into the main cobbled area of the stable. It was then she realised that the wooden horse stall she'd just touched was the only thing left intact in the building. The hayloft above her head was no longer there, hence the clear view of the sky through the holes in the roof. Her mind immediately went back to the days of her childhood when she'd so often played up there. Moving the bales to make a "house" where she'd have tea parties with her doll. Using the bales to cover her when playing hide and seek. And, of course, sneaking up there with Tommy in the early days of their courtship. Despite the damage around her, the memories came flooding back.

She moved along the cobbles, taking great care with her footing. She now understood Charlie's concerns – all it needed was one slip, a bump against a pillar and the roof could come down. Everything inside the building was a charred mess which could disintegrate from the smallest of touches – as she'd already found out. She'd walked halfway along when she came to a halt. She could go no further. Burnt-out beams were piled high in front of her along with the rotten floorboards from the hay loft. To her left, the old water troughs were rolled on their sides. As she moved her foot to turn around, she felt something hard beneath it. Bending down, she saw a buckle lying in the dirt. The blackened leather strap, which had once been a bridle, fell away as she picked it up. Molly rubbed it with the paper handkerchief Charlie had given her earlier and a tiny bit of metallic sheen glowed back at her. It was this action which caused a long-forgotten memory to slam into her mind. She'd been arguing with Albie, the way brothers and sisters do, and in a fit of rage, she'd emptied a bucket of water over his head. The action in itself wasn't the worst part – it was the fact that it had been early December and the water was half frozen which had really gotten her into serious trouble. Albie had ended up in bed with a chill and, as a punishment, her father had made her polish all the tack in the stables for the next three weeks. Oh, how she had come to loathe that job. Now, however, as she stood there in that space, she'd give anything to be back there again, listening to her father whistle as he worked away, keeping an eye on her to make sure she didn't slip away when his back was turned. Oh, what she would give now to hear that whistle once more – she would even sit and polish tack for a hundred weeks if she had to.

That was when the tears began to fall as it finally really hit her that she would never see her family again.

Charlie came to sit beside her and straightened the throw around her shoulders. 'Hey, how are you doing?' he asked her in a soft voice.

He'd been so kind, once again, when he saw her begin to panic as she'd stood in the middle of the stables. He'd come immediately to her side, and while talking very gently, had carefully guided her back out into the sunlight. He'd taken her in his arms and held her tightly while the tears poured out of her. Eventually, she was all cried out but the shivering hadn't stopped. Charlie said it was the shock of everything coming to the fore and he was surprised that it had taken this long to happen. They'd made their way out of the stable yard and headed straight back to the windmill, luckily not meeting anyone along the way.

She could feel Charlie's warmth seeping through the blanket as he held her by his side and it helped to calm her down. Gradually, the shivering ceased and she began to yawn as a heavy tiredness flowed through her body.

She woke for a few brief seconds as Charlie pulled some blankets over her but, the first she became aware of being in her bed, was when the sunlight played across her face the following morning.

Chapter Twenty-Two

'Morning, Molly, how are you feeling this morning? I've just put the kettle on; would you like tea, coffee or hot chocolate?'

'Good morning, Charlie. Tea, please.'

'Coming right up.' As Charlie busied himself getting the teapot and tealeaves prepared, it had not escaped his notice that Molly hadn't answered his first question. He took this to mean she was still feeling unsettled and he didn't want to push her on the point. He watched her moving around as he poured the hot water into the teapot.

'What would you like for breakfast? I've got bacon and eggs – we could have a good old English fry-up, or toast if you would prefer something lighter?'

Molly looked over and shrugged her shoulders. 'I'm not really hungry. I'll just stick with a cup of tea, thank you.'

Charlie thought for a moment, as he allowed the tea to brew. Molly had to eat something, she hadn't had anything since lunchtime yesterday and that had only been a light sandwich. He was used to women in his past not eating breakfast but that was usually because they were on some diet or another and he'd never given it a second thought. In fact, if he was being honest with himself, he was generally glad when they declined as it meant he could get rid of them quicker and get his space back to himself. In this case, however, it was a completely different situation. He'd taken on this responsibility for Molly and her situation and he needed to ensure she stayed healthy. He had to tread carefully here because, if he came across as being bossy and overbearing by demanding she eat something, her stubborn streak would kick in and there would be no persuading her otherwise.

He swirled the teapot and, as he filled the mugs on the worktop, inspiration came to him.

'Okay, no problem. Here's your tea. Do you mind if I go ahead and cook something for myself? I haven't eaten anything decent since lunch yesterday and I'm famished.'

Molly walked over to the breakfast bar, picked up her mug and gave him a wan smile. 'No, of course not, you go ahead.'

She walked back to the sofa and perched on the edge, nursing the hot drink in her hands, just as she had the night before.

Charlie set about cooking his fry-up. He was going for the full enchilada here – bacon, sausages, eggs, mushrooms, baked beans, eggy bread (he preferred that to fried bread) but no tomatoes as he couldn't stand them. Ugh!

He whistled as he worked, striving to create an appearance of nonchalance. Very soon the air was rich with the smell of sausages and bacon. Normally he'd open a window to let the smell out, but not today as was he was relying on it to kickstart Molly's taste buds. He'd yet to meet someone who could resist the heady scent of bacon frying. Even his most ardent vegan friends had told him that this was the one thing which really tested their resolve.

He glanced over while making a fresh pot of tea and saw her nose twitch as the various delicious aromas wafted her way. He laid out two place settings on the breakfast bar and dried the two plates he'd been warming up. He really hoped his plan worked otherwise a lot of food was about to go to waste. Or, if truth be told, to his waist as he would be unable to resist having seconds.

'Molly, I've made a fresh pot of tea if you're ready for a top-up.'

She stood up and returned to the kitchen. When she saw the two laden plates in front of her, she looked at Charlie. 'I said I wasn't hungry.'

'I know but I was taught to share and I could not, in all justice, sit here eating while you did not. I'm not going to force you to eat but I think a couple of mouthfuls might be good for you.'

Molly gave him a hard stare but didn't argue any further. She sat up on the barstool, waited for him to sit down and then, picking up her cutlery, began to slowly eat.

Molly was fuming! She had made it quite clear she didn't want anything! How could she possibly eat when her head was buzzing and her heart was aching. Typical bloody man, she thought. She never cussed as a rule but this was an occasion which merited it. Why do they always think they know better? Okay, she was prepared to concede that the smell of the bacon cooking had made her mouth water a little… Okay, a lot, but that was by the by! Charlie had not respected her wishes.

She threw him a quick side glance to see if he was watching her but he appeared to be concentrating fully on his own plateful. She looked down at hers. It did all look quite tasty and the small bite of sausage she'd forced down had been delicious. Maybe it wouldn't hurt to have another couple of mouthfuls…

Ten minutes later, she placed her knife and fork neatly on the plate, having used the last piece of eggy bread to mop up the remains of the egg yolk. Charlie, without saying a word, picked up the empty plates and took them over to the sink. 'Would you like some toast and marmalade to finish off?'

Oh goodness, her stomach screamed, no more! 'Thank you, Charlie, but I am absolutely full. I don't believe I could eat another morsel.'

'Okay. More tea?'

'That I could do. I like your tea, it's good.'

'Thanks. When I have the time, I like to make a proper brew with tealeaves, teabags just don't taste the same.'

'Teabags?'

Charlie took a small tin from the cupboard and brought it over to show her, explaining how they had come to be invented by a woman sending out samples of her tea products to potential buyers. 'They're convenient when you're in a hurry but nothing beats the flavour of proper leaves. Now that we have infusers in our teapots,' he showed her the little metal holder inside the teapot, 'it's much less messy and no need to faff about with tea strainers when pouring.'

Molly picked up the teapot to take a closer look. 'My, that is really clever. Such a simple and effective idea. You're correct, this makes far more sense than trying to pour through a strainer.' She gave him a smile. 'It would appear the twenty-first century has really made some incredible advances. Light at the push of a button and teapots which keep the leaves inside. Whatever next?'

'Are you taking the piss, Molly Smythe?'

'The *what*?'

'Sorry. Are you teasing me? Taking the mickey?'

She gave him a big smile as she chuckled, 'Yes, I am teasing you. Although I do mean what I say, the progress I have seen is quite incomprehensible. Just as I think I am coming to terms with the change, something else comes along and I'm all at sixes and sevens again.'

'Well, you guys were the start of it all.'

'I'm sorry?'

'So many advancements were made during the Victorian era. Things like trains, manufacturing and machine tools, all came about during the 1800s and early 1900s. The Victorians were great innovators and paved the way for many new inventions. Prince Albert was quite a forward-thinking man and even arranged for a vast exhibition to be held in London where countries from around the world sent their best products and inventors to share their ideas and increase trade.'

'You are talking about the Great Exhibition in Hyde Park?'

'That's right, did you hear about it?'

'Charlie, I went to it!'

Molly couldn't prevent her giggles upon seeing Charlie's shocked expression. His jaw really had just dropped open.

'You… you… you *went* to the Great Exhibition? Seriously?'

'Yes, I did. Lord Featheringstone arranged it. He initially sent all the business owners in the village as he thought it would be beneficial for them. He'd been there on the day it opened and had found it most impressive. My father, being the village blacksmith, was among the business owners and the whole family went with him. It was quite an adventure for we had to stay in London for a few days. The exhibition was vast and more than one day was required to see it all. When the business owners returned, singing the praises of all they had seen, Lord

Featheringstone made provisions for the remaining villagers to attend. He knew many things would change because of it and he wished for his tenants to be prepared. People are not always open to change, especially where there are machines involved which may take over their jobs. He thought standing in front of them and seeing everything close up might help.'

'And did it?'

'Charlie, we're a small, rural, village. It takes a while for progress to reach us although some of the farmers have begun looking at threshing machines. I don't know much about those but I've heard talk at the inn. I also know Betsy is a bit worried about these new trains because, if they become more popular, coach travel will cease and she will lose her main source of custom. I do not disagree with progress, Charlie, but it can leave innocent casualties in its wake.'

Charlie got to his feet and began cleaning up the detritus around the kitchen. Molly watched him. 'Are you alright, Charlie? Have I said something to upset or annoy you?'

'No, Molly, not at all. I'm just trying to get my head around the fact I am speaking to someone who witnessed the Great Exhibition first hand. Someone who walked around that magnificent structure and experienced the sights and sounds and grandeur of it. It's something I would have loved to see. I'm rather jealous, if I'm being honest. Knowing you've met Charles Dickens was bad enough but that you've also attended the Great Exhibition… Well, that has blown my mind. It's simply… well… wow!'

Molly said nothing but, strangely, knowing that Charlie had moments where he too felt mixed up in his head helped her to feel better.

'Is there anything you wish to do today, Molly?'

Molly glanced out of the window. The early morning

sun had disappeared and the sky was now grey and overcast. In her experience, this meant a storm was brewing.

'No, I would be happy to stay indoors today, if that's acceptable for you?'

'I was thinking about returning to London, I don't think there's much to be gained by staying here any longer.'

'Oh! Do we have to leave today?'

'No, we can stay here another couple of days, it's not a problem. I just thought you might want to get on with trying to find out more about your family.'

'I do but… I don't feel ready to leave yet. I think I'm still adjusting to what I saw yesterday… I can't quite say…'

'It's okay, Molls, we'll go when you feel it's right.'

'Thank you, Charlie.'

She turned away and walked over to the window to look up at the grey clouds tumbling above her head. They expressed how she felt inside – as though everything was tumbling down and mixing itself up. She knew going to London, where Charlie could access more information, was unavoidable but, right now, something inside was holding her here, almost pinning her down and, when the thought of leaving the village came into her head, it pulled and tugged at her insides, telling her it was not yet the right time.

Chapter Twenty-Three

Lower Ditchley – 1860

Damien Featheringstone stood looking around him in surprise. The workmen were packing up their tools and making their way to the cart which stood waiting to take them home. The land where the Smythe's cottage had stood was now cleared of all debris and rubble. The scorched earth was the only sign that it had ever been there at all. In time, the grass and weeds would grow and its very existence would be forgotten.

The wall his father had requested was built and extended all the way up to the roof of the stables, level with the yard wall on the other side. From this angle, neither the yard to the rear of the stables, nor the courtyard to the front, were visible. This should be sufficient to stop anyone trying to enter the unsafe buildings. The inn was now closed and boarded up at the front. No one in the village was interested in taking up the tenancy and his father hadn't yet decided what to do next. For now, the building was to remain unoccupied.

From the corner of his eye, Damien saw the foreman approaching. He walked up the lane to increase the distance between him and the cart where all the workmen were now sitting and waited for the foreman to join him.

Damien got straight to the point. 'Did you find anything?'

He chose to ignore the look of distaste the foreman gave him before he answered. 'Aye, sir, we did find a few items of interest.'

'Such as?'

'Some bones which may be human although that is not certain. Two rings which looked like wedding rings and a couple of teeth. I did tell the men to take care whilst cleaning up but, if they didn't know what they were looking for, it is possible any other remains were removed within the rubble. The few bones I found were barely recognisable and it is only from past experience that I knew what they were.'

'And these "items", where are they now?'

The foreman nodded towards a dense bush a few yards away. 'In a box, under that bush. There wasn't much so the box is not big.'

'Good. Now remember, this must never be discussed with anyone again.'

'Once I receive the balance of the agreed remuneration, sir, no further words on the matter will pass my lips.'

Damien handed over another purse of coins and walked back to stare at the wall until the foreman had joined his workmen on the cart and it moved off.

He waited for a few more minutes and, once satisfied he was alone, he went over to the bush and bent down to peer underneath the foliage. He could just about make out a box close to the stump. He knelt on the grass and pushed his hand in, groping about for a few seconds until his fingers brushed against the rough wooden container. He managed to grasp it and pulled it out towards him. He looked at the roughly made casket – it was only marginally bigger than his wife's jewellery box. Resisting the urge to look inside, Damien stood up, tucked it under his arm and took the slightly longer, but less used, route back to the manor. He knew exactly what he was doing with this.

Thirty minutes later, he stood on the edge of the riverbank. The recent heavy rain had enhanced the speed at which the river was flowing and the water created white foamy peaks as it skipped over the stones and rocks. Damien finally opened the box to look inside. The foreman had not lied when he'd said there was little within. The two rings had been wrapped in a bit of cloth and they nestled in the corner. The rest of the contents were… well… he would have to take the foreman's word that these were bones for he would not have known it himself. There were some knobbly pieces which he assumed were joints like finger knuckles, perhaps, and other fragments which could have come from… well… anywhere. He felt the weight of the box and then looked around for some heavy stones which he placed inside. He weighed it again and nodded with satisfaction. He shuddered as he replaced the lid but didn't feel the slightest bit of remorse as he held all that was left of the Smythe family in his hand.

He stood up, pulled his arm back and, with all his might, threw the box as far as he could into the deepest part of the river. The extra stones did as he'd intended and the box quickly sunk below the surface.

Damien brushed his hands together to remove a few bits of dirt and turned away to hurry home, glad that the whole situation had now finally been dealt with.

Chapter Twenty-Four

Lower Ditchley – Present Day

Molly walked into the lounge, put Sukie's holdalls down at her feet and announced, 'Right, Charlie, I am ready to go to London.'

'What? Now?' He looked at the clock which read three thirty in the afternoon.

'Yes, now. It is time. I am ready.'

'Okay. Well, give me a couple of hours to get my stuff together and close up the mill. We'll head off at six when the rush hour traffic has passed.'

'As you wish. I will begin to clear up in here while you prepare yourself.'

Molly walked over to the kitchen to tidy up while Charlie thumped up the stairs. It was the strangest thing, she mused, while filling the sink with hot, soapy water. She'd been lying on her bed, thinking about everything she'd been through in the last few weeks and the emotions she'd experienced three days ago at the stables. As the catalogue of events ran in circles around her head, the tugging sensation in her stomach, which had been constantly there from the moment she'd been pulled from the river, had suddenly ceased. One moment it was there, and the next… Gone! Just like that! It was as though she had been released – like when you are in a game of "tug-of-war", holding tightly onto the rope and feeling yourself being pulled while you try to resist and then, suddenly, you are on your backside on the ground, the tension has gone and there is a feeling of relief. Well, that was how she felt now – relieved and almost light-hearted. Something had shifted, she didn't know what, but she was now ready to leave the village. There was nothing more to hold her here.

Two hours later, Molly was beginning to reconsider her bold declaration of being ready to leave. It wasn't that she was worried about going to the capital, it was more the means of how they were getting there.

When Charlie had rebuilt the windmill, he'd added a garage at the side – "to protect the cars from the tree sap and bird poop" was how he'd so delicately put it – and so this was the first time she'd been this close to a "motor car". Or "car", as Charlie said it was more commonly called.

While he'd been putting their bags in the "boot" – which actually wasn't too dissimilar to some of the more expensive coaches which had passed through the inn – the interior of the "car" was something else entirely. Charlie had turned the engine on and the low, thrumming noise could be felt when she put her hands on one of the seats. Charlie said he would not normally "leave the engine running as it wasn't good for the environment" – whatever that meant – but he wanted her to get used to the feel and sound before they drove off. Apparently, he didn't want her to become "hysterical" when they were halfway down the motor way. He'd laughed when she had given him what he now called "one of her looks". Molly may not have any idea of these strange things he was talking about but what she did know was that she had never been "hysterical" in her life and she was not about to start now.

'That's everything,' he called over to her. 'I just need to check all the windows are closed and secure the front door, then we'll be heading off. I suggest you get in the car so you know how it feels before we go.'

Molly did as he advised, gingerly sitting in one of the seats and looking around her as she pulled the door closed. A few minutes later, Charlie opened the door. 'Molly, you can't sit there, you need to move.'

'Why, what's wrong with this seat?'

'Can you drive a car?'

'You know I can't, Charlie, don't ask such silly questions.'

'Then, Molly, we're not going to get very far while you're sitting in the driver's seat.'

She looked at the wheel thing in front of her which she had been gripping tightly. 'Oh! I thought this was for me to hold onto, to make sure I didn't fall about.'

'No, that is what I use to steer the car and make it turn.'

'I see. Then I suppose I had better move.' She heard him snort as he helped her out. 'Are you laughing at me again, Charlie Rowland?'

'I'm trying really hard not to, Molly, but it is quite funny.'

Molly looked at him for a second or two before beginning to chuckle herself. 'I don't know why I am laughing, it wasn't that funny, but I can't quite help myself.'

Charlie grinned at her, as he walked her round to the passenger's side of the car. 'It's good to laugh sometimes, even when it is over the silliest of things.'

'Are you now calling me a silly thing?'

Charlie glanced at her as she got into the car a second time. 'Are you teasing me again, Molly Smythe?'

'I might be…' she grinned up at him.

'Well, lady, I suggest you belt up!'

'Excuse me?'

'Hah! Gotcha!' Charlie leaned in and pulled a strap at the side of her head. 'You need to "belt up". Or, in other words, put your seat belt on. This keeps you safe and stops you "falling about".'

'Oh, I see.' It dawned on her that Charlie had purposely used an expression full of double-meaning to tease her. 'You are becoming very cheeky, Mr Charles Rowland.'

'You started it, Miss Molly Smythe, so don't blame me.'

He grinned at her as he stretched over and put the buckle into the lock by her side. 'How does that feel, is it alright?'

He looked her in the eye and, from nowhere, she suddenly felt light-headed and slightly dizzy. She'd been this close to Charlie before but this… This felt quite different. She could smell the lemon scent of his perfume, the peppermint aroma from the mint he'd just eaten and something else. A deeper, more manly odour and it was singing to her senses.

'Molly, I asked if this felt okay?'

'Oh, sorry, Charlie, yes, it feels fine, thank you. I was just taking a moment to decide.'

'Great stuff.'

He moved away and closed the door. As he walked round to the other side of the car, Molly took the few seconds of being alone to draw a few deep breaths and clear her head. What on earth had just happened? What was that all about?

Charlie got in beside her and, in an attempt to redress

her scrambled senses, she said, ‘Now it is *your* turn to “belt up”!’

They both chuckled and Charlie set the vehicle in motion.

Molly gripped the thick handle on the door beside her as the car moved slowly over the gravel. This felt so strange. The car had sounded much louder outside than it did inside. What was more surprising was how little movement there was. In a coach, one rocked from side to side and felt every tiny bump on the road. Now, she felt nothing – not even any rocking when they made a sharp turn onto the lane. Molly realised she felt quite secure within the confines of the car and began to relax. When Charlie started to move faster, once they were on the main road, she allowed herself to unwind, released her hold on the door handle and, placing her hands in her lap, she began taking in the sights around her.

She thought back to when she’d once bemoaned the lack of thrills and adventure in her life – well, she could moan no more for she was now embarking on a bigger adventure than she could have ever possibly imagined.

Chapter Twenty-Five

Lower Ditchley – 1860

All the villagers had turned out to give Patrick, the stable-hand, a good send-off. Damien Featheringstone stood beside his father with his wife, Audrine, on his other side. She was leaning heavily on his arm as the hot sun beat down upon her, giving her even more discomfort than the babe inside her. Damien glanced at her swollen belly – you would be forgiven for thinking the birth was imminent, given the size of her protruding stomach, but the reality was, she still had another two months before she was full term. Under normal circumstances, Audrine was a beautiful woman but pregnancy had not agreed with her and she had blown up considerably. All he heard about was the swollen ankles, how nothing fitted, she couldn't sleep and her face was all puffy and moon-shaped.

On the other side of his father stood Beatrice, his sister. There was only eighteen months between them but, from the way she acted sometimes, it felt more like eighteen years. Still unmarried, it was now generally accepted that she was destined to be an old maid.

He listened to the vicar droning on – how much longer was this going to take? He stared up at the blue, cloudless sky and let his mind wander, thinking about nothing in particular.

Finally, the service was over and he led Audrine back to the carriage, Beatrice and his father walking behind.

'Aren't you coming back to the house, Damien?' Audrine asked him, as he settled her inside the sweltering black box. Why on earth hadn't the coachman parked it in the shade of the tree by the gate? The stupid fool! He'd be speaking to him about that later.

'No, my dear, I have business to attend to. Besides, you need to rest, standing about in this heat would not have been good for the baby. Or for you,' he added belatedly.

He stood back to let his father and sister board the coach, not speaking a word to either of them. He watched until it disappeared around the bend and then turned back towards the churchyard. He was now alone, everyone else had returned home, impatient to get about their business.

He turned his face up towards the sun, his eyes closed and drew a deep breath before making his way to the far side of the cemetery and the family burial plot.

He stopped when he reached an ornately carved, floral headstone which marked the site of his mother's grave. He knelt by the graveside and gently brushed away some old leaves which had blown over it. Some weeds had popped up and he removed them with an impatient hand. He'd only been here a few weeks ago, how could the damn things grow so quickly? Finally satisfied the grave was tidy once more, he pulled from his coat pocket a small posy of meadow flowers which he'd collected that morning, and placed it in the little vase at the foot of the headstone. He rested his hand on the warm stone as he bent his head and the sense of loss made its way through his body again. It was over thirty years since his mother had died and he had never stopped missing her.

He sat down on the ground and, leaning against the headstone, told his mother the latest news regarding the baby and the list of various ailments Audrine was suffering with. He was sure he could hear his mother's laughter on the wind. It wasn't long until he'd run out of words and he just sat there, letting the memories of the past flow over him.

His entrance into this world, so he'd been informed, had been a difficult one. He'd come out backside first and, in doing so, had caused his mother to haemorrhage heavily. At one point, they thought she was going to die there and then, but they eventually managed to slow the bleeding and she made it through the night. For all that she survived, however, her previous good health didn't return and she was bed-bound for her remaining days. Her husband – his father – being totally besotted with his wife, blamed him for her condition. He'd overheard conversations between the staff about how Eustace had refused to hold him as a baby and would leave his mother's room when the nanny took him to her, refusing to even look his way. His mother tried many times to sway her husband towards his son but to no avail.

As he grew older, Damien spent most of his waking hours with his mother. He adored her. She would read to him, play silly card games and board games with him and cuddle him as hard as she was able. The more distance his father put between them, the more he gravitated to his mother for affection. She voiced her love for him every day and he returned the sentiment with as much vigour as a four-year-old is able.

He didn't remember her actually dying but he couldn't forget the day she was buried. It had been a cold, frosty day. He always remembered that because they used to play a game on the cold winter mornings where they'd try to find funny shapes and people's faces in the frosty patterns on the bedroom window. He'd been happy that it was frosty because he thought his mother would have liked that.

Unfortunately, when he'd tried to convey the thought to his father, it hadn't gone down so well. Unconsciously, Damien put his hands over his ears as if trying to block out the cruel voice which rang in his head.

'You stupid little brat! What do you know of anything? You killed your mother, you are the reason she's dead. She's gone from me forever and it's your fault. I wish you had died! I wish you had never been born for then she would still be here with me. Get out of my sight, you life-sucking little leech, I never want to set eyes upon you again. GO!'

The shock of the verbal attack had caused a sharp pain inside him and, as he'd ran from the room, he'd caught the smirk on his sister's face. He was never able to forget his father's words for she repeated them to him often over the years. She lorded over him the fact she was the favoured child although, truth be told, he'd have known without her ever having to say a word. He watched from the shadows as she bloomed under the soft, gentle tones of their father's voice and blossomed in the warmth of his love and affection. Damien got the scraps of his father's attention and that usually consisted of harsh words and venomous put-downs. No matter how much he tried to please his father, he never succeeded. In time, and after many failed attempts, he eventually learnt the lesson – if you don't love, if you don't care, if you don't feel, then you don't get hurt. He'd switched off his emotions and, since doing so, nothing more had touched him. Nothing ever affected him.

He felt nothing. He was now as cold on the inside as he appeared on the outside.

Damien stood up, brushed down his coat and, placing a kiss on his fingers, laid his hand on the gravestone once more.

A few seconds passed before he turned and strode towards the church gate. As he passed through, it suddenly came to him what the pain in his chest had been, on the day of his mother's funeral – it was the first time he'd felt hate.

Chapter Twenty-Six

London – Present Day

Charlie held the door of his London apartment open for Molly to walk through. She'd fallen asleep on the journey down from Oxfordshire and he'd had to waken her when they arrived downstairs in the underground car park. She was still quite groggy and hadn't really registered anything unusual on the way up. He'd expected something to be said when they'd gotten in the lift but she'd simply leant against him with her eyes still closed, pretty much oblivious to what was going on around her.

He took a breath and caught a slight hint of furniture polish in the air – oh good, Babs, his cleaner, had been in today. She'd have opened the windows and let the fresh air waft through the rooms. He hated the musty smell which built up after a few days and, with this being such an old building, mustiness had permeated the walls over the centuries and it liked to seep out every now and then.

He guided his semi-comatose lodger over to the sofa and gently sat her down. He closed the blinds on the windows as he didn't feel Molly was quite up to seeing the London skyline just yet. Usually, it was the first thing he gravitated towards when he returned home. Nothing filled his senses with joy as much as looking over London at night. While he loved the sense of peace when he was at the windmill, the real thrill of living came when he was in the capital. This was his city. He'd been born here and he'd been bred here. This was his home.

He walked over to the kitchen and put the kettle on before taking Molly's things into the spare room which was now hers for as long as she needed it.

He quickly appraised the room as he set her holdalls by the wardrobe – it was nicely decorated and had its own en-suite facility but it was a little bland. He made a mental note to say she could do what she liked with it in order to make it feel more homely.

He went back out and, having made tea, he placed a mug in her hands. After a couple of sips, she began to come back to life.

'Oh, have we arrived? I missed it all. Why didn't you wake me? I wanted to see how London looks now.'

'I was concerned it might be too much for you, all at once. But, don't worry,' Charlie said, 'we've got all the time in the world to see the sights. I promise, you won't miss anything.'

Charlie saw her look of dismay and felt a tiny little twist deep down in his gut. He felt bad that he hadn't wakened her sooner and felt compelled to make it up to her.

'Actually, I do have something a little more special to show you. You need to wait about an hour, until it is fully dark, but I promise you, it'll be worth the wait.'

'Alright, if that is what you suggest.'

'I do, but, in the meantime, let me show you to your bedroom and then we'll sort out something to eat. Are you hungry?'

'I am now you have brought the subject up.'

'Then I suggest we have pizza. It's another Italian dish which I have a feeling you'll like.

'Okay, close your eyes, give me your hand and trust me.'

Molly let Charlie take her hand and guide her across the room. She heard a click and then a cool breeze wrapped itself around her. She pulled the throw Charlie had placed over her shoulders a little closer. She allowed him to push her forward until he placed the hand he was holding onto something very smooth and rather cold.

'Okay, you can open your eyes now.'

Molly took a moment before doing as Charlie said. What was she about to see? Was it wonderful? Would she be scared? She didn't want to be scared but all these new experiences—

No! Stop it! She pushed down the quiver that was slowly building inside. It's an adventure, she must keep reminding herself of that… This is all an adventure.

She slowly opened her eyes and looked around. Beneath her, a large expanse of water flowed swiftly along. A boat, the size of which she had never seen before, sailed past all lit up and music could be heard floating over the waves. She could see people dancing through the brightly lit windows.

She turned to Charlie. 'Is that… Is that the River Thames?'

'Yup, it sure is.'

'I didn't realise it was so… immense.'

'It looks wider at night because of the lights reflecting in it. It's a bit less daunting during the day.'

'I see. We're very high up, is this safe?'

'It's totally safe. This building is an old converted warehouse and has stood here for centuries. It has several homes within it and we call them flats or apartments.'

'Why two names? Why not just one name?'

Charlie shrugged. 'I suppose some people think "apartment" sounds rather American…'

'But the word is French.'

'You've heard the term before?'

Molly had to choke down the sigh which had almost escaped. 'Charlie,' she said with as much patience as she could muster, 'the word "apartment" has been part of the English language for some time. Charles Dickens has used it in several of his books. Please stop thinking I am stupid.'

'I'm sorry, Molly, I don't think you're stupid, I simply didn't realise it was a word you would have come across in rural England. I haven't read any of Mr Dickens books so didn't know he had used it within them.'

She gave him a brisk nod as she accepted his apology. She must try to be less reactive, she thought, this situation was difficult for both of them. 'So, what do you prefer to call this – is it a flat or an apartment?'

'Actually, this is the topmost flat and it's called "The Penthouse". Those are the most special apartments of all.'

'Is it a flat or an apartment, Charlie? You keep using both names? It's confusing me.'

'I… erm… well, I tend to use both…'

Molly made a little "hmph" of annoyance before she replied, 'So, how do you know all these flapartments are special? Have you been in every one?'

'Flapartments?'

'Since you can't decide which terminology to use, that seems a reasonable compromise.'

'Flapartments! I love it!' He grinned at her widely, his white teeth glinting in the light from the room behind them. 'And, to answer your question, yes, I have been in all of them but only because I designed them!'

'You designed this building?'

'Yes. It was an old disused warehouse, left over from when the Thames used to be the main transport route for the city. When the trains became more popular, due to their speed and ability to deliver produce much faster, the boats and shipping trade began to peter out and the warehouses were no longer required. They lay empty for many years, slowly decaying until, in the 1980s, someone decided to renovate them into luxury homes and offices. The move was a massive success and almost every warehouse along the Thames has now been renovated. They are in high demand and have completely changed the face of the city.'

'I see.' She looked at the unusual, but not unpleasant, vista in front of her. 'I think I can understand why.'

She cast her eyes over the brightly lit buildings on the other side of the river and admired both the beauty of them standing proud against the inky night sky and their reflections twinkling in the water below.

'Is it the lectricity thing which is making them so pretty?'

'That's right. The electricity means they can use all sorts of different effects to make the buildings stand out and be noticed.'

Molly was aware that, this time, Charlie had corrected her error without making it obvious he was doing so. She appreciated this little piece of thoughtfulness for it was hard enough trying to understand this new world she was in without thinking he was always laughing at her. She knew he wasn't doing it out of malice but that didn't prevent her from feeling stupid.

She gave a small shiver. Despite the throw around her shoulders, it was a little nippy up here, right above the water.

'Come on, let's get back inside, Molly, it's quite breezy tonight.'

Charlie closed the full-length glass doors but she stood looking out for a moment or two longer until he called over to her, 'Come, let me show you around the rest of the flapartment. It is, after all, going to be your home for the foreseeable future.'

With reluctance, she peeled herself away from the mesmerising sight of the lights on the water and followed Charlie as he took her on a tour of her new home.

Chapter Twenty-Seven

Charlie smiled at Molly over his coffee mug when she walked into the lounge the next morning.

'Hey,' he said, 'how did you sleep? Is the bed okay? If it's not, we can easily change it. I want your time here to be as pleasant as possible.'

'Charlie, a few weeks ago, I was sleeping on a horsehair mattress. Everything since has been an improvement on that. I had a perfect sleep and, I confess, I did not want to rise this morning. I could have stayed there much longer.'

'So why didn't you? It's Sunday, you could have enjoyed a nice, long lie. Many people do on Sundays.'

'What? But what about attending church? When does that happen?'

'Ah!' Charlie had forgotten that religion was followed more closely in the past than it was today. He looked at Molly again and it suddenly hit him that she was dressed more conservatively than she had been of late. Yes, she was still wearing Sukie's clothes but today she had donned a skirt which almost touched her ankles and a blouse with a high neck and long sleeves which had been turned over at the cuffs. She had dressed the best she could in a manner that would be appropriate for attending church.

He looked at his watch – if he was quick, he could grab a shower and be dressed in time for them to make the morning service at the church up the road.

'Molly, you make yourself something to eat while I get myself ready. If you want to go to church, then that's what we'll do.'

Two hours later, Charlie listened to Molly as she sang the last hymn of the service. She had a sweet voice and it had made the time pass a little quicker. He wasn't a churchey person although he had no issues with those who followed a faith. It simply wasn't for him.

They both blinked a few times as they stepped out from the muted shade of the vestibule into the bright noon sunlight.

'So, how was the service? Was it different from what you're used to?'

'Oh, yes!' Molly's eyes were shining. 'It was lovely. All the talk of loving our neighbours, and caring for people who are different from ourselves, was so good. Our vicar in the village simply tells us every week that we're all going to hell unless we repent and forsake our sins. I confess,' she gave a small giggle, 'that by the time we leave the church, my thoughts are so ungodly, I expect a big finger to drop from the sky and smite me down.'

Charlie laughed. 'Like I said before, much has changed although I'm sure there are still vicars who preach fire and brimstone on a regular basis. I can try to find one for next week if you wish?'

Molly laughed again. 'No thank you, Charlie. I think I prefer the more kindly approach to worship.'

'Okay, but, if you change your mind, just let me know. Now, would you like to take a walk around the area and look in some of the local shops?'

‘The shops are open on a Sunday?’ He looked down at Molly’s incredulous expression.

‘They sure are!’

‘Charlie Rowland, I must say that this twenty-first century is really quite decadent.’

‘I think we would prefer to say “relaxed” or “free”, Molly. You may attend church if you wish, that is a personal choice. You can dress in whatever manner you choose, that is also personal choice. There are still people who think they have the right to judge their neighbours – I’m sure you had those in your village too – but, on the whole, people today have, and enjoy, more freedom within their lives.’

He stood patiently while she mulled this over and was surprised to feel his stomach give a little tumble when she suddenly smiled up at him.

‘Charlie, I like “freedom”. I’ve always detested the old wives in the village who poked their noses into other people’s business, they used to annoy me *so* much. “Molly Smythe, don’t you think you’re too old to be running about with your hair loose like that? It makes you look wanton…” or “Shouldn’t you be looking to get wed again, Molly Smythe? You don’t want to be left on the shelf, you know, a woman needs a husband.” They were so small of mind!’

Charlie smiled at her mimicry of the older ladies whose judgement she’d had to endure. ‘How did you respond to them?’

‘I just smiled sweetly, asked after their health and walked on as quickly as possible.’

‘Were you biting your tongue as you “walked on”?’ he asked.

Molly laughed at his reply. ‘Charlie, I think you are beginning to know me just a little too well.’

‘So, do you want to look around the area or would you

prefer to return home? It's up to you.'

'Oh, go on then. Lead me astray and take me exploring.'

He'd turned to lead the way when he felt Molly softly touch his jacket. He looked down to see her child-sized hand lying in the crook of his arm. A wave of protectiveness rushed through him and he put his own hand over it as he tucked his arm more tightly to his side. 'Come on then, let's start with Hays Galleria. I think you'll like that and it's not too far from here.'

'Oh, Charlie, my feet are aching!' Molly sat on the sofa in the lounge, rubbing her toes. 'We must have walked for miles.'

'Not quite but it probably seemed so because of all you have seen.'

She flopped back and closed her eyes, her head spinning with all the glorious new sights, sounds and smells which had bombarded her senses in the last few hours. There had been so many wonders and she knew her mouth had dropped open on several occasions. She'd given a good impression of being some kind of village idiot more than once… Or twice, for that matter.

'Did you enjoy yourself?'

Molly opened her eyes and pulled herself up into a more ladylike position. This sofa was a long way from the upright, rather solid, settees she had sat on at the manor. Charlie's sofa was soft and inviting and virtually begged you to throw off your shoes, pull up your feet and curl up in the embrace of the cushions which wrapped themselves around you when you sat down. It did not encourage a ladylike posture in any way.

'Yes, I did enjoy myself. Thank you for being my guide, I really appreciate it. I will confess, however, that everything I have seen is running amok in my head right now. I think it might take a day or two for my thoughts to settle.'

'That's only to be expected, Molly. There are so many changes for you to come to terms with and it will take quite some time for you to adjust. Hopefully, though, we might be able to return you to 1860 before you have seen too much.'

'Are you wanting rid of me, Charlie?'

'No, not at all, I just know how much— You're winding me up again aren't you?'

She began to laugh. Charlie was so like her brother at times and she'd always been able to tease him most successfully.

'You're quite the little minx, you nearly always get me!' Charlie was grinning as he replied.

'Yes, I know!'

'Right, for that, young lady, there'll be no Sunday dinner for you.'

As soon as Charlie mentioned food, her stomach let out the most unladylike of rumbles and she felt her face heat up with embarrassment. 'Oh, my goodness! How rude, please excuse me.'

Charlie's bark of laughter made her feel less mortified but even so…

'Okay, I'll be kind, you may have your dinner. Come and talk to me in the kitchen while I prepare it.'

'Charlie, I know how to cook, please let me do it. You can't keep running about after me, it's not right.'

'Molly, you need to learn your way around a modern kitchen before I'll feel safe letting you loose in one. I'm sure you're an excellent cook but I think it would be better to do a few trial runs before you take over.' His smile took the sting out of his words.

As Molly watched Charlie from her seat at the table, she saw that he was right. He'd placed a pork joint in the "slow cooker" before they'd gone out and he was now putting "frozen potatoes" in the oven and "frozen vegetables" in the pots on top. Thankfully, the kitchen was equipped with an Aga and she knew where she was with those. It was the only bit of equipment which didn't scare her and that had to be a good start. The rest would come, however, she'd make sure of that.

Chapter Twenty-Eight

Charlie stood in Berkeley Square and watched Elsa move around inside the showroom. He recalled the last time he'd stood here, just over two years ago, when he'd been trying to pluck up the courage to go in and ask her out. It had taken three attempts to win her over but he'd succeeded in the end. Their relationship had lasted almost six months but he'd pushed her too far, too soon, and their engagement had been very short-lived. In the end, however, Elsa had been right to call it all off – he hadn't really been in love with her, not the way you should be when you plan to marry someone. He'd been in love with the challenge she'd presented and it was only his pride which had been broken, not his heart as he'd suspected. He was now thankful he'd made his peace with her last year at Jeff's wedding, for he was here to ask her for a particularly large favour. Molly needed proper clothes to wear, not Sukie's castoffs, and Elsa was the only person he knew who could be trusted to help.

He checked once more that the coast was clear and crossed the road. He took a deep breath as he walked up the steps at the front of his brother's art gallery and pushed open the door.

The buzzer went off as he stepped inside and Elsa came through from the showroom at the back.

'Good morning, how may I help— Charlie? What are you doing here? Is Jeff okay? Has something happened?'

Charlie registered her concern and immediately realised that this was the first time he'd been in the showroom since Elsa had broken off their engagement. No wonder she was thinking the worst. He quickly reassured her that Jeff was absolutely fine.

'I'm sorry I gave you such a shock, I'm afraid I didn't stop to consider what you might think when I walked in.'

'Well, I'm delighted to hear that Jeff is okay but it does leave me wondering why you're here. I'm sure you haven't dropped by just to shoot the breeze.'

Charlie tried to think where to begin. He needed her help. After a moment of silence, that was how he started.

'Elsa, I need your assistance but, before I go into detail, I need to give you some background and it's going to require you to engage every iota of your imagination.'

'I see. Well, in that case, why don't you go up to the roof terrace and I'll meet you there in a few minutes. I need to drag Fliss from the stock room and ask her to cover the floor.'

While he waited for Elsa to join him, Charlie thought back over the night before. He'd explained to Molly that he had go to the office today, for a few hours, and it would be necessary to leave her alone in the apartment. She'd fully understood but he'd been concerned over what she could do to pass the time in his absence. When he'd said as much, Molly had laughed and pointed towards his bookshelf. 'You are leaving me alone with all these books and wondering how I will pass my time? I can think of nothing better than to be in a position where I can just sit and read for many hours without interruption. This will be luxury.'

When he'd left that morning, Molly was already fully engrossed in "The Picture of Dorian Gray" by Oscar Wilde and a few Charles Dickens novels were lined up on the table too. He'd carefully vetted what books he felt would be appropriate for her to read at this time. Whilst Wilde may have been a few years after her time, he was certainly acceptable reading matter. Some other books on his shelves were most certainly not.

'I've brought you a coffee. I'm guessing you still take it white with no sugar?'

'Oh, thank you, Elsa. That's perfect.' He took a few sips as he waited for Elsa to sit down and make herself comfortable.

Then he began to speak.

Elsa listened to Charlie and Molly's story. Some might say it was Molly's story but, without Charlie's input, she'd have drowned and there would be no story at all. And it did, as he'd advised, require her to use every iota of her imagination. Time travel? Was this the proof it was possible? She also, however, understood his concerns. If news of Molly's existence in this world were to become public knowledge, it would cause a rumpus and a half.

'Charlie, I need to ask… Are you *sure* this is all genuine? Are you positive you're not the victim of some elaborate scam?'

'Sukie asked pretty much the same thing and, I'll be honest, Elsa, during those first few days, I wondered about it too. But Molly has been able to tell me so many details that only someone from that time period would know. And to be able to sustain that level of pretence for several weeks would really take some doing. I'm quite sure it's real.'

'I see. Well, if you're convinced, Charlie, then that's good enough for me.'

'Elsa, you don't seem to be fazed by this. Why not? I did expect you to be a little… Well… you know!'

'Charlie, why did you share this with me?'

'Because… I suppose I've always felt I could tell you things that no one else would understand.'

'Such as your father?'

'Yes, exactly that. You have this aura about you. I dunno… it's like some kind of "other worldliness" that made me feel you were the *only* person I could tell this to.'

Elsa nodded but said nothing. Charlie had no way of knowing how close he was to the truth. She could never tell him, or anyone else for that matter, how she had in fact spent time in another world. That she'd sat in Death's waiting room, listening to her dead husband tell her she had one year to get her sorry apology for an act together or she too would be dead – for ever! If she were to try sharing *that* story with anyone, she'd most certainly be locked up in a padded cell and they'd throw away the key. So yes, in this instance, Charlie was right – she *was* the only person who could really understand a situation that was so far removed from the norm.

'Fair enough, but why are you telling me? Why are you here, Charlie?'

He looked her square in the eye. 'Because, I need your help, Elsa.'

'In what way?'

'Molly needs clothes and other personal items. She's currently wearing Sukie's castoffs but she looks like she got dressed in a charity shop. They don't fit properly and don't really match.'

'Why can't you take her shopping?'

‘She needs *everything*, Elsa, from shoes, to clothes, to coats and erm… underwear.’

Elsa couldn’t hold back the sudden yelp of laughter. Charlie had gone a soft shade of pink as he uttered the last requirement.

‘Charlie Rowland, I never thought I’d see the day when you would blush over some ladies’ underwear!’

‘Ha ha! This is different. Seeing your girlfriend’s undies is one thing but seeing those of well… your lodger, I suppose, is quite different. Plus, you need to remember, she’s a Victorian lady, I don’t think she’d feel entirely comfortable with a man taking her shopping.’

Elsa gave him a little sideways look. ‘Are you sure she’s only a lodger?’

Charlie started slightly at her question.

‘Err, yes, I am. Quite sure. I’m… err… just looking out for her…’

Before she could probe any further, her mobile rang. She took the call and, when she’d finished, she said, ‘I need to pop downstairs for a few minutes. I’ll be back shortly, DON’T go away! Get yourself a drink from the fridge or, if you prefer, a warm drink from the machine.’

She made her way down the stairs and dealt with the client who’d popped in to enquire about reserving a Danny Delaney painting which had been featured in their new “Coming Soon” catalogue. As she walked back up to the roof terrace, Elsa couldn’t help but ponder over Charlie’s response to her question regarding his relationship with Molly. While she didn’t doubt that everything was quite innocent between them, she could sense Charlie was feeling more than he was letting on. What she couldn’t work out was if he did merely feel responsible for her or if it went deeper than that. If it was the latter, one thing was for sure, Charlie most certainly didn’t know himself. She was interested to see how this would all pan out and it was that which aided her decision.

She sat back down beside him. 'Okay, I'll help out. I've checked the diaries and I can have a day off on Friday to take Molly out on the town for some retail therapy.'

Charlie took a hold of her hand and squeezed it tightly. 'Thank you so much, Elsa, I really do appreciate this.'

'No problem. Now, help me to make a list of what Molly needs and in what other areas I can help.'

'There is one thing…' Charlie's voice trailed off and this time he was bright red and unable to meet her eye.

'What?'

'Could you help her with… um… ladies' toiletries? And explain how to use them?'

'Do you mean like soap and deodorant?'

'Not soap, she's okay on that regard and she's worked out the deodorant. It's the "other" toiletries. You know, the monthly ones…'

'Oh, my goodness! Of course! I didn't think about those. Do you think…? Has she…?'

'I don't know!' Charlie blustered, 'It's not really come up as a topic of conversation!'

'Okay, okay, keep yer cravat on! I'll be sure to have that talk with her.' Elsa jotted it on her tablet. 'Anything else?'

'She'll need swimming costumes.'

Elsa raised an eyebrow. 'Swimming costumes?'

'We're working on the assumption that the only way back to her time is through the same portal in the middle of the river. For Molly to be successful, she'll need to dive or jump into the centre of it and then swim underwater back to the point where she originally fell in. She currently can't swim so, until she can, she'll be going nowhere.'

'I see.' She added "Swimmies" to her list.

'I've got some money here for you, if it's not enough, let me know.' He took an envelope from his inside jacket pocket and handed it over. It was larger than Elsa had expected and it landed on the table with a thunk.

'Good grief, Charlie, how much is in there?'

'Two and a half grand. Is that enough?'

'I would say so! I don't plan on taking her to Gucci and Armani!'

'Why not? You wear designer clothes – are you suggesting Molly isn't good enough?'

Elsa noted again how instantly protective Charlie was. 'No, Charlie, I'm not suggesting that at all. Yes, I have designer pieces in my wardrobe but I also have some high street brands in there too. Don't worry, if it's not enough, I'll let you know the difference and you can do a transfer. It's not a problem.'

'Thank you. And there's one last, little, teeny, thing…'

'What now?'

'Do you mind explaining our money to her? I think she'd appreciate someone else's voice in her ear as she learns yet another change from her own way of life. And, she might be more comfortable if the discussion was with you. I don't want to risk any offence by having her think she's a "kept woman" or whatever term they used back then.'

'Blimey, Charlie. Don't you think you're overthinking things here?'

'Maybe, possibly… but you'll see for yourself on Friday. We don't appreciate how much our world has changed from the one Molly was born in. I'm just doing what I can to make the transition as painless as possible.'

'But, Charlie, what's she going to do when she goes back? How's she going to cope? Can she even get back?'

'That, Elsa, is something none of us know. Right now, I'm just trying to do the best I can for her.' He let out a small sigh.

'Hey, don't fret about it.' She patted his arm. 'You're already doing your best. No one can ask for more than that.'

'Thank you, Elsa. And thank you for being so cool and understanding.'

'No problem, Charlie. Thank you for trusting me.' She stood up. 'Right, I need to get back to work. Bring Molly to my flat on Friday morning, say about 9.30. We can have breakfast and I'll go through some stuff with her before we head out.'

'She likes croissants.' Charlie smiled as he spoke.

'Then croissants it shall be!'

They walked back down to the showroom and Elsa kissed Charlie on the cheek before waving him off. She stared out into the pretty square opposite for several minutes after he'd disappeared from view. There was no question now in her mind that Charlie was beginning to fall for this woman. Elsa just hoped he didn't fall too hard because this was a situation which could only end in heartbreak.

Chapter Twenty-Nine

Charlie put his arm around Molly's shoulders and pulled her closer to his side. He could feel her trembling against him and understood her fear – the London Underground during the rush hour would instil the fear of God into anyone, never mind someone so out of their natural time. It didn't help that she was so petite for it made seeing where she was going almost impossible when a mass of tall bodies surrounded her.

A couple of nights earlier, however, he'd had the good sense to introduce her to the tube system at the considerably quieter time of nine o'clock at night, so this wasn't her first rodeo, so to speak. After getting on and off the trains a few times, and learning how to read the map whenever a change was needed, Molly had begun to enjoy herself. Charlie had tested her by writing down a small route, which required several changes, and challenged her to accomplish it. She'd only made one small error but had quickly worked that out and rectified it. She'd "passed" with flying colours. It was at this point that he began to notice just how intelligent Molly was. It wasn't that he'd thought she was stupid, not by a long chalk, but because he was constantly having to explain things to her, it had impeded his ability to look beyond her lack of knowledge. This was when it also occurred to him that, for all the educating he'd done over the last few weeks, he'd never had to explain anything twice. She always got it first time around.

He looked down at her now, pressed up hard against him, and caught her eye. 'Are you okay?'

'Yes,' she nodded. 'It's as you said – very, very busy. I guess your understanding of busy and mine are quite far apart. I wasn't expecting anything like this. I thought I would still have the ability to actually be able to move. I'm quite sure that, if I raised my feet off the ground, the crowd would carry me along.'

Charlie smiled at her reply. 'I do believe that theory has been tried and tested a few times and has been successful.'

She giggled at this and, in doing so, began to relax. He felt the tension ease out of her shoulders just as the train began to pull into the station.

'Right, Molls, make sure you hold on tight – this is always the worst part.' He pulled her in front of him and prepared himself for the rugby scrum that was getting on the tube at this time of the day.

'There, that wasn't so bad, was it? You've survived the tube during the rush hour. That almost makes you a true Londoner now.'

Molly looked at Charlie and replied in her driest tone, 'If standing in a metal container, squashed up against a large number of complete strangers, whilst being hurled around under the ground at goodness only knows what speed, is what is required to be a "true Londoner" then I am quite happy to remain a countryside yokel. *That* is not an experience I wish to repeat again any time soon.'

Charlie chuckled at her reply. 'You soon get used to it.'

'I would really rather not!'

'Come on, give me your hand so I don't lose you. It gets busy around here.'

Molly looked about her as Charlie took her hand in his. Physical contact between them was actually quite rare given they had been residing under the same roof for the last three weeks and yet, in the last hour, they'd barely stopped touching. She was surprised to find she quite liked the feel of Charlie when he was this close and her hand didn't mind being held in his. Whenever she'd been courted by some of the young men in the village, in the years after Tommy had died, she'd always found their presence bothersome. On one occasion, she'd declined to walk out with a chap because he breathed too heavily and it annoyed her. Her mother had despaired of her ever meeting someone else but, luckily, her father had understood. He had always said that when you meet the right person, you just fit right in together. That was how it had been with him and her mother and he had no problem with Molly taking as long as was needed to find her perfect fit.

She didn't think Charlie was her "perfect fit" – he couldn't be, her situation deemed it impossible – but it was good to know that being this close to him was not going to be a problem.

'Where are we? What is this place called?'

'That big road back there, where we came out of the tube station was Piccadilly. We're now making our way into Berkeley Square. This area is called Mayfair and it's considered to be extremely "well to-do". That building over there,' he pointed to a large cream-coloured shop with paintings displayed in the windows, 'belongs to my brother, Jeff, and that's where Elsa works. Before it was a shop, it was my family home and it's where I grew up.'

Molly turned to him. 'So, that would make you "well to-do" then? Is that correct?'

'Not really, not as far as the socialites are concerned. My mother was an actress and so our family was "new money". As you know, you are only considered to be someone of worth in England if your fortunes can be traced back to the cavemen.'

'I thought Sukie said there was less emphasis upon the class structure now than what I grew up with?'

'Oh, there is. She's right. The class system doesn't dictate most people's lives the way it once did, but it's still there, lurking in the background.'

'In other words, while things have changed, in some ways they haven't changed at all, they're simply less obvious.'

Charlie grinned at her. 'Couldn't have put it better myself. Right, this is Elsa's flat. Now, before we go down, are you okay? Elsa is a truly lovely, kind person and I know she'll look after you today and ensure you have a fun time. There's no need to be nervous.'

'I was nervous last night, Charlie, but after what you have put me through to get here this morning, meeting the Queen would not bother me now! I am quite fine. But thank you for checking with me, I do appreciate your concern.'

She followed him down the stairs to Elsa's basement flat and waited for his knock on the door to be answered. She was actually still a bit nervous but there was no need to concern him with that. Charlie worried enough about her as it was.

When the door was opened, Molly found herself looking at an extremely beautiful woman not much taller than herself. She had stunning midnight blue eyes and shining, golden hair. Most importantly, however, she had a smile which went all the way up to her eyes.

'Hey, guys, you're here. Come in, come in.' She stepped back to allow Molly and Charlie to enter.

Molly followed Charlie down the hallway into the lounge.

'Where's Puddle, Elsa?'

'Outside, digging up the garden as usual. I wasn't sure if Molly liked dogs or not so popped him out there for now.'

'Alright if I go out to see him?'

'Of course.' Elsa turned to Molly and stuck out her hand. 'Hi, Molly, since Charlie is too obsessed with my dog to bother introducing us properly, we may as well do it ourselves. I'm Elsa and it's a pleasure to meet you.'

Molly looked closely at Elsa. The welcoming smile was still on her face. Molly had met many women who behaved one way in front of a man but were less than friendly when there were no men around to impress. It appeared, however, that Elsa wasn't one of them. Friendliness was oozing from her. Molly took the proffered hand and shook it while returning the greeting. 'I also like dogs, so if Puddle wants to come indoors, I will be okay. Thank you for your consideration.'

'Not a problem, Molly. He's a big lump of a thing so I didn't want him bowling you over. Although, he's getting on a bit these days so would mostly likely push you over then lick you to death!' Elsa giggled as she walked over to call Charlie and Puddle back indoors.

'I've got the coffee on, Charlie, if you would like one.'

'Thanks for the offer, Elsa, but I need to get to the office. Knowing that Molls would be with you today, I arranged for one of our foreign clients to come in for a long-overdue meeting, so I'd better be on my way.'

He turned towards Molly and took a hold of her hands. 'I'm sure you ladies are going to have a great time. Try to enjoy yourself and, if you have any concerns, just tell Elsa. She's adorable and she'll understand. Okay?'

Molly saw the concern in Charlie's face and realised that letting her out of his sight was worrying him. 'Charlie, I am going to be fine. I know you wouldn't leave me with just anyone. If you trust Elsa, then so do I. We have already had this conversation so go to work.'

He gave her a quick kiss on the forehead before saying his goodbyes. As Elsa showed him out, Molly lightly touched the area where his kiss had landed with her fingertips. That had been unexpected but, once again, not at all unpleasant. In fact, the tingling on her skin was rather nice. Before she had the chance to dwell further on this, Elsa was back standing in front of her.

'Charlie tells me you like croissants so let's have some for breakfast before we go out. Would you like tea or coffee to drink? Or, I can do hot chocolate if you prefer?'

'I really like hot chocolate, if I may have some of that, please?'

'Coming right up.'

'Did Charlie tell you I liked hot chocolate?'

Elsa grinned at her. 'No, but he did tell me you'd spent your first few days at the manor with Sukie. She's my best friend and I know how much she likes hot chocolate so there was a good chance you'd had some.'

'You know Sukie?'

'Since I was about seven or eight years old. We met at school and have been best friends ever since.'

Molly felt the last vestiges of nervous tension melt away. If Elsa was best friends with Sukie, then she had to be a good person. 'Sukie has been very kind to me, Elsa. I owe her a great debt of gratitude. Even when she had difficulty believing my story, she was still kind to me. That meant a great deal.'

'Sukie's like that, kind right down to her last bone. She's also incredibly loyal so her first concern would have been for Charlie and making sure you were not trying to pull some kind of scam. Your story is, after all, highly unusual and really, in truth, quite unlikely.'

Molly thought for a moment before replying. 'Elsa, for you and Sukie, it is a story. For me, however, it is my life. If you are all struggling to understand it, think how it is for me having to actually live it.'

Elsa looked at her. 'Good point, well made. Anyway, let's leave that there and move on, eh? While I sort out breakfast, you can open this present I've bought you. Here you go.'

Molly gasped as Elsa pulled a pretty bag out from behind the chair and passed it across to her. 'Oh, Elsa, that is so pretty. Thank you. You are so kind.'

'Urm, Molly, that's only the wrapping. The gift is inside…'

'You mean this bag is only the gift wrapping? But it's lovely. This alone would be a really nice gift.'

'Then I really hope that what's inside is equally as pleasing. Come and sit here at the breakfast bar to open it.'

Molly did as Elsa suggested while noting that Elsa's kitchen also opened out into her lounge area, just like the one at the windmill and in Charlie's flapartment. It must be a modern thing. She perched herself upon one of the tall chairs and, looking inside the gift-wrapping bag, saw an item wrapped up in flimsy pink paper. She pulled it out and carefully opened it. Once again, she let out a gasp of delight for, nestled inside was a pretty black and white check, with black leather, handbag. It had a gold clasp on the front and two long black handles. Her eyes were shining with joy when she looked at Elsa. 'This is for me?'

‘It sure is, Molly. Every woman needs her handbag and I guessed you may not have brought yours with you, given the circumstances of how you arrived here.’

‘You’re quite correct, Elsa. I did not think that day, “Oh, I’m going to practically drown myself later, I must take my handbag with me…” I will ensure I am more prepared in future.’

Elsa looked at her in surprise and then joined in with Molly as she laughed, realising she was joking.

‘Yes, Molly, it was most lax. Let that be a lesson to you.’

‘I consider myself suitably chastised.’

The two women chuckled at their shared humour and Molly felt a small flicker of friendship spark inside her. She was beginning to like Elsa and hoped Elsa felt the same.

‘Well, go on then, open it up and look inside.’

Molly returned her attention to her new handbag and ran her hand over the front of it. The top of the bag and the flap with the clasp was in a fabric, dog-tooth check while the body was made of black leather. It was really smart. She did as she was instructed and opened it up, squealing like a child when she saw more items all wrapped up inside. She pulled out the first present but, before she could open it, Elsa said, ‘Oh, leave that one for last.’

Putting it aside, Molly took out the next gift and, upon opening it, found a small round, gold box. ‘Oh, a snuff box?’ she said.

‘Ah, no! It’s a compact. You do know what a compact is, don’t you?’

Molly shook her head so Elsa leant over, pushed the little button at the front and opened the case to reveal the mirror and face powder inside.

‘Every lady should have a compact in her handbag to check her face and hair is tidy. This,’ Elsa took her hand

and dusted a little of the powder on the back of it, ‘removes any shine on your nose and chin. Once upon a time, women wouldn’t leave the house without one but, these days, they’re less popular. I got one for you as I thought you’d probably have had one.’

Molly shook her head. ‘I’ve never seen anything like this before but I do really like it. Thank you.’ She put it down and pulled out her other gifts which were a box of three cotton handkerchiefs, a small notebook with a pencil and a little book titled “London A Z Mini”. She opened it up to find lots of small map-like things inside. Elsa placed a mug of hot chocolate and a plate of warm croissants in front of her.

‘That is what we call a street map and it helps you to find places. Here, let me show you.’ She opened the book to a page which had been marked with a small piece of paper. ‘This yellow dot here,’ Elsa pointed to the page, ‘is where we are now. This is where my flat is in London. This here,’ she pointed to a blue dot, ‘is where you and Charlie got off the train this morning.’

‘Piccadilly?’ Molly answered.

‘That’s right! Now, if you follow this line here, that represents the street you walked along to get to my flat. And this line here,’ Elsa pointed again, ‘is the street we’ll walk along when we go out shopping. This bigger, thicker, line is where most of the shops are and it is a large street. That’s why it’s more pronounced than these other streets which are small.’

‘I see. How clever!’

‘At the back, all the streets and roads are listed in alphabetical order along with the page number on and the grid reference to help you find the location you’re looking for.’

Molly flipped through to the back, ran her eye down the list until she found what she was looking for. She turned to a different page, stared at it for a few seconds, referred back to the index again and then finally put her finger on a street in the middle of the page. 'That's where Charlie lives!'

Elsa looked at where she was pointing. 'Hey, go you, Molly-girl! Well done. That's bang on!'

Molly felt a swell of pride inside her. She'd conquered another challenge. It might only be a little one but they all added up over time.

'You've got one gift left to open.'

Molly opened the last package and discovered a money purse inside which matched her handbag. Upon Elsa's urging, she looked inside to find coins and paper notes all tucked up in their respective sections.

'Now, before we head out, Molly, I need to explain how our money works today because it's all quite different from your time. I think, though, that you'll find it easy to understand. Now if you place all the coins and notes on the worktop here, I'll go through it with you.'

Molly did as Elsa requested and, for the next hour, she learnt about decimalisation and what value each coin and note held. Finally, Elsa said, 'Well, Molly, I think you've got the hang of all that so, if you're ready, shall we go and do some shopping?'

'Yes please. I am now looking forward to it.' She picked up the money in front of her and passed it over to Elsa.

'Oh no, Molly, this is *your* money.' Elsa pushed it back towards her.

'I can't take money from you, Elsa, that wouldn't be correct.' Molly felt her face flush with shame. Since she'd left school, she'd worked for her money and didn't feel right taking money she hadn't earned.

'Molly, this is from Charlie. The gifts are from me, but the money is from Charlie. He wants you to have some independence and not feel that you always have to ask him for funds whenever you need to buy things.'

'But… it doesn't feel… right…'

'Molly, I do understand but there will be things you'll need to purchase that you really don't want to be asking Charlie to get for you. Things like protection when you have your monthly lady things.'

'Oh!' Just as the heat had been leaving Molly's face, it did a swift U-turn and rushed right back up again.

'And that brings me to something else we need to talk about.'

'Actually, there is no need, Elsa, Sukie went through all that with me and provided me with items to use at that time. But you are correct in that, when I require more, I do not want to ask Charlie to buy them for me. Thank you for thinking of that and saving me from that shame.'

'Hey! There is no "shame" in having periods, Molly. You're a woman and that's how it all works. It is what it is.'

'I see. Okay. Well, I think we can end this discussion now and go out. I am growing rather excited at seeing more of London and doing some twenty-first century shopping.'

Elsa smiled widely at her. 'Then, let's get going, Molly! This is going to be so much fun. I could shop for England and those stores don't know what's about to hit them!'

Chapter Thirty

Elsa tried not to laugh at Charlie's face when he arrived that evening to take Molly home. She'd sent him a text to say the front door was open and to just come through when he arrived. He'd walked out into the garden where she and Molly were sitting on the patio, drinking prosecco, and laughing as they recalled the antics of the day they'd spent together. All of their purchases were piled up in the lounge and there were a lot of bags.

'I'm beginning to question my wisdom in sending you out shopping. Molly, is there anything left in London for other people to buy?'

'Of course, there is, Charlie. That would be all the clothes which are too big for either of us. On the other hand, there might be a slight shortage of items in our sizes!'

Molly giggled as she spoke and Elsa threw her a smile. Now that she was finally dressed in clothes which fitted her properly, Molly's confidence had grown. She was no longer wearing hand-me-downs and having her own clothes had made such a difference.

When they'd first arrived on Oxford Street – Molly had led them there using her new map book – Elsa had taken her to the large high street department store where she'd been all measured up and her new underwear had been purchased. Elsa had explained that this was day-to-day underwear and that they'd visit a specialist lingerie shop later to get some extra special items. From there, Elsa had found out just how much fun it would be to become a personal shopper for that was how it had felt sorting Molly out. There had been a couple of moments when Elsa had handed over clothing that Molly felt was too revealing and Elsa had had to make a point of remembering why Molly had these concerns. On the whole, however, she'd managed to persuade her into some items and had accepted defeat on others. The funniest part of the day had been buying the swimming costumes. Molly simply couldn't accept that these miniscule items were acceptable attire to wear when in the water. Elsa had shown her a range of bikinis in an attempt to prove that the swimming costumes were, in fact, rather modest, but to no avail. Luckily, Elsa had remembered the specialist sports shop at the bottom of Regent Street and, after dumping the bulk of their shopping back at her flat, she'd taken Molly there in a trip which turned out to be more successful. They stocked professional swimming equipment, some of which covered more than the standard costumes, and Molly was more easily persuaded into those.

All in all, it had been a great day out and they'd celebrated with afternoon tea at The Ritz before returning to the flat to crack open a bottle of wine.

Elsa had really enjoyed getting to know Molly and had found her acerbic wit very funny. She'd had her laughing most of the day although there had been a few occasions when her nineteenth century upbringing had required some twenty-first century updating, such as reassuring her that wearing a dress which displayed her ankles did not make her a harlot or putting on a touch of makeup would not suggest she was wanton. When Molly had asked what other advancements there had been for women since her time, she'd been both shocked and delighted to know women now had the vote, they could open bank accounts without permission from husbands or fathers and that, most importantly of all, in the eyes of the law, they were equal to men, although Elsa was quick to point out that just because this was law, it did not actually make it reality and the fight was still ongoing on this issue.

Molly had declared she wanted to be a part of this revolution and was now sitting wearing a lovely lemon-yellow dress which revealed not only her ankles but also quite a bit of her shapely calves. She'd shown further "bravery" by allowing Elsa to put a little bit of eyeshadow and mascara on her. Only a touch – just enough to emphasise her large brown eyes. Nothing else was needed for she was glowing with joy from the fun day she'd had.

'Can I get you a drink, Charlie? I've got some beers in the fridge.'

'Thanks, Elsa, but I'll pass, if that's alright. I need to get home sharpish – I've got a conference call with Japan later this evening.'

'No problem. I'll just go and call a taxi because I don't think you want to be carting this lot onto the tube.'

'You've got that right,' he smiled.

'I'll just use the erm… facilities, Elsa.' Molly placed her empty glass on the table, glancing at Charlie as she stood up. Elsa saw her hesitate for a moment, looking up at Charlie through her enhanced lashes, before moving indoors to go to the loo.

'Charlie Rowland, you can be a right asshole sometimes!' Elsa rounded on him as she made her cutting remark in a loud whisper.

'Eh? What?'

'Didn't you notice Molly's new outfit? How pretty she looks?'

'Of course, I did! She looks very nice.'

'Then maybe you could try *telling* her that! She was waiting for you to say something, you blind idiot.'

'Molly's not like that, she's got her own mind and wouldn't care what I thought.'

'You seriously believe that?'

'Elsa, I've known her a bit longer than you have, so yes, I do know that.'

'And I've been a woman a lot longer than you have, Charlie, so trust me, she *does* care what you think. Make life easier for yourself, just tell her, okay?'

'Okay. I'll compliment her new outfit but I'm quite sure she won't care either way.'

Molly looked in the bathroom mirror and tried to wipe the black streaks off her face. Why was she so bothered if Charlie hadn't noticed her new dress? She hadn't dressed up to impress him so what did it matter if he'd been oblivious to how she looked? Her strong words, however, didn't make her feel any better and the tears threatened to spill over once again. She looked in the bathroom cupboard and found a bottle of the same lotion Elsa had given her to take the mascara off before she went to bed that night. Tearing off a few squares of toilet roll, she poured out a small drop of the cream and wiped it gently on her face as she'd been shown earlier.

Once all the monstrous streaks were gone, Molly splashed her face with cold water to reduce the redness her crying had caused. When she looked in the mirror again, her unadorned face looked back. Her eyes were still red-rimmed and her cheeks were flushed but at least she looked better than she had a few minutes ago. She took a few deep breaths then made her way back down the hallway to the lounge.

'Hey, Molly, I've put a few bottles of prosecco in a bag for you to take with you. I know Charlie's probably only got beer in his fridge. Have some when you get home to celebrate your day and all that you've achieved. You did really well today and should be proud of how well you coped.'

Molly tried to return Elsa's bright smile but the shine had been taken off the day for her. 'Thank you, Elsa, but I am not used to drinking alcohol and I would not wish to become inebriated. I'm not quite ready to be that defiant. Maybe I should save some of my new-found disorderly behaviour for another day.'

Before Elsa could reply, there was a knock on the door, announcing the arrival of the taxi. They gathered up all the shopping bags between them and took them out. When they were loaded into the vehicle, there was just about enough space for Molly and Charlie to squeeze in.

Molly leant forward to thank Elsa for looking after her so well and found herself wrapped in a tight embrace. 'The pleasure was all mine, Molly. I had a great time. Give me a phone call on Monday and we'll arrange to meet again next week.'

Molly couldn't help but smile at Elsa's invite. 'I would really like that, but I don't know what you mean.'

'Don't worry, Molls, Charlie will explain it to you.'

'I will ask him and I am already looking forward to spending more time in your company.' Elsa gave her another hug before closing the taxi door and Molly turned to wave as the taxi moved off. When she was out of sight, Molly turned back to look at all the bags piled up in front of her. She looked at Charlie and said quietly, 'Thank you very much for buying all these for me. It was really kind of you. I am quite indebted to you.'

'No, you're not, Molly, they're a gift. I hope you've had a good day with Elsa and got some nice things. I look forward to seeing you in them. And, if it's not too impertinent to say so, I think you look very pretty in that dress. The colour really suits you.'

Molly felt a burst of joy skip though her at his words. He *had* noticed and the thought thrilled her more than it really should.

Charlie saw the happiness flash across Molly's face and realised Elsa had been right – she had hoped he would notice. He didn't have a problem with telling Molly how lovely she looked. No, what he had a problem with was how he'd felt when he'd walked out onto Elsa's patio and had seen her sitting in her new attire. The lemon of her dress had made her dark brown hair look almost black and the smattering of makeup had enhanced her already beautiful, brown eyes. He'd felt more than a small flutter in his gut when his eyes had settled on her. He wasn't in the mood, however, to question his reaction and so pushed his thoughts away while making a quick decision. He smiled at Molly as he said, 'It would be a terrible waste to just go home, now that you're all gussied up, so why don't we drop your shopping off at the flat and pop out for dinner. I know a nice Greek restaurant which you may like. We can continue working on your "Foods of the World" project.'

'I thought you had to "talk to Japan" – that's what you said to Elsa?'

‘That’s not until much later this evening. We have time for dinner.’

Her cheerful giggle was music to his ears. ‘Well, Charlie, I do think it is more your project than mine but dinner would be very nice, thank you.’

She leaned over and gave him a small kiss on the cheek before turning away to look out of the window at the passing buildings. Charlie sat back and, for the remainder of the journey, mused over the tingling sensation on his face where her lips had briefly touched him.

Chapter Thirty-One

'Hey, Charlie, good morning. How's it all going? Did you have a good weekend?'

Charlie looked up to see his niece, Amber, standing in the door of his office. 'Hi, Amber, it wasn't too bad, how about yours?'

'I spent Saturday with Grandma and Sunday chilling out followed by some studying.'

'Nice!'

'Yeah, it was. Well, apart from maybe the studying, I could've done without that.'

'Needs must though! You don't get to be a top architect without it.'

'Aw damn! Shatter my hopes, why don't ya!' She threw him a smile before giving a small wave and walking off down the corridor.

Charlie smiled at her retreating back and then smiled even more as he recalled exactly how he'd spent his weekend…

'Molly, you need to come out, I can't teach you to swim

while you're still in the changing room.'

'No, I can't. It's not decent…' came the muffled reply.

It was Saturday afternoon and Charlie had brought Molly down to the gym and spa in the basement of the building. There was also a rooftop infinity pool but, in this hot weather, he knew it would be busy, which also meant the indoor pool would most likely be quiet. His assumption had been correct and they had the whole area to themselves. Well, he had it to himself right now because Molly seemed to have developed an extreme case of modesty and was refusing to let him see her in her swimming costume.

'Molly, I'm going to walk over to the side of the pool and turn my back. If you come out and get into the water, I won't see anything. You don't need to be scared of the water. Just walk down the steps and hold on tight to the rail until I come in beside you. Okay?'

He couldn't quite make out her reply but took it as an affirmation. He went to stand by the pool and waited. A minute or two went by then he heard the splash of water as she walked through the disinfecting pool. A few seconds later this was followed by a sharp gasp as she got into the main pool.

'My goodness, Charlie, you could have warned me it would be cold.'

'It's not that cold, you'll get used to it in a moment or two. Are you in now? Can I turn around?'

'Yes, I'm in.'

He made his way over to the steps and collected the plastic blow-up ring he'd placed there earlier. He slipped into the pool and stood next to Molly. She was wearing a full body swimsuit, very similar to those worn by professional swimmers, and, although it covered a great deal of skin, it also clung rather tightly to her body thus leaving little to the imagination. Charlie dragged his eyes away from her lovely curves and focused on the task in hand. They were both standing in the shallow end of the pool but the water was halfway up Molly's chest. He took the ring and said, 'Lift both your arms right up so I can put this on you.'

'Why, what is it and what does it do?'

'We call it a rubber ring and it'll keep you afloat. You can't learn to swim with your feet on the bottom. This will keep you safe.'

Molly let him place the ring around her and he had to bite down on the inside of his cheeks so as not to laugh at her expression when she suddenly found herself up on her tiptoes as the ring had settled under her armpits and lifted her upwards in the water.

'Charlie Rowland, are you sure you know what you are doing? Are you qualified to teach this to me?'

'I don't know about "qualified", Molly, but I used to swim for the county when I was a teenager so I certainly know what I'm doing.'

'Show me!'

'I'm sorry?'

'Show me! Let me see you swim. How can I trust you to teach this to me if I haven't seen you actually swimming?'

'Alright. I'll swim to the other side and back. I'll do front crawl there and breaststroke back. Pay attention to what I'm doing on the way back as that's the one I'll be teaching you first.'

He turned around and kicked off. Just over a minute later, he was back.

'Well? Did that satisfy you?'

'How often do you swim?'

'Three to four times a week. Molly, trust me, I know what I'm doing.'

‘Oh, alright.’ She let out a big sigh. ‘Let us get on with it then. What do I need to do?’

‘Well, today is an easy day. I just want you to get used to the feel of being in the water. We’re going to have some fun with this ball. The ring will keep you upright so all you have to do, to move around, is kick your legs like this.’ He gripped the side of the pool to show her how to move her legs, ‘and do this with your hands and arms.’ He moved his arms in a circular motion, showing her how the water moved when his hands went into it.

‘Now it’s your turn.’ He took her hands, told her to kick her legs and gently guided her away from the edge.

Molly clung tightly onto his hands at first but, once she realised the plastic ring really did stop her from going under the water, she relaxed and her confidence grew. She began to move around on her own, using a combination of the leg and arm movements he’d shown her. When Charlie threw the multi-coloured beachball at her, she’d been shocked for all of about ten seconds before grabbing a hold and throwing it back. They’d messed about like that for almost an hour and the reluctance Molly had displayed when getting into the pool was evident again when he said it was time to get out.

‘Oh, do we have to? A little while longer… Please…’

He gave in on the first request but was firm on the second. ‘No, Molls, we need to get out now. You’ll be absolutely shattered tonight. You don’t feel it now, but you’ve used a lot of energy. That’s enough for one day.’

When she got out, Molly made no mention about her attire or modesty, she just made her way quickly back to the ladies’ changing room, her teeth beginning to chatter as she grew cold. He yelled at her to use the showers before heading towards his own changing rooms.

‘So, how was that then? Did you enjoy yourself?’

They’d just walked into the apartment.

‘It was wonderful, Charlie. I didn’t want to stop.’

‘Yes, I gathered that!’ he grinned at her.

‘It was much easier than I thought it would be. If I’d known swimming was that simple, I’d have learnt it years ago.’

‘Then you really would have been the talk of the village since it was considered “unseemly” for ladies to swim back then. And besides, today wasn’t swimming. Today was just playing so you could grow comfortable being in the water. After this, it’s going to be harder and there’ll probably be days when you hate me for pushing you on, but it’ll be worth it in the end.’

‘Oh, so I can’t swim yet?’

‘Not yet, but I know how determined you can be, so I don’t think it’ll take long. And, once you begin to master the strokes, it’s just a case of building up your strength. If the current under the river is as forceful as you say, then we need to make sure you’re strong enough to fight it when the time comes.’

Molly nodded her understanding at what he was saying. She opened her mouth to speak but instead a large yawn came out.

Charlie laughed. ‘See, I told you you’d be knackered. Why don’t we have an early dinner? I’ll stick some pizza in the oven and then you can head off to bed afterwards. You need to be bright-eyed and bushy-tailed for tomorrow. There’s a lot to see at the Science Museum and you don’t want to be half asleep when we get there.’

The visit to the Science Museum in Kensington had been Elsa’s idea. When Charlie had mentioned to her the fun he was going to have explaining to Molly how a telephone worked, Elsa had come up with this brainwave. As she’d said, the history of all technology was there and fully explained in a way that might be easier for Molly to understand. He'd given a great deal of thought to the matter of how much new technology he should allow Molly to learn. On one hand, he didn't want to make life more difficult for her while she was here in the twenty-first century but there was too much tech stuff around for him to be able to avoid her knowing about it. On the other hand, when – or if – she was able to return to her own time, how would she cope with knowing about things that hadn't even been dreamt about, never mind invented? Was he opening her up to all sorts of issues by teaching her these things? Talk about damned if you do and damned if you don't!

In the end, he'd decided to ask Molly what she wanted to do. After all, who was he to be making these decisions for her? He'd broached the subject in the Greek restaurant on Friday evening and, initially, Molly hadn't known what choice to make. Over small buffet platefuls of dolmades, dips with pitta bread – she took a particular liking to taramasalata – moussaka, souvlaki and baklava, they discussed the pros and cons of the current situation and how best to move forward. Charlie hadn't had time to delve further into the census archives and, even if he did find her and her family on there – which was not guaranteed as the early census offerings had been quite sparse – it still wouldn't solve the question of what had become of the Smythes after that. Molly was adamant she wasn't going anywhere until she knew what had happened to them for it was only by knowing that she'd be able to change theirs, and her own, destiny. The more they talked, the clearer it became that Molly was going to be his "lodger" for some time to come – not only because she still had to learn to swim but because they had a mystery to solve too. With this in mind, they both mutually concluded it would be more to her benefit to learn as much as she could about this modern world she now inhabited as there was a limit on how long she could remain innocent of all that surrounded her. Once the decision had been reached, there was no longer a question about visiting the Science Museum with a view to beginning her education and so, here they were, strolling through the ground floor of the exhibits while Molly gawped at the sights around her. It was a touch unfortunate that they had to walk through the stunning Space exhibition to reach the area where air flight was revealed as Charlie felt learning it the other way around may have been more beneficial. As they strolled along, Molly read every plaque and education board and even made some notes in the little notepad Elsa had given her. She asked pertinent questions and wrote down the answers. When they reached the area which covered flight, she gasped aloud, 'Oh my goodness, he was right!'

'Who was right?' Charlie looked at her with surprise.

'Charles Dickens. When we met, he mentioned that one day man would be able to fly.'

'He did? How on earth did he know that?'

'Well, he made a funny joke and one of the customers in the pub replied with, "Oh yes, and pigs will fly" to which Mr Dickens said, "Not quite yet but they will one day." When we pressed him to explain his comment, he informed us that he was interested in science, although more along the lines of chemistry and medicine, but he had friends who were keen to replicate the flight of birds and great advances were being made in the field. I thought it all very interesting and it thrills me to see that he was right. Have you ever been in one of these machines, Charlie?'

'I have, many times, and it's a wonderful experience.'

Molly gave a wistful sigh. 'Oh, I am sure it is. To be up in the air, flying like a bird… My, that would be such a delight.'

For the rest of the day, they took their time walking around the extensive array of exhibits and Molly learned about space, flight, telecommunications, computers and television. When they reached the latter, she turned to Charlie. 'Is this what that black thing is in your flapartment? A tevelision?'

'Yes, it's a television.' He, once again, subtly corrected her pronunciation although he found it rather endearing when she got her words slightly mixed up. He adored her "flapartment" and was quite happy for her to continue calling it that; her mixed-up, made-up words made their conversations fun and colourful.

They were just making their way to the remaining exhibits in the basement, the History of the Home, when the announcement came over that the museum would be closing shortly and could all visitors now begin to make their way to the exit.

'Oh, that's a bummer,' said Charlie.

'Is something amiss?'

'Yes… No… Not really, I purposely kept the best bit till last and now we've run out of time.'

'What did you want me to see?'

'It's the history of household objects and how they've changed since they were first invented so some of the items you know from your time are quite different now.'

Molly rounded on him, her brown eyes sizzling. 'Charlie Rowland, are you actually trying to say that I would have found household items more interesting than airplanes and spaceplanes? That a kitchen spoon would have more appeal than seeing what the surface of the moon looks like? If that is what you believe, then you need to work harder on understanding me better.' With those words, she'd made a sharp turn towards the exit, leaving him to rush after her, a silly grin on his face from her heated reprimand.

The sudden shrill of the telephone on his desk brought

Charlie out of his reverie and back to Monday morning in the office. As he picked up the receiver, he realised that a silly grin had, again, found its way onto his face.

Chapter Thirty-Two

It was Tuesday morning and Molly had just picked up the map book Elsa had given her and was looking at it closely. It was quite small, however, so she wandered over to Charlie's bookshelves and was pleased to find he had a larger version. Elsa had told her that most people who lived in London had one of these because the city was so big. Thankfully, it turned out that Charlie was "most people".

She took it back to the breakfast bar and opened it up. There, that was much better. The larger version marked out the local attractions more clearly and she was keen to go out for a bit of exploring. She made bright pink dots in her pocket-sized map using a colourful pen she had found on Charlie's writing desk in the corner of the room. She didn't plan to walk too far – an hour or so would be enough for her first trip out alone.

She picked up the small satchel she'd bought when shopping with Elsa. Elsa had explained she should wear it across her body to prevent thieves trying to steal it. Charlie had brought home one of the touchy-button things for her last night. She frowned as she tried to remember what he'd called it... Oh yes, a mobile! He'd shown her how to use it and he'd done something to it so she didn't have to remember numbers, she only had to touch his name and his mobile would ring. Elsa's name was also on it. Molly liked the idea that she could speak to either of them at any time and it was this item, going into her bag, that was giving her the courage to venture out alone. If she did get lost, she would be able to touchy-button either Charlie or Elsa to come and find her. Not that she intended to get lost. She'd copied down the address of the flapartment from one of Charlie's letters on his desk and this was securely secreted in a pocket on her trousers… No, jeans! These were jeans. She was wearing the blue pair with a white cotton top and the trainers Sukie had given her. A cardigan was on the table by the door. She'd plaited her hair in one long strand down her back and, when she'd looked in her bedroom mirror earlier, she'd been pleased to see that she looked just like the other women she'd seen when out with Elsa. Given her unusual situation, it would ill behove her to stand out from the crowd.

She checked her bag once more to ensure she had what she needed and, satisfied that she did, Molly picked up her cardigan and stepped out of the front door. One thing she didn't need to worry about was door keys because Charlie had yet another push-button thing to open the door and she had memorised the code when he'd been tapping it in.

Down on the street, she turned in the opposite direction from that which Charlie had taken the previous week and began to slowly walk along the cobbled road. She made a point of having a good look around to familiarise herself with the neighbouring buildings so she could find her way back more easily, although the route she was planning to walk had looked quite straightforward on the map.

She passed a quirky old building and, when she took a closer look, she was quite shocked to see it was an old prison and that people were queuing up to enter! A peek through a small window revealed a dark, dingy space and she shuddered at the thought of going inside. She took a moment to read the plaque on the wall outside, shaking her head as she reached the bottom. It really was quite strange, she thought as she walked away, what these modern people liked to look at. Who would ever have thought an old prison would become a tourist attraction? Well, it certainly wasn't for her, that was for sure.

Molly continued to gaze up and around as she walked to the end of the street. The buildings around her were all mixed-up – some shouted out their old age while others were clearly more recently constructed and seeing them standing side-by-side was rather quite interesting. She turned right and found herself walking towards the side of the river. A sharp breeze was coming off it and she pulled on her cardigan to ward it off. She took out the notepad from her bag and looked at the first name she'd written on there – "The Anchor Pub". And there it was, to her left, looking all old and history-ridden. She'd worked out a route earlier and the pub confirmed she was going the right way.

She strolled along the river walkway and enjoyed taking in the views of the huge, looming buildings on the opposite bank while, at the same time, watching the people around her and listening to snippets of their conversation. Many of them appeared to be speaking in foreign tongues which lent credence to both Charlie and Elsa's comments that London was always busy with tourists from all around the country and all around the world.

There was so much to see and soon, Molly began to feel her head was on a swivel as it turned this way and that, trying to see everything around her. She didn't want to miss anything and often stopped just to look about. When she'd done this for the third time and had been bumped, then cursed, by people walking behind her, she learned to move out of the way before grinding to a halt.

Eventually, she came to the building she'd been aiming towards – Shakespeare's Globe Theatre – and it was not at all what she had been expecting. 'What on earth…?' she muttered aloud, when she looked at the beautiful white, round and fully intact building in front of her. She had anticipated seeing a glorious ruin of what had once been – after all, how old must the building be now – but instead, her eyes were feasting on something quite splendid. She walked a little closer and couldn't quite keep in the little squeak which escaped when she read that it was possible to have a guided tour. She'd enjoyed reading Shakespeare's plays in the past and she would love to see where they would have been performed. She didn't feel brave enough to go in by herself but she was certainly going to ask Charlie if they could come here for a proper visit.

The excitement in her tummy spurred her on and she decided to walk a little further along the river walkway. It was rather pleasing and, with no traffic to deal with, she could feel her confidence growing with each step.

A few hours later, Molly stepped back into the flat and let the door slam behind her, unable to catch it due to the weight of the shopping bags in her hands. She'd had a wonderful morning. She'd found a small market area called Gabriel's Wharf with little shops full of all sorts of treasures. She had been very tempted to purchase many items but, in the end, had settled for a small pencil drawing of a public house called "The Grapes". It was a pretty picture of a pub with numerous floral hanging baskets adorning its frontage. Her reason for buying it, however, had been because she remembered Charles Dickens mentioning it when they'd met. It was his favourite place to visit although Betsy's inn was a close second. Molly had always suspected he'd only added the latter part of his sentence because he'd noticed Betsy hovering nearby and he had no wish to offend her. Once she was able to drag herself away from the pretty shops, she made her way back to the flat but, upon hearing the stall holders shouting their wares to all and sundry in Borough Market, she made a small detour and found herself in some kind of food utopia. The stalls practically bowed under the weight of the delicacies upon them. From game birds to meat to cheese to breads to fruit and vegetables every colour of the rainbow – her eyes almost fell out of her head in pleasant surprise. The smells were rich as they weaved themselves around her. Occasionally, she would go with her mother to the market in Chipping Norton but, while busy and lively, it was nothing like this. As she walked through the stalls, she suddenly had the idea to cook a nice meal for Charlie – a small gesture of thanks for all he'd done for her. She was limited in her resources to be able to show her gratitude towards him but a nice, home-cooked meal would surely go some way. Now, with her arms laden, she walked over and placed the bags on the counter. Thank goodness Charlie had an Aga range here in his flapartment for this was one thing in his home that she knew how to work. She removed her cardigan, took down the apron she found on a hook in the corner, put it on and, after turning it up around her waist several times to avoid tripping over it, washed her hands and set to work to prepare her mini-feast.

Charlie pressed the numbers on the door pad and wearily pushed the door open. It had been a frantic day in the office with back-to-back meetings – the result of the meetings he'd postponed by staying those few weeks longer at the mill with Molly. Now, all he wanted to do was crash on the sofa, order in a pizza and relax with a couple of bottles of beer.

As the door closed behind him, however, his olfactory sense was immediately assaulted by a sharp, acrid smell and his hair flew up as a sharp breeze caught and lifted it. He placed his briefcase on the floor by the hallway table and walked through to the lounge. The disgusting odour increased and he felt it catch on the back of his throat. The doors out to the balcony were flung wide open. He quickly looked around for Molly but there was no sign of her. His pulse began to race with panic as he all but ran to her bedroom. He knocked on the door but there was no reply. He knocked a second time and called her name. He heard her calling him faintly and was about to enter when he realised her voice had come from the direction of the lounge. He walked back in and that was when he saw her, sitting huddled up on one of the deck chairs out on the balcony. She was so petite that, from a certain angle, he hadn't been able to see her.

He walked out to join her and was dismayed to see her red-rimmed eyes and blotchy face peering up at him.

'Hey, what's wrong? What's happened? Are you alright?' Without thinking, he gathered her up in his arms and sat down, placing her on his lap and holding her tightly against him. He felt an ache in his chest at seeing her so upset.

'Oh, Ch-Ch-Charlie,' she hiccupped, 'I am so sorry.'

'What for? Tell me what's upset you so much.'

She pointed to one of his large roasting tins, sitting in the furthest corner of the balcony. It contained a black, disgusting-looking mass surrounded by a small pool of water.

'Molly, what is that? Or, should I perhaps say, what *was* that?'

Molly began to weep again and it took another few

minutes of soothing her and uttering platitudes before she finally composed herself enough to speak.

'I went out for a walk today and, on the way back home, I found the market around the corner.'

'You went out? On your own?'

'Yes, I did. I am capable of doing some things myself!'

Charlie suppressed a little smile as Molly's fire reignited itself. This was better and far more in line with what he was used to.

'Okay, okay. So why are you so upset?'

'I decided to cook dinner to say thank you for all you have done to help me. I know it's not much but it's the best I can manage.'

'There was no need to do that—'

'Will you stop interrupting please, this is difficult enough.'

'Okay but I'm going to take a guess that the tin over there contains what is left of this dinner you were cooking.'

'I beg your pardon? It most certainly does not, Charlie Rowland! Cooking is something I am more than capable of doing, I'll have you know! In fact,' her little nose raised itself up into the air and sniffed, 'I'd say dinner is coming along nicely and will be ready within the hour.'

Charlie followed her lead and also sniffed the air. Now that the evil, nose-hair burning stench had been diluted with the slightly less pungent aroma from the Thames, he could smell something far more pleasing – something sweet, tangy and meaty.

'So, if that's not dinner,' he nodded towards the incinerated object, 'then what was it?'

'Well, after I'd put everything in to cook, I decided to clean the flapartment. I polished the surfaces, swept the floor and cleaned the kitchen and bathroom. I then decided to iron the shirts you had left in the machinery-washer. I found your iron and the board in the cupboard and, after setting up the board, I put the iron on the Aga to warm up while I looked for a jug to put some water in. When I returned to the iron, it wasn't hot enough so I set it back down on the stove and went into my bedroom to find hangers to put your shirts on. I had to move some of my clothes to get enough spare hangers and it took me longer than I intended for, the next thing I knew, there was a terrible smell and, when I came back to the kitchen, that is what I found.'

Charlie felt a surge of horror rush around the veins which had suddenly turned icy-cold. Not over the loss of his iron but at the thought that there could have been a much more serious accident. Thankfully the plastic casing on the iron had only melted and hadn't, as some items may have done, burst into flames. He pulled Molly tightly to him.

'Look, it was just a silly accident and the important thing is that you were not harmed. It was also quick thinking to put it into a roasting pan and put water on it.'

'Once again, Charlie, I'm not an idiot. I don't understand why your iron broke but I didn't do anything I haven't done many, many times before.'

'I know you're not an idiot, Molly, trust me, I've definitely worked that one out. But why are you so upset, it's only an iron?'

Molly wriggled off his lap and sat down on the deckchair next to him. 'I am upset because I have ruined your iron and could have set fire to your home. I know I didn't but the thought crossed my mind that it could have happened. Then, I grew more upset because I have enjoyed a good day. I went gone out alone, did some exploring, didn't get lost and even sorted out dinner. I actually felt as though I was regaining some kind of control over my life. I was excited about being able to do more and finally starting to understand this new life I am living and then, *that* happened,' she pointed at the now-defunct iron, 'and I went right back to feeling hopeless and helpless again.'

'Molly,' Charlie twisted in his seat in order to face her, 'look at me.' He placed a finger under her chin and gently lifted her face up so that her eyes met his. 'You have done so well today. You were incredibly brave, going out all alone, and I am extremely proud of you. Don't be so hard on yourself. You had a small setback. If I had bought an ordinary iron, instead of some new-fangled, cordless thing, you would have realised that it worked differently from what you have been used to. You would have realised because you're not stupid. As you keep telling me!'

'But—'

'No, Molly, no buts. Count how many good things happened today and how many bad. What is one small, insignificant, little bad point compared to the several, big good points you have achieved?'

'Well… when you say it aloud like that… I suppose today was quite good.'

'There's no suppose about it, you did great. Now, do I have time to grab a shower before dinner is ready?'

'Yes, you do, I need to put the vegetables on to boil.'

'Smashing!' Charlie raised himself up out of the deckchair.

They walked back into the lounge and, as he headed in the direction of his bedroom while Molly went over to the kitchen area, he stopped and turned back to face her. 'May I ask what we're having for dinner, Molls?'

'Of course. Pork roasted in honey and apricots with roasted honey parsnips, boiled carrots and boiled small potatoes in butter. Dessert is steamed pudding with custard.'

Charlie's mouth immediately began to water. 'Would that happen to be Bird's custard?'

'Of course, Charlie, it's the best.'

As he got ready for his shower, Charlie found himself humming the tune to "Food Glorious Food" from the musical film "Oliver" and chuckled as he thought how appropriate it was on so many levels.

Chapter Thirty-Three

'Molly, are you ready yet? Come on, at this rate the museum will be closing by the time we get there.'

'Oh, keep your hair on, I'll be there in a minute.'

Charlie rolled his eyes at the words which came floating down the hallway. Ever since Molly had found out how the television worked, her vocabulary had become decidedly more colourful. She'd picked up many "modernisms" and he wasn't altogether sure if he liked them or not. He'd been rather fond of her quaint, old-fashioned, lady-like way of speaking and, while she still spoke "properly", it was now littered with various current and trendy expressions.

His cheeks lifted with a smile at the memory of her first venture into modern-day speech. He'd come home one Friday evening from work and, as had now become their routine, they were going out for dinner. The choice had been between Indian or Turkish and Molly had replied with, 'Oh, whatever, I don't mind.'

It took a few seconds for her words to sink in and Charlie was halfway to the fridge when he stopped in his tracks, turned around and asked, 'What did you just say?'

‘I said,’ came the slightly sarcastic reply, ‘Oh, whatever, I don’t mind.’

‘Where did you pick that expression up from?’ Charlie’s niece, Saffy, often used this but, at sixteen, she could get away with it. Hearing it fall from the mouth of a Victorian lady was quite a different matter.

‘From the talkyvision.’

‘The *what*?’

‘The talkyvision! Over there in the corner.’ She’d pointed at the television. When they’d come home from the Science Museum, Charlie had decided it was probably for the best that she didn’t watch television, even though she’d learnt about it there. He’d purposefully kept her away from it for fear of her learning too much about her future, his past and which could cause way too many headaches and heartache for them both. Did she need to know there had been two massive world wars which had caused so many deaths and had bred such appalling horrors? Was it necessary for her to learn of the Spanish Flu which had spread across Europe, hot on the heels of the First World War and had caused nearly the same number of deaths as those who’d fallen as heroes? Charlie had felt that, with the hope of being able to get Molly back to her own time, these were things she was better to be in ignorance of.

‘You mean “television”. How did you figure out how to work it?’

‘Babs came in today and showed me. She gave me a fright to begin with, when she just walked in the door and began demanding to know who I was and what I was doing here. I told her the story we came up with about being a distant cousin who had recently lost my parents and was staying with you for a time. She then mentioned it was rather quiet in the flapartment and asked why I didn’t have the talkyvision on. I said I didn’t know how to work it so she showed me.’

‘Oh, great!’ Charlie sighed. Babs had been away on holiday and he’d forgotten to cancel her visit. ‘So how did you explain your lack of technological knowledge?’

‘I said my parents were rather protective and didn’t agree with many modern-day inventions.’

‘And that satisfied her?’ He knew what Babs was like. She had a way of winkling information out of you even when you were adamant you were telling her nothing. Charlie was convinced she was wasted as a cleaner and would have been far better placed in MI6.

‘It seemed to. She showed me what to do, how to use another pushy-button thing and I’ve been looking at it since she left.’

‘And what do you think?’ Charlie couldn’t hide his curiosity over how such a thing would be perceived by someone from her era.

‘I’m not quite sure. I don’t fully understand how it all works but it does seem rather clever. I think I might grow to like it.’

Well, that had turned out to be quite the understatement. Molly had fallen fully in love with the television – or talkyvision as she still called it – and now watched it almost every afternoon when he was at work. Her morning routine involved a few hours in the gym and swimming pool followed by exploring London. Her swimming had come on leaps and bounds and she was now focused on building up her stamina, hence the gym sessions to strengthen her up.

‘Okay, I’m good! Let’s go.’

Molly appeared in front of him and brought him back to the present. Today they were visiting the Victoria & Albert museum in Kensington and they were both looking forward to it. When Charlie had explained it was not unlike the Great Exhibition in that it covered designs and innovations from around the world and across the centuries, Molly had been keen to visit and relive the experience of the Great Exhibition once again.

Molly walked down the stairs in front of him at the tube and Charlie admired the style she was beginning to display with her clothes sense. Now that she had the freedom to dress as she wished, she was allowing her imagination to run wild. Some days she was a little too eclectic for his tastes but other days, like today, she got it just right. She was wearing a pair of navy blue, close fitting – but not tight – capri pants, a white T-shirt top all tucked in and an open, pale yellow, cotton shirt. Underneath all her modern attire, however, she was still a Victorian lady and didn't like the sun on her face so she'd purchased a straw hat with a wide brim. This would then be decorated with various scarves, flowers or ribbons which matched the outfit she was wearing. Today, she'd plaited yellow, navy and white ribbons and had tied them around the crown. A matching plait had been fed through the hoops on her trousers and tied around her waist. A pair of bright yellow Sketchers on her feet finished off the ensemble. With her long dark hair swept up in a loose bun at the nape of her neck, she looked fresh, carefree and colourful. As they waited for the tube train to arrive, she gave him a bright, cheery smile and it struck him that she looked completely happy. Her eyes were sparkling and she gave the impression of being full of joy.

They managed to find a couple of seats and it dawned on Charlie, as they sat down, that he hadn't asked Molly how she was feeling in several weeks. He was appalled at how he now took her presence in his life for granted and he'd stopped thinking about her feelings. She gave the impression that she was coping and had come to terms with her changed circumstances but this could all be a front, a brave face, and inside she was still fighting the fear of living this new kind of life. What a damned fool he was!

Yet again, he was only thinking of himself. He was such a stupid, selfish, man!

While he was mentally flagellating himself, a deep, sarcastic voice above him said, 'If you take your eyes out of your head, darlin', you could get an even closer look.'

Charlie looked up to find a gentleman dressed in ladies' attire, with his face fully made up and his hair all teased into place, standing in front of him. He was a drag queen and Molly was staring right at him.

Immediately realising the awkwardness of the situation, Charlie spoke up. 'Please accept our apologies, my friend has had a sheltered upbringing and there are some aspects of life which are still new to her— Ouch!'

He turned to look at Molly who had just stuck a rather sharp little elbow deep into his ribs.

'Charlie, I am perfectly capable of speaking for myself.' Her eyes were sparkling in annoyance.

She turned back to face the man towering above them. 'My apologies for staring, I didn't mean to be rude, but I was actually looking at your dress and thinking that, if you put some elastic on either side of the waist, it would stop the hemline drooping at the front!'

Chapter Thirty-Four

Molly looked around her, trying to take in the vibrancy of Earl's Court while attempting to keep up with Maggie May or May Not's long stride. Her interest in Maggie's outfit had immediately thawed any animosity and, when the seat next to her in the carriage had become free, Maggie had immediately sat beside her. She'd kindly informed her that, when in full attire, most drag queens prefer to be referred to as female. Molly had thanked her for clarifying this and, after that, they'd spent the next few stops discussing the problems of ladies' dresses not sitting quite right on her less-than-lady-shaped physique and how best to resolve this. When she'd confessed to being useless with a needle and thread, Molly had found herself offering her services. Charlie had asked, with more than a little incredulity in his voice, if she was capable of this, Molly had sweetly – but pointedly – reminded him that she had been a seamstress first and foremost before she met him. The few alterations Maggie required would take her no time at all to fix. The South Kensington tube stop for the V&A had been ignored and they'd alighted two stops later at Earl's Court. When they came out of the tube station, Molly had immediately picked up that this area had a different feel to the other London locations she had visited. She would have struggled to say what exactly made it different but it was just something she could feel.

Maggie took them down a side street and, within a few minutes, they were being led up a flight of stairs to her flat. When she flung the door open and stood back to let them enter, Molly let out a gasp of wonder when she walked in. It wasn't the vast, high ceilinged room that had taken her breath away, or the brilliant sunlight spilling in through the high, beautifully arched windows. Nor was it the glorious wrought-iron spiral staircase which led up to a mezzanine area above her head. No, what had rendered her speechless and wide-eyed was the abundance of colour surrounding her. Every wall was resplendent with bright, swirling murals. Lamps were draped in colourful scarves. The two sofas had vibrant red and orange throws over them with large purple cushions chucked in for good measure. The only area in the room which retained a semblance of normality was the dark wooden flooring but even that was broken up with a plethora of rugs – all of which clashed magnificently with each other.

In the far corner, beside one of the windows, was a bright red and gold Chinese silk screen and next to it, a rail of dresses, skirts and blouses, some of which were on hangers, some were draped on the end and others were thrown messily over the top. There was also a table covered with fabric and something else which she had heard of but never actually seen up close. A sewing machine.

She walked over and gently touched it, feeling the cold smooth surface under her fingers.

'Would you guys like some tea or coffee?' Maggie called over from the kitchen underneath the wrought-iron balcony which Molly could now see housed a bed. Long velvet curtains hung from the ceiling above it and these could be drawn to allow privacy from the downstairs area.

'Tea for me, please,' she called back.

'Me too, please,' added Charlie, 'white, no sugar for both.' He walked over to stand next to her. 'Do you know what that is?' he asked, looking at her hand which was still stroking the beautifully decorated item.

'Yes, it's a sewing machine. I read about these a few years ago, when they were first invented and I saw a picture when we visited the Science Museum but I've never been this close to one. It's beautiful.'

'Yes, she sure is.' Maggie arrived beside them and handed over two mugs of strong tea.

'She?' asked Molly.

'Yes, this is my Sylvie. She belonged to my great-grandmother and I call her Sylvie in her memory. She was quite the dress-maker, I've been told, but unfortunately her abilities did not run in the family.'

'Would you fare better, perhaps, with an electric one?'

'Oh, Charlie, definitely not. I tried one, once, and nearly attached my finger to a winged collar. It was not pretty and I never did manage to get the blood stain out. No, this nice little manual number is much better and I find it far easier to control.'

'How does it work?'

Maggie looked at Molly in surprise. 'You're a seamstress but you've never used a sewing machine?'

'My parents weren't big on technology so I do all my sewing by hand.'

'But surely when you went to college, you used a machine then.'

'I… err… didn't go to college. I was taught by my mother and other ladies in the village. The rest is my own skill and talent.' Molly pulled herself up straight and said with pride, 'I am very good at what I do and my skills were often requested by the ladies of the manor when alterations were required – especially when they held their fancy balls and the gowns required attention.'

'Well, anyone who has worked on ball gowns, using only a needle and thread, is more than good enough for me.'

Molly smiled. 'I would be keen to learn how this machine works. I think it would be useful to know.'

'Well, let me go and change into something more practical and I'll show you.'

Ten minutes later, Maggie reappeared at Molly's side. The wig and makeup had been removed and she was wearing a pair of jeans and a t-shirt.

'My goodness, Maggie, how different you look.' Molly was more than a little surprised by the transformation. In her bright, colourful attire, Maggie had come across as larger-than-life but now she was just normal and a bit ordinary.'

'It's okay, Molly, you can call me Frank now. I'm only "Maggie" when the full ensemble is on.'

'I see. Okay.' She smiled at Frank and returned her attention to the pile of clothing she'd gathered in front of her. She knew Charlie was confused by her easy acceptance of Frank being dressed as a woman but she remembered being taught in school that, in the times of William Shakespeare, women were not permitted to act in theatres and so men had dressed up for the female roles. She wasn't quite sure if that was still the case as there were lots of women actors in the talkyvision when she'd been watching it. She would ask Charlie more about this later but, right now, she had a dress to fix for Maggie.

Frank sat beside her and began to teach her how to work the sewing machine. She had a few false starts on the piece of scrap material he was training her on but it didn't take long to get the hang of it and, after thirty minutes, Frank declared she was now better than him. Molly knew he was merely being complimentary but she also knew it wouldn't take long for her to fully get the hang of this.

While she'd been waiting for Frank to change, she'd looked through his box of haberdashery items and had found it severely lacking in basic requirements. A few spools of thread in red, black, and white, a tin of pins and some needles were all he had to offer. Fortunately, she'd previously spent a few hours inspecting how her new clothes had been made and, as such, knew how to commandeer some suitable alternatives from other items of Frank's clothing which Frank said he was happy for her to deconstruct – another new word to add to her ever-expanding vocabulary. With a pair of scissors in hand, she shooed Frank away and began to work her magic.

Chapter Thirty-Five

Charlie was looking at the vast array of photographs which adorned the wall. Most of them featured Maggie standing with a plethora of well-known celebrities. Frank watched Molly work for a few minutes before wandering over to stand beside him.

'I see you've met Pete Wallace,' Charlie said, pointing to one of the pictures.

'Yes,' Frank replied with a smile. 'He did a video a few years ago which featured some drag queens and I was lucky enough to be one of them. He's a really decent bloke. Some of today's celebs are quite stuck-up, but he wasn't, he was lovely.'

'Yeah, I know him and his wife well, he's a really down-to-earth chap. They both are, if I'm being honest.'

'There's not many up there I'd choose to work with a second time but I definitely would with Pete. He was a lot of fun.'

'Does Maggie get much work? Is there a big demand for her services?'

'More than you'd probably realise. People like Lily

Savage, and then RuPaul, have helped to pave the way for drag to become more acceptable. Don't get me wrong, we're nowhere near being considered "normal" yet, and we still have to deal with a lot of bias and discrimination, but it's getting better.'

'I hope you don't mind me asking – and please forgive me if I'm being rude – are all drag queens gay?' Charlie was genuinely interested and hoped Frank could see that.

'You're not being rude, Charlie. I'm always happy to answer questions when I knew they're being asked out of a genuine desire to learn. It's when folks ask with the intention of arguing, or baiting me so they can put me down, that I have an issue. To answer your question, not every drag artist is gay although I think it would be fair to say the majority are. I'm currently working with a theatre troupe, we're putting on a show up the West End in December, and all the cast are gay men along with most of the backstage staff. It sort of works better that way.'

'I see.' Charlie nodded as he took on board what Frank was saying.

'You can also get female drag artists.'

'You can?'

Frank smiled at Charlie's shocked reply. 'Oh yes! Currently not as commonly found as male queens but they're a growing breed.'

'Wow! I didn't know that.'

Charlie walked away from the photographs and Frank invited him to sit in one of the chairs by the fireplace.

After a moment, Charlie said, 'May I ask, are you gay?'

'I am,' Frank nodded. 'Does that bother you?'

Charlie instantly shook his head. 'Not in the slightest. My father had a good friend many years ago who was gay. He was a lovely man and I couldn't understand why he wasn't married. I asked my dad one day – I must have been about fourteen – and he explained to me that Mike was homosexual and what that meant. He also explained how many people were less than accepting of this and why that was wrong. As such, I've always been aware and it doesn't bother me.'

'Your dad sounds like an amazing man.'

'He was.' Charlie felt a little tug on his heart as he thought about the man who had been such a positive influence in his life. Not wishing to grow maudlin, he gave a small cough before saying, 'When did you realise you were gay? Once again, if you don't mind me asking? And please, if I'm being rude or overstepping the mark, do say so.'

'I realised I was gay in my mid-teens when I kissed my first girlfriend and felt nothing. The other boys in the class were talking about getting hard-ons and feeling their girlfriends up but I had absolutely no desire to do that. On the other hand, however, when a picture of Mark Owen *did* produce those kinds of results and desires, then I realised I was going to be walking a different path in life than what I had grown up expecting.'

'I see. How were your family when you came out?'

Frank didn't reply immediately and Charlie was about to apologise for asking the question when Frank suddenly said, 'They weren't quite as understanding as I had thought they'd be. I'm thinking of the various words which would best describe my father's reaction. Disgusted, annoyed, disgraced, angry, and furious would all fit when it came to his response that day. *"Positively evil"* however was the expression he threw at me when I broke the news.'

'Oh, Frank, that's terrible. That must have been dreadful for you. What kind of reaction had you been expecting?'

Frank gave a small shrug. 'I'd always been good at art and I'd been practising my makeup skills for a few years so I knew I was good at it. I dressed up, did my hair and makeup, and presented myself, in full drag mode, to my family. I could remember my dad laughing at Lily Savage when she did that quiz show on the TV so I didn't understand why he was so angry with me when he found her so funny. With the benefit of age and hindsight, I've since learnt that it's because she was not his problem, she was someone else's problem. Some other man was being laughed at by his work colleagues, being told he was less of a bloke because he'd fathered a freak. His words, by the way, not mine. Now, I had brought my "freakiness" into our house and he didn't like it. Not one single, tiny, bit!'

'Do you ever see your father or your family?'

Frank sighed and stared into the cold mug of tea in his hand. 'Rarely. Sometimes at Christmas, when my mum begs me to go home, but I always feel excluded. My dad focuses all his attention on my brother and will barely even look at me when he passes the gravy. If I try to talk to him, he just blanks me.'

'Do you visit as Frank or Maggie?'

'I've tried both but it makes no difference. My mum attempts to make up for his rejection but no one can replace your dad. I want the same relationship he has with my brother but…' Frank's voice tapered off and Charlie looked away as Frank blinked a few times to clear the tears which had welled up in his eyes.

'I'll be honest, Charlie, it always hurts to think of my dad. If I'd been a serial killer, or had committed some heinous crime, then I could understand my father's rejection. But all I've done is be gay and that was hardly a choice. After all, who would actually *choose* to be something that is slandered, ridiculed and defiled by a large portion of society. People who try to make out being gay is a lifestyle choice really do need their heads read!'

'So, how did you get into the whole drag scene thing?'

Instantly, the sadness left Frank's face. Clearly this was

a happier topic for him.

'I left home a week after I came out. I was going off to university and would have been leaving anyway. I simply didn't go back home at the end of term. I found a small flat share in London and managed to get a job helping backstage in one of the theatres on Shaftsbury Avenue. When the makeup artists were doing their thing, I paid attention. I learnt how to enhance what I already knew and I also learnt how everything works behind the scenes. The great thing about being the general dogsbody is that you are sent anywhere and everywhere. For an eighteen-year-old boy who desperately wanted to learn, it was the best form of education. This saw me through to the end of my uni course and I graduated with a degree in acting. My mum was there to see it but no one else from my family bothered to attend…' he paused for a moment. 'I try not to think about it because, even now, it still causes me a lot of pain.'

'A degree in acting? Is that what brought you to the drag scene?'

'Well, Charlie, I'm not going to lie and make out life has been a barrel of laughs to get to this point. I had a few small acting roles in various programmes,' he named a few well-known soaps and crime dramas, 'but I was too shy. I didn't have the self-belief needed to push myself forward at auditions or interviews. One day, however, I went for an audition where I was required to dress in drag. It was the first time I'd donned such an outfit since the day I came out. I suppose, in a way, I kind of blamed the drag for my dad's shitty reaction. I know now that, no matter what I wore, it would have made no difference.'

'I'm guessing you got the part?'

'Hell, no! I was rubbish! But it did make me realise that I felt considerably more sure of myself, when I was in drag, than I did at any other time so I did it again. And again.

And again. I discovered I had an abundance of confidence when I was in full battle dress. I morphed from being a rather meek chap – which I am, I know that – into this full-on, mouthy, take-no-crap, woman. When I'm Maggie, I can take on the world. Nothing scares me, nothing worries me. I become invincible!'

'So, what is Maggie doing now? Is she in this show in December?'

'She sure is.' Charlie couldn't help but return the smile which cracked open Frank's face and shone as brightly as the noon day sun. 'I'm directing, and starring in, "Barry, The Queen of Balham" at the Horseshoe Theatre in Covent Garden. It's a send up of the film, "Priscilla, Queen of the Desert".'

'I like the sound of that. Molly hasn't yet been to the theatre, I'm sure she'd love to attend and see you in all your glory.'

They both looked over at Molly whose head was bent over her sewing. She was also smiling and humming quietly as she worked.

Frank looked back at Charlie. 'What's the story there? I can sense that she's… well… different but I don't know how.'

'It's nothing untoward. She had a particularly sheltered upbringing, like she told you. No technology of any kind. She's recently lost her parents and is now leaning to adjust to what is, essentially, a whole new way of life. She might be naïve in some ways but don't let that fool you, she's as sharp as a tack and misses nothing.'

'And her relationship to you?'

'Distant cousin. I'm simply looking after her and helping her to find her feet.'

'I see.'

Frank watched Charlie as he looked over at Molly. The expression on his face was most certainly *not* the look one gave a cousin, no matter how distant they were. Frank knew what love looked like and he was looking at it right now. Charlie clearly, on the other hand, had no idea about his feelings. Frank found himself warming to this lovely not-yet-together couple and hoped they realised their feelings for each other soon. There wasn't enough love in this world – the more there was to fill it, the better it would be.

Chapter Thirty-Six

Molly stood in the huge haberdashery department in the John Lewis store on Oxford Street and tried to contain the excitement rushing around inside her. Hilda's Haberdashery in Lower Ditchley had always been a thrill to visit with the bales of pretty cottons, ladies' gloves and gorgeous Nottingham laces but this… This was a whole new adventure altogether. The bales of fabric extended all along one far wall and reached almost to the ceiling. There were also stands dotted around the floor with even more colourful treasures on them. Added to this were rails and rails of buttons, hooks, tie-laces, ribbons and even a substance called "Velcro" which was new to her but she could already imagine a million uses for it.

Elsa appeared by her side. 'Let's look at the list you've made and see how much we can get here.'

'Elsa, we should be able to get everything here. This place is breath-taking!' Her eyes were shining in delight at all the wonderful sights in front of her.

When Molly had finished her alterations on MaggieFrank's dress, she'd made her put it back on and had been delighted to see the hemline now sitting perfectly. The small adjustment had worked a treat and, in making the dress sit properly, it had enhanced her appearance considerably. MaggieFrank had been so delighted she'd immediately asked Molly if she would mind taking the rest of the wardrobe under her wing. Naturally, she'd be paid for her services. Molly had said yes straight away and they'd agree what times she would visit so they could work together. They'd also agreed she could call her MaggieFrank because Molly kept getting confused using two different names.

Charlie had been rather quiet on the way home – they hadn't made it to the museum – and, when Molly had asked why, he'd explained that he was merely concerned for her. The more she was adapting to this world, and making a new life for herself, the more difficult it would be when she returned back to her time. How would she be able to go back to the life she'd once lived when she knew what the future held? A future she would never see?

Molly understood his concerns; they tumbled around in her head often enough when she went to bed at night. But, what else could she do? She had to adapt to the life she was living now. Her swimming had improved greatly so she had no qualms that, if the time came when the portal thing appeared back in the river, she'd be able to go through it and survive to get out on the other side. That couldn't happen though until they'd solved the issue of what had happened to her family. Charlie had looked up Lower Ditchley on the computer and had managed to find the census for 1841 and 1851. Well, he'd found what should have been the census for those years. The one dated 1841 had been sparse to almost non-existent. Molly had recalled that the man who'd collected the paperwork had not impressed her father and he'd expressed his doubts about the paperwork actually ever reaching its intended destination. It appeared his suspicions were founded. Charlie had then looked up the 1851 census and, while he'd found more details regarding the village, a number of pages hadn't stood the test of time and were badly deteriorated. If there had been a record of her family on them, it was now lost. Not to be deterred, he then checked out the 1861 census. This had been more detailed but there was no mention of her family within it. This discovery brought that search to a dead end. Charlie had tried some lateral thinking and had asked Molly about her mother's side of the family – maybe they could trace something through that line – but she'd given him a small defeated shrug, telling him her mother had refused to talk about her past and she didn't even know her maiden name. They were stumped and neither knew what to do next.

With this lack of information in hand, Molly had patiently explained to Charlie that, while she completely understood all of his concerns, she couldn't just sit around waiting for something to happen. She needed to work, she didn't want to be dependent on him for everything and she wanted to feel she was making a contribution. She had always worked and, having not done so for the last few months, she'd finally come to miss it. She hadn't realised just how much until she'd been sitting sewing Maggie's dress. Now that her fingers had been busy again, she wanted to keep them that way. Luckily, Charlie had understood and he'd – albeit reluctantly – given her his blessing to work with MaggieFrank. Not that, she'd silently told herself at the time, she actually needed his blessing but it made for a nicer atmosphere in the flapartment to have it.

When she'd told Elsa on the talkyphone that she now had a job and what it entailed, Elsa had straight away offered to take her to the best shop in town for all her sewing requirements. Elsa had also said how impressed she was that Molly was learning to work this new technology. Molly explained to her how she'd created a little system of calling all the new devices she was encountering a name which told her what each one did rather than trying to remember the given name. So, there was the talkyphone because you talked into it, the talkyvison because it talked when you watched and the pea-see buttonbook because you pushed its buttons and it gave you stuff to read.

'Right, I think that's the lot,' said Elsa, as she placed the packet of hooks and eyes in the basket.

Molly looked down her list and checked the contents of the basket. Satisfied nothing had been missed, she made her way to the till to pay. She was just putting her change in her purse when, while smiling her thanks at the cashier, something caught the corner of her eye. She turned and saw one of the sales ladies on the floor returning a bale of midnight blue satin to the shelf. She picked up her bag of sewing goodies and made her way over for a closer look. Elsa followed behind.

'What have you seen now, Molly?'

'This satin – the colour would be perfect for MaggieFrank. Some of her outfits aren't the right shade for her natural colouring but this… This would be stunning on her.' She turned to catch the attention of a nearby sales assistant and set about purchasing a small sample.

'I'll take this to MaggieFrank and see what she thinks. I've got a few ideas of what I could make with this.'

Once she'd paid for this extra piece of shopping, she dragged Elsa out of the department and up to ladies clothing.

'And we're here because…?' asked Elsa. 'Do you need more clothes?'

'Oh no! I've got lots of clothes now, I definitely don't need more. We're here, Elsa, so I may take a closer look at your modern designs and techniques. I've studied the clothing we bought, and also Charlie's suits, but I want to look at some more of these wonderful zip things because nearly all modern clothing seems to have them.'

The two women spent a good hour inspecting all the dresses, skirts, trousers and tops. Molly was especially taken with the idea of a hidden zip down the side seam of a dress. 'My, but this is a clever idea. It enhances the waistline beautifully.' She made a note in one of the little notebooks she carried around in her handbag. She now had four different notepads, each for its own topic, where she made notes or wrote in questions for later discussion with Charlie.

'How's Charlie taken to you working with MaggieFrank? I wouldn't have thought hanging out with drag queens would be his thing.'

'He and MaggieFrank got along rather well. They talked about art and the places they have seen around the world. MaggieFrank had a lot of photographs on the walls of her flapartment so they had plenty to discuss. As for the working thing…' She hesitated a moment before repeating Charlie's fears.

Elsa nodded as she listened. 'I get where he's coming from, Molls. Every time we meet up, I see a change in you. I've noticed how settled you are becoming in this life and while, yes, I think it's wonderful that you are adapting so well, I do also worry about what will happen when you have to go back.'

'Elsa, I think the expression is, "I will cross that bridge when I come to it". We don't know if the portal thing will come back or not. Since she returned from Austria, Sukie goes to the river almost every day to see if it is there. So far, she hasn't seen anything. I can't sit in limbo, just waiting and hoping. Rightly or wrongly, I have to embrace the life I'm now living in and enjoy all these miracles that my generation of people could barely even have dreamt about. Now, take me to the nearest Costa Coffee and let me buy you a large hot chocolate with cake to say thank you for helping me today.'

'Well,' laughed Elsa, 'if you're going to be making offers like that, you can stick around as long as you like!'

They linked arms and, giggling like teenagers, made their way out of the store.

Chapter Thirty-Seven

'Molly? Molly? Are you here? Molly?'

Molly came out of the bathroom, the towel still in her hands as she dried them. 'Yes, I'm here, what's all the noise about?'

Her breath was squashed out of her body as MaggieFrank rushed over and pulled her into a huge bear hug.

'Oh, Molly, have I ever got some exciting news for you. Come, sit down.'

She let herself be led over to the sofa and, once she was perched on the edge, MaggieFrank bounced down beside her.

'As you can see,' she said, 'I wore your beautiful creation to the theatre today and EVERYONE fell in love with it. They were all quite jealous, especially Francine Fury and it takes a lot for that sarky bitch to be jealous of anything.'

'Well, I am very happy your friends liked it. It does look exceptionally well on you.'

And it did. MaggieFrank had been delighted with the satin sample Molly had brought round for her to consider and, between them, they'd created a design which Molly was confident she could create and MaggieFrank was equally confident would look fabulous.

The outfit, which became MaggieFrank's pride and joy, was a calf-length pencil skirt, split up the side, and lined with a glorious, vibrant pink lining which occasionally peeked out as she walked. The matching jacket, however, was the pièce de résistance. It was long in length, reaching almost to the top of the thighs, and perfectly fitted to display MaggieFrank's hourglass figure. A pink belt, which matched the lining of the skirt, showed the waist off exquisitely. The outstanding part of the design, however, had been the shoulders. When in a decorous frame of mind, MaggieFrank could wear it with the detachable epaulettes in situ and it would look smart. If she was feeling wildly flamboyant, however, the epaulettes could be removed, two vast, padded shoulder pads could be attached inside and the hidden darts would expand to fit them. A second pair of larger epaulettes could then be attached. To finish the outfit off, a small pill-box hat had been covered in the same blue satin and adorned with a large pink bow at the back.

Molly was incredibly proud of the creation although she was too modest to bask in her pride. Her Victorian upbringing was still in evidence in several ways; self-pride being a sin was one of them.

'But, it gets *even better* than that, my tiny little pocket-doll. The girls want you to come and work at the theatre in the wardrobe department. Our current seamstress, while good at what she does, is better suited to repairs and alterations of the stage outfits. We need someone with imagination, flair and the ability to create outstanding creations. I've told everyone you would be perfect for the role. How about it? Are you up for it?'

Molly looked at MaggieFrank but couldn't speak. The surprise of the request had completely taken away her ability to think and all she could do was stare.

'Well, Molls, aren't you going to say something? Would you like to come and work with my ladies in the theatre?'

'I… I… I'm not sure what to say, MaggieFrank. You have taken my breath away with your question. This is something I did not expect to hear or to be asked.'

MaggieFrank took hold of her hands. 'Molly, you have great talent in these here tiny fingers,' she raised her hands up to her mouth and gently placed a kiss on the back of each. 'It would be sacrilege for them not to be put to better use than just designing frocks for little old me! These hands are meant to make big, beautiful, eye-catching, outfits. You have style, Molly, and you have class. It's your time to let it shine!'

MaggieFrank's extravagant declaration was too much for Molly and she doubled over while the sound of her laughter flew all the way up to the high ceiling of the flapartment.

'Oh, MaggieFrank,' she finally managed to choke out, 'you do make me laugh. You are funny.'

'Be that as it may, sweet cheeks, but you have yet to answer my question.'

'Let me speak with Charlie. I would like to discuss it with him first before I give you an answer. May I take a day or two to consider your kind offer?'

'Of course, but I don't see what business it is of Charlie's. It's your decision and no one else's. You're not living with your overbearing parents now; you get to make up your own mind.'

'My parents were not overbearing, they simply looked out for me the best way they knew how. There is a big difference. And I know I don't *have* to discuss this with Charlie, but I am choosing to. I will let you know my answer, MaggieFrank, in two days.'

When Molly broke the news to Charlie that night, after dinner, he was as surprised and as shocked as she herself had been. It took him a few sips of his beer before he asked the same question she'd been asking herself all the way home – how did she feel about the offer?

And the truth was, she was excited by it. As a seamstress, being presented with the opportunity to display your work in front of an audience was as good as it could get. Creating beautiful dresses and outfits is another form of art and the creator wishes to receive the same praise and accolades as any artist who paints pictures or moulds sculptures. It was also an opportunity that would never have come her way had she still been at home with her parents in Lower Ditchley.

Molly said as much to Charlie. She could see that, beneath his apparent joy at the news, he was worried and she understood why but there was little she could do to appease his concerns. Eventually, after a few minutes of silence had passed, he gave her a small smile. 'It's your choice to make, Molly. If you want to do it, then I'll support you the best that I can. My brother works in the art world so I fully understand your reasoning. Do you mind if I speak to MaggieFrank to go over your working hours, rate of pay etc? I want to be sure they're not taking advantage of you.'

'Oops! I didn't even think to ask those questions! I was so excited at being asked… Doh!' She slapped her hand against her head.

Charlie rolled his eyes as he asked, 'Have you been watching The Simpsons again?'

‘Hmm, might have been…’ She gave him a cheeky grin and a wink as she left the room.

When she returned to the lounge after her shower, a short while later, Charlie informed her that the show was due to open on the first of December and was currently set to run until Christmas Eve. The option was there to extend the run in the New Year if it sold well. He’d arranged with MaggieFrank that she would work on a consultancy basis with an hourly rate and he, Charlie, would sort out a new bank account – in his name but for her own personal use – and her fees would be paid into it.

‘Due to your lack of identification, opening an account in your name would be impossible. The only way around it would be false papers and I’d rather not go there. Not right now, anyway. The more your presence is logged in official circles, the more likely you are to be discovered and the whole time-travelling thing would come to light. It’s imperative that you “stay under the radar” as much as possible.’

‘I don’t know what that means but I’m guessing it’s another expression for “lying low” and that I do understand.’ And she did, for it was a concern she also shared, but not enough to keep her from taking this chance to indulge herself in her desire to let her talent shine.

The following Monday, Molly stood beside MaggieFrank in a sparse old rehearsal room in Vauxhall. The lights were on and the rain battered against the window, the sound echoing off the bare, badly painted, walls. Along one wall, there were several clothing rails, jam-packed full of outfits in innumerable colours. Molly could also see two tables, each bearing a sewing machine, pushed back against the wall and scraps of material littered the floor beneath them. A much older lady was trying to thread a needle and making little puffs of annoyance each time she failed. 'That's Imelda,' MaggieFrank whispered in her ear. 'Now you know why I was so keen for you to join us.'

'Surely you could have found someone with more theatrical costume experience than myself?'

'We're drag queens, darling, which means we're not everyone's cup of lapsang souchong,' drawled a voice on her other side.

Molly turned to look at the newcomer who was so brightly attired in an orange and yellow suit, with makeup and wig to match, she shone like a beacon. Suddenly, the rehearsal room felt considerably less drab.

'Molly, I would like you to meet Fifi Firelight. Fifi, this is Molly who's going to be working on our costumes.'

'Oh, sweetie, was it you who created that gorgeous little satin number Maggie was wearing last week? It was divine. I'm gonna work at keeping you on side, honey, because I want you to make me look awesome.'

'Fifi, I don't think I'll need to try too hard because you already are.'

'Oh, I love you already!' came the reply as Molly found herself swept up in an elaborate hug.

While this exchange had been going on, several other queens had come in and were now gathering at the far end where a make-do stage had been marked out. Some were wearing quite elaborate outfits; others were more subtle but they were all equally eye-catching and exotic. MaggieFrank introduced her and explained what her position was. Molly tried to catch and remember all their names but knew it would take her a few days to get them right. Her eyes were dazzled by the array of colours surrounding her and she felt decidedly underdressed in her black jeans, white shirt and black boots. She was glad she'd chosen to wear the bright red coat she'd bought when Charlie had taken her to Camden Market a few weeks before otherwise she'd have totally faded into the background.

MaggieFrank was handing out papers to the ladies in the room when he stopped, turned around and said loudly, 'Okay, where the hell is she? Where's Tallulah?'

As if on cue, the double doors were flung wide open and a vision in red tartan strode in. Molly caught her breath as the tallest person she'd ever seen made her way across the floor towards them. She caught sight of the high heels on the boots the vision was wearing but, even without those, this queen was one tall lady.

'Did I hear some pipsqueak dare to utter my name?' The voice was deep, rich and full-bodied.

'Always with the grand entrances eh, Tallulah? Maybe you could try opening and walking through just one door.'

'Maggie, I did do that, just the once, and that was once too often. I—' She stopped as her eyes settled upon Molly who, surrounded as she was by the other ladies, had not been immediately noticeable.

'Oh, my dear sweet Lord, what *has* the cat dragged in now?'

'Tallulah—'

'It's alright, Maggie, I can speak for myself.' Molly placed her handbag on the floor and slipped off her coat which she handed to Fifi. She calmly stepped forward and made a show of looking Tallulah up and down before replying, 'Oh, my goodness, look what the dog threw up!'

She heard the collective intake of breath in the room but she didn't take her eyes off Tallulah.

'*What* did you just say?' There was no mistaking the sinister undertone in the question.

Molly let out a loud sigh, leant over and grabbed a nearby plastic chair which she pulled towards her. Placing her hand on MaggieFrank's arm, she stepped up onto it and, in doing so, came eye-to-eye with Tallulah.

'I said, "Oh, my goodness, look what the dog threw up!" Does sound not travel up this far or are you just a bit mutt 'n' jeff?'

'Do you know who you are talking to?'

'Nope, and I'm guessing that's going to piss you off even more. However, I will tell you who YOU are talking to – your new wardrobe mistress so, unless you want to walk out onto the stage looking like you got dressed on a dung heap, you had better start displaying some manners.'

Molly glared into the beautifully made-up eyes and waited. A moment later, a smile cracked open the perfect face and a large, but well-manicured, hand was held out.

'Tallulah Strumpet.'

'Molly Smythe.'

They shook hands and Tallulah helped her down off the chair.

'My, but aren't you a feisty little thing. It's not many who face up to me, I can tell you.'

Molly didn't reply and just gave her a small smile. She picked up her belongings and walked over towards the wardrobe corner where MaggieFrank caught up with her a moment later.

'Molly, where on earth did all that come from? You were superb,' she whispered.

Molly stuck her hands in her jeans pockets to stop them trembling and took a few short, sharp breaths. She couldn't believe she had stood up to Tallulah like that but was thrilled that she had done. She sneaked a glance over her shoulder and seeing no one close by, she leaned into MaggieFrank and whispered back, 'Thank *you* for the pre-warning, for I knew what to expect although… I think I've been watching too much EastEnders!'

Chapter Thirty-Eight

Charlie was sitting in the front of the stalls, a few rows back from the stage, in the Horseshoe Theatre. His laptop was perched on his knees while he waited for the show to begin. This evening was the first dress-rehearsal of "Barry, The Queen of Balham" and Molly was in attendance to ensure all the outfits looked right under the stage lights. Charlie didn't want her making her way home alone later so he'd come over after work. He wasn't on his own however as a few close friends and family were also there to provide feedback on the performance.

Just as the house lights went down, Molly appeared and sat down in the seat next to him.

'What are you doing down here? Shouldn't you be backstage helping with costume changes?'

'Imelda's doing that. I'm here to watch how the outfits perform.'

'I'm sorry, what?'

'I need to be sure the outfits move smoothly through the dance routines. If "Barry" raises his arms in the air, I need to know how the lights make the outfit look or, if it needs to be taken in or out. I have to ensure buttons don't gape and feather boas don't obstruct or constrict. Stuff like that.'

'Would you not have picked that out before now, at the rehearsal room?'

'No, because the angle is different. The rooms only have a marked-out stage so I was watching straight on. Here, the stage is raised and the audience will be looking upwards, so I need to see what they will see.'

Just then, she jotted down a couple of lines in her notebook and Charlie felt a massive swell of pride rise up within him. Molly had truly blossomed the last few months as the drag queens had worked on building up her confidence. After her initial set-to with Tallulah, the Amazonian queen had taken Molly under her wing and had looked after her, teaching her many different things about life, clothes, makeup, and philosophy amongst others. Outside of her acting life, Tallulah was a fully qualified, practising, psychiatrist. Charlie had been most surprised to learn this but he'd appreciated the knowledge she'd passed on to Molly.

The first half of the show passed quickly and Charlie was surprised when they announced the intermission. He'd found himself, quite unexpectedly, immersed in the story of Barry, who worked in a dead-end office job in the City but who dreamed of becoming a famous drag artist. Some of the musical numbers were lip-synched but others were sung live – usually those where the lyrics had been altered to fit the show. "It's Raining Men" had become "It's Draining Me" as Barry sang about his daily commute on the Northern Line each morning and the lack of seating most of the time. The lines:

"Someone is rising,
Everyone's ready to go,
A rugby scrum's forming,

You don't wanna be too slow,
Because today, it's the first time,
In living memory,
That a seat has become vacant,
Before we've reached the Ci-i-ty."

had gotten a good chuckle from those sitting around him.

'I'll be back shortly,' Molly whispered to him as she left to go backstage and her departure left him feeling a little bereft. He'd enjoyed watching the performance with her beside him and hearing her giggle even though she must have heard the lines a thousand times.

Charlie let out a sigh. He hadn't seen it coming but he now knew he was deeply in love with Molly. He hadn't meant for it to happen – it *shouldn't* have happened, given the situation – but it had. She'd grown on him, little by little, every day until now he felt empty and lost when they were apart. He did less overtime hours in the office, preferring to work at home where he could see her curled up on the sofa reading or watching the soaps on the talkyvision. She'd brightened up his world with her views on life, her laughter and her silly names for items which had now become the norm in their household. He could have done without the frequent viewings of the film "Oliver" but the sound of Molly's sweet voice singing the songs as she sewed was more than worth it. He didn't know what he should say or do, so he was saying and doing nothing for now. They were due to head back to Lower Ditchley immediately after the Christmas Eve show in order to spend the holidays with Jeff and Jenny. It was going to be a full house with his mum and nieces, Amber and Saffy, also joining them so he and Molly would stay at the mill. He was hoping to see Sukie while they were there, as she was the only other person he could speak to. Elsa had become a close friend of Molly's and he didn't want to put her in an awkward position by confiding in her.

'Hey, Charlie, what do you think of the show so far?'

Charlie smiled at Maggie who'd just sat down in the seat Molly had occupied.

'Rubbish!' he laughed, as he gave the traditional answer to the question. Maggie chortled at the response.

'Nah, seriously, Maggie, it's good. I'm really enjoying it. I think it'll go down well.'

'I hope so. We'll know more by the end of the week when we have the press preview. We need them to give us good feedback if we're to stand a chance of getting tight little bums on seats.'

'I'll keep my fingers crossed for you but they should like it, it's a lot of fun.'

Maggie smiled at him. 'What do you think of the costumes? Hasn't Molly done well?'

'They're amazing! I didn't realise just how talented she is.'

'She's more than talented, Charlie, she's exceptional. Her best skill is understanding exactly what we have in mind despite being rubbish at describing it. And, somehow, she always manages to take our ideas and make them even better than we could have imagined. I hope she stays in the business, Charlie, she could go far.'

'That'll be her choice, Maggie, although she has loved doing this, these last few months. Anyway, to change the subject, may I ask you a small favour before you scurry back off again?'

'Sure, what is it?'

'It's my works Christmas Ball on the eighteenth of December and I want to take Molly. She's never been an actual guest at a ball, having only ever helped out behind the scenes, and I just know that you would be the perfect person to help her with an outfit. I want her to feel as special as the Queen and for the event to be one she'll remember forever.'

'I think we can do that. The other queens will want to help too as we all love our little sewing bee. We will make her special beyond her wildest dreams.'

'I DON'T want her turning up in drag, mind!'

Maggie laughed. 'Don't you worry, Charlie, Molly is in the safest of hands. She'll look and feel utterly amazing and fabulous, I promise.' The lights dimmed and Charlie felt Maggie gently squeeze his shoulder before standing up and disappearing down the aisle.

Charlie paced up and down the aisle of the theatre while glancing at his watch again. Time was passing and they had to go. As Chairman of the company, it didn't look good if he turned up late to the office Christmas party. He liked to be there early to greet his employees and their partners as they arrived. His staff worked hard and he liked to make sure they always felt appreciated. He also had a limousine waiting outside and the West End traffic, which was always a nightmare at the best of times, would be even worse this close to Christmas. He'd been told to pick Molly up from the theatre so at least they didn't have too far to go. It would have been much worse if she'd been at home at the flapartment.

Maggie appeared by his side. 'Okay, Charlie, face the stage and close your eyes.'

He turned and did as he was told. He heard the swishing sound of the curtains parting.

'Okay,' Maggie whispered in his ear, 'Open!'

Charlie did so and there was Molly standing alone on the stage, a single spotlight shining upon her. The breath flew out of his body and his head actually swam for the first few seconds. Maggie had kept her promise – Molly looked *beyond* beautiful.

She was wearing a long, dark red, fitted dress. The straps were full and off the shoulders, curling gently around the tops of her arms. Her hair had been teased into a million curls and had been arranged in a half-up, half-down do, which gave her added height but still showed off the length.

As he walked slowly towards the stage, he could see she was wearing full makeup but it was subtle and served only to enhance her already gorgeous and perfect features. There was nothing at all to suggest she had been at the mercy of a troupe of drag artists.

He whispered to Maggie, 'The dress… It looks familiar…?'

'Julia Roberts, Pretty Woman. When we were looking at pictures, to get an idea of what Molly liked, that was the one she wanted. We suggested something similar but she was adamant – she wanted a dress exactly like it, so that is what she got.'

'She looks unbelievable, Maggie, she really does.'

'Well, don't tell me, tell her that! You haven't said a word yet, you lovestruck fool!' Before Charlie could respond to Maggie's comment, he felt a hand on his back give him a gentle push. He made his way to the steps at the side and walked up to Molly, noting the uncertainty in her eyes as she turned towards him. He felt his heart tighten – he'd caused that by not speaking sooner. He came to a halt in front of her and whispered, 'You look absolutely beautiful. You have taken my breath away. You are gorgeous and I feel deeply honoured to have you walking by my side this evening. Please, allow me to escort you to our car.' He offered her his arm and the feel of her small, white-gloved, hand settling upon it soothed the tumbling sensations in his soul. The peace she always created within him spread through his body and, as they walked out of the theatre, he couldn't have wiped the happy smile off his face if you had paid him.

Chapter Thirty-Nine

Molly sat straight up against the leather seating in the car and allowed Charlie to present her with another glass of Champagne. She really shouldn't, she'd had so many already tonight, but she didn't care. What had begun as a wonderful night had now turned sour…

When they left the theatre, Charlie led her to a long, black, shining car which he called a limo. He explained, as it moved into the traffic, that this was a special car he'd hired for the occasion. He opened a small bottle of Champagne, handed her a glass, and toasted her and her first ball. She smiled happily before turning to gaze with excitement out of the car window as they travelled up Regent Street and along Oxford Street. The pretty blue and white Christmas lights were strung across them overhead and the dazzling store windows were enticing her, never mind the passers-by. It didn't take long to reach their destination and Charlie helped her out of the car. Once inside, he took their outerwear to the cloakroom before leading her upstairs to the function suite where, when they entered through the double swing doors, her eyes lit up like beacons for the ballroom, in the upmarket London hotel, had been beautifully decorated with fake snow, fake snowmen and a plethora of bright, shining, twinkling, Christmas trees, bedecked with ornaments of all shapes and sizes. Charlie went off to get them both a drink and she slowly walked round, taking a closer look at the decorations. It was amusing her greatly to see figurines dangling from the branches which were dressed in Victorian clothing and depicting, what she overheard one woman say, "a quaint, Dickensian, Christmas theme". She supposed they had gotten that right to a point, as the clothing was accurate for the period of time Charles Dickens was alive, but hearing people discussing it as though it had been a most idyllic time had her grimacing inside. She wished she could tell them the truth, that it was mostly only the middle and upper classes who got to spend Christmas with their families. The masters and mistresses of the households still expected the servants to help them get up and dressed, light their fires, cook and serve their breakfasts and continue to run the tight ship they were used to while they sat back and talked about the importance of spending the festive period with those you cared for. She wished she could say that, for many other families, especially those who worked in the retail trade, it was a time of misery. They worked twice as long for no extra pay and were often collapsing with exhaustion by the time Christmas Day arrived. If their place of work was closed for the day, they were not paid and thus they worried how they would cope with the shortfall in their wages for that week.

Molly pretended to look closer at one of the figurines as she listened to the same woman talk to her colleagues about how she'd have loved to have lived in those times when life was less about money and more about family. Molly sneaked a glance at the woman's perfectly made-up, line-free face and her soft, smooth hands – both of which suggested she'd never really had to do any hard work or hard worrying in her life. When Charlie returned to her side with glasses of Champagne for them both, she quickly steered him away and moved to the other side of the room where the dining tables were laid out and there was less chance of her saying something out of turn.

After the meal had been eaten, and the plates cleared away, Charlie quietly asked her how the fare had compared to her previous Christmas meals.

She whispered back, 'Quite different for we've never had turkey. It was too expensive for us so we normally had beef.' He was surprised by her answer but, before he could reply, the lady sitting on his other side snared his attention for which Molly was relieved as she didn't want to get into a discussion on the differences from her Christmas last year, with her parents and brother, to her Christmas this year in a different century. She'd watched all the adverts on the talkyvision for Christmas gifts and family Christmas dinners and was surprised to see the "commercialism", which had begun in her era, had not diminished over time. It seemed to have only gotten worse.

At the end of the meal, the serving staff, whom Molly made sure to thank for their services that evening, moved the tables away and a man called a "dee-jay" appeared on the raised dais in the far corner of the room and loud music had begun playing. She recognised several of the songs from the radio which was always playing quietly in the sewing room at the theatre. Imelda loved her music and couldn't, she said, bear the silence when the radio was off.

Molly sat watching the people gyrating on the dance floor for a few minutes. Having grown up dancing waltzes, polkas and quadrilles, to see this freedom of movement and expression was quite eye opening. She thought back to the day in Sukie's lounge when she'd first heard modern music and remembered how good it had felt when they'd both allowed the music to dictate how they moved. She turned to Charlie and asked him why they weren't dancing.

'Do you want to?' he asked her.

'Yes please, very much.'

'Come on then.' He held out his hand, led her onto the dance floor and into the midst of all the other dancers. Just at that moment, the music changed and a song she'd heard frequently on the radio came on. It was a Christmas themed song by a band called Spade? Slayed? She wasn't sure but she really liked it and, when everyone around her joined in with singing the chorus rather loudly, she was there with them when it came around again. Charlie was a good dance partner and he twirled her around, pulled her towards him, pushed her from him and also gave her space to find her own rhythm. She couldn't recall ever feeling this happy and free. The joy felt like it was bubbling inside her and there were several times when she burst out laughing for no reason other than sheer happiness.

Just as the pain in her feet began to feel unbearable – these high heels might add a few inches but they were as painful as anything – the tempo of the music changed. Around her, couples took to the floor and were soon entwined around each other. She looked at Charlie and he held his arms out to her. She hesitated for the briefest of heartbeats before moving inside them and allowing her head to lie against his shirt. She could feel his chest moving up and down under her cheek and the soothing sound of the music lulled her into a semi-conscious state. It felt so nice, so warm, so comforting, so right. At one point, she looked up to see Charlie looking down at her, an unreadable expression on his face. She continued to gaze into his eyes until he leant down and placed a soft, warm kiss on her lips. She felt herself, and her body, responding and the kiss lasted until the final notes of the song faded away. She pulled away and Charlie, with a smile, returned her to their seats and asked her to wait while he retrieved their coats from the cloakroom.

She was just draining the last of the wine from her glass when the woman she'd heard waxing lyrical about Dickensian Christmases dropped down onto the seat next to her. She was looking considerably less "put together" now than she had been earlier and Molly noticed the slur in her voice when she spoke.

'So, you're Charlie's new bit of fanshy are you? I'd heard he wash sheeing shomeone but I'd exshpected shomething better than a shmall, little, nothing like you. Well, jusht to let you know, he never shtays for long and he always comesh back to me. You'll shee, your time with him ish running out and he'll be mine onesh again.'

'Excuse me?' Molly turned to face the woman.

'I shaid he'll shoon come running back to me. He always doesh. We have a conec-shun you shee…' She gave a drunken hiccup. 'You're hish latest novelty but you'll shoon wear off. They alwaysh do—'

'Molly, are you ready?'

She spun round at the sound of Charlie's voice and saw him looking at the woman beside her through narrowed eyes. The look on his face was one of distaste. 'Annette, how are you? Have you enjoyed yourself this evening?'

Annette stood up and ran her fingers down the buttons of Charlie's shirt. 'Oh, Charlie, how lovely to shee you. I wanted to give you a Chrishtmas kissh. Come here, you gorgeoush man, let me run my tongue around your gumsh…'

Charlie gently, but firmly, pushed Annette back down onto her chair. 'I don't think so, Annette, it wouldn't be proper. Where's Eddie?'

Annette gave a sullen shrug. 'I dunno!'

'Annette, there you are. I told you to meet me by the stairs. I've been waiting there for fifteen minutes.' A harried looking man came rushing over and placed a stole around the woman's shoulders.

'Hi, Charlie, I hope she hasn't been making trouble.' He gave a small, wry, smile.

'Not at all, Eddie, not at all. I think she may have enjoyed the free bar a little too much; I don't fancy the headache she's going to have in the morning. If you need to come into the office a little later due to caring for your wife, then that won't be a problem.'

'Thank you, Charlie. Hopefully it won't be necessary but I appreciate the offer.' He put his arm around his wife's waist and carefully led her towards the doors.

'Are you ready, Molly? Here, let me put your cloak on for you.' He swung the beautiful red cloak Imelda and Fifi had created around her and fastened it at her throat. The faux-fur lining felt warm in here but she knew she'd appreciate it when they got outside. She made to walk towards the same doors as Annette and Eddie but Charlie stopped her. 'No, Molly, this way.'

He led her to a door marked "Private" and, when they passed through it, she found they were standing at the top of a narrow, carpeted stairway. 'Just follow it all the way to the bottom, Molly. There's an exit door when we get there.'

Sure enough, the door stating "Exit" loomed up as they turned the last bend. She stood aside for Charlie to open it and, when he did, there was the limo sitting quietly outside, the driver standing waiting by the door, and opening it as they walked towards him.

As soon as the limo door was closed on them, Charlie reached across and opened another bottle of Champagne, passing a glass to her. 'That was my little secret escape route. I arranged it with the hotel manager when we had our first Christmas Ball here nine years ago. It saves me having to run the gauntlet of getting past my drunken employees who either wish to tell me how much they love their job – which is nice – or how much they hate it – which is not so nice. Sometimes the secretaries get a bit over-amorous and that is just embarrassing for all parties. So, sneaking out the backdoor helps to save everyone's blushes in the morning.'

Molly accepted the glass of wine, knowing she shouldn't but feeling so angry, she didn't care. She took a long drink before asking, 'Who is she, Charlie? Who was that woman?'

'What? Annette? She's no one. She's the drunk wife of one of my senior architects. Nothing more.'

Molly turned her stern gaze upon him. '*No one*? You think I am foolish enough to believe those words? She would not have touched you in such a familiar manner if she had been "no one".'

Charlie didn't reply.

'Well? Are you going to treat me as though I am simple in the head?'

'Fine! We have a bit of history but it was a long time ago. We had an on/off relationship for about eighteen months. Eventually I knocked it on the head for good as it was going nowhere. That was over five years ago. I didn't see her again until two years back when she rocked up at the Christmas Ball on Eddie's arm. He introduced her as his fiancée and then last year as his wife. Both times she's made a drunken play for me. Eddie is a decent bloke and I have no wish to embarrass him so I say nothing and just try to make life a little easier for them both the next day. I'm sure Annette would be mortified if she knew what she actually said to me.'

'I see. And what about what she said to me?'

Charlie sat up and looked at her. 'What do you mean? What did she say?'

Molly repeated the one-sided conversation and was annoyed to feel tears welling up in her eyes as she spoke.

'Oh, Molly, Molly, my Molly, come here.' She let him pull her into his arms and hold her tightly against him. 'Let me promise and assure you, Annette is very much in my past and she will stay there. Nothing could ever make me re-ignite the relationship we once had. Apart from her being married – I don't do married women – there is nothing in my heart for her. I belong to only one woman now. A woman who lives in my home, uses crazy words to describe inanimate objects, who makes me laugh and smile every day, makes me feel joy like I've never felt it before, makes me feel love like I never knew it could be felt and who is here in my arms right now. I only want to be with one woman, Molly, and it is you. Rightly or wrongly, I love you with every fibre of my being and I never, *ever*, want to be with anyone else again. I only want you.'

Molly looked up and saw the sincerity in his eyes which matched the sincerity in his voice and felt her heart fill up with happiness.

He loved her.

Charlie loved her.

And, in that moment, she knew she loved him too.

With a smile playing on her lips, she took both of their wine glasses, placed them in the holders and, as they drove under the bright lights of Piccadilly Circus, she kissed him again, whispering against his lips, 'I love you, Charlie Rowland. Rightly or wrongly, my heart will be yours for ever more.'

Chapter Forty

Charlie swept in the gate and drove up the driveway. He pulled onto the parking bay and the outdoor security light flicked on. He switched off the engine and let the silence settle around him. Well, it should have been silence but Molly, having fallen asleep halfway up the M40 motorway, was making sweet little chirruping sounds as she slept. Charlie now knew she did this occasionally, usually when she was in a deep sleep, and it always made him smile. He sometimes teased her in the morning and called her his little songbird. She would always reply that, if they were going for nicknames based on sleeping noises, then he could only be a bull elephant because, when he started snoring, he could be heard for miles. Charlie smiled again as the memory of her sassy reply came to mind.

The night of the ball would be imprinted in his memory forever as the night he finally understood the expression "making love". When they'd returned to the flapartment, Molly had made a beeline for his bedroom and he'd followed her in surprise. Even though they'd spent the remainder of the journey home lip-locked and tightly wrapped up in each other's arms, he had still expected her Victorian values to take precedence over her emotions and for their relationship to remain fairly chaste. When he'd spoken this thought aloud, she'd replied, 'I'm a widow, Charlie, not a simpering virgin. I have known the delights of the marital bed and I am also aware that women enjoying the "pleasures of the flesh" is more widely accepted in this time. Elsa was thorough in bringing me up to date on what rights women now have and the freedom of expression we are permitted. So, get your kit off and get in that bed!'

As he'd walked towards her, he'd replied, 'Molly, you *really* need to stop watching EastEnders!'

Charlie stepped out of the car and the frosty leaves crunched under his feet as he walked round to the passenger side. He carefully opened the door and lifted Molly up into his arms, thankful he'd had the foresight to undo her seatbelt before he'd gotten out. He made his way to the front door and was just tapping in the numbers on the lock when Molly stirred and began to waken up.

'Are we there yet?' she asked sleepily, while snuggling further into his chest.

'Yes, my darling, we're here.'

'Hmmm, nice. Is good here…' she mumbled, as she dropped off to sleep again.

Charlie carried her up the stairs and took her straight to her bedroom where he laid her on the bed and removed her boots and jacket before pulling the quilt up over her. He smoothed away the loose strands of hair, which had escaped from her plait, from her face. He wasn't surprised she was this tired – she'd been doing long hours at the theatre for the last remaining shows and they had finally caught up with her. She hadn't intended to do so many nights – she and Imelda were supposed to alternate their shifts – but Imelda had come down with a nasty cold and

Molly had insisted she stay at home to recover and she'd cover the shifts. Thankfully, tonight had been the last performance in the West End for the immediate future. The show had been rather successful and there had been an invitation to tour around the country for the next four months, commencing after the New Year. It would then return to the Horseshoe Theatre in June for an extended run. Molly had declined the invitation to travel the UK with the troupe but had said she'd be delighted to return to them when they were back at the theatre.

Charlie had been pleased with Molly's decision although he'd done his damnedest to ensure he didn't influence her thinking and had let her make her choice under her own steam. As she'd pointed out, while things were considerably better for her now than when she'd first arrived in this century, straying too far from Charlie and Elsa – her little support team – was too risky. Besides, she was falling in love with London and, now that she was a lady of leisure for the next few months, she wanted to continue exploring and finding out more about it. She'd made a point of informing Charlie that she was going nowhere until they'd visited Charles Dickens' house.

With a smile still sitting on his lips, Charlie leant over and placed a soft kiss on Molly's cheek before putting out the bedside lamp and closing the door behind him. He went back out to the car and spent the next ten minutes unloading their bags and the Christmas presents for tomorrow.

They were spending Christmas Day over at the Little Gatehouse with Jeff, Jenny, his mother, his niece, Amber, and her adopted sister, Saffy. He hoped they were all kind to Molly because, when the whole family got together, it could be noisy and chaotic. He also suspected there would be many questions directed at Molly once it became known they were a couple. He'd have to ensure he deflected as many as possible because the last thing either of them wanted was for the truth to come out.

Charlie made his way to his own room, stripped off and fell into his own bed, letting out a grateful sigh as his head hit the pillows. He was asleep himself within minutes.

At some point in the night, he awoke briefly to feel the mattress dip and a small body push itself against his. He turned around and spooned into Molly's back, pulling her tightly against his chest.

'Why did you put me in the other room?' she asked quietly.

'I didn't like to presume you'd want to sleep beside me now that we're back here in the village. I was worried you may not feel it was right.'

'I want to be with you always, Charlie, right beside you. Don't do that again.'

Her breathing had slowed and deepened before he could answer, 'I won't, my darling, I promise. I'll always keep you here by my side.'

Within seconds, he too was asleep, feeling far more relaxed now his love was back in his arms.

'Charlie, come and give me a hand with making the tea and coffee. No, Jenny, you stay there, darling. You've worked hard this morning preparing that wonderful Christmas dinner, now it's time to relax. Let me do these.'

Charlie stood as his older brother bent down to kiss his wife. Yesterday had been their first wedding anniversary so today had been a double celebration. It still surprised him at times to see Jeff so loved up – his brother had never been one for dating but he'd found out last year that Jeff had had a brief fling in his early twenties with a woman whom he'd carried in his heart ever since. Unfortunately, the lady had died many years previously but not before she'd given birth to Amber, Jeff's daughter. Finding out he was a father, twenty-five years after the event, had been quite a shocker but, the one thing Charlie could always say about his brother, he always faced up to his responsibilities and he never walked away from a challenge. Amber had been adopted but her "parents" had died in an accident and this was when she'd found out the truth about her birth. Saffy was the natural child of Amber's adoptive parents but Amber had stayed by her side when the truth came out. Saffy now lived with Jeff and Jenny and Amber worked in Charlie's office in London as a trainee architect. In the space of barely six months, Jeff had become a husband and a father and it suited him to the ground. He looked relaxed and happy – far more than Charlie could ever recall him being. 'If this is what love does for you,' Charlie thought to himself, 'then I'll have a piece of that too.' He was so lost in his thoughts, of spending his own life with Molly, that he didn't hear Jeff speaking to him.

'Oi, Bro? Hello? Earth calling Charlie?'

The snap of the fingers in front of his face had him moving quickly backwards. 'Uh? What?'

'I asked if you wanted tea, coffee or something stronger. Where were you, you were miles away?'

'Oh, sorry, tea please. I was actually thinking about you and how happy you are, Jeff. If it's possible for a man to glow with joy, then you are doing it. It's good to see.'

'Thanks, Charlie. To be honest, I don't think I've ever been as happy as I am now. I fall in love with Jenny more every day and Amber and I are really beginning to feel like father and daughter. It's all good.'

'I'm glad, Jeff, you deserve this happiness.'

'Hey, little bro, don't be sounding too envious, I think you'll be in the same boat yourself before too long.'

'What do you mean?'

‘Oh, Charlie, I wasn’t born yesterday. One would have to be blind not to see the spark between you and Molly. I know you introduced her as a friend but you can’t hide the relationship between you.’

‘Does everyone know?’

‘Yes.’

‘Even Mum?’

‘Yes.’

‘Oh blimey! I thought we were being discreet.’

‘Well… you’re both being discreet… in that you’re not making out on the dining table but your eyes and body language are telling us all that that is exactly what you’d like to be doing!’

Charlie felt his face flame scarlet and Jeff laughed at his discomfort.

‘Don’t fret it, Charlie. It had to happen to you sometime and Molly seems absolutely delightful. Mother is enchanted by her so half the battle is already won.’

‘You make it sound like we’re a done deal!’

‘Well, if you’re not, you should be. You’re both perfect for each other.’

‘Things aren’t always what they seem, Jeff,’ Charlie replied quietly.

Jeff stopped unloading the dishwasher and turned to face him. ‘Is there a problem, Charlie?’ The earlier humour in his voice had disappeared.

Charlie hesitated for a moment, desperate to tell his brother the truth about Molly. He opened his mouth, about to speak out, when the kitchen door opened and Saffy stuck her head round. ‘Jeff, your mum wants to know if you’ve gone to India to pick the tea because you’re taking so long!’

Charlie burst out laughing at Saffy’s cheeky words, accompanied by her cheeky grin, and the moment for sharing his secret was lost.

‘Tell everyone we’ll be back in a few minutes, once I’ve reloaded the dishwasher. And, any more of that cheek, and you won’t get your Christmas present.’

Saffy skipped off down the hallway, leaving a trail of laughter behind her.

‘Am I allowed to enquire what her present is?’

Jeff peeked out the kitchen door to ensure the coast was clear before he replied, ‘Jenny and I are going to ask her if we can adopt her. We want her to be a legal member of the family.’

‘Wow, Jeff! That is wonderful news. Do you think she’ll be happy with that?’

‘Only one way to find out, Charlie. Let’s go.’ He picked up the tray on the table, gestured to Charlie to pick up the other one with the mince pies and shortbread on it and made his way back to the lounge.

Ten minutes later, the hysterical screams of ‘yes, yes, yes’ from Saffy confirmed to everyone that she was more than happy with her Christmas present.

Chapter Forty-One

'Can I pour you more tea, dear? There's plenty in the pot.'

Molly turned to the soft voice by her side and, with a smile, picked up her teacup and saucer and allowed it to be refilled.

'Thank you, Rose,' she replied.

It was the day after Boxing Day and Charlie had asked Molly if she wanted to accompany him to visit the two older ladies they'd met that summer's day on the village green – the day they'd broken into the old stables. He'd explained how fond he was of them and that he often spent time with them when he was in the village. She'd agreed to join him and was having a most interesting afternoon. She'd been quite shocked to learn they were both in their nineties for they neither looked nor acted as though they carried such an age. Doris had quite an acerbic tongue and a quick humour and Molly knew that this was the kind of "old lady" she wanted to be. Doris had fire in her belly and Molly could identify with that. Rose, on the other hand, was mild-mannered and softly spoken. She had a gentleness about her which made you want to hold and protect her. It appeared, however, that she could easily hold her own against Doris's stronger character and, more than once, she told Doris to pin her lips together, no one wanted to be lectured. They were very sweet to see although Molly would never say as much to Doris – she knew she'd get short shrift if she did.

When Doris said she'd lived in the village all her life, as had her family for several generations before her, Molly leant forward with a view to asking a number of questions. It was Charlie's warning cough which caught her and made her put her words together more carefully.

'Do you know exactly how long your family have lived in Lower Ditchley, Doris?'

'Oh, lass, I think at least three hundred years, if not longer. I'm sure if I checked the parish records, I'd find them going all the way back to when time began.'

'Have you never looked, Doris?'

Doris turned towards Charlie and thought for a moment before answering his question. 'I can't say that I have. It's not something I've ever given much thought to. I suppose, when a place is in your blood, you sort of take it for granted.'

'Does it feel strange to have lived so long?' Molly sat back with a gasp. 'I am terribly sorry, Doris, that was quite rude of me. Please, forgive my impertinence.'

'Now then, lass, don't you worry there, I don't mind you asking at all. It's nice for people to take an interest rather than just pegging me as the old bird in the village.'

'I'm quite sure they don't say that, Doris, behave yourself.'

'I'm quite sure that they do, young Charlie, and they'd be right, we are the old birds of the village—'

'You speak for yourself, Doris. I've only just turned ninety – a mere spring chicken!'

Doris laughed at Rose's sharp reply before she returned to Molly's question. 'Molly, it has most certainly been an interesting life, let me tell you. When I look at how things are now to how they were when I was a child... Well, it takes my breath away. I can recall sitting at my grandmother's knee, learning how to crotchet a lace collar – now it's cheaper to buy modern imports from China. Back then, the nearest we ever got to China was the best dinner service locked away in the cabinet in the front parlour!'

'What was your grandmother's name? Were you named after her?'

'I was named after my father's mother. My older sister, Charlotte, was named for our mother's mother.'

'Not Charlotte Bakewell?' Molly gasped.

'That was her maiden name – how did you know that?' Doris peered at Molly through narrowed eyes.

'I... err... I was reading my grandmother's old diaries earlier this year and I recall that name being mentioned.'

'I see. What was your grandmother's name?'

'Erm... Alice Parsons.' Molly quickly made up a name to ensure no suspicion was raised.

'Hmmm, I can't say that name rings any bells.'

'My grandmother was quite a bit older but, if I recall correctly, she used to sometimes babysit Charlotte.'

'I see.'

Molly realised she'd had a close shave and so steered the conversation back to the wonders Doris and Rose had seen invented in their lifetime.

'I tell you, Molly lass, if you were to pick up the younger me and just drop her into this world we live in now, she'd most likely have some kind of breakdown. Can you imagine going from a life of hard work and drudgery to the kind of luxury we have now? It would freak you out no end. I'm glad I've lived through these times; when I look back, I realise it really has been quite an experience.'

'What would you say has been the highlight of your life, Doris? As in, what's been invented that you've enjoyed or appreciated the most?'

Molly waited while Doris thought for a moment. 'You know, it's very hard to choose as there have been so many but, if I was forced, I think I would have to say it was "The Big One" rollercoaster at Blackpool Pleasure Beach. I darn well loved that thing! Only went on it for the first time last year but, let me tell you, it was the best thrill of my entire life!'

'They're amazing ladies and I can't believe their age. That is impressive.'

Molly and Charlie were making their way back to the windmill. There was a frosty nip in the air and their breath was visible in front of them as they talked.

'They most certainly are amazing and I love spending time with them, listening to the stories of the things they've seen and experienced. As Doris said, the life she was born into was quite different to the one she now leads.'

'Does that help you to understand how it was for me when we first met?'

'It absolutely does. It only fully dawned on me today, as I listened to them talking with you, that you are probably much more familiar with their early years than I'll ever be.'

'But, even so, they were born the best part of seventy or so years after my time so there would have been many changes in those years that I could never have imagined back then.'

'So, did you know Charlotte Bakewell, Doris's grandmother?'

‘Yes, I did and she is… was… a right cheeky little madam. Rather bossy and likes to get her own way all the time. If I’m being honest, I find her quite annoying.’

‘Cheeky, bossy and likes getting her own way…? Are you sure you’re not related?’

Charlie ducked the swipe that came in his direction, laughing as he did so.

‘Is that how you see me?’

Charlie stopped and drew Molly into his arms. He placed a warm kiss on her nose before replying, ‘Molly, when I look at you, I see a strong-willed woman who knows her own mind and won’t take any nonsense from anyone. I’ll happily bet that, in her childhood, she was described as bossy and annoying because she always liked to get her own way.’

Molly looked at him for a few seconds before breaking into giggles. ‘Oh, my goodness, when you put it like that… Maybe there’s hope for Charlotte after all.’

‘Well, Doris didn’t turn out so badly so I’m going to take a guess on Charlotte growing up to be a fine woman indeed.’

They came to the path that ran behind the manor, down to the mill and the river. Through the naked boughs of the trees, they were able to catch a glimpse of the darkened building.

‘I’m sorry that Sukie’s not here for the holidays, I had hoped to see her again. I don’t feel I ever thanked her properly for looking after me.’

‘It was unfortunate that Pete decided at the last minute to return to Austria – I’d been looking forward to catching up with them also. Mind you, it might be a blessing in disguise that they’re not here.’

‘What makes you say that?’ Molly burrowed in closer to Charlie.

‘Well, for a start, I don’t think she’d be too happy at the turn our relationship has taken.’

‘Why?’

‘Molly, I’m supposed to be finding a way of returning you to your own time. Us becoming involved with each other means I’m less inclined to search too hard and, worse, if we do find a way back for you, how are we going to cope with being separated? If I’m being honest, the thought of spending a single day without you, makes me feel quite ill. I daren’t even think how I would get through the rest of my life knowing I would never see you again.’

‘I know.’ Molly sighed. ‘The very idea of leaving you is more than I can bear but not knowing what happened to my family is hard too. To be in the situation, where I have to make a choice, is something I simply cannot bring myself to consider. Maybe being unable to do anything is the best place to be.’

‘I think you might be right, Molls. While there is nothing we can do at this time, we might as well enjoy the freedom from the responsibility. There’s no point in worrying about it until it arrives on our doorstep.’

‘I absolutely agree. And, talking about doorsteps, Charlie Rowland, I’ll race you to ours! Last one there makes the hot chocolate.’

Molly was already sprinting ahead before Charlie could even begin to quicken his step. ‘Never mind “making the hot chocolate”, young lady, it’s where I’m going to drink it from you should be concerned about…’

Molly let out a squeal and began running faster while Charlie, his laughter flying around on the wind, sprinted along behind her.

Chapter Forty-Two

Molly lay in the circle of Charlie's arms and watched the rain lash down against the bedroom window.

'Is there anything you have a fancy to do today?' Charlie nuzzled into her neck and she squirmed as his morning stubble tickled her.

'Not really…' she sighed. The truth was, she was bored. It was the last weekend in February and she'd begun to really miss her drag queens and her job. She was counting down the days until they arrived back in London but there were still a few months to go. She'd returned to the sightseeing she'd enjoyed before she met MaggieFrank but the wet, wintery, weather took the joy out of it. Molly didn't mind the rain, and London was still impressive in the wet, but she truly dazzled when the sun shone upon her and Molly preferred to see her in all her shining glory.

'I know,' said Charlie, 'Why don't we go to the Victoria & Albert Museum? We never did make it there the last time we tried. How about it? Do you think we might make it this time without you picking up strangers on the tube?'

Molly laughed at his comment and felt herself brighten at Charlie's suggestion.

'I think that is a good idea. May we get a McDonald's breakfast on the way?' She'd become rather partial to their sausage and egg muffiny things and the hash browns were rather tasty too.

'Of course, we can! When have I ever refused a Maccy D's breakfast?'

'Then let's get to it!' Molly threw back the quilt and quite literally jumped out of bed. A moment later, the shower was running in her en-suite bathroom. Charlie had asked her to move her belongings into his bedroom but she'd declined. When asked why, her reply had been it wasn't practical. 'If I move in here, it means one of us will always be waiting for the shower to be free, or the mirror to be free, or we'd be tripping over each other as we got dressed. If I leave my things in the other bedroom, and shower room, we have space to get ourselves ready and no one is waiting on the other. You know it makes good sense.'

And she was proved correct again as they stepped into the hallway at the same time, both fully dressed and ready to go.

'Now do you believe me when I say keeping our own rooms is a good idea?'

Charlie wrapped his arms around her and kissed her. 'It sure is, dear. Anything you say, dear. You are always right, dear,' he murmured against her mouth.

'Oh, away with you.' She pushed him hard against his chest.

They were both still laughing as they closed the front door and made their way down the stairs.

‘Oh, Charlie, this is beautiful.’ They’d just walked into the main hall of the V&A and Molly was gazing around her as she took in the splendour of the building. Charlie had to agree with her. From an architectural point of view, the Victoria & Albert Museum really was quite special. Creating stunning buildings was something the Victorians had excelled at although the Georgians hadn’t been too shoddy either. The combination of marble and granite, sweeping staircases with beautifully carved balustrades, sparkling floors and majestic pillars all worked together to create a stunningly visual building. Charlie had visited the museum many times and it never ceased to take his breath away.

‘How would you like to work this, Molls? Start from the earliest and go forward through the centuries or head upstairs to the 1800s – your era – and go backwards through time?’

‘I think it is better to start at the beginning – after all, I already know what to expect in the 1800s. I do believe I have first-hand experience of that one.’ She grinned as she replied.

‘Come on then.’ Charlie gestured to his right and led her towards the Medieval and Renaissance department.

A few hours later, they were resting their weary feet under a table in the café. A couple of slices of cake and cups of coffee had helped to revive their spirits. Molly was utterly entranced by all the museum had on show. She’d said that, in many ways, it reminded her of the Great Exhibition but this was better for, although it was busy, it was nowhere near as packed as the exhibition had been and there was more time to spend admiring the items on display. It had been impossible to stand still for more than a few seconds on her visit to the Great Exhibition, as it had been so crowded and you were swept along amidst the hustle and bustle of the sheer volume of visitors.

'Shall we make our way up to the 19th century displays? It's the only one left for us to visit.'

'Do you think it's worth it? Like I said, I'm more than a little familiar with that period of time.'

'You might as well. I'm sure there will be some items which will be pleasing for you to look at.'

'Okay. Since we've seen everything else, I suppose it would be wrong to leave it out.'

They made their way up to the third floor. These display rooms covered the period from 1760 to 1900 so there were more than a few bits and pieces which were new to Molly.

They slowly walked through the rooms and, eventually, found themselves in a larger room with quite a few book displays. Molly immediately became more alert and gravitated towards them, her interests lying more in the books than the ceramics. Charlie had noticed this as they'd walked around the museum and had begun to wonder if he'd have been better taking her to the big Waterstones bookshop down on Piccadilly, as he was sure that would have been more fascinating for her. He turned to see where she was and found her, nose and hands pressed up against a glass cabinet, staring hard at the contents within.

He walked over to her side and whispered, 'You really shouldn't touch the display cabinets, Molls, some of them have alarms on them and you may cause a bit of a stir.'

She turned to look at him and he started when he saw how pale she'd become and the tears in her eyes.

'Molly, what's wrong? You look as though you've seen a ghost? What is it?' He looked through the glass to see what had caused her upset.

'Those diaries…' She pointed to a number of volumes placed on a small shelf. The label at the side read, "The Diaries of Simon Caldwell – 1854 to 1864".

'What about them, Molly?'

She stared at the display and the tears began to slip down her face. 'I know Simon,' she whispered. 'He visited our village and stayed at the inn.'

She turned to look at Charlie.

'Charlie, I'm in those diaries…'

Chapter Forty-Three

Molly allowed Charlie to lead her to a nearby bench and sit her down. He sat beside her and took her hand.

'Tell me more.'

She paused for a moment to gather her thoughts, still coming to terms with the shock of seeing Simon's books in front of her. Eventually she began to speak.

'In the summer of 1857, Simon arrived in our village and took a room at the inn for a week. He explained to Betsy and I that he was a diarist. He travelled around the country and wrote about the places where he stayed. He'd been inspired to do this when he'd realised how important diaries are for passing on information to those who came after. His words, not mine. He wanted to record as much as he could about the ordinary people, who lived the most ordinary lives, because he felt they were the ones who really shaped the nation. He spent time with my father, making notes on his normal day, how he worked and the effects the hard labour of being a blacksmith had had on him over the years. At night, he would sit in the public bar in the inn and listen to the stories of the villagers and everything would be written down. He made notes of all their names and their professions. One evening, when it was quieter than usual, I noticed he was drawing. When I approached him, he showed me a sketch of myself.' She turned to look at Charlie. 'Charlie, Sukie couldn't find proof of my having existed when she looked in the church. You've been unable to find anything when you looked on the pea-see thing. I *know* you will find me in those diaries. We need to get a closer look at them.'

Charlie nodded. 'Hang on a minute, let me make a phone call.'

He took his phone from his pocket, stood up and walked over to the other side of the room where it was quiet. Molly looked down at her hands, twisting over and under themselves in her lap. Their motions matched those of her stomach which was churning so badly, she feared her earlier slice of cake may make a reappearance. Eventually, Charlie returned to sit by her side.

'Right, I've spoken to my friend, Chris. As luck would have it, she's here today so she's making her way up to see us. This isn't her department but she's good friends with the lady who's in charge so she's going to have a word with her.'

'Thank you, Charlie,' she whispered.

Charlie laid his hand on top of hers and stilled their movements. 'Hey, try not to worry. I know,' he said, putting his other hand up to stop her making a comment, 'easier said than done. I understand but we don't know what's contained within those volumes and there's no point getting all worked up until we do.'

Molly nodded, leaned into his side and waited for his friend to appear. While she knew she was in the diary in 1857, for Simon had shown her the sketch he'd drawn of her and Betsy laughing when they'd sat down for a chat, he may never have returned to the village and she could be getting all worked up over nothing. Her inner sense, however, was telling her there was something in those books she needed to see.

Finally, in what felt like hours but was, in reality, only ten minutes, a woman strode through the door and made her way straight to them. She was slim built with a small pixie face and short cropped, spiky hair which was dyed bright pink. She walked straight over to Charlie and, when he stood up, threw her arms around him and gave him a tight hug.

'Hey, you old reprobate, how're you doing? It's been a while.'

'I'm very well, thanks, Chris. How are you? You're looking great.'

'All is good, my friend, all is good.'

Molly watched the exchange and was surprised to find that, in amongst all the other emotions running through her right now, there was still some room for a bit of jealousy in there. Who was this woman and how did she know Charlie so well?

Charlie turned to her. 'Molly, please meet Chris – she's the lady in charge of the Architecture department. We met at university and we've been friends ever since. Our paths often cross when sites are being dug out in preparation for new building works and we find items of interest where the foundations need to go.'

As she shook hands with Chris, Molly noticed the wedding ring on her left hand and her little bout of jealousy immediately subsided. There was nothing to worry about here.

'So, what's sparked your interest and why?'

Molly led Chris over to the display cabinet with the diary volumes inside.

'I would really like a closer look at those diaries, please. I believe they may have information in them which is pertinent to me.'

'Really? In what way?'

'I've been researching my family tree and my great-grandmother mentioned in a letter that Simon Caldwell had visited the village she lived in at the time and that he'd written about her in his diary plus sketched a picture of her. I would dearly like to see it but I'm also hoping he may have revisited at a later date and that there may be more information about her in her later years.'

Chris nodded as she listened to Molly's explanation. 'Okay, let me go and see who's around. It's Sunday so I can't promise a result today – you were lucky I was here, Charlie. We had a late shipment arrive on Friday and I came in today to get a jump start on cataloguing it.'

'Or, to translate, Steve went out on a climb and you couldn't be bothered to stay at home on your own.'

Chris laughed. 'You know us far too well.' She turned to Molly. 'It's impossible to keep anything to yourself when you've been mates with someone for over twenty years. Right, wait here, let me go and see who I can find.'

Within moments, she was back with a young man following in her wake. 'Right, we have mostly good news, and a small bit of bad. The bad news is you can't have access to the original volumes because they're rather delicate. The good news, however, is that the contents were scanned for the archive records and we can sort out copies. If you would care to give Josh here your email address, and what dates you require, he'll be able to sort that out for you on Tuesday.'

'Tuesday?' Molly couldn't keep the disappointment from her voice.

'I'm afraid Archives is closed on Mondays.' Chris gave her an apologetic smile.

'Tuesday will be fine. Thank you, Chris, for helping me. You are very kind.' Molly shook Chris's hand.

Chris looked at Charlie. 'I like your friend, she has far better manners than you.'

'Such a cheeky woman!' Charlie grinned at them both.

'Right, it's almost closing time and I need to get back to my department. Charlie, we must sort out dinner – it's been too long and I know Steve would love to see you. Give us some dates and we'll sort something out.'

'Will do!' Molly watched him as he gave Chris another hug and was pleased to note it held nothing more than friendship.

'If you would care to give me your contact details, and the dates you're interested in, I'll sort that out for you.' Josh held out a pad and pen.

Charlie scribbled down his email address and then looked at Molly. 'What dates do you need?'

She thought for a moment. 'Definitely 1857 and then everything from 1860 onwards.' She looked at Josh. 'Sorry if that seems quite a lot but those are the years we have the least amount of information on.'

'No, that's not a problem. I'll have to check how they've been scanned and archived. It may well be you end up with all of the diaries as that might be easier.'

'That won't be a problem. Whatever is the least amount of trouble for you is absolutely fine.'

'I just need to make a note of their reference number. It was lovely to meet you.' Josh shook their hands, jotted down the catalogue number of the diaries and walked off, leaving them alone in front of the cabinet.

'Are you okay?' Charlie put his arm around Molly's shoulders and squeezed gently.

'Err… I'm not quite sure. I feel all… jumbled up.'

'Come and sit down. We need to leave soon, it's almost closing time, but you can take a few minutes to collect yourself. Do you think there might be answers within those volumes?'

'Simon was insistent that he intended to revisit the village one day. He said his plan was to return to the places he'd been and see how they had changed, or not, since his previous visit. The villagers had been kind and friendly to him and he was adamant he'd be back one day as he'd made friends within our little community. I believe he meant it.'

Charlie took out his phone and tapped on the screen. A minute later he read out, 'Well, this is the short version… *"Simon Caldwell was a diarist in the later 1800s. His diaries were recently discovered within an old trunk, hidden at the back of an attic in a house in Wimbledon. Realising what they contained, the ten volumes were donated to the Victoria & Albert Museum. Simon Caldwell died in February 1865, aged 49."* So, we have to hope he got back to Lower Ditchley before December 1864 which, according to this, is when the diaries stop.'

Molly took one last look at the brightly patterned books in front of her, saddened to know the kindly author of them had not enjoyed the long life he'd hoped for. She straightened up. 'Come on, Charlie, let's go. There's nothing more for us here today.'

Charlie took her hand and they walked towards the door. Just as they were leaving the room, Molly looked back at the glass cabinet. She really hoped she was right and that she would soon find the answers she sought.

Chapter Forty-Four

Molly was pacing the floor in the flapartment. Charlie had just phoned to say he'd received an email from Josh, with the diaries attached, but was about to go into a meeting he couldn't get out of so they would need to wait until this evening to go through them. She looked at the clock – it wasn't even noon yet. She needed something to keep her occupied until then. A sudden thought came into her head; she rushed into the kitchen and began rummaging in the cupboards. A smile crossed her face and, a few minutes later, she was donning her coat, grabbing her handbag and sailing out the front door.

By the time Charlie got home that evening, just after five, the smell of baked goods had not only permeated the whole of the flat but had also wended its way down the stairs. Molly smiled when he came into the lounge and walked over to the kitchen.

She watched as he took in the array of cakes and bread lined up on the counter. 'Molly, what on earth have you been doing?'

'Err… Baking, silly! I thought that was obvious.'

‘Yes, I can see that, but… So much? There’s enough here to feed an army!’

‘I needed to occupy myself, Charlie. I couldn’t just sit and wait for you to come home. It’s been a long time since I’ve baked. In fact…,’ she paused, ‘the last time I baked was the day we met. I’d been helping my mother to complete an order for Betsy…’ Her voice trailed off and her face fell as the memory hit her. She’d been so focused on her task throughout the afternoon, she’d quite forgotten that.

‘Well, it all looks – and smells – utterly delicious. What have we got?’ Charlie gave her such a big smile that she couldn’t resist smiling back.

‘Fruit cake, lemon drizzle loaf, a cottage loaf, lady fingers, jam fancies and iced buns.’

‘And you did all this from memory?’

‘Not quite. I bought a recipe book when I went to purchase the ingredients – you had nothing in your cupboards that was of any use! Not even baking tins.’

‘It’s not really my forte, Molls. You know pasta and fry-ups are where my basic skills lie!’

‘Well, reading, and trying, new recipes kept me from thinking and worrying too much about Simon’s diaries. Do you have them?’

‘I do.’ Charlie pointed to his briefcase which he’d placed on the dining table as he’d walked past. ‘They emailed over the whole batch but I’ve only printed off the relevant years. I did two copies so we can both work on them. Let me get changed and we can begin going through them.’ He looked at the baking in front of him. ‘Would you like me to order in a takeaway or shall we work our way through this lot?’

‘Why don’t I sort out a meat and cheese platter and we can make up sandwiches with the bread. I’ll make a pot of tea.’

‘That sounds good to me.’

By the time Charlie returned to the kitchen, Molly had sliced up the bread, plated the meat and cheese, brewed the tea and placed a selection of the cakes on plates. They were sitting to one side of the table, leaving space on the other side for them to spread out the paperwork.

She sat down and waited for Charlie to retrieve the diaries from his case. He took out two brown envelopes and handed one to her.

‘Both copies are identical. I’ve printed off all of 1857 and then it jumps to 1860. I haven’t read anything as I felt it was only right for us to do it together. Do you want to open yours first?’

Molly looked down at the envelope. She desperately wanted to rip it open and read through as quickly as possible but, at the same time, she wanted to turn away and never look because what she might find could be too terrible to bear. She looked up at Charlie and her fear must have been clear to see on her face because he leant over and took her hand.

‘I know this must be frightening, Molly, but we have to do it. We have to find out if there is anything here which will go towards solving the puzzle. There may be nothing but we have to look.’

She nodded and, picking up the envelope, slowly opened it. She pulled out the thick wad of paper inside and placed it on the table in front of her. Charlie poured them tea while she leafed through, looking for the first page which was relevant to her. When she found it, she sat back and picked up her cup, nursing it in her hands and finding some comfort in its warmth. The familiarity of the motion gave her the courage to lean forward and begin reading. A few minutes passed in silence and then she looked up at Charlie.

‘Go to page…’ she looked down, ‘seventy-three. That’s where you’ll find me.’

Molly sat back and waited while Charlie read. She forced herself to eat some bread and butter. She didn’t want it, and certainly didn’t feel in the least bit hungry, but aware she hadn’t eaten all day, she knew she had to. Whatever came next, it would be better faced on a stomach that wasn’t empty.

She watched Charlie turn the page and the gasp which followed was not a surprise as she had been expecting it. He’d found Simon’s sketch of her and Betsy. She turned the page of her own copy and looked down. Simon had possessed a talented hand for drawing and he had captured her likeness well. There was no doubt it was her. She looked over at Charlie and saw him gently running his finger over the picture. He looked up at her and the expression on his face could only be described as awe.

‘It’s you. It is definitely you. I… I…’ he looked down at the picture again. ‘I don’t know what to say.’

‘I did tell you about this, Charlie.’

‘I know but… Well… Seeing it in front of me like this… It makes it all feel very real.’

‘Are you saying you’ve never believed me?’ Molly could understand his surprise at seeing the picture but was confused by his shocked reaction.

‘No… I mean, yes, I’ve always believed you but there’s something about having cold hard evidence in front of me… It’s hard to explain. I suppose it’s like… It’s like being told someone has died. You know it’s happened, you’re aware of the situation but it’s not until you see the body in front of you that the reality fully sinks in. Until that moment, a part of you can’t believe the truth of the matter.’ He looked back down at the sketch. ‘This is the moment when the reality is finally sinking in.’

Molly didn’t reply for there was nothing she could say.

She'd always felt that while Charlie had accepted the truth in her words, he'd never fully understood her situation. The way in which he'd just described it had made sense and she could see his point of view quite clearly. This was the only piece of evidence they had to prove everything she'd told him was real.

'This Simon chap seems to have been quite taken with you and your family. He speaks highly of you all and has written of his admiration for the hard work your father and brother put in daily at the forge. He also writes about the generous hospitality shown to him by you and your mother when he was invited to tea on more than one occasion. To quote, *"Alice and Molly Smythe have kindly invited me to partake of their tea-time meal again tomorrow when I made comment on how much I had enjoyed their company. While John Smythe may be a labouring man, he is well-read and his discussions on the politics of our time were informed and accurate. He is also a reasonable man who takes the time to listen to the opinion of others and structures his response accordingly. What engaged me most, however, is that he not only permits the womenfolk of his family to speak of such manly matters but that he appears to actively encourage them to do so. Miss Molly spoke most eloquently on the suppression of women and her father appeared to almost burst with pride when she did so. Such forward-thinking company is one which I must take pleasure in once more before I move on from this charming village."* You clearly made an impression there, Molly.' Charlie looked at her with a smile. 'So, you *have* always been a feisty gal, then!'

'I have, although I was never aware of my father being proud of the fact. I often had the impression that he found it troublesome and wished me to behave in a manner akin to that of the other ladies in the village.'

'Sometimes it takes an outside eye to notice these

things.'

Perhaps…' Molly looked back down and began turning the pages until she found Simon's entries for July 1860.

'On the date I arrived here in your time, Simon appears to have been somewhere near Manchester. I guess this is where we need to begin reading from.'

Charlie flicked through until he found the same page she was reading.

'It looks like he puts headers above his diary dates when he arrives in a new location. See, if you look at these pages,' he pulled a couple out of the pile, 'here is the name of the town or village underlined. That should make it quicker to find any further reference to Lower Ditchley. We've got four years to cover – why don't I take 1861 and 62 and you can go through 63 and 64?'

Molly nodded her agreement. If they split the years between them, they split the time it would take. 'Shall I put the kettle on for more tea?' she asked, perversely trying to delay the moment of commencing her search.

'I think wine might be better. You begin reading, I'll sort it out.'

Charlie got up and Molly wondered if he'd guessed her reasoning behind the request. If he had, he wasn't falling for it and, with no other reason she could find to put off the task any longer, she began to work through the pages in front of her.

Chapter Forty-Five

Charlie sat back in his chair and watched Molly skim-read the paperwork as he stretched his arms above his head and rubbed his eyes. They'd been reading for about forty minutes and Simon Caldwell's writing was small and curvaceous which made reading it arduous. Had he realised this earlier, he would've had the copies enlarged for easier reading. He turned a few more pages and then stopped. He felt his blood first run cold in his veins before it began to pound in his head for, on the entry dated the 15th of September 1862, Simon Caldwell had returned to the village.

He looked back over at Molly and saw she was still engrossed. She didn't appear to have noticed the change in his breathing which he was aware was now quick, short and shallow. He made an effort to calm himself and began to read. It didn't take long, for the entry was only a few pages but, when he had finished, his first thought was, Oh, shit! How the hell was he going to tell Molly what he'd just read? She had to know, there was no question of him not telling her, but it was going to break her heart and it was the pain he was about to inflict upon her that was hurting him the most. He re-read the passage a few more times, ensuring he had understood it correctly, although there was no possible way he could have misunderstood. It was clearly written with no room for misinterpretation. He drew in a deep breath, held it for a second and then spoke.

'Molly, I've found it.'

Her head shot up and the smile on it quickly faded when she looked at him. 'I can see from your face that it's not good news you have for me.'

Unable to speak, he shook his head.

'What page is it on?' She frantically began to turn the papers but Charlie placed his hand on the pile to stop her.'

'Molly, it might be better for me to read it to you first.'

She looked at him for a few seconds and then nodded. He saw the tears already gathering in her eyes and he hated what he was about to tell her. He picked up the relevant pages and, in a quiet voice, began reading:

"It is with a sore and heavy heart that I write my diary entry tonight. On my way homeward to London, I made a last-minute change to my plans and took the decision to detour to Lower Ditchley. I was passing within ten miles of the village and it came to me that I should like to engage once more in conversation with Mr John Smythe. The last few months of travelling have found me in the presence of many disagreeable companions and I had care to spend some hours in more pleasing company. Those last few miles were traversed in anticipation of such an event. I had purchased some pleasing wares in Birmingham and I believed both the ribbons and spices which I had tucked away in my trunk would give pleasure to Molly and Alice Smythe. It would have been rude to arrive empty-handed.

My anticipation, however, had been in vain for, upon my arrival in the village, I could see immediately that much had changed. The coaching inn where I had rested so well on my previous visit was closed and boarded up. I tied up my horse and, having advised my man-servant to make enquires on where else we may rest for the night, I walked round to the blacksmith's cottage. It was with the greatest of shocks that I found only an empty patch of ground, overgrown with weeds. Upon stepping back to the far side of the lane, I was able to get a view of the rooftop belonging to the stable block behind the inn. To my eyes, it appeared scorched and in a poor state of repair. There was nothing more in the vicinity that could answer the questions which now filled my head. I made my way back to my horse and was met by my servant who informed me he had secured us rooms at the newer establishment over by the village green. While it did not have stabling facilities, they had an arrangement with a local farmer who would be able to accommodate our steeds for the night.

I left my man to sort out the details and entered the establishment which would provide the roof over my head this night. My first request of the landlord was a glass of gin for I needed something strong to ease the turmoil inside of me. It was clear something untoward had occurred and the lack of stables within the immediate location of the village had me fearing to hear more of what had occurred to my friend and his family. However, hear it I had to do and, upon the consumption of a further two gins, I asked the landlord for information. The silence which befell the room, upon uttering my question, was immediate and I felt all eyes therein come to rest upon me.

The landlord uttered a gruff reply that it was a matter which no one spoke of and it was best for it to be left well alone. He turned away and declined to speak further. No one else was forthcoming with information and it was with more than a little frustration that I ate my evening meal. I tried to catch the eye of the other occupants in the room but none would engage with me.

Thankfully, however, the landlady was not one to be so reticent and I finally got the answers I sought when it was time to retire to my bedchamber. The lady of the inn was placing a pitcher of fresh water upon the washstand when I entered. She crept towards the chamber door and, after checking the hallway was clear, she closed it behind her and made her way to my side. In a quiet voice, she informed me that the villagers had been forbidden to speak of the incident which I had enquired of, however, as she had been a close friend of Alice Smythe's and had been aware of the bond I'd forged with the family, she felt it only right to impart the events of that night to me.

She began with the sad news that a fire had broken out in the forge in July 1860 and, due to the slightly isolated location of the cottage from the rest of the village, no one had been aware until it had taken full hold of the blacksmith's cottage. By the time help had been called for, it was too late and the cottage had been fully engulfed in flames when the villagers arrived on the scene. The ferocity of the fire, for it had been a hot summer with little rain, had quashed any hope of saving anyone within. When the flames and smouldering had finally eased a few days later, the lord of the manor had ordered the area to be cleared up. At the same time, a rumour began to spread that John Smythe had set the fire with his own hand due to being in debt and being unable to cope with the shame of this as he was a proud man. The rumour made him out to be unscrupulous and that he'd removed his family in the night in order that people would think they had all perished. The suggestion then followed that he'd done this in order to flee from those he owed and begin a new life elsewhere, free from these responsibilities.

The kind lady advised me that, despite knowing how upstanding John Smythe was, the villagers had been all too quick to listen to this untruth and it was now the belief of many that this was fact. The lack of bodily evidence when the cottage remains were cleared away, only served to uphold the rumour. There were some villagers who did not agree with this aspersion cast upon John Smythe's character but they soon learned to keep their thoughts to themselves when threats were made against them for being in league with John and his plans. The kindly lady then bid me goodnight and, after extracting a promise that I would not repeat to a living soul the details she had imparted to me, left me with my own thoughts on the matter.

I have spent the last few hours unable to find sleep, as my mind continues to consider all it has learnt this evening. I confess that my thoughts have turned to foul play and my belief that a miscarriage of justice has occurred for any man who has known John Smythe, no matter how briefly, would know he is a person of honour and integrity. The bearer of a grudge has been at the root of this travesty but, with the passage of time and no one alive who seems to really care, I suspect they will never be found and brought to justice. I shall pray for the rest of my days that they reap what they have sown in the hereafter for I have faith that the good Lord will demand recompense for the untimely demise of these kind and worthy people.

Now I, though I fear I shall not, must try to sleep for I leave tomorrow to return to London. I no longer wish to remain here a moment longer than I must."

Charlie looked up to see Molly rocking backwards and forward in her chair. Her arms were wrapped around her chest and the tears poured down her face. A low keening sound was falling from her lips.

He stood up and moved to sit in the chair beside her, putting his arms around her and holding her tightly. He didn't say a word for there was nothing he could say. There were no words which could ease her pain right now, he just had to let her cry herself out. They would talk when she was ready.

After a while, Molly's sobbing slowed and finally stopped although her breathing was disjointed and broken as she gulped on the air around her. Charlie got to his feet and picked her up, carrying her over to the sofa where he sat down and placed her on his lap. She laid her head on his shoulder and sat there quietly while he held her tightly.

'It's all my fault,' she eventually said.

'What?' He pulled back to look at her. 'How have you worked that one out?'

'I overheard Damien Featheringstone tell his evil little henchman to take revenge on my father for having slighted him earlier that day. I was about to make my way home to warn him when I slipped and fell in the river. Had I not done that, I would have been there and could have prevented this happening.'

'Or, you could have been in the cottage and been killed yourself. You may have had an inkling that something bad was going to happen but I'm sure something like this would never have entered your head.'

'No, I did not think that even Stan Alderly could be so foolish as to raise a fire in the midst of a hot, dry summer, but I clearly gave him credit where none was deserved.'

Charlie noticed Molly's speech had slipped back into its Victorian pattern. No doubt the shock, plus reading Simon's diaries, had brought it about.

Molly raised her head and looked into his eyes. 'So, now I know what happened, I must return to preparing myself so that I am ready for the moment when I can get back to my time.'

'But Molly—'

She placed her hand on his lips. 'No, Charlie, please do not speak. I know what I have to do and that is to find my way back. I have to prevent that fire.'

The following day, Molly made her way up to the rooftop pool and began to swim thirty lengths. Her swimming had greatly improved since she'd first ventured down to the basement pool with Charlie but it was now time to up the ante! She had to make sure she was strong enough to swim against the underwater current in the river and she also had to work on swimming in cold water for, even in the heat of the summer, the river had been icy down below the surface and that had not helped her when she'd fallen in.

It took her an hour and a half to complete her mission and, when she'd finished her thirtieth lap, she barely had the energy to drag herself out of the pool. She knew if Charlie was here, he'd have berated her for being stupid and pig-headed but, so far, this was the only thing that had managed to cease the endless diatribe going around her head. Her heart agreed with Charlie in that there was little she could have done to prevent the incident occurring but her head refused to give in and kept telling her otherwise. It was going around and around with no sign of stopping. She'd only slept last night because Charlie had insisted on her taking a sleeping tablet when they went to bed. He'd offered to stay home with her today but she'd refused him. She'd already known how her day, and future days, would be structured, mostly dividing her time between the swimming pool and the gym. She needed to be strong, and she had to be prepared for the day when she could get back. She didn't know how it was going to happen, or even *if* it would happen, but at least by being prepared, she could cope with the uncertainty for now.

The days passed and, as they grew longer when February moved into March, Molly's strength also grew. Her arms had always been strong due to carting bags of flour about for her mother but now they were even stronger and so were her legs. By the end of March, she could swim her thirty lengths in half an hour and was barely out of breath when she was done. She would then go to the gym where a further two hours would pass as she worked out on the equipment before finishing off with a half-hour sprint on the running machine.

It was the last day of March, and she'd just returned to the flapartment from her daily gym session, when a strange sensation hit her as she stood keying the number into the entry pad. She walked through the door and let it bang closed behind her. She stood for a moment trying to figure out what it was she was feeling. It was a strange kind of knowing, a sort of certainty about something but she didn't know what. She spent the day trying to pin down this elusive emotion but to no avail. It was only when Charlie returned home that evening, and gave her the sad news that his lovely friend Doris had passed away and they would be returning to the village for the funeral, that the strange sensation finally made sense.

It was time to go home.

Chapter Forty-Six

Charlie stood at the side of Doris's grave and watched the coffin being gently lowered. Molly stood to his right and Sukie stood next to her. Before they'd gone into the church for the funeral service earlier, Sukie had come over and said hello, providing Molly with the opportunity she'd been waiting on to thank Sukie for all the help and understanding she'd given her in the summer. They'd all sat together in the church while Jeremy had given Doris a glowing send-off. It had been a happy event, in its own way, for Doris had made it perfectly clear that she wanted her long life to be celebrated, not mourned. No black was permitted and no flowers either bar one soft pink rose on her coffin. To his left, was his brother Jeff, his wife Jenny, her mother, Bernice and her close friend, Sadie. They were all wearing bright, garish, Hawaiian shirts and he knew Doris would most certainly have approved. He overheard Sadie telling Bernice and Jenny that Doris was a woman after her own heart and this was exactly the kind of funeral she wanted when her time came. He hadn't realised Doris and Sadie were friends but it transpired they'd developed a bond the year before when the WI had arranged a day-trip to Blackpool for the older residents in the village and they'd both discovered a love of rollercoasters when they'd visited the amusement park there. It helped to ease some of the sadness in his heart, knowing Doris had continued to wring every last bit of pleasure out of life, regardless of her age. He was really going to miss her and her dry, pithy, comments. She'd been a force of nature and many had loved her for it, not just him.

When the final words had been spoken and people were moving away from the churchyard and heading towards The Cabookeria for the party afterwards – no way was there to be a funeral breakfast, Doris had insisted on it being called a party – he caught up with Rose to see how she was holding up.

'I'm fine, Charlie, thank you for asking.' Her soft voice was strong as she looked him in the eye. 'We both had our lives planned, ready for the day we could no longer be together. I'll be moving into the retirement village beside Sadie and Bernice and renting out our cottage. It would be too difficult to live there on my own, with all our memories around us and so we'd both agreed on this course of action, regardless of who went first. It's a good plan because I'll be too busy to grieve overly much and that's for the best. We had sixty years together – we were both incredibly lucky. Why should I be sad when I have been so blessed? It's time for new adventures – I have to move on, it's what Doris wanted.'

Charlie gave her a hug and watched her move off with Sadie and Bernice on either side. He knew they'd look after her well but that didn't move the lump sitting in his throat. She was right – most people didn't get those many years with their loved ones. He looked over at Molly and couldn't help but wonder if he'd be lucky enough to get six months with her by his side, never mind sixty years.

Molly stood in the conservatory area of the tearoom, gazing out at the stables opposite. The last time she'd sat here looking at them felt like a lifetime ago. Her life had changed beyond recognition these last months and she knew that, with each passing day, it would be harder to go back if the opportunity ever arose. When she'd first landed here in the twenty-first century, all she'd wanted was to get right back in the water and go home to her parents, her brother, and her own way of life. Now, however, she'd had a taste of this modern lifestyle and could no longer say with any certainty that she wanted to return to her own time. It wasn't just the better life she was living, or the independence she was enjoying, it was also Charlie. She loved him with every fibre of her soul, and being apart from him for more than a few hours was hard enough – how could she ever survive never seeing him again?

'Penny for them?'

She jumped at the soft voice whispering in her ear. 'Charlie! Don't do that! You scared the wits out of me!'

'Sorry, gorgeous. You were looking far too serious and, while this may be a funeral party, Doris would not be happy at the lack of a smile on your face. Come, they've cleared the floor for some dancing. Show me how they did it back in the 1800s.'

Molly followed him and moved gracefully into his arms. 'I can tell you now, dancing was a little more sedate than what I've seen around here. Headbanging and air guitars hadn't yet found their way into the middle-class lounge parties.'

'Then I can only say it was their loss!'

Molly chuckled at Charlie's droll reply. 'Charlie, on this occasion, I would have to quite agree.'

It was later in the evening, as they were walking back to the windmill, that Sukie caught up with them. She'd left the party earlier to help Pete put the twins to bed and had been keeping an eye out for Molly and Charlie's return. The trees were still a bit woody, the new leaves had yet to finish growing, and she'd spotted the torchlight along the path.

'Hey, you two, wait up.'

She caught up and made a point of inserting herself in between them.

'So, how are things going? Have you made any progress in solving the mystery?'

Charlie filled her in on the discovery at the museum and how they now knew what had happened to Molly's family.

'Oh, Molly, I'm so sorry to hear that. How are you feeling? You must be so muddled up inside.'

'It's… strange. I think that's the best word for it. On one hand, I miss my family terribly yet, on the other, being here makes it feel very far removed and quite unreal.'

'Do you still want to find your way home?' Sukie asked her gently.

'Yes, of course I do. I want to either save my family or seek justice for them.'

Sukie tried to see the expression on Molly's face but it was too dark. Her voice, however, had been a little less convincing than it should have been.

They arrived at the mill and Charlie asked if she'd like to join them for a hot chocolate.

'Charlie Rowland, you always know how to get on my good side. I would love one.'

Once inside, Molly headed up to the second floor to get changed, leaving Sukie and Charlie to sort out the beverage. The minute she heard the bedroom door click closed, Sukie rounded on Charlie, her eyes blazing with anger.

'Charlie Rowland, what the *hell* are you playing at? Why on earth have you become involved with Molly? Are you truly incapable of keeping your dick in your pants?'

'Whoa! Just a minute there, Sukie, don't be so quick to judge! Do you know how it feels to be a twenty-four-hour babysitter? Watching someone's every move and having to answer question after question after question? It is exhausting! While you were off in Austria, chilling out and living your life, I had to put mine on hold to look after Molly. Living a normal life was near-on impossible those first few months – I couldn't risk introducing her to my friends for fear she would let slip how she came to be here and terrified about the consequences if she did. We have lived in each other's pockets for the last eight months and it was inevitable that we would gravitate towards each other.'

'But—'

'No, Sukie, let me finish! Molly is amazing! She's funny, witty, kind, clever, intelligent and she has coped wonderfully with all the challenges she's had to face. Neither of us can even begin to imagine what she's had to take on board in order to cope with this crazy, new world she's found herself thrust into. But coped with it she has – with grace, with style and with panache! And, somewhere along the line, we fell in love.'

'Oh, Charlie, you silly, love-struck fool. Don't you see that you've simply made it harder for both of you? She's two hundred years older than you, for goodness' sake. How on earth could you ever have imagined this could work?'

'One-hundred and fifty-four, actually.'

'Excuse me?'

'In her time, Molly is thirty-five. I'm forty-one. So, she's only one-hundred and—'

'Okay, I get it!' Sukie looked at him in exasperation.

'Sukie,' Charlie took hold of her hand and looked into her eyes. She could see the pleading in his, begging her to try and understand. 'I didn't plan for this to happen, I'm quite sure Molly didn't either. But it has and, right now, I'm just living for the moment, trying to make the most of the time we have together because I don't know how long it's going to last.'

'You've made the decision for her to go back to her own time much harder for her, you know that, don't you? You or her family is a choice Molly should never have had to make.'

'It might be that she can never go back, then it's not a problem.'

Sukie tried not to sigh at the petulance in Charlie's voice. It was like listening to Poppy, when she was trying to make an argument she was never going to win.

'Charlie, Molly being here has put the universe out of sync. The opportunity *will* present itself for her to return to her own time and you had both better be prepared for it.'

She leant in and gave him a hug. She didn't want to be cruel but it was vital that they both knew what was at stake here. She wished with all her heart that it could be different for she cared deeply for Charlie and would love to see him happy and content.

'I'm going to head off now, tell Molly I'll see her soon. Are you staying long?'

'We're going back to London on Monday morning.'

'Then why not join us for lunch on Sunday? I know Pete would love to see you.'

'We'll see. I'll need to run it by Molly first.'

'Okay, let me know. No, you stay here,' Sukie halted Charlie as he made to follow her. 'I'll let myself out.' She pecked him on the cheek and made her way down the stairs.

She closed the mill door behind her and began walking up the path back to the manor. When she reached the bend, she turned around to look back and saw the silhouette of Charlie and Molly embracing through the window. Her heart ached for them both for common sense told her it was inevitable that, one day, they would have to part.

Chapter Forty-Seven

Molly sat hidden in the bushes. She could hear Charlie calling her name but she didn't want him to find her. She hoped he wouldn't come too far down the path for then he would see what she had seen – the shimmer was back on the river.

That morning, when she'd woken up, she hadn't felt any different from how she woke up any other day. She'd turned over and snuggled into Charlie's back, peppering it with soft, feathery kisses until he too was awake. They'd both decided they wanted a nice, lazy day. Molly had taken a swim in the river the previous morning and was happy to pass on getting wet and cold today. It was a fine spring day, outside the window, but the temperature was still low so a long cuddle in bed, eating breakfast and watching a film was the perfect choice.

Charlie had introduced her to Sukie's favourite film, The Sound of Music, and she'd adored it. The songs were so catchy and she'd found herself humming snippets of them as she'd showered and tidied up afterwards.

She'd just put the vacuum away in the cupboard – she'd never thought there would ever be a day when cleaning the rugs would be so easy – when she was overcome with a sudden urge to walk along the river. She hadn't given it much thought for it was an urge she'd often had in the past; the feeling of being cooped up indoors and just needing some time outdoors to revive her spirits.

She'd grabbed her jacket and called out to Charlie that she'd be back shortly. He'd offered to accompany her but she'd declined, saying she needed a little time alone.

She and Charlie had walked this way so many times over the months since the previous summer, always looking for something which never materialised, so, when she saw it today, it took a few seconds for it to sink in. In fact, she'd walked right past before coming to a halt and doing a swift turn on her heel to go back and look again.

And there it was – the silvery brightness on top of the water. There was no mistaking it for sunlight this time for the sun had disappeared behind the clouds and the sky had a grey, overcast hue.

Molly had sat down between the roots of the old, stunted hollow and stared across the river. Her heart was pounding and her hands were shaking. She had to choose what to do next but she didn't know *what* to do next. Her heart was here with Charlie but her family, and her real life, lay on the other side of that pool of shining water. She should never have been here and she should never have seen all that she had seen or had the wonderful experiences which she'd enjoyed so much. So much change which lay in a future that could never be hers.

She didn't know how long she'd been sitting, staring into the growing dusk, when Charlie's voice broke into her thoughts. She heard him calling her name but couldn't bring herself to call back. She didn't want him to find her, for then he'd see the river and everything between them would change. She quietly slipped down behind the nearby bushes and the irony of the situation was not lost on her that she'd taken the very same stance to avoid being seen by Damien Featheringstone on that fateful day.

She heard the cracking of a twig as Charlie drew near and she held her breath, knowing that he was close. For a moment there was silence and then she heard him murmur, 'Oh shit!' A second later, he spoke again, 'Molly, you can come out from wherever you're hiding, I can see it. It's back.'

She let out a sigh and stood up. 'I'm sorry, Charlie, I saw it and… well…' She couldn't finish her sentence as the tears began to roll down her face.

'Hey, come here.' Charlie took her into his arms and pulled her tightly against him. 'I don't know what to do,' she sobbed.

'Yes, you do,' he whispered into her hair. 'You do know. You've always known. You have to go back. You have to try and save your family. You'll never be able to forgive yourself if you turn away from them now.'

'But, what if it's too late? What if I get there and I'm all alone because they're dead? I don't know how this time portal thing works.'

'Neither do I, my love, but, if they are already gone, then you have to get justice for them. You have to make sure there's a gravestone for them in the churchyard – you have to ensure they are never forgotten.'

'Will you come with me, Charlie?' She looked up at him.

'I can't, Molly, it would be wrong. I don't want to lose you, I wish I could keep you here by my side for ever, but that's not how it should be. We've been lucky to have this time together and I will cherish it for as long as I live.'

'A love that will span two centuries?'

'A love that is timeless.'

Molly held onto Charlie until darkness had almost fallen. Eventually, she looked up and said, 'Well, I suppose I had better get ready before it disappears.'

She took Charlie's hand and they walked back towards the mill for the last time.

Charlie stood on the riverside path, kicking at a stone buried in the earth, while listening to Sukie going through the details one last time with Molly, ensuring she was clear on what had to be done.

'Tell me again what you need to do, Molly.'

Molly looked at Sukie who was holding a bag in her hand.

'I put this across my shoulders, get into the water, make my way to the shimmer, jump up and dive into it then swim down to the riverbed. From there, I need to swim to my left to take me back upstream so that, when I come back up, I'm away from the shimmer and, hopefully, back in my own time.'

Charlie looked over the water at the shimmer. It really was there. Part of him had hoped they'd imagined it and, when they got back, it would have gone.

But it wasn't.

It was very much there and Molly was very much going.

'That's right.' Sukie nodded. 'What else?'

'In this bag is a towel to dry myself along with my original clothing. I need to change into it, place my swimming costume and the towel in the bag, and hide it over there in the hollow tree because no one must ever find them.'

Charlie walked away until he came to the hollow stump. Unable to hold himself up a moment longer, he sat down with his back against it and faced the water. He couldn't even begin to describe the pain inside him. His head kept saying, *You knew she'd have to go one day*, while his heart was screaming, *How can she be leaving us?* Of course, he'd always *known* Molly couldn't stay with him forever but that hadn't stopped him from hoping that she might.

'Cool!' Sukie gave Molly a high-five and, despite his sadness, Charlie smiled. Molly so loved those little actions – thumbs-ups and fist bumps – they tickled her. Sukie carried on talking. 'I've also put in a small box of items you can sell, should you find you need to. You don't know what you're going back to, Molly, but they'll give you some security.' She pulled Molly into her arms. 'Good luck, I hope it all works out for you.'

He caught Molly's gaze and tried to give her his brightest smile – he didn't want to make this any harder for her than it already was – but knew he'd failed miserably when she turned back to Sukie and he heard her whisper, 'Please, look after him for me, Sukie. Tell him to find happiness – I don't want him to waste his life pining over a corpse, for that is what I will soon be for you both.'

'I'll take care of him, I promise.'

Sukie moved away, gathering up the last bits and pieces into the waterproof bag. Molly walked towards him and he got to his feet.

She stopped in front of him and placed her small, perfect hands on his face. Charlie grasped them tightly within his own and pressed hard against them, trying to imprint their shape onto his cheeks forever.

'Charlie, I can't even begin to thank you—'

'Don't! Don't thank me, Molly, please.'

'But—'

'Molly, you have nothing to thank me for. You have brought so much fun, and colour, and laughter, and love into my life that I should be thanking you. I love you so much, my Molly, and I'm glad you allowed me to share this time with you.'

She gazed up at him in silence for a few seconds before slowly nodding. She got it. She understood. Saying "thank you" made it all feel like it had been some kind of favour or business transaction when it was so much more than that.

Her hands slid down to his chest, and he wrapped his arms around her one last time, holding her close, never wanting to let go. He felt her lips reach his chin and he lowered his head to bring his mouth to hers. Their last kiss. He poured everything he had into it and felt her tremble against him. He knew his tears were mixing with hers.

A small cough from nearby brought them apart. Charlie clasped Molly's hands between his as he looked into her dark-brown eyes for the last time.

'I love you, Molly Smythe, with everything that I am and everything I ever will be.'

'Charlie, I will love you until the end of time. Our love will be timeless. It will last forever.'

She took a step back and gently pulled her hands from his, not knowing that she had also pulled his heart from him too.

He watched her walk back to Sukie, take the waterproof bag from her hands, sling it over her shoulders and make her way into the river where she swam over to the shimmer, and, after raising her arm in a brief wave, she rose up out of the water and dived right into the middle of the silvery ripples.

Charlie stood staring at the spot where she had last been, willing her to reappear. When she didn't, he lifted his foot as though to take off his shoe but then he felt a gentle, but firm, hand circle his wrist.

'No, Charlie, you can't go after her.'

His shoulders dropped and began to shake as the sobs ripped out of him. Through the blur of his tears he could make out the shimmer growing smaller and smaller until, finally, it was gone.

He staggered over to the hollow stump and slumped down onto the ground once more. The rough bark at his back was the only thing that seemed to be real right now.

He was vaguely aware of Sukie sitting down and waiting with him. There was silence all around and even the river seemed to have stilled its path for no sound came from it. After a time, Sukie stood, switched on her phone torch leaned into the hollow trunk and, with a bit of a rummage, pulled out the bag she'd handed to Molly only moments before. She shook off the old leaves and dirt which had accumulated on top of it, sat back down beside him, and opened it up. Inside was the musty, disintegrated remains of the towel and swimming costume and a plastic storage box. The box was still fully intact and, when she opened it, there was a small book and an envelope with Charlie's name on it. Sukie gently placed the box on his lap. He picked it up and held it in his hands for a few seconds, running his fingers over the faded ink on the envelope. Once again, his eyes filled with tears, this time at the sight of Molly's beautiful cursive writing. Writing he'd no longer see on post-it notes dotted around the flapartment, in journals lying open as she made her notes on all her new experiences or on bits of paper as she planned her walking routes around London.

He carefully opened the old, fragile stationery and, with the heels of his hands, wiped the tears from his face. He didn't want to mar the last letter he would ever receive from her.

He gently took the folded pages out, turned them over, opened them up and began to read:

My darling Charlie...

Chapter Forty-Eight

Lower Ditchley 1860

Molly burst up out of the water and drew in a sharp gasp of air. It was late dusk and the trees on the riverbank loomed above her like motionless shadows. She swam to the shore and used the exposed tree roots to pull herself out.

The first thing she noticed was that it was warm. The air was thick and heavy which suggested it had been a hot day and it had very little intention of cooling down as night fell. She peered into the darkness around her and spotted the old tree stump a short distance down the path. She quickly made her way to it and pushed her way into the thicket behind it to dry off and change. She felt her heart lurch as she began pulling on her old stays and corsets. The weight of the bag, when she'd been in the river, had been a reminder of the excessive number of layers she'd once worn. Now, she was having to don them again and each item felt like a punch in her stomach, dragging her further and further away from Charlie and shackling her back down into her own time. A ball and chain around her ankle could not have weighed her down any more than her completed outfit did.

She rolled the swimming costume inside the towel and was putting it back in the bag when her fingers brushed against something at the bottom. She pulled out a small box – it was the thing Charlie had called "Tupperware". She opened it and found some pretty jewels and a note. She recognised Sukie's handwriting but it was too dark to read what she'd written so she closed the box back up and placed it back in the waterproof bag, put the damp, rolled-up towel on top and shoved it deep inside the hollow stump. She brushed some dry leaves, twigs and dirt over the top and turned to make her way back to the village. Right now, she had other issues which were a priority – she could come back for a closer look at the contents of the box once she knew how the land lay. She really had no idea what she was going to find and her stomach was churning furiously.

She'd just walked past the spot where she'd exited the river when her foot kicked something on the edge of the pathway. She bent down and found the basket she'd dropped when she'd first fallen in the river. She picked it up and, finding a few berries still inside, ran her fingers over them – they still felt fresh. Oh, my goodness, she thought, was it possible that she'd arrived back on the same day she'd left? Could she really be that lucky?

The thought lent speed to her heels and, throwing the basket back on the ground, she picked up her skirts and began to run. Maybe, she might just be able to change history after all. When she reached the fork in the path that led to the windmill, she faltered for a few seconds as the memories of walking along it, hand-in-hand with Charlie, hit her. She mentally berated herself for allowing these thoughts to intrude on her mission. There would be plenty of time to indulge herself in the pain of her lost love later. With a mental shake, she picked up her pace once more and it wasn't long before she reached the village green. The church clock had read nine thirty as she'd scurried past. That explained why it was so quiet – everyone would be abed due to rising considerably earlier on the lighter mornings.

She ran across the green and saw the inn looking exactly as it once had. Some of the windows were open and Betsy's laughter floated out and danced in the air.

Molly had just reached the duck pond when her nostrils twitched. A smell she'd hoped not to encounter was assailing them.

Smoke!

Her breath was now coming in short gasps and a sharp pain was stabbing at her side. She ran down the side lane towards the cottage and a groan slipped from her lips as she saw the red dancing flames licking their way up the side of the cottage, growing closer to the stable roof.

She stopped still, bent forward to pull some breath into her lungs and then screamed as loud as she possibly could, 'FIRE! FIRE! FIRE!'

She ran into the cottage and saw her father dozing in his chair next to the fireplace. She ran over and shook him roughly.

'Father, Father! Wake up! The cottage is on fire! Father! Wake up!' She pushed him hard and heard his grunt as he came too.

'Huh? What? Molly, what's all the fuss? Why are you so late home? Where—'

'Father, the cottage is on fire. Quickly, go and get help. Hurry!'

'Your mother? Albie? Are they out?' There was no missing the panic in his voice. She pushed her father towards the cottage door.

‘Father, go and get help. I’ll find Mother and Albie – GO NOW!’

Molly ran towards the stairs; the smoke was growing thicker by the minute and it was getting harder to breathe. She knew she had to keep low – Charlie had gone through all this with her, just in case she fell back into her timeline at the same point where she’d left it. She climbed the stairs on all fours and made her way along to her parents’ bedroom, screaming for her mother as she went. She arrived at the door just as Alice opened it and, not giving her mother a chance to speak, Molly quickly told her what was happening.

‘Come quickly, Mother, I’ll need you to help me move Albie – you know how deeply he sleeps.’

The two women ran back to the small box room at the top of the stairs and began pushing and pulling the young man from his bed. Molly glanced out of the door, over her mother’s shoulder and saw a small red flicker in the far corner. The fire had reached the cottage roof. Given the lack of rain over recent weeks, the thatch would be as dry as a bone and would be perfect tinder for a hungry fire to consume. Fear lashed through Molly and, turning back to her somnolent brother, she slapped him hard across face to bring him to his senses. All those days in the gym had left their mark and the action had the desired effect – Albie was suddenly fully awake.

Molly left her mother and Albie to escape while she ran to her own bedroom. She opened the window, grabbed the trunk which rested beneath it, heaved it up and pushed it through. She ran back to her parents’ bedroom, feeling the heat of the flames as she ran through the door, opened their window and did the same with whatever of their belongings she could lay her hands on. She saw the villagers running down the lane towards the cottage and some of the women began grabbing the possessions strewn on the ground below, moving them away from the burning building.

'Molly! Get out of there now!'

She looked down and saw her mother and Albie standing beneath the window, both urging her to make her escape before it was too late. She ran to the stairs but the flames were already creeping up the treads. Suddenly, there was a loud "whoomph" above her head as the dry thatch of the cottage roof turned red and fiery. She dropped to her knees as a terrifying thought hit her. She was trapped!

For the briefest of seconds, she froze. This was it. She'd saved her family but at what cost? Just then, she heard Charlie's voice, when he was pushing her to try harder in the gym, *'You can do this, Molly, you can do anything. Go on, show me what you've got!'*

She spun around and ran back into her own bedroom. The flames were just beginning to feed on the doorframe as she slammed the door closed behind her. She dragged her bed over to the window she'd flung her trunk out of mere moments earlier and stripped the sheets off. Smoky tendrils were floating in under the gap in the door and the wood was starting to blister from the heat on the other side. She hurriedly knotted the sheets together and tied one end as tightly as she could to the end of the bed. About to lower herself out, Molly's eye fell on her bedside table and, despite the flames now forcing themselves around all four edges of the door, she lunged across and snatched up the small book lying there. She pushed it inside her bodice, ran back to the window, grabbed hold of the knotted sheets and pushed herself through the gap just as the door went up in a blaze, the flames leaping to her bed and turning the horsehair mattress into a blazing inferno within seconds.

Strong hands pulled her away from the cottage just as the flames flew out the window above her head. She was carried away and laid down on the grass opposite the cottage. Her mother held her hand as her father and brother, along with the other men of the village, threw buckets of water onto the flames. From where she lay, she could see how extensively the fire had spread. It was all across the roof of the stable and Betsy and her husband were hanging out of the upper windows of the inn, pouring buckets of water down the walls to stop the fire consuming that building too.

Molly started to shake as the realisation of what she was seeing began to sink in. She had seen the after-effects of this fire but now she was seeing it happen and she had been too late to prevent it. It was only as her mother held and soothed her in her arms that Molly came to her senses. She may have been too late to prevent the devastation the fire was causing but she had saved her family and that was all that mattered. She began sobbing heavily and fell into the arms of the mother she believed she would never see again.

Chapter Forty-Nine

Molly and her family stood looking at the ruins of their home and the family business. The stables had been rendered unsafe and, after the body of Patrick had been brought out, no one had wanted to enter them anyway. The villagers were all in mourning over the death of the gentle young man whose greatest love had been the horses in his care and whom he'd died saving.

The weather had broken and the torrential rains had dampened down the remains of the cottage. Her father and Albie had already searched through the ruins for anything which could be salvaged but to no avail. Such had been the ferocity of the flames, nothing had survived. Her father and mother had both hailed her quick thinking in throwing out some of their belongings for it meant they were not entirely destitute, although they were not far off. It was with some small fortune that Lord Featheringstone had insisted upon giving them while he arranged for one of the vacant workers' cottages to be cleared out, which, he'd informed her father, they could have use of for as long as was needed.

No one had been able to work out how the fire had begun and, although Molly knew Stan Alderly was behind it, she had no way of proving it and to speak out against him without proof, would only cause further trouble. She had to – as Elsa would say – "suck it up" and listen to her father being blamed for not dampening down the forge properly. No one was taking him to task over it; the general view was that everyone makes mistakes and he was being sorely punished for his by losing his home and his livelihood. Molly had taken him to one side and had told him exactly what had happened for she didn't want him to be carrying guilt he did not deserve. When he asked her why she'd been late home that evening, Molly had said she'd fallen in the river and hadn't wanted to be a laughing stock, walking through the village dripping wet, so she'd stayed in the woods until she'd dried out. Her father had given her a strange look but hadn't questioned her any further on the matter.

Taking one last look at where their home had stood, the four of them turned and walked away in silence. They came around the front of the inn and saw Betsy overseeing her belongings being loaded up onto a waiting cart. Her jolly spark had left her, in the wake of the fire, and she had no desire to continue running the inn. She'd told Molly that the loss of Patrick had hit her and her husband greatly and, while he was not their son, they'd cared for him deeply and would grieve over his death for some time to come. They did not need to be reminded of it every time they looked out of the window. They were going to stay with family on the other side of Oxford and the inn was being put up for sale.

The Smythes had just crossed the village green, heading back in the direction of the manor, when a voice hailed them from behind. They looked to see the postman scurrying towards them, waving an envelope in his hand.

He handed it to Alice and, having voiced his condolences for their misfortune, trotted away, leaving Alice holding the letter with a concerned look on her face.

'He's replied,' was all she said to her husband. John took her hand and they resumed their journey. Albie and Molly looked at each other in puzzlement. Albie shrugged and they both followed on behind.

Later that evening, in the library of the manor, Alice and John asked Molly and her brother to sit with them as they had some news to share. Alice brought out the letter she'd received earlier that day and laid it on the table in front of them.

'Albie, Molly… Due to the circumstances we now find ourselves in, I have had no choice but to make contact with the family from whom I have been estranged for nearly forty years. It is not the desire of your father, nor I, to be reliant upon the charity of others. I sent a letter last week and today received this reply from your uncle.'

'We have an uncle?' Albie's face was a picture of incredulity. Molly knew her own expression perfectly reflected his.

'Yes, Albie, you have an uncle. His name is Martin, after my father, and he is younger than me by seven years.'

'Oh! That's the same age difference as Albie and myself!'

'Yes, Molly, the irony of that was not lost on me.'

'But, Mother, you've never made mention of him or any of your family. Why? Whenever we have asked, you have always changed the subject.'

'When I met your father, Molly, my affections for him were immediate and he returned those affections. It was no secret that my father had a wish for me to marry another and I knew I could not do this. Your father and I eloped. Upon our return, my father disowned me and told me I was no longer welcome within the family. My mother had died only a few years before and, with no one to talk sense into him, his ill-temper was taken out upon me. We have not spoken since.'

'And our uncle? Why did he follow your father's orders? Surely he should have stood up against him?'

'He was eleven-years-old, Albie, only a child although, when the time came that he was old enough to exert his own will, he did send the occasional letter but bid me not to reply for fear our father would intercept the correspondence.'

'But you have written to him now?'

Alice looked down at the letter lying on the table before answering Molly's question. 'Yes, I have. On the morning of the…' she paused for a moment, 'the fire, I received a letter from Martin informing me our father had passed away six months previously.' She held up a hand to stop Molly from asking the obvious question. 'He was unable to contact me sooner for my father had left specific instructions in his will that this was to be the case. I wrote back and informed him of our change of circumstance, and he has replied with haste,' she pointed to the letter on the table, 'to invite us all to be his guests until such times as alternative arrangements can be made. He has made a rather unusual comment in that he believes this will not be long-term, so I have hope that he may be in a position to offer some assistance.'

'Have you replied to him?'

Alice smiled faintly at Albie. 'Not yet. I, firstly, had to discuss it with your father and then discuss it with you. Neither of you are children – you are adults with your lives here in the village and you need to decide if moving to Oxford is something you wish to do.'

'Oxford? I didn't realise they were so close.'

'Close in distance, Molly, but so far apart in the ways that matter.' Her father took her hand and gave it a gentle squeeze as he spoke. These were the first words he'd uttered since they'd sat down.

'How will it work for you?' Molly looked at her parents. Her father was fifty-five years and her mother fifty-four. They were not young and there was no knowing what kind of living they could find in the city.

'I still have strength in my arms, girl, I'm sure I can find some kind of employment which will suit.'

'And I can look for something which will suit my baking skills.'

Molly looked at the sorrowful faces of her parents. They were trying so hard to be brave. She knew that inside, however, they must be scared. The way of life they'd shared together all these years had disintegrated in front of their very eyes and the future was now quite unknown to them.

'I will do what I can to help. I will find work as a seamstress – I'm sure there must be a need for ladies who can sew in such a big city. Albie,' she looked at her brother, 'you're very quiet – what are your thoughts?'

'I… I will be staying here in the village,' he whispered quietly.

'WHAT? But why, Albie? Why would you not join us?' Molly asked in surprise.

'Because I am betrothed to be wed.'

'You're WHAT?' It was difficult to tell which of the three voices carried the most shock.

'You're betrothed? To whom?' Molly could scarce believe her ears. Albie had been courting and none of them had known.

'Victoria Meadows, the innkeeper's daughter. We've been walking out for a few months and I asked her to marry me the evening before the fire.'

'But, son, you never made mention of this. Why have you held your tongue?'

'I was waiting that evening for Molly to return home so I could share the news with us all together. The events of that night, and the days since, have been such that it felt wrong to tell you. I would have held my peace on the matter longer had it not been for this discussion.'

'What will you do, Albie?' Alice spoke softly.

'Lord Featheringstone has offered me a position working in the stables. His man there is finding some of the tasks burdensome due to his years and I would help him with a view to taking on his role when he can no longer manage. The position also comes with a small cottage.'

'I see! Well, Albie, please let me be the first to congratulate you on your splendid news. I am quite happy for you and Victoria is a nice girl. I'm sure you will both have many happy years together.'

Molly watched her mother stand and pull Albie into a tight hug, her father waiting by her side to give his own good wishes once his wife had relinquished her son. Molly remained sitting as the pangs of jealousy stabbing at her heart would have made standing quite impossible. She was happy for Albie – she did not begrudge him this happiness in any way – but it only served to remind her of the love she had walked away from. She was fully aware the decision to do so had been hers and hers alone but even knowing she'd saved her family did little to ease the loss she was feeling.

'Are you not going to congratulate me, sister?'

Molly looked up at Albie's words. With the greatest possible effort, she pushed the pain aside and pulled a smile onto her face. She stood and threw her arms around her brother. 'Of course, I congratulate you, Albie, it is the very best of news although I should make a point of giving

Victoria my condolences for being stuck with you – have you told her your snoring could drown out a brass band?'

'You're such a horrible big sister, Molly Smythe, I will be so delighted to be away from you.'

'Oh, you talk like a big man but I know you'll miss me, little brother, for I know I will miss you.'

'You are right, I will miss you, Molly. Promise me you'll look after Mother and Father – this talk of moving to the city concerns me greatly.'

'Don't you fret, Albie, I'll make sure they come to no harm.'

Molly looked over at her parents and accepted the responsibility her brother had placed on her shoulders, hoping that it might just help her to find a way through the torment and pain in her soul.

"And so, my Charlie, we take up residence with my uncle tomorrow. I do not know if I will return this way again.

I cannot ever thank you enough for the care you gave to me. You took me under your wing and showed me nothing but kindness and generosity. You even showed me love and I will hold those memories close to my heart for the rest of my days.

Please also thank Sukie for her generous gifts. I wish I was in a position to return the jewels but I do not know what our future will be so I, reluctantly, have chosen to hold onto them for now. Please also tell her that, if she should care to visit the vestry in the church, she will find the missing records for the 1800s underneath the large walnut bookcase, pushed back against the wall. How it came to be missing in your time, I do not know, but I have my suspicions that Damien Featheringstone may have been trying to hide evidence of his involvement. His demeanour has been quite shifty since the fire and I trust him less than I ever did before. I have taken it upon myself to place the book out of view to ensure the continuity through time.

Finally, before I say this last farewell to you, my love, I give you a gift to remember me by. It is my most treasured item and I want for you to have it. It is my copy of "Oliver Twist" and has been signed by Mr Dickens. Please look after it as much as I have done and think of me whenever you see it upon your bookshelf.

Now I must go. We depart shortly and I must place this in the hollow where I trust you will find it one day.

I love you, Charlie, and will do so for the rest of my time on this earth.

Yours forever,

Molly.
xxx"

Charlie stared at the signature on the letter for some time before folding it up and putting it carefully back in the box. He glanced at the book but decided not to remove it until he was back at the mill – there was no telling how delicate it might be.

'So, let me see if I have understood this correctly, Molly has given you a signed copy of "Oliver Twist"?'

'Yes, she has.'

'Wow!'

'Indeed.'

He stood up, brushed some bits of dirt and leaves from his trousers and turned back towards the windmill. Sukie made to follow him but he stopped her.

'Sukie, I am *more* than grateful for everything you have done for Molly and myself and, in time, I'm sure I'll be able to talk with you about it but, right now, I really need to be alone. Please…?'

'Of course, Charlie, of course. Call me to let me know you're okay.'

'I don't know if I'll ever be "okay" again…'

'Then just call me so I know you're alive.'

Charlie gave her a hug, picked up the plastic box and slowly walked back to the mill, each footstep sending daggers of agonising pain up into his heart as he tried to accept that the woman, who he loved more than he'd ever thought possible, had now been dead for over a century.

Chapter Fifty

Oxford – 1860

Molly stood looking at the huge imposing house in front of her, her mother and father by her side. Set back from the road, the building screamed of money and affluence, with its vast bay windows set on either side of a large, double-sized, front door. The roof had several steep aspects, facing in a number of directions and the garden at the front was landscaped with trees which, in time, would be a natural divider from the garden to the driveway.

The afternoon sun shone upon the pale brickwork, making it look warm and welcoming. Suddenly, the door began to open and, before the aperture was barely wide enough to squeeze through, a man slipped out and began running towards them. As he drew close, Molly could see her mother's eyes on his face and Albie's grin on his mouth. There was no mistaking this man for anything other than her mother's brother and her uncle.

'Alice! Oh, my beautiful sister, welcome home. It has been far too long.' Her mother didn't get a chance to speak before she was swept up in a hug which lifted her off her feet and swung her around. When she was stationary once more, introductions were made and Uncle Martin exclaimed loudly how he would have known Molly for his niece, even without the introduction, for she had the beauty of her mother all over her.

He ushered them indoors and showed them to their suite of rooms. As they'd walked up the beautiful oak staircase, her mother stopped to gaze at one of the oil paintings hanging there. A small sob escaped from her as she turned away and followed her brother. When Molly took a closer look, she saw it was a portrait of her grandfather. She glanced back at her mother and saw her father's hand come to rest on her back as he tried to comfort her.

Martin – Molly felt strange thinking of him as "Uncle Martin" for she didn't know this man and it was a moniker she felt to be too familiar for now – led them along a corridor and stopped at a wooden door. 'Alice, John, this is your suite of rooms. I hope you'll find them to be comfortable but, if there is anything further which you require, please do let me know. You've suffered a most horrific experience and I simply want to make your transition as painless as possible.'

He turned to face Molly. 'Molly, if you follow this corridor along there and turn at the end, you'll find the door to your suite of rooms. It's the only door along there so you don't need to worry about entering another room in error. As a young lady, it is only appropriate for you to have your own suite. Once again, I hope you find it to your liking but, if there is anything more that you need, you only have to say.'

With his open and friendly grin sitting on his face once more, Martin turned back to his sister and brother-in-law. 'Once you are feeling refreshed, please join me in the drawing room which is to the right as you come down the stairs. We have much to talk about and even more to catch up on.'

He gave Alice one more hug and hurried off back the way they'd came.

Molly left her parents to explore their rooms and made her way to the suite she'd been assigned. This house was a far cry from the cottage where she'd grown up. How had her mother managed to adapt from what, Molly suspected, was a life of easy comfort to the harder life dictated to her by village living and being the wife of a blacksmith?

She came to the door of her rooms and pushed it gently open. The room was quite beautiful and, despite the dark green wallpaper adorning the walls, was rather bright thanks to the double-aspect windows which faced out to the front of the house. A small sofa was situated there upon the patterned rug which covered most of the floor. A lady's writing desk was placed in the corner and, directly above, were two wall-brackets containing a pair of brass oil-lamps. She placed the bag she was carrying on the chair by the fireplace and made her way through to the next room which was swamped by a huge carved wooden bed with a canopy over the top. The walls were lilac in hue and the silk of the canopy matched. Had she not spent several days as Sukie's guest at the manor, Molly would have thought this to be the most beautiful suite of rooms she'd ever seen. However, she had been Sukie's guest, and this made her realise that, whilst these rooms were exceptionally nice, they were not quite as beautiful as Sukie's.

She peeked through another door, over by the corner and found a fully installed bathroom, complete with a flushing toilet. With all these modern items being in situ, Molly began to wonder just how old the house was. The layout of the rooms suggested they hadn't been adapted to accommodate the latter discovery.

Somewhere in the house, she heard a clock chiming three. She quickly took off her outer clothes, smoothed down the dress she was wearing – she only had two now – and washed her hands and face. She brushed out her hair and, once it had been re-braided, she left her rooms and met her parents as they came out of theirs. The three of them made their way down to the drawing room and Molly noticed her mother kept her eyes averted as they passed her father's portrait. Molly had no such qualms and took a second look. The face looking down at her was quite inscrutable and she was unable to discern what kind of man her grandfather had been.

A short time later, Molly sat perched on the edge of the large sofa which dominated the drawing room, her mother and father sitting by her side. A saucer was carefully balanced on her lap although the matching teacup had halted halfway on its journey towards her lips. The words her uncle had just uttered had rendered her, and her parents, quite incapable of both speech and motion.

Eventually, her father was able to ask, 'Martin, I'm sorry but, please may I ask you to repeat what you have just said?'

'I understand, John, it is probably quite a shock to you all although I had hoped more for it being a pleasant surprise. Although, given the circumstances, I can see why you'd be shocked. Let me explain further. Alice, as the years passed, and Father began to grow infirm with age, he came to regret the manner in which he had treated you at the time of your marriage. He often expressed the wish that he had not been so hasty in his manner with you. He was, however, as you well know, a very proud man. Too proud really for it prevented him making contact with you, reacquainting himself with you and meeting his grandchildren. When he had this house built, and we moved out here, he didn't sell the house on Wellington Square as I'd believed but had, instead, rented it out to a colleague with the monthly payments being paid into a separate bank account. This was only discovered upon his death, when his will was read out. Both the house *and* the bank account have been bequeathed to you. I would have brought this news to you sooner but he also specified that you were not to be contacted until six months after his death. On this latter request, I can offer no explanation as to why, nor can his lawyer.'

'But… this is so unexpected, Martin, I don't know what to say.' Alice took a sip of her tea, her face quite pale. Molly suspected hers looked pretty much the same.

'I do hope this news goes some way to alleviating the distress of recent events. John,' Martin looked at her father, 'you haven't said anything yet, are you comfortable with this news?'

'Well, Martin, I'm not uncomfortable with it. It is a great relief to know we are not destitute like we had believed we were this morning. It will be quite a change for me as I have always lived in the country but, if as I have surmised, this is the house Alice grew up in, then I'm quite sure we will both soon feel at home.'

'Martin, are you not aggrieved with Father for leaving that house to me?'

'Oh, Alice, of course not. I inherited this pile of bricks over our head, his really quite successful business and an extremely overflowing pot of coins. I have no need of the townhouse and, even if I had inherited it, I would have gifted it to you as you are now in need of a home. Tomorrow, once you are rested, we will travel into Oxford so you may view the property and we can discuss any alterations or decoration you may wish to see done before you move in. You may stay here for as long as it takes to be ready to your satisfaction.'

'Oh, we can do any work needed, once we move in, Martin. We don't wish to impose upon your hospitality any longer than necessary.'

'You are not imposing, my dear sister-in-law.' Cecily, Martin's wife spoke for the first time since they'd been introduced. 'Nothing could give me the greatest of pleasure than to spend time getting to know Martin's family. He has always spoken of you with deep fondness.'

Alice blushed at Cecily's words and they began to talk about her children. Martin and John were in deep discussion over what state the townhouse might be in and what updating might be required.

Molly sat listening to the chatter but chose not to participate. The effort of putting on her brave face was getting to her and she was tired. What she really wanted to do was make her excuses, leave the company and head up to her suite of rooms where she could lock the door behind her and sob until she was quite bereft of tears. With all that had happened since her return, she'd not had a moment to herself where she could immerse herself in her pain. She'd had to be strong for her family, but that strength had begun to seep away and she desperately needed some time to be alone. Thankfully, this good news had given her parents renewed spirit and freed her up, for the time being at least, to partake in some solitude. She looked at the clock upon the mantel – soon they would be sitting down for dinner and, after that, she would feign tiredness which would see her abed early and she could finally acquaint herself with the sorrow which was beginning to consume her very being.

Chapter Fifty-One

Lower Ditchley – Present Day

Charlie sat in the pub with Robbie, Jeff and Pete. It was the weekly quiz night and, as he'd been holed up in the windmill for the best part of three weeks now, Jeff had insisted, nay… *demanded*, that he join them this evening. Jeff had expressed his concern for Charlie and he was right to do so. It was nine months since Molly had left and the pain of her loss was still as acute today as it had been the night she'd gone home. When asked where she was, he kept it simple by saying she'd returned to her family as they'd needed her. It was, after all, the truth.

Sukie had found the book of the parish records right where Molly had told her to look and they'd both been in awe when they'd seen Molly's name recorded there, as she'd told them it would be. Sukie and Elsa had both done their utmost to chivvy him along and keep his spirits up. Elsa and he had become better friends as they shared their memories of Molly and how she'd affected them in the short time she'd been a part of their lives. MaggieFrank had also become a part of their little group, although he remained in the dark regarding the true facts of how Molly arrived in the twenty-first century. The drag queens had been quite emotional when they'd returned from their UK tour only to discover their little sewing bee had spread her wings and flown home to her hive. Tallulah had taken the news especially badly and had been unable to perform for two days. MaggieFrank had informed Charlie that this was a first because, despite being the biggest drag bitch between here and John O'Groats, Tallulah was also the ultimate professional and absolutely nothing ever came between her and a performance. She was the queen of the stage and she gave it up for nothing and to no one.

Charlie let out a sigh as he glanced around the pub. He *so* did not want to be here but, knowing how Jeff was worrying about him, he'd come out to try and put his mind at ease.

'And, the next subject is… History. There'll be a ten-minute "drink-and-pee" break and then we'll resume.' Percy slipped down off her barstool on the small stage and made her way to the bar to help out with the immediate rush following her announcement.

Jeff turned to face him as Robbie and Pete went to get in some more pints. They'd long since worked out that dragging Pete along was akin to Moses parting the waters – the villagers just stood back to let him pass and they got served almost instantly.

'Still hurting, bro?' he asked.

'Yeah, like a bastard!' Charlie looked at his older brother. 'How long does it take to go away? How long until the hurt stops hurting?'

'I'm not sure it ever really does, Charlie, you simply learn to live with it. Eventually, it goes off and hides in a dark corner and, just when you think you're over it, WHAM, it comes out of nowhere and kicks you in the nuts when you least expect it.'

'It wasn't like this with Elsa.'

'Do you remember the conversation we had when I found out Amber was my daughter?'

Charlie thought back and a vague memory of sitting waiting for a Chinese takeaway surfaced at the back of his mind.

'The one we had the night you introduced Amber to Mum?'

'That's the one. Can you recall what I said about Elsa?'

Charlie stared down at his hands for a moment, mentally going through their chat. When he looked up, his vision was blurred and he couldn't see Jeff properly for the tears which filled his eyes. 'You said I was never properly in love with Elsa and it was only my pride that was hurt.'

'Do you agree with me now?'

'Yes.' The reply was a mere whisper.

'I'm sorry, Charlie, I wouldn't wish what you're feeling on anyone. I'd do anything to take it away.'

Charlie gave a small smile at Jeff's reply. 'Unfortunately, there are some things that big brothers just can't fix.'

Robbie and Pete arrived back from the bar with their drinks, bringing the conversation to an end. Charlie didn't mind as talking about his feelings was about as much fun as root canal work without anaesthetic.

Percy the landlord made her way back to the stage for the final section of the quiz. Soon, everyone had their heads down, trying to work out the answers, which meant Charlie was free to be alone with his thoughts. His attention was soon grabbed, however, when Percy read out her next question.

'Question nine. In what year was Prince Albert's Great Exhibition held?'

Charlie watched his fellow teammates look blankly at

each other. He leant forward and whispered, '1851! How can you not know that?'

'Not my bag, man, I'm here for the footie questions!' Robbie grinned at him as he wrote down the answer.

'Right! Final question of the night. When was the novel "Oliver Twist" first published?'

Charlie leaned in again. 'This is a trick question. It was first serialised from 1837 to 1839. It was then published in two volumes in 1839.'

'So, what's the answer?'

Charlie shrugged. 'Put them both down and then you're covered.'

'For someone who's never read any of the classics, how on earth do you know that?' Jeff asked him.

Charlie buried his face in his pint glass, mumbling he just did, as he raised it up for a drink.

'If everyone has finished writing down their answers, please swap your papers with the table next to you.' Percy barked out her orders as if the participants were first-time quizzers even though it was a weekly event and usually with the same crowd.

Ten minutes later she announced, 'It seems we have a tie, ladies and gentlemen. The "Rock 'n' Rowlands" and "Sukie's Sassy Cats" both have fifty-seven points.'

There was a round of applause before Percy stated she would be asking one more question and whoever answered first would be declared the winner.

'Good luck, big boy, you're going to need it!' Sam from the bakery gave him a nudge in the back and a big, bold, wink, living up to the "sassy" part of her group's name.

'Right! Silence please. Only members of the two tied teams can answer. The tie-break question is another history one and the winner will be the team who calls out the correct answer first.'

Charlie heard a small groan go up from the ladies

behind him.

'This is a local history question – In what year did the old stables, behind what is now The Cabookeria, burn down?'

'July 1860.'

'Well done, Charlie! That's spot on although adding the month doesn't get you any extra points. Ladies and gentlemen, this week's winners are the "Rock 'n' Rowlands". Give them a big round of applause.'

'Okay, bro, how the hell did you know *that* one?'

'Oh, Jeff! Who project-managed the conversion of the shop? Learning the history of the building, and the surrounding land, was part of the remit.'

'Of course, I never thought of that.'

Charlie slapped his brother on the back and breathed a sigh of relief that his bluff had worked. He looked over at the ladies on the next table and caught Sukie's eye. She gave him a little smile and a nod before turning to Pete and giving her husband a winner's kiss.

Charlie bade goodnight to Jeff, Jenny, Sukie and Pete as they all went their separate ways when they reached the Little Gatehouse. The light from his torch wavered slightly from side to side as he walked along the tree covered path. His attempt to slip away unnoticed from the pub earlier had been foiled when his teammates had declared him the hero of the night and plied him with a few more beers than he'd become used to. Once upon a time, in his younger days, he could have drunk them all under the table but that was long behind him and he rarely ever had more than a few bottles a week.

When he reached the mill, he stumbled up the stairs, bypassing the lounge and went straight to his bedroom. It didn't take long for him to get ready for bed and, before he put the lamp out, he went through what had become his bedtime ritual. He lifted his pillow, removed Molly's edition of "Oliver Twist", opened the cover to see the signature inside and, kissing his fingertips, he gently touched them again her name. After staring at it for a moment, he put it back under the pillow which he then plumped up before switching off the lamp and lay thinking of Molly until he eventually fell asleep.

Chapter Fifty-Two

Oxford; Summer – 1861

Molly fanned herself with her hand. It was hot, humid and sticky and she really wished she was back in Lower Ditchley where she could have taken herself off for a walk along the river where there was always a cool breeze. Mind you, she thought to herself, given what had happened the last time she did that, maybe it was better that she couldn't. She let out a sigh. It was just over a year since she'd left Charlie to come home and her heartache hadn't lessened in the time that had passed. She had tried to push him from her mind – there had been the renovation of the new house to distract her and, when they'd moved in, her mother had allocated two rooms for her to work in as she began growing her small sewing business. Her Aunt Cecily had pointed a few of her lady friends in her direction after she'd helped with redesigning some of her older gowns and frocks which were no longer fashionable. However, as much as she enjoyed her sewing, she knew her heart really wasn't in it. It was simply another means of occupying herself in order to prevent thoughts of Charlie, MaggieFrank, Tallulah and Elsa invading her head. She hadn't known her friends all that long but they had become so dear to her and she missed them all. She let out another, larger sigh and started when her mother snapped at her.

'Molly! Will you please stop sighing! What is wrong with you, girl?'

'Sorry, Mother, it's just this heat. I'm not used to being in the city in the summer. It never felt like this back in the village.'

Her mother's tone softened as she replied. 'I understand. I forget this is still all new to you.'

Molly stood. 'I think I'll go for a walk down to the river. With luck, it might be a bit fresher down there.'

'What? On your own? Do you think you should?'

'Mother, I'm a grown woman, I think I'll be okay.'

'I'll come with you – I could do with a walk.' Her father folded his newspaper and put it on the table by the side of his chair.

'Oh, John, you know Cecily will be here shortly, I'm sure she'd love to see you.'

'Now then, dear,' he took his wife's hand in his, 'I think we all know that once you and Cecily begin talking, the rest of us fade into the background. I'm quite sure we will not be missed.' He kissed Alice on the forehead and then turned to Molly.

'Well, come on then, let's go.'

Molly gathered up her bag and parasol while her father put his hat on. When they were outside on the pavement, he offered her his arm and, once her hand was tucked within it, they strolled in a companionable silence towards the river.

When they reached the water, they found it to be quite busy as the students from the university were out on their punts, courting couples strolled along the bank and nannies with their charges called out time again for them to keep away from the water's edge. The noisy bluster occupied them for a time until they came to a vacant bench where her father invited her to sit with him.

They gazed out across the river for a short time until her father said, 'You've been through, haven't you, lass?'

'I beg your pardon?' Molly turned to look at her father but he continued to stare straight ahead.

'You heard me, Molly. I said, "You've been through"!'

'Through what?' She felt a small trickle of sweat slip down her back.

'Oh, Molly, you never were a good liar.' Her father finally turned his head and looked at her. 'You've been through the river, haven't you? You've been in another place that is not here.'

'But… How… How could you know that?'

'You've not been the same since the night of the fire. At first, I put it down to the upheaval and the change in our living circumstances but I now know it to be more than that. Comments you have made and things you have done, lead me to believe I am correct. You've been forward in time.'

'What could possibly make you think such a thing, Father?'

Her father picked up one of her hands, placed it between his own and said seven words she'd never expected to hear.

'Because I have been through it myself.'

Molly sat and watched the boats on the river for several seconds. Had she really heard her father correctly? She turned her head to look at him and found him watching her closely as she took in what he'd said.

'I'm sorry, Father, what did you just say?'

'You heard me the first time, Molly.'

'You've been through the… the shimmer? You've been in the future?'

'Yes, Molly, and not just once.'

She couldn't answer him this time and she felt her mouth open and close several times before something finally came out.

'When?' was the only word she could manage.

Her father sat back and she turned around to face him. She could see him trying to think of how to tell her his secret.

'The first time it happened, I was eighteen. It was a hot summer, just like this, and I'd gone down to the river to cool off after a busy day working the forge with my father. I put my clothes under a bush and jumped in. I went under the water a few times to wash the sweat out of my hair. When I came back up, I noticed a bright area just along from where I was and, thinking it was sunlight, I swam towards it. I dived underneath and came up in the middle of it. It felt like sunlight on my face and I never gave it a second thought. I splashed about for a little while longer and then got out. I walked back to where I'd left my clothes but they were gone. I looked around to see if I'd mistaken where I'd left them but to no avail. I didn't actually notice that the bushes and trees were thicker and taller, I was too annoyed that my clothes were missing and I would have to walk back to the village in my long johns. I was dreading everyone laughing at me. I then had the idea to go to the manor house for I had a friend who worked in the stables and I figured I could ask him to lend me a few items, just to get me home. However, when I arrived there, it was all quite different. There were only a few horses and they no longer had carriages – they had a thing called a motor car. I will never forget it – it was called a "Rolls Royce Phantom". A thing of beauty that was.'

'What year was it?'

'1932. And let me tell you, it was one almighty shock!'

'What did you do? How did you manage? How long were you there?'

'I used my common sense, lass. It only took a few moments to realise something was quite wrong so I played simple and pretended not to understand so much. I managed to imply that I was good with horses and was looking for a job. I led them to believe I had been washing in the river when my clothes were stolen. Fred was the head stableman and he looked out for me. He let me sleep in a room above the stables, lent me some clothing and gave me a job. I was there for about four months until, one day, while walking along the riverbank, I saw the silvery glistening upon the water again and realised that everything had changed when I swam into it. I decided to see if I was right so removed the clothes I was wearing, jumped in and, when I came out of the river a few minutes later, my own clothes – the ones I'd placed under a bush – were waiting for me right there. It was dusk by this time, so only a few hours had passed and when I returned home, no one knew I had been missing. It was the same day, just a few hours later.'

'How many times have you been through?'

'Only twice, my dear.'

'*Only* twice…' Molly flashed him a look which backed up the sarcasm in her voice. 'And the second time?'

'It was ten years later. I was having a difficult time. Your grandfather had died only a month before and I wasn't dealing with it very well. I'd worked with him since I was thirteen and, now, I was alone. The forge was busy, I was struggling to keep up with the work and I was missing him badly. One evening, I'd gone for a walk by the river to try to clear my head when I saw the shimmering thing again. I'd often looked for it in the years that had passed but this was the first time I'd come across it again. Without any hesitation, I jumped in the river and made my way straight to it. I dived underneath and, when I came back up, I was in 1959.'

'Oh, my goodness. What did you do that time?'

'Being the second time around, I had a better idea of what to expect and I was slightly better prepared in my head. After all, I'd had ten years of coming to terms with my first adventure.' Her father smiled at her. 'Once more, I made my way to the manor house but, this time, things were quite different again. They had no horses at all for a start off and barely any staff. The cook was in her late fifties and the housekeeper wasn't much younger. They both looked after the latest Lord Featheringstone. He was a single man, unmarried, and they both expressed doubts that he ever would wed. Much of the manor had been closed up and he was living in a small suite of rooms. I offered my services as a handyman and helped out with repairs in the house and some maintenance in the garden. That was when I came across things like showers for washing in, the importance of boiling water to control disease and a few other things which I've since forgotten. I also saw a thing called a television.'

'You saw a talkyvision? And you've never said a word about it?'

Her father laughed at her made-up word. 'How could I tell anyone? Look around you – these people today would never understand.'

'How long were you there?'

'This time I stayed about nine months. I wanted to explore a bit more and see things I knew I'd never otherwise see. Oh, Molly, it was so good.' He squeezed her hand and she realised he was quite enjoying indulging himself in his memories.

'Why did you come back if you liked it so much?'

'You and your mother. Your mother was expecting Albie and I was missing you all so much. I had dealt with the loss of my father and I knew I couldn't desert you both and my unborn child. I had to get back to my family.'

'Have you ever regretted coming back?'

'No!' There was no hesitation in her father's answer. 'I have never regretted coming back. My only wish has always been that I could have taken you all forward. It's a better life, an easier life and there isn't a parent alive whose biggest desire isn't to give their children a better life than the one they have lived.'

Molly nodded. 'I can see that and I don't disagree, it was a different life. Better? I am in some doubt about that for the people I met still had their troubles, they were simply different troubles to the kind we have.'

'I suppose that is true.' Her father nodded. 'Did you like it, Molly? What year did you arrive in? How did you cope? How long were you there for?'

For the next hour Molly talked, while her father listened, about the things she had seen, the experiences she'd had and the people she had met. She wasn't aware of the frequency with which Charlie's name came into her story although her father was left in no doubt that this "Charlie" had become more than just the guardian angel who had taken her under his wing.

As she talked, Molly became more animated and excited as she relived those months in the twenty-first century. When she had finally worn herself out with talking, her father asked, 'Molly, were you in love with Charlie? Please, be honest with me.'

She looked him straight in the eye, and replied, 'Father, I loved him more than I could ever possibly begin to tell you. We were a perfect fit. It felt like dancing whenever we were together. We walked at the same pace and always in step. When we did tasks around the flapartment, it was as though every move had been choreographed to make us flow and ebb together. When he held me, our heartbeats were as one. He was, is, and will always be, my one true love.'

She looked down at her hands, twisting in her lap, and tried to blink away the tears which had filled her eyes before saying, 'What made you ask, Father?'

'Because, my beautiful daughter, I have just sat here and watched you truly come alive in front of me. I can't recall ever seeing you look so happy and joyful. I am heartsore that you gave it all up to come back to us even though I am fully aware that, had you not done so, we would now be dead. You have made a great sacrifice for us and no one will ever convince me otherwise. Giving up the person you love more than anything, is one of the hardest things to go through. I know this for, when I fell in love with Alice, your mother, I tried to resist her, knowing our different class would impede any possible matching. It didn't take long for us both to realise, however, that being apart was only making us miserable and that was why we eloped – it was the only way we could be together.'

Molly looked up again at her father and held his hand. 'Father, had I chosen to stay with Charlie, I could not, in all fairness, have enjoyed our life together knowing that I had put my happiness before my family. I will be honest and tell you that, before the shimmer reappeared, I did have moments of doubt when I didn't know what I would do but, as soon as the way back presented itself, I knew I had to come home and save you all. To use a funny expression from the twenty-first century, it was a "no brainer"!'

Her father laughed at her words. 'No brainer… I like that one!' He gathered her in his arms and held her close. Molly clung to him as the pain inside her crashed around like waves on a beach. It had been a blessed relief to share her secret and to talk about Charlie but it has also reawakened the deep ache she'd been suppressing for so long.

After a time, her father spoke above her head. 'Well, my little Molly-dolly,' he used the childhood pet name he hadn't spoken for many a long year, 'if you are lucky enough to get a second chance to go through the shimmer, promise me you'll take it! Promise me you will go and find your Charlie and be happy with him.'

'Are you jesting with me, Father? Are you giving me your blessing to leave you all behind?' Molly pulled herself away to look up at her father's face.

'I could not be less in jest, Molly. I am not only giving you my blessing but I am *telling* you to go. I don't know what you'll find, I can't guarantee your Charlie will have waited for you but I have never seen you look so exuberant or so vital as I have this last hour. I see now how you have changed and, it feels to me, that this is no longer your time. Promise me, Molly, that if the opportunity should come again, you will take it. Don't play me false, that will not be fair to either of us. Be true to me, your Charlie but, most of all, be true to your heart.'

'We'll see, Father. I do not wish to make a promise I may be unable to keep for you.'

Her father picked up her hands in his and, clenching them tightly, he looked into her eyes.

'Molly, you are so beautiful, my gorgeous girl, and it's time for me to uncaged the free spirit within you. You are worthy of so much more than the life you are living now and, as your father, I am absolutely determined that you should have it. I would give you the world if I could but, since I can't, I am giving you the next best thing – another world instead. Molly,' his tone was fierce, 'I *demand* that you take the chance should it ever reappear for you. Don't waste it. You are worth a better life than this, you deserve the love Charlie holds for you. You MUST go. Now, I insist you make the promise.'

'But what of you, Mother and Albie? I can't just go and leave you—'

'Albie has his own life now with his bride and the child which will be here soon. Your mother and I are quite content and our later years will be very comfortable thanks to her inheritance. You also deserve your happiness and you must go wherever you need to find it.'

Releasing her hands, her father lifted one of his and, with his thumb, wiped away the tear slipping down her face. 'Hush, my beautiful girl, do not cry. Just make your promise.'

Molly looked away from him and gazed across the river for a time. How could she make such a promise? How could she leave the family she'd given up everything to save? But then a small voice in her head whispered, *how can you live without Charlie?* As the minutes passed, the voice grew louder and louder until finally it was all she could hear, screaming inside her, *HOW CAN I LIVE WITHOUT CHARLIE?*

Finally, she looked at her father and whispered softly, with tears in her voice, 'I promise.'

He took her in his arms once again and held her tightly as she sobbed on his shoulder. After a time, her tears were spent and they sat side by side on the bench watching the sunbeams dance across the water as dusk came down and the sun began to set.

Chapter Fifty-Three

Oxford – Summer 1861

'I'll go, Father, you stay there.'

Molly motioned to her father to remain seated at the breakfast table as he made to rise upon hearing the clatter of the letterbox and the small thump of the mail landing on the floor.

She was sorting through the various pamphlets and cards when she let out a small exclamation of joy.

'We've got a letter from Albie. Here, Mother, you read it.' She thrust the envelope with her brother's vibrant scrawl upon it, into her mother's hand and poured them all a fresh cup of tea while she opened it.

'My dear family,' she began…

"I hope this letter finds you all in good health. We are both well although Victoria is convinced, she carries a cannonball in her belly and not a babe as we first thought. She says the weight is like that of a small horse and has taken to asking if we have giants somewhere in our family.

I do believe she will be willing the next six or eight weeks to pass with some haste and for the babe to be born at its earliest convenience. I try to help as much as possible but there are limits to my abilities in this area. Victoria is not the only one wishing for this time to pass with speed.

Work is going well and I am taking on more tasks. My pay has increased accordingly and this is good news with our child on the way. I have found I am greatly enjoying working with the horses in this new role and, sorry, Father, I do not miss the forge at all.

The purpose of this letter, besides wishing you well, is to impart some news. How this will affect you remains to be seen as I know you hold no importance to the concerned party.

Four days past brought about the untimely demise of Lord Featheringstone's son, Damien. Against my advice, he insisted on taking out his favoured horse for a gallop over the fields. Now that the harvest is in, the horses have more freedom in their travels and Master Damien was keen for his mare to stretch out her legs. I had noticed one of her shoes was not fitting properly and impressed upon him the need to take her to the smith in Upper Ditchley with some urgency. He informed me he had only been to them the week before and did not see any need to revisit. Once again, I tried to urge him of the need to return his mare to them for they had not done a good job and this could be a problem for him. We have always known, Father, the work done by our old competitors was of poor quality and the evidence was there before me, in front of my eyes. Master Damien did not heed my advice and set off on his jaunt with only one intention – to ride his mare as hard and as fast as he could.

We have been told that he was only moments into his gallop when his horse stumbled before coming to a dead halt, most likely the result of the ill-fitting shoe, and he was propelled forward over its head and onto the ground. This resulted in the horse being frit and she reared up, coming back down with her hooves right onto his head. The doctor, however, states that it is unlikely he felt these blows as his neck was broken and he was, most probably, already dead.

By the time you receive this letter, the funeral will have taken place. I would like to say Lord Featheringstone is suffering with great grief over this but he appears to be quite unmoved. We have, as you know, long suspected that he held little regard for his son and his current demeanour would support this.

In other news – well there is not much. The coaching inn continues to sit empty and is now boarded up. The Inn on the Green is enjoying the upturn in trade now that the larger competition is no more.

Well, I must bid you farewell now. Dusk is coming down and it is not so easy to see what I have written. I will ensure you are alerted as soon as the babe is with us and I hope you find your way here to visit and meet your grandchild. Lord Featheringstone has bid me to advise you he will make accommodation available for you at the manor in order that your stay will be a comfortable one.

May the Lord keep you all well until then,

Your loving son and daughter,

Albie and Victoria."

Alice placed the letter on the table while looking at Molly and John. There was silence around the table as the news sank in. Eventually, Molly spoke out.

'I know it is wrong to speak ill of the dead but I am not sorry to hear this news.'

'Molly!'

'No, Mother, it is true. I will not play false with my

words and make out to be upset when I am not. He was a man with badness in his soul and the world will be a better place without him.'

'But what of his wife and child? She is now a widow and he is fatherless. Have you no pity for them?'

'From what I heard, his wife will not miss him so much as she may make out and the child will have a better role model in his grandfather than it would have done with his father.'

'The devil has called back his own, Alice, and that can be no bad thing. Now, let us move on from this topic and speak of something which holds a greater interest for us all – the new addition to our family. It is not long now and we must pray for Victoria to have a safe birth.'

'Indeed, Father, I wonder if they will have a boy or a girl.'

'Well, Molly, one thing is guaranteed…'

'What's that, Father?'

'It will definitely be one or the other!'

'Oh you!' Alice swiped at her husband with her napkin as she stood to clear the table. The room was filled with laughter and the other contents of Albie's letter were soon forgotten.

It was seven weeks and two days later that the news they were waiting for arrived. Victoria had given birth to a baby boy and they were invited to visit post haste in order to meet him. He had been named John Wilfred, after his respective grandfathers, and he'd already proven he had a hearty pair of lungs on him. Rooms had been prepared at the manor for their imminent arrival so there was no need to respond to the letter, they were merely requested to arrive at their earliest convenience.

The very next morning they set off, for Alice had also been preparing for the big event and had organised their travelling needs and requirements several weeks in advance. It was late afternoon by the time they entered Lower Ditchley and Molly now knew how royalty felt for all the villagers had run over to their carriage, when they'd realised who was within, and had begun waving to them as they drove by. Molly hung out of the window and made promises to visit before they left again. As she sat back in her seat, it dawned on her that she had missed her old home more than she'd been aware of. Seeing it all now, in full autumnal bloom and with the ducks swimming on the pond, brought a lump to her throat which she struggled to push down. It didn't take long for the carriage to arrive in front of the manor and it felt really strange to alight from it and walk through the front door once again. The last time she'd entered by the front, she'd been in Sukie's care and had been adjusting to all the modern changes it had undergone. Now, it was once more the manor she had known since her childhood and she felt quite disjointed. Her two worlds were coming together and it was making her senses feel all out of sorts.

A maid showed them to their suite of rooms and she breathed a sigh of relief to find they had been housed in a different wing to that which Sukie had placed her in. To have been in the same room would have been just a step too far.

That night they remained at the manor and dined with Lord Featheringstone and his daughter-in-law. He informed them his daughter was currently overseas at this time. The discussion turned to the news of Alice's father and his passing and Lord Featheringstone – 'Please, call me Eustace, there is no longer the need to stand on occasion with each other. You are now my guests, not my tenants, and we must adjust accordingly,' – expressed his regret that they had not been reconciled before her father's death but he was glad the silly old fool had seen the error of his ways in the end and had ensured she was looked after in his will. Eustace then went on to share some of his memories of a younger Martin Browning and the evening turned out to be quite jovial.

The following day they made their way over to Albie's cottage and met the new family member amidst lots of cooing and doting. When Molly was finally able to prise John Jnr from her mother's arms, she couldn't help but feel a little bereft that this was an opportunity she would never experience. Children had never been a desire for her but that had all changed when she'd fallen in love with Charlie. They'd never spoken of children and she didn't know if he wished to be a father but, for her, it was the ultimate expression of a mutual love when a child is created from two hearts.

That day, and subsequent days, were spent getting to know baby John, catching up with Victoria and helping her through the early days of motherhood. At night, Molly would make her way to the library in the manor and curl up in her favourite chair – just as she had done since she was a child – and re-read some of her favourite books.

It was in there one night, when Lord Eustace – just calling him Eustace was a step too far for her – came in and asked if he may sit with her awhile, for he had a matter he wished to discuss with her. Molly felt she was hardly in a position to refuse so closed her book and waved her hand to the seat opposite.

'So, Molly, how does it feel to be back in the village? Is it strange now you have adapted to city life?'

'Not at all, Lord Eustace. I realised, on the day we returned, that my heart lies here and that I have missed it more than I knew.'

'You're happy to be back then?'

'It is nice to have my family all together again. It's been too long and I like seeing my parents so happy, especially my mother.'

'Indeed, I'm sure it is. Molly,' Lord Eustace leant forward in his seat towards her. 'I have a proposition for you.'

'A proposition? Whatever do you mean?'

She sat back against the chair, not quite sure what to expect next.

'Proposition may be the wrong word to use. An offer of employment would be better.'

Molly's interest was sparked and it was she who now leant forward to hear more.

'I see.'

'Audrine, my daughter-in-law, is not coping so well with the loss of her husband. She seems to have taken into herself – I'm not sure if you've noticed how quiet she is at dinner. Anyway, her son now requires a nanny-cum-governess and I think this would be a situation you may be rather well suited for.'

'Oh!' Molly sat back in her chair. This was not what she had been expecting to hear.

'I hope I have not offended you with this offer, Molly? You would not be considered a servant, if that is what you are thinking. Nannies and governesses hold a high rank among the staff and you would have your own, quite comfortable, suite of rooms next to those of the child.'

'I'm just surprised, Lord Eustace, it's a role I have never given much thought to.'

'I've heard tell that you managed the village children well when you assisted the church and school with their day trips and that you often minded children for other families when they had to work late in the fields during the harvesting. So, you do have some experience of this nature. You are also well-read thanks in no small part to having all of these books,' he swept his hand around him as he indicated the contents of the well-kept library they were sitting in, 'to read as you grew up. You have good penmanship so are quite qualified to teach him his letters as he grows older.'

Molly didn't know how to reply. The idea was not an unpleasant one and it would be nice to be back in the village again even if it meant being tormented with memories of Charlie most of the time.

'May I take some time to consider your offer, Lord Eustace? I don't wish to appear ungrateful – I simply need to establish if it will be a benefit for my family.'

'Of course, Molly. All I ask is if you could let me know the outcome of your decision in a timely manner. If you should choose to decline, then I would like to offer the position out in order to give Audrine some respite as soon as possible.'

'Forgive me if I am speaking out of turn, Lord Eustace, but the tales I heard suggested there was little affection between Master Damien and his wife but her lapse into grief would say differently.'

'I confess, I too am surprised and I now suspect she was more swayed towards my son than I was led to believe. What she ever saw in him, I will never know for he was not a good person in any way – evil from the day he was born, that one – but we all have our crosses to bear. Clearly, he was hers. I hope she recovers herself soon for the child needs his mother even if he is no longer a babe in arms and the time has come for him to be less nursed and more cared for.'

Molly gave him a small smile.

'I promise to give your offer the most serious consideration and I will return my answer to you at my earliest opportunity.'

‘Thank you, Molly. Now, I will take my leave and give you room for your thoughts.’

The door closed behind him, leaving Molly staring out of the window into the garden as she sat thinking over this latest twist in her life.

Chapter Fifty-Four

Lower Ditchley – Present Day

Charlie stood looking at his reflection in the mirror. There were a few extra wrinkles around his eyes and a couple of new furrows on his forehead but, all in all, he still looked pretty good for a man nearing his mid-forties. The first year after Molly had left had been rough. Every day had been worked through in seconds and minutes with each one feeling like an eternity until, eventually, one day he found the strength to pack away the items she'd left behind. Well, most of them that is. There were still a few little bits dotted about such as the novelty cat-shaped salt and pepper cruets she'd bought because she loved them so much or her special teacup and saucer set because she'd preferred to drink her tea from a cup rather than a mug. The lavender she had potted that spring, out on one of the mill balconies, had flowered well and he'd made sure to tend to it regularly. Charlie had never been one for plants and most died once they'd crossed his thresholds. The lavender, however, had flourished under his ministrations.

The last year had been better. His outlook began to slowly improve once he'd taken the step of packing up her things, even though he hadn't actually gotten rid of them – that would have been a step too far. No, they were in a box upstairs in the loft, although he knew he'd have to remove them permanently if he wanted to keep making changes to his life. He reconnected with his friends and began to enjoy going out again. He no longer had to rely on his brother or Robbie to drag him out, he was happy to join them on their quiz nights at the pub and the "Rock 'n' Rowlands" had become the team to beat. A new quiz league was being put together with other surrounding villages and Percy the landlady was keen for them to hold a good position within it. Now that he was spending most of his time at the windmill, only going back to London a couple of days a week to check in with the office and do what he had to do in the flapartment, he was gradually becoming more immersed in the village lifestyle and he found it both warming and comforting. It had brought a new perspective on his life and he was closer to his family than he'd ever been. His mother had moved into the retirement village a mile up the road and his brother and nieces were just over the other side of the manor estate – barely a ten-minute walk from the mill.

Suddenly, his musings were rudely interrupted by a sharp knock on the door which was then flung open before he had a chance to speak.

'For sure, man, are you not ready yet? We're going to be late. Here, let me sort that for you or we'll never be away!'

Robbie stepped over and quickly finished off tying the royal-blue cravat at Charlie's neck, grabbed the charcoal jacket of his morning suit and helped him into it. He pulled it too at the front and swept his hands over the shoulders and down the arms.

‘Sure, man, yer looking grand! Just need to get this buttonhole in place.’ He picked up the yellow rosebud with gypsophila decoration, swiftly popped it into place and stood back to admire his handiwork.

‘Smashing! Now come on, let’s go or we’ll be late.’ He swept the top hat off the bed, handed it to Charlie and rushed back out of the room. Charlie followed behind with a bemused look on his face.

They were walking out the mill door when the decorated limousine pulled up in front of them. Charlie closed the door behind him, giving it an extra tug to ensure the lock clicked into place and walked around to the other side of the car. He stood for a moment to allow the warmth of the early summer sunshine to dance on his face before opening the door and slipping inside.

Once he was seated, Robbie leant forward and tapped the chauffeur on the shoulder.

‘Time to go, Mr Driver Chap! We only have a few minutes so please make it swift. No bride likes to be upstaged by people arriving at the church *after* her and even less so when those people are the best man and groom!’

He sat back in the seat, looked at Charlie, and gave him a light punch on the arm.

‘For sure, Charlie, today’s going to be a grand day, so it is!’

Chapter Fifty-Five

Lower Ditchley – 1862

Molly sighed and looked out of the window. It was late spring and the flowers were finally blooming around the grounds of the manor. The days were growing longer and the winter chill had finally ceased. Birdsong filled the air once more and everyone was feeling better within themselves. Cook had begun singing again in the kitchen as she could once more leave the back door open to let out the oppressive heat of the ovens. Now that Molly's mother was no longer in the village to make the bread orders, cook was having to do this task herself and was none too happy about it.

Molly had been in her new position for almost three months and, had more or less, gotten herself sorted and a routine established. It had been her intention to join the household of Lord Eustace before the end of the year but when her clientele of well-heeled ladies heard she would be leaving, and not available to make up their gowns for the forthcoming Christmas season, there had been quite an outcry and she had been almost forced to stay until all the festivities had ceased. As such, it had been early February when she'd taken up her new post.

It had felt strange the first few weeks – she had adapted to city life more that she'd realised and initially missed the hustle and bustle. It hadn't taken long, however, for her to fall back into the ways of the village and, when she'd re-established her friendship with Hilda in the haberdashery shop, she found herself occupied with small sewing tasks once more in her spare time. It had been nice to reacquaint herself with her friends although she did miss Betsy and it was always painful to see the closed-up inn when she went into the village.

She heard a noise behind her and, turning around, saw that young Michael had woken up. She gathered him up in her arms and gave him a quick cuddle before setting him at his small table for something to eat. She popped his little cup of milk down in front of him and he drank it while she prepared his luncheon.

'Once you've eaten that all up, shall we take a walk down to the river and see if Mrs Duck is out with her new babies? We can take the leftover bread to feed them if you like, just don't tell cook or she'll be annoyed that we're feeding her hard work to the water-fowl.'

Michael's blue eyes lit up at her suggestion and the last vestiges of sleep left his chubby baby face. Molly felt her heartstrings tug at his sweet little smile, his mouth rimmed with the milk he'd been drinking. He was such a sweet child and, although he bore a strong resemblance to his father, his nature was all from his mother. Audrine had since come through her grief and, after the initial period of mourning was over and she could stop wearing the black clothing she found so oppressive, her demeanour began to lighten too. She started to take an interest in her son once more and, in the beginning, had been almost annoyed to find Molly taking charge of him. Molly, however, had wasted no time in befriending the young mother and they were now well acquainted. Audrine often spent her afternoons in the nursery playing with Michael and enjoyed the time before bed when she read him his bedtime story.

'Finis-ed, Molly. Me done now.'

She looked over and saw Michael's plate was empty bar the crusts from his sandwich.

'You haven't eaten your crusts, young man.'

'I not likes them, Molly. Yucky!'

Molly smiled inwardly. She had detested the bread crusts when she'd been a child and it had taken many years for her to learn to eat them willingly. She was not going to berate the child for something she herself had once done.

'Alright then, we'll let the ducks have them. Come, let me dress you for the outdoors and we can get on our way.'

Thirty minutes later, Molly was holding the collar of Michael's coat tightly in her hand as he leant forward to throw the bread out to the birds on the water. It had been a pleasing stroll and, on the way, they had stopped to see Seth at the mill. Michael loved to see the giant sails spin round in the wind and Seth enjoyed the company of the child. Today had been a sad visit, however, as Seth had imparted the news that the mill would be closed at the end of the year. He was no longer able-bodied enough to tend it and, with no family to pick up the reins in his wake, they either had to find someone from outside the village to take his place or close it down. He and Lord Eustace had discussed the issue and both had agreed that, with all the new inventions occurring every day and the growing army of machinery making jobs such as his less in demand, the simplest thing would be to close the mill down and bring their flour orders in from the city. The cost of maintaining the building, plus wages, would be more than the cost of buying their flour ready milled from other sources. Lord Eustace had kindly offered Seth a small cottage to reside in for as long as he required it. It had been sad to hear the news even though Molly already knew when the mill had closed down, thanks to Charlie telling her.

'Mo' bwead, Molly, mo' bwead!'

'Sorry, little man, but it's all gone. See, the bag is empty.' She knelt beside him and let Michael look inside the small holdall they'd brought the bread in.

'Aw.' His mouth turned down and, looking as though he was about to cry, Molly quickly took his hand and said in a jolly, happy voice, 'We'll walk along the path a little more and see if we can find a pretty stone for you to take back for your mama.'

Michael's face brightened immediately and, taking Molly's hand, he began pulling her along the path.

They were a few feet away from the old hollow stump when Michael let out a small cry of joy. He let go of her hand and bent down to pick up a flat stone. He handed it to Molly for her to have a closer look. Seeing that it was a bit dirty, she bent down and dipped it in the water to clean the muck off. She dried it on the hem of her skirt and showed Michael his pretty prize. The stone had a number of different coloured rings around it and would make a nice little paperweight.

As she straightened up, something caught the corner of her eye and, when she turned for a closer look, she let out the loudest of gasps. The shimmer was back on the water. She took Michael's hand and walked along the path for a closer look. Every day, since she'd come to work at the manor, she'd made a point of walking along the river, hoping to see the shimmer but it was never there. The disappointment always sat in her stomach like a brick and this was how she knew her father was right – she didn't belong in this time anymore. The few doubts she'd had were long since quashed and her heart and soul had told that, should the day ever come where she found the shimmer again, there would be no hesitation, she would happily jump in that river and, no matter where she came out on the other side, she'd grasp that new life with joy and enthusiasm. She had already written a letter for her father to let him know and it was now sitting in a drawer just waiting to be sent. Next to it was a special belt she had made with Sukie's jewels sewn into it. These were the two most important items in her room and she now had to get back as quickly as possible to retrieve them. She didn't know how long the shimmer had been there for and how much longer it would last.

She grabbed Michael and lifted him up into her arms, ignoring his protests that he didn't want to be carried and wished to walk. She ran as quickly as she was able, cursing the length of her skirts as they impeded her progress. By the time she made it to the front door of the manor, she was red in the face and out of breath. She knew she shouldn't enter by the main door – even nannies have some limits and she should go around the back – but she didn't care, she wasn't going to be here much longer for it to matter.

Molly turned the door handle and bumped it open with her hip. To her delight, Audrine was just walking out of the drawing room as she stepped into the hallway.

'Here, Audrine, take him. He has a gift for you.' She thrust Michael into his mother's arms and scurried over to the stairs, running up them two at a time. She heard Audrine call her name, and the questioning confusion in her voice, but she wasn't hanging around to explain. She threw open the door of her rooms, hurried over to the tallboy and, pulling the drawer open, lifted the skirt of her dress to tie the jewel belt underneath, putting in a double knot to ensure it didn't come loose in the water. Molly dropped her skirts, picked up a length of fine rope, a small piece of ragged cotton, the letter for her father and, not even bothering to close the drawer, ran back down the stairs, placed the letter on the silver tray in the hallway where all outgoing post went and skipped to the front door. She paused for a moment to look about her. Audrine's voice floated out of the drawing room where she was thanking Michael for his pretty stone and making him laugh. She knew they would be alright. She wasn't really needed here and, with her father's blessing, she was free to go.

Molly opened the door and turned towards the river. She didn't bother to follow the path and took the quicker route by running across the well-tended lawns. She was soon back on the riverbank and, thankfully, the shimmer was still there. She paused for a moment to establish where she should enter the water, and the distance she'd need to swim underneath, to ensure she came back up in the correct spot. Her swimming would be a bit rusty, as there had been little opportunity to practise since she'd come back, but she'd made sure she'd kept up with her ability to hold her breath under water by doing so every week in her bath.

She had initially intended to wear the swimming costume stored in the hollow trunk but, when she'd last inspected it, the fabric had begun to rot and had several holes so she now had to improvise. She took the piece of rope, bent over to place it between her feet and pulled it upwards, hoisting up her skirts and petticoats and freeing up her legs. She'd given this matter a great deal of thought and knew she'd most likely fail in her task if her legs were encumbered by the length of her skirts. She tied the rope around her waist and immediately appreciated once more the freedom of being released from the confines of her attire.

The final thing left for her to do, was to push the small bit of rag down underneath the roots of the old stumpy tree and place some stones upon it. When this task was completed, she turned around and slipped down into the water, waiting for a moment – just as Charlie had taught her – to allow her body to adjust to the temperature before she made her way towards the middle of the river. She took a few tentative strokes around the water first, just to refresh her memory and was pleased to note how quickly it all came back to her. Once she felt confident, she swam over to her chosen spot, drew in the deepest breath she could and dived under the water.

Chapter Fifty-Six

Molly swam down towards the riverbed and felt the current pull at her. This time, however, she let herself go with it. She was heading in the opposite direction to when she'd come back and didn't need to worry about fighting it. When she figured she was in the right place, she placed her feet on the stony gravel of the riverbed, gave an almighty push upwards and came up through the water right in the middle of the shimmer. Exactly where she'd hoped to be.

Using all her strength, for the weight of her wet clothing was pulling her down, she managed to swim to the riverbank and, making good use of the tree roots once again, hauled herself out of the water. She lay where she landed for some time, getting her breath back and letting the sun warm her up.

When she had the energy to move, Molly stood and made her way to the old tree stump where she tried to locate the rag she'd placed there a few minutes earlier. After brushing away some old leaves and some dirt, she found the stones and checked they were still in the same formation as she had laid them. Satisfied that they were, she pushed them out of the way and rummaged around trying to find the rag but it was gone. There was nothing there. She stood back up with a smile, her question answered. She was in the future again although she didn't know when but it had to be a number of years for the cotton scrap to have wasted away. Oh well, there was only one way to find out. She untied the rope around her waist, allowing her skirts to drop, and began walking in the direction of the mill. She would need to see that to have a better idea of what year she was in.

When Molly rounded the bend and saw the mill up ahead, she stopped. Her heart began to beat faster and she could feel the blood pounding in her head. What was she going to find? Was she too late for Charlie? Had he met someone else? Did he have a new family? Was he even alive? Or been born yet? So many questions and no way of finding out by just standing here staring into the distance.

Her breath coming in short gasps, Molly set off once more and drew to a halt when she arrived at the windmill. Her initial fears were instantly allayed – the mill had been renovated and didn't look too different from when she had last seen it. She walked around and saw the pot of lavender she had planted, now in full bloom, still sitting up on the small balcony area, exactly where she had placed it. This was looking promising. She had arrived after the time of her previous arrival – that meant Sukie, Charlie and Elsa would know her. Her biggest worry had been landing in a year earlier than before and no one would know who she was. She felt her heartbeat slow down and her breathing eased back into its usual rhythm.

She turned and walked back the other way towards the front door. A car was parked nearby but it was different from the one Charlie had driven – had he bought a new one or was someone else now living in the mill?

She stepped up and knocked on the door. After a few minutes, she knocked again. No one was answering and, when she looked up and saw all the windows were closed, she made the assumption that no one was home.

Molly sat on the step and mulled over what to do next. The mill had the same kind of push-button lock that Charlie had on his London flat and she'd known the codes for both of them. Should she try it and see if the door opened? She didn't want to be breaking in but her wet clothes were now causing her to shiver and she had to get out of them soon. She could have a quick look around and, if it appeared that Charlie no longer lived here, then she would make her way up to the manor. She knew it was highly unlikely that Sukie would have moved as she'd made it clear to Molly how much she loved their home and she'd said she never wanted to leave it.

Her mind made up, Molly cast her eye around to double check no one was coming and, satisfied nobody was going to suddenly scream "thief" at her, she pushed the buttons and turned the handle. The lock gave way and the door opened. She slipped inside and closed it behind her. The hallway gave no indication of who now lived there so she went upstairs and into the lounge. It only took one quick glance to know Charlie was still here. All the furniture was in the same place, the same books were on the shelves and the same lamps still sat in the same nooks. She walked over to the desk in front of the French windows and saw paperwork with his handwriting sitting there.

This was good. This was very good.

She still needed to know what date and year it was so she looked about for the buttons to switch on the talkyvision. She pressed the button for the guide to come up and there was the date. She was thrilled to note she'd come back towards the end of May – a little over two years from when she'd left.

Just then, her teeth began to chatter and her shivering intensified. Regardless of his current situation, she was quite sure Charlie would not begrudge her a nice hot shower to wash the river off and maybe a cup of tea afterwards. She made her way up to the next floor and into the room which had once been hers. She opened the wardrobe but found it empty. The same with the drawers in the dressing table. Molly walked along the hallway and into Charlie's room. She had to find something else to wear, at least until her clothing had dried. She entered the bedroom and saw Charlie's bathrobe lying across the chair. That'll do, she thought. She was turning to leave when she noticed the photographs by the side of the bed. These were new and she stepped closer for a look. There were four small frames – the first was of Charlie and Jeff with their arms around their mother, the second was Charlie with Jenny, Amber and Saffy, the third was Charlie with Jenny and Jeff but the fourth was Charlie embracing another woman who she didn't know. There was something slightly familiar about her but Molly couldn't place who she was. She picked up the photograph for a closer look, holding it for a moment as she took in the happy smile on Charlie's face before replacing it where it had been and trying to ignore the heavy feeling in her chest as she walked out, closing the door behind her.

When she came back down the stairs, forty-five minutes later, she felt restored and in a better place. A good, hot, powerful shower could do that to a body, she thought. She went into the kitchen, switched the kettle on and was thrilled, when she opened the cupboard, to find her little cup and saucer still sitting there. She placed them on the worktop and it was as she was getting the milk from the fridge that her world shattered around her and the hope which had been building up inside her was taken out and smashed to smithereens, for there on the calendar, on the line for today's date and circled several times, was one word written in large, capital letters – WEDDING.

Chapter Fifty-Seven

Charlie looked at his watch and, seeing the time, decided he could now leave. He looked at the guests still dancing on the dancefloor and wondered where they got their energy from. He was done in and needed to get out of there. He looked around the function suite and saw his nieces on the far side, gyrating away to the disco beat pounding out of the speakers. He decided to leave them be – he'd catch up with them another time.

He slipped out through one of the side doors and made his way back towards the manor. The windmill was on the other side of the estate from the function suite so it would be the best part of fifteen minutes till he was home. Mind you, he thought, the way his head was feeling after a few too many glasses of champagne, a walk in the crisp night air would probably do him the power of good.

When he reached the Little Gatehouse, he looked up as he retrieved a torch from the small storage-box he kept in the garden there. The windows were closed and in darkness which suggested Jenny and Jeff were already in bed. They did have to be up for the shop tomorrow so he wasn't surprised. He walked a small distance along the path before switching the torch on as he didn't want to disturb them. This area of the estate remained unlit and, although Pete and Sukie had said they would put in some lighting, Charlie had told them not to bother doing so – he was more than happy to use a torch to light his way on dark nights. He didn't want to see the trees and bushes being uprooted just to make his life a little more convenient. He heard an owl hoot nearby and some rustling in the undergrowth as some small animal or another heeded the warning to stay out of Mr Owl's sight otherwise it may become Mr Owl's supper. Charlie gave a small smile and carried on.

When he saw the mill looming up in front of him, he switched off the torch as the security lights came on, helping him to see as he punched the numbers into the keypad on the door. He didn't bother to put the light on when he stepped inside and made straight for the stairs up to the lounge. He suddenly had a desire for a cup of hot chocolate. How unusual, he thought, he hadn't had hot chocolate since Molly had left and now, out of nowhere, he had a longing for one. Thankfully, he always had some in the cupboard for Sukie when she visited and, as he switched on the lamp at the top of the stairs, he was busy wondering if he had enough milk when he turned around and let out a yell.

'AARRGGHHHHH! WHAT THE HELL—'

A small figure, wrapped in white, was lying curled up on the sofa. It was asleep and the noise he'd just made didn't appear to have disturbed it. He stepped closer and, as he did so, he noticed the small teacup and saucer sitting on the coffee table. He stopped in his tracks. Was it possible? Could it be…?

With no warning, he went all light-headed and dizzy and stars danced in front of his eyes. He grabbed the back of the sofa and waited for the sensation to pass before, while holding his breath, he approached the body lying in front of him. The face was hidden away in the crook of an arm and it was his bathrobe which engulfed the rest of the being. It was, however, the sight of some long dark tendrils of hair hanging over the crooked arm which had his hope firing up. He, ever so gently, shook the comatose sleeper.

'Molly,' he whispered, 'is that you? Molly, wake up, it's me, Charlie.'

The small squeak that squeezed out from under the arm was all he needed to hear.

It was his Molly!

She'd come back to him!

She had returned!

Barely allowing her time to move or stretch, he gathered her up in his arms and began to shower her face with kisses.

'Molly, oh my goodness, my Molly, my Molly. How I've missed you. A day has not passed—'

With his eyes closed in joy, Charlie didn't see the small fist coming at him from the side and was only aware of it when it landed full force on the side of his jaw.

'Owwwwww!'

He broke his hold on her as his hand came up to rub his throbbing face. As he did so, she rolled away from him and onto the floor.

'What was that for?' He looked up at her as she stood in front of him.

'You bounder! You loathsome man! How dare you say those words to me. How dare you utter such lies! You are beyond contempt.'

'Molly, what are you talking about?' He couldn't understand why Molly was saying these things to him.

'You, sir,' she pointed at him, 'are a married man and yet you sit there telling me you have missed me. I think you have not. It did not take you long to find someone to take my place. Two years, Charlie, only two years and yet, here you are, on your wedding day speaking such words to me when another woman is waiting for your affections to be hers. Where is she? I want to speak with her.'

Charlie watched with raised eyebrows as Molly spun around, almost tripping over the hem of the bathrobe which was trailing on the floor behind her.

'Molly! Molly!' When she continued to ignore him, he shouted, 'MOLLY! JUST STOP!'

He got up and put his hands on her shoulders. 'Why do you think I am married?'

'Do you play me for a fool, Charlie Rowland?' He let out a groan of frustration as she wriggled away from him and stepped around the coffee table, putting it between them.

'No, Molly, I do not think you are a fool but, right now, I want you to stop shouting at me and explain why you believe I am married. Which, if you would care to listen, I am not.'

'Your suit. Is that not the suit a man would wear to be wed in?'

'Yes, it is but—'

'And I have seen it with my own eyes.'

'Seen *what*?' All he wanted to do was gather his little wild songbird up in his arms and hold her tightly for the rest of forever and yet, here she was, throwing all sorts of wild accusations at him.

Molly stomped off to the kitchen and returned with his calendar in her hand. She thrust it under his face and pointed at the date.

'There! Wedding! In nice big letters so you would see it every day. So, are you going to tell me now that you didn't get married today?'

'Yes, Molly, that's exactly what I am going to tell you. NO! Enough! It's my turn to speak.' He held up a hand as her mouth opened to begin berating him again.

'Molly, I *was* at a wedding today, but not as the groom. I was the best man. Robbie's best man, to be exact. Robbie and Sam got married today. It was written in large letters on the calendar to remind me I still had a speech to prepare. Nothing more than that.'

'So, you're not married?'

'No, I'm not.'

'But there is another woman now who holds your affections.'

'Err… Nope! It's still only you. Why do you think there's someone else?'

'When I was in your room, getting this robe, I saw the photographs by the side of the bed. There was one woman with red-gold hair who I didn't know.'

'That's Mandy, Jenny's daughter. She's a sort of niece and also far too young to be of interest to me.'

'So… There is no one else?'

'Molly, come here, my love.' He patted the sofa beside him. When she sat down, he turned to face her and looked into her big brown eyes. He could see the redness around them and surmised that, having seen the calendar, she'd made her incorrect assumption and, most likely, had shed many tears after which she'd fallen asleep. He reached up and smoothed down her hair before cupping her chin softly in his hand.

'My darling, sweetest, adorable, Molly. I have thought about you every single day since you left. At first it hurt like hell but then, eventually, the pain eased and I was able to think of you with joy. Joy that I had been able to meet someone as wonderful as you and had been allowed to love you for that short time. I could never replace what we had with someone else and I was slowly beginning to accept that there would never be another woman in my life who could fill the space you left behind. To have you here beside me again, fills me with more happiness than I am able to express to you.'

The tears began to slip down her face and, unable to hold back any longer, he pulled her into his arms and began kissing her again. This time she responded and he was in no doubt that his Molly had returned to him.

Several hours, and a few cups of hot chocolate later, they were lying on the sofa almost all talked out as they caught up with what had occurred since they'd last been together. Charlie was as shocked as Molly had been when she told him about her father's adventures but he was also glad that she'd had someone she could talk to about her own experiences – he didn't like to think how it must have been, keeping all that to herself.

Finally, they grew quiet and were content with just lying in each other's arms. After a time, Charlie asked, 'So, what now, Molly? Are you staying this time?'

Molly propped herself up on her elbow and looked down at him.

'Do you think I can? Will it be possible?'

'Of course, why would it not be?'

'But what about the people you were scared of before? The ones who would not be nice if they found out I had come through time?'

'We'll find a way of working it out. I've seen a film where a man who couldn't die had to keep finding new identities to stop people noticing this – maybe we can employ some of his tactics.'

He looked up at her and felt his breath catch in his chest, unable to really believe she was by his side again.

'So, Molly, I'll ask you again – are you here to stay this time?'

She leant down and kissed him. 'Charlie, I will be by your side for ever, if you will have me.'

'Molly, I want you here with me until the end of time.'

'Then I will stay.'

She laid her head upon his chest and Charlie wrapped his arms around her, holding on tightly, determined to never let her go again. As they drifted off to sleep, his last waking thought was how their love had survived through time. It was, indeed, timeless.

Chapter Fifty-Eight

Lower Ditchley – 1884

Frank Wilson Snr. passed the signed paperwork back to the agent and waited for him to hand over the keys to the building in front of them. He'd waited a long time for this moment, doing all his research and viewing many, many properties, looking for the right one.

He waved as the agent set off, leaving him standing in front of the old boarded up coaching inn. The building looked sad and sorry for itself right now but, once it had been cleaned up, it would look good.

He stepped forward and unlocked the front door, catching his breath as he did so. The smell of smoke still lingered in the air although it would clear when all the boards were removed from the windows and fresh air was allowed back in.

Careful not to brush up against the dusty surfaces, Frank made his way to the middle of the room where he turned to view his new purchase. In his mind's eye, he could already see the new layout he had planned. To his left, he would install a bank of drawers which would hold all the small, fiddley items of his ironmongers premises and, in front of that he'd place his work counter. He would have shelves of items on the shop floor which he hoped the local clientele would be persuaded to buy.

He'd done his homework thoroughly and knew there was no such facility for many miles and the local people in Lower Ditchley, plus the nearby surrounding villages, found it a bother to have to go all the way to Oxford to purchase the smaller items required to mend their day-to-day items. The general consensus, among those he had spoken with, was that an ironmongers in the village would be very well received.

Well, here he was, soon to be ready to give them what they needed.

He walked into the back room, the light from the front door not quite reaching in here, and stepped over to the double doors which led out onto the yard. He threw them wide and the sunlight flew in through the opening. He cast his eye around the room. It was dark and dingy with only one or two small windows. However, it would not be thus for long. Oh no! Soon it would be filled from top to bottom with bright, shining daylight and every corner would be clearly lit, for Frank Wilson Snr had a plan to build himself a quite large, and utterly glorious, conservatory…

A Rock 'n' Roll Lovestyle

Not everyone wants to be famous...

Sukie McClaren is a thirty-something singleton. She's a cat lover, a Sound of Music Fanatic, and a happily independent, woman with a razor-sharp tongue. She enjoys her anonymity so when she is sent to Salzburg on a business trip, all she is hoping for is some time to see the locations in her favourite film. Befriending the world's number one rock star is the last thing on her mind.

Pete Wallace is a cynical, reclusive rock-star and the world's Number One, male solo artist. After a three-year hiatus, he's preparing to go back on the road again. A week in Salzburg, schmoozing with the music press, is one of his worst nightmares. Making new friends is the last thing on his mind.

When Pete and Sukie meet, sparks fly, but despite Sukie's reservations over his fame, their friendship flourishes. However, when life throws up a cold, calculating Italian, intent on seeking vengeance, Sukie has to make tough decisions.

Could their new friendship die, before it has a chance to bloom?

An Artisan Lovestyle

When falling in love is the only way to stay alive...

Elsa Clairmont was widowed barely five years after marrying her childhood sweetheart. She has struggled to come to terms with the loss and, six years later, has almost ceased to live herself. She does just enough to get by.

Danny Delaney is the ultimate 'Mr Nice Guy'. He's kind, caring and sweet. A talented artist in his teens, his abusive mother ruined his career in art and he turned his back on his exceptional gift. Now, he does just enough to get by.

On New Year's Eve, both Danny and Elsa are involved in unrelated accidents which leads to them having to make some serious lifestyle changes and face up to the consequences of their actions. They need to *begin* living if they want to *keep* living. Will they succeed in altering the paths of their lives? Will they find love before it's too late?

An uplifting tale of second chances and appreciating every opportunity life gives you.

An Incidental Lovestyle

It only takes one small incident to change your life...

Jenny Marshall is your stereotypical, middle-aged, spinster. She works in a library, has two cats and likes cake. She has her dreams but not the courage to chase them.

Jeff Rowland fell in love at first sight with Jenny four years ago but hasn't seen her since. When they bump into each other again, he realises his feelings haven't changed.

When Jenny's car breaks down on a cold winter's day, it sets off a chain of events which brings them together in a way neither could ever have imagined. Both, however, have dark secrets in their past which begin to seep into their present.

Will these secrets bring them closer together?

Or will they shatter their relationship beyond repair?